BEAR GOES TO TOWN

Anthony Browne

Hamish Hamilton · *London*

Other books by Anthony Browne

Through the Magic Mirror
A Walk in the Park
Bear Hunt
A Bear-y Tale
The Little Bear Book
The Visitors Who Came to Stay
(with Annalena McAfee)
Knock Knock Who's There?
(with Sally Grindley)

HAMISH HAMILTON LTD

Published by the Penguin Group
27 Wrights Lane, London W8 5TZ, England
Penguin Books USA Inc, 375 Hudson Street, New York, New York 10014, USA
Penguin Books Australia Ltd, Ringwood, Victoria, Australia
Penguin Books Canada Ltd, 10 Alcorn Avenue, Toronto, Ontario, Canada, M4V 3B2
Penguin Books (NZ) Ltd, 182-190 Wairau Road, Auckland 10, New Zealand
Penguin Books Ltd, Registered Offices: Harmondsworth, Middlesex, England

First published in Great Britain 1982 by Hamish Hamilton Ltd

5 7 9 10 8 6

British Library Cataloguing in Publication Data
CIP data for this book is available from the British Library

ISBN 0-241-10817-9

Printed in Italy by Printers srl–Trento

One day Bear went to town.

There were a lot of people rushing about. It was rush hour. Bear was small and people could not see him. They knocked him down.

Bear saw big yellow eyes looking down at him.

“What is that?” asked Cat, looking at Bear’s pencil.
“It’s my magic pencil,” said Bear.
“Then draw me something to eat,” said Cat.

Bear drew lots of different kinds of food.
"Will that do?" Bear asked.
"Yes, thank you," said Cat and gobbled everything up.
Bear and Cat stood outside a butcher's shop.

Bear did not like the look of the butcher.

Bear and Cat stood outside a bear shop.
"I wonder if people eat them," thought Bear.
Look out, Cat!

HELP . . . !

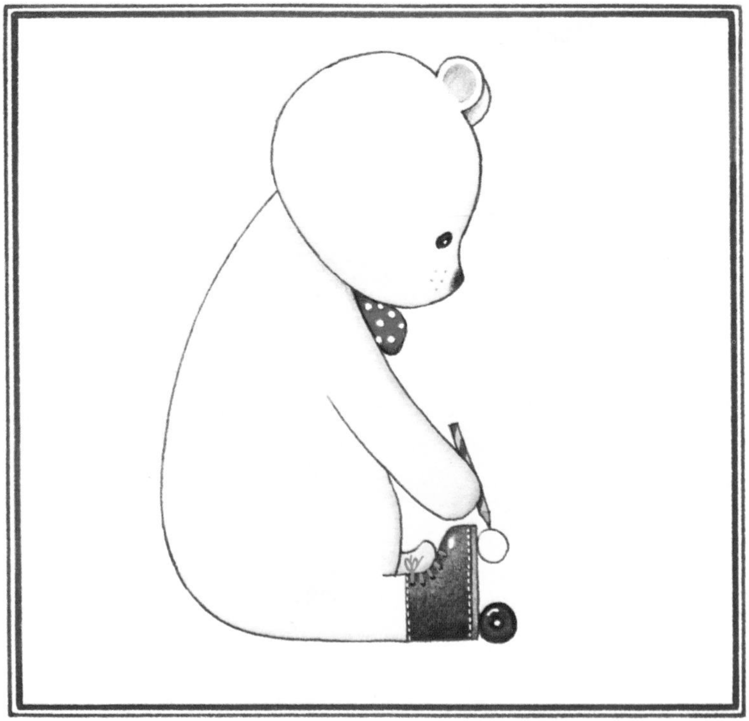

Cat was thrown into a van. Bear drew himself a pair of roller skates and hurried after him.

·DEAD END STREET·

The van turned into a gateway and stopped in a yard.

The driver locked Cat in a shed.
"Mmmm. Most odd," muttered Bear. As the guard's back was turned, Bear went round to the side of the building and drew himself a ladder.

Bear got to work with his pencil again and sawed through the bars on the shed window.

He climbed in.

"You took your time," Cat said.

“What is this place?” Bear asked.
“We don’t know,” said Cow, “but can you get us out?”

Bear used his pencil. “Follow me,” he said.

Sheep refused to leave.

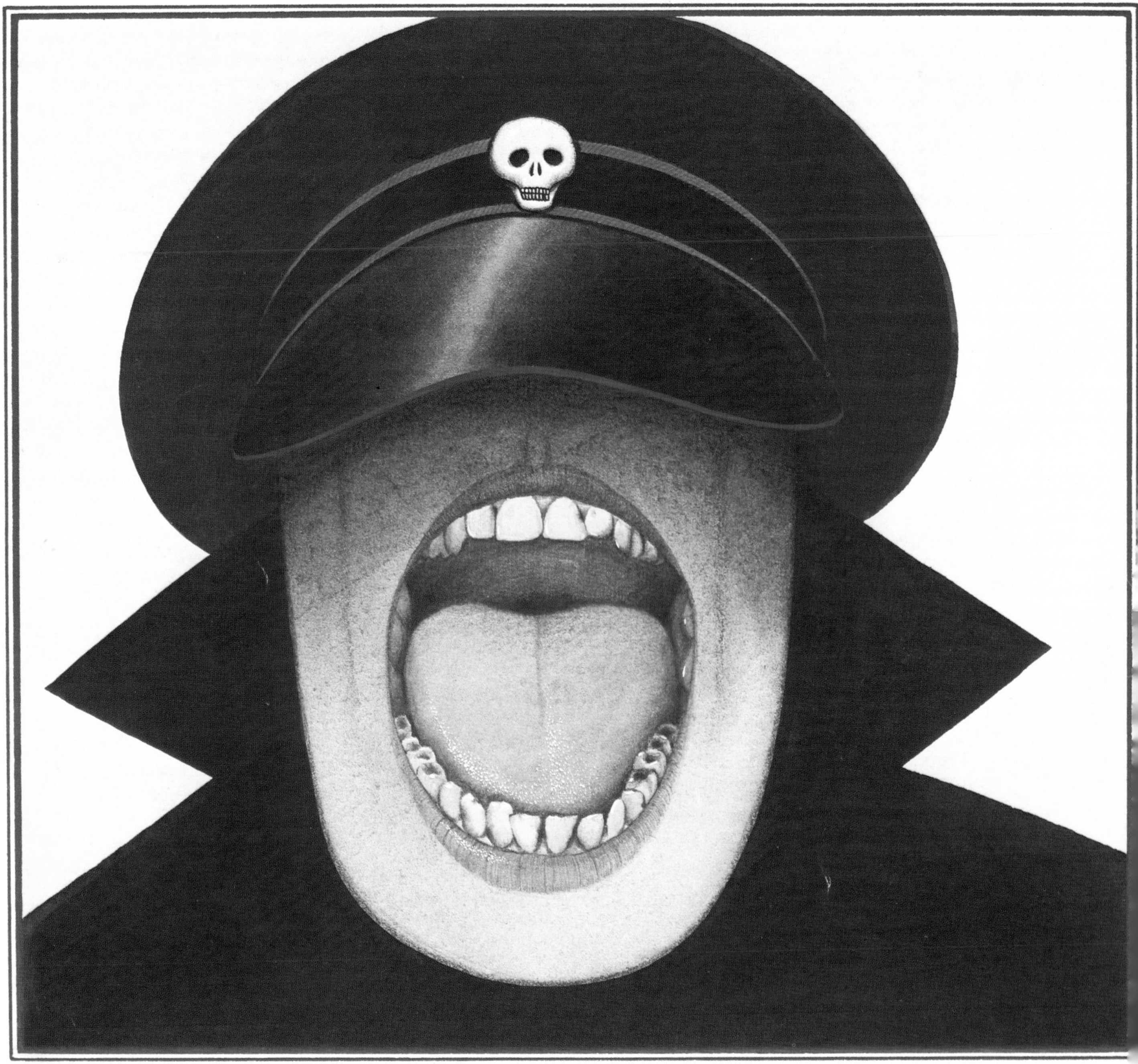

STOP!!!

Guards chased the animals across the yard.

"Banana skins, I think," said Bear and began to draw.

Whooooooops.

Look out behind you, Bear!

“Tacks, I think,” said Bear and drew some.

Psssssssss.

The animals got away.

“Where are we?” asked Cockerel.
“In the middle of nowhere,” Bear replied.
“I like it here,” said Pig.
“We don’t want to be eaten . . .”
“. . . or beaten,” added Dog.
“Yes, it’s a dog’s life,” sighed Cat.
“Easy,” said Bear and began to draw.

"Thank you, Bear."

And Bear walked on.

Beyond Reason

Gwen Kirkwood

ROBERT HALE · LONDON

First published in Great Britain 2014

ISBN 978-0-7198-1381-4

Robert Hale Limited
Clerkenwell House
Clerkenwell Green
London EC1R 0HT

www.halebooks.com

2 4 6 8 10 9 7 5 3 1

Typeset in Palatino
Printed in the UK by Berforts Information Press Ltd

www.savingsbanksmuseum.co.uk

There is a small museum in a cottage in the village of Ruthwell near the Solway Firth. This was the community meeting room where the Reverend Doctor Henry Duncan started the first Trustee Savings Bank for ordinary working men and women in 1810. The movement quickly spread in Britain and abroad. Many articles and books have been written about the Reverend Duncan and his other achievements and these can be seen on the internet.

This novel is purely fiction but the author has borrowed some of the banking principles from the Reverend Duncan for the purpose of the story. All events and places are imaginary and the characters bear no connection to any persons living or dead. The only real names are those of Annan, Dumfries and Edinburgh.

Chapter One

Billy Scott's eyes were troubled as they rested on his wife's thickening waistline, then moved to their four-year-old son, Andrew. The little boy was finely boned with the same air of fragility, the same smoky-blue eyes and fair curly hair as himself. Mary caught his eye and read his thoughts.

'I saw my father having one of his wee chats with you when we came out of the kirk,' she said. 'You shouldn't take any notice, Billy. It's his habit after all the years of being the dominie. He forgets you're no longer one of his pupils.'

'Aye, but he means well. I love you so much, Mary.' His voice was low, soft as the sigh of an evening breeze. 'I love you both. I want to do what is best for you.'

'I know you do, Billy.' Mary sank onto the parched strip of grass beside his chair and took his hand, holding it against her cheek. 'I know you love us. That's all that matters to me.'

They were sitting outside their little whitewashed cottage, enjoying the peace of the Sunday afternoon, knowing the fine spell of weather could not last much longer. This part of south-west Scotland rarely enjoyed more than a fortnight without a shower of rain, but grass, trees and flowers flourished all around their small village. Mary looked up into her husband's face.

'I fear your father may have been right, lass,' he sighed wistfully. 'I want to give you so much, yet scarcely a week goes by now without me losing hours of work.'

'You can't help your cough, Billy. Mr Cole understands. He told

Father you are the best assistant he has ever had – both at the tailoring and with the books. When you're well he—'

'That's the trouble, I'm never as well as I ought to be. I remember the way my father went, and Donald and wee Agnes. I didna believe the consumption could strike me down as well. I've so many plans, so many dreams for you and our bairnies.'

'It hasn't struck you down, and it won't,' Mary vowed with determination.

'You're the best wife a man could have, Mary, but your father knows how the coughing disease can wipe out whole families. 'Tis what he was afraid of. I understand that and. . . .'

'Did he say he feared the consumption? He didn't, did he Billy?' Mary's tone was indignant. She loved her father. She had been the only surviving child of the four babies her mother had borne, and her parents had loved her well, perhaps too well. She had been fourteen when her mother died, only weeks after the birth of her last baby. She had grown even closer to her father then, but that did not give him the right to criticize and dictate to her beloved Billy.

'He – he just asked if my cough was improving. He reminded me I should soon have another wee one depending on me.' He smiled down at her, his eyes twinkling suddenly. 'As though I could forget.' He stroked her cheek with a gentle finger. 'I hope this one is a wee girl, just like you.'

'Whatever it is, we shall love it so don't you worry about anything, Billy Scott.'

'But I do. I'm not afraid for myself, but I canna bear the thought of leaving you with a family to raise on your own. That's what happened to my mother, but she had Uncle Sam to help her. You'd have nobody to turn to if anything happened to me.'

'Nothing is going to happen to you. Don't even think about it. My father has been getting at you. I can always tell. I shall have a word with him.'

'No, no, lass, don't do that. We were talking about the savings bank the Reverend Drummond has started in our own village Society Room. He says we can start with sixpence a week, not like the banks for rich men where you need ten pounds to open an account. Nor will it be like the Craft Guilds who only look after their own members. Your father says the minister is a wise man. He has planned this savings bank for the benefit of all the people in his parish. He's going to London to get the Members of Parliament to pass a special act. This bank is for people like us, working men and women wi'little money to spare but who want to prepare for a rainy day and can only afford to save a penny or two.'

'Aye, the minister is a great man for encouraging thrift,' Mary nodded. 'He doesna believe in spending money on a funeral wake when folks can scarce afford bread for their bairns. Yet neither he, nor my father, would see a body starve.'

'Aye, that's so. You must promise me, Mary. You'll not hold a wake for me. . . .'

'Billy! We're too young to think about funerals. My father. . . .'

'He's only concerned for your future, lass. I promised we'll make sure our wee Andrew gets his education. I told him we put a wee bit in the china teapot every week. That seemed to please him.'

'It would.' Mary smiled. 'Already he has been teaching Andrew his letters, and he knows all his numbers up to twenty,' she added proudly.

'Imagine, Mary, the world's first commercial savings bank, here in our own wee village. We, the parishioners, are to elect our own trustees. The minister plans to hold a meeting every year on the first Saturday of August at six o'clock.' The light died from his eyes and his earnest face grew pensive. 'Your father was telling me all about it but he says to be a member we have to save four shillings a year, or pay a penalty of a shilling. Do you think we could manage four shillings in a twelvemonth, Mary?'

'We shall try, if 'tis for the sake of our children.'

'Aye, we must save a farthing whenever we can. When we've saved sixpence we'll deposit it in the bank.'

'How shall we know it is safe? Can we get it back if we need it?'

'Your father said you would ask that,' Billy chuckled. 'The Reverend Drummond and two other trustees will keep it in a strongbox with separate keys so that one man cannot open it on his own. The minister will lodge the money in a bank in Dumfries to earn interest for the depositors.'

'You mean we would get back more money than we put in?' Mary asked.

'Aye, so your father says. Anyone who stays a member for three years will get five per cent interest.'

'My father thinks the Reverend Drummond is a fine minister. I suppose we can trust his opinion on that. I shall try to be very thrifty. I would hate to lose a shilling in a penalty.'

'So would I, but it would be worse to lose it all in a fire like poor Mrs Chalmers. You're a good wife, Mary.' He stroked her shining dark hair lovingly and bent his head, intending to kiss her, but he saw Andrew's wide eyes fixed upon them. The little boy came running and threw himself into his mother's arms.

'Please to make a daisy chain for your hair, Mama?' He handed her a bunch of flowers clutched in his fist. His parents smiled, warm in their shared happiness, content in their plans for the future of their family.

A month later, on a glorious day towards the end of June, Billy announced that Thomas Glover had asked him to go fishing with him and his father.

'It's a good chance to earn a wee bit extra money for our savings bank card.' He was very enthusiastic about the savings bank. Mary knew it was his way of proving to her father that he was a good and provident son-in-law.

'I wish you wouldna go, Billy,' she pleaded. 'We're managing fine and you might catch a cold and set off your coughing.'

'Thomas thinks the salt air will be good for me. Clear my chest.'

'We practically live beside the sea! Sometimes I think it will be at our door when the tides are high. Anyway, Thomas is a tough hunk of a man, with or without the sea air. He and his cousin still have a hand in the smuggling, I've heard. I don't want you in trouble too.'

'His father will be with us today.'

'Just as well, but neither of them have your brains, or your skill.' She knew how much Billy yearned to be bursting with good health and energy like some of the fishermen and ploughboys who had been his companions at her father's school. 'I wouldn't change you for a dozen Thomases,' she added softly, giving him a beguiling look from under her lashes.

He grinned and gave her a hug, but he was determined to earn all the money he could. He would prove to the dominie that he was worthy of his only daughter.

It was late that afternoon when Mary glanced out of the window to check on Andrew. He was playing with four-year-old Charlie Hughes, who lived in the cottage next to theirs. His mother, Lucy, was inclined to be slovenly but she had a kind heart. She often kept Andrew occupied for an hour or so now that the baby was nearly due.

The two boys were happy enough, but Mary frowned when she looked beyond the garden to the mist obscuring the top of Criffel. The big hill, rising high above the Solway Firth, gave a reliable indication of the weather. It had been etched clearly against the skyline for days now while the sun shone from a sky as blue as the speedwell. When the weather was fine, Mary was often filled with awe at the glorious spectacle of the sunset gilding the top of their little mountain and the Galloway Hills, cloaking them in a mantle of gold and crimson. But there were times when everything was obscured by cold, damp mist and Mary knew it would be like that before night. Would Billy be back before the rain came? She prayed fervently that he would, but she knew the boats sailed with the tides.

In spite of her reassurances, she worried secretly about Billy's increased bouts of coughing. Once or twice she thought she had detected spots of blood on the white handkerchiefs he used during his work in the tailor's shop. Her anxiety increased as the sky darkened ominously, although sunset was still several hours away – indeed at this time of year it was scarcely dark at all when the weather was good. Now it felt more like autumn. She called Andrew inside and gave him his supper, washed him and sang softly as she tucked him up in his crib, but all the time her thoughts were on her husband.

Big drops of rain plopped slowly onto the dry earth outside the cottage door. They fell faster and faster. Soon it was impossible to see through the streaming window pane. Mary could not settle to darn. She began to knit and dropped some stitches. She sorted a pile of clothes. She rearranged the cups on the shelf. She stared at the slow pendulum of the wig-wag clock on the wall. Surely it could not be keeping time? At length, she opened the big family Bible, which had belonged to Billy's family. For once, it brought her little comfort. It had fallen open at the list of births recorded there; the marriages were few, the deaths were many. She closed it with a faint moan and went to stand at the window.

Mary had no idea how long she stood there, unseeing. The rain had slackened to a steady drizzle and the whole world seemed grey and shrouded. Then her eyes widened. A tall, thin figure was hurrying along the merse, shoulders hunched, head bowed against the incessant rain.

'Billy!' she breathed in relief. 'Oh, Billy. Thank God.' Without further thought, she pulled her shawl around her and grabbed Billy's tweed coat from behind the door. She ran out of the little cottage, down the garden, past the pigsty and out onto the grassy tussocks which made up the foreshore. It did not occur to her that her husband was already soaked to the skin and ten more minutes without his coat would make little difference now. She hurried, hampered by her bulky figure, stepping over the watery inlets, jumping over wider ones in her haste to reach her husband. Her dark hair was wet and flattened to her head. She blinked the raindrops from her lashes. Perhaps it was that which caused her to miss the treacherous little gully hidden between two high green tussocks. Before she realized what had happened she had fallen heavily, one leg caught in a stagnant pool. For a moment she lay winded. She didn't know she had screamed but Billy heard and raised his head, peering through the drizzle. He saw Mary struggling to haul herself to her feet. He began to run.

'Oh, lass,' he panted. 'My ain lassie! What are ye doing out here?' He began to cough with the effort of his brief sprint.

'Your coat. Put it on.' She gasped as a sudden pain took her breath away. The baby was nearly due, she remembered. Surely it wouldn't come yet. Not now. 'Must get you home, Billy. A hot bath. I'll put mustard in. The kettle is on. My big pan is on the rib. Oh – oh!' She couldn't prevent the gasp as pain shot through her.

'Mary, lass, dinna worry about me. Let me help you back to

the house.' He pulled on his coat and pulled her close, holding it around them both as they stumbled towards their cottage. Just before they reached the gate, a stab of pain brought Mary almost to her knees.

'I – I think the babe is coming,' she gasped when the pain subsided.

'Oh, my lassie.' Billy's voice was choked with loving concern as he helped her to the house, trying hard to stifle the coughing which racked his thin frame.

'You must get dry and warm,' Mary gasped weakly. 'Please, Billy. I'll be all right if you help me onto the bed and let me lie down.' He removed her shawl and wet shoes and helped her to the bed in the alcove beside the fireplace. In the corner, Andrew slept peacefully in the large crib which had once been his grandfather's. Billy brought the towel and gently rubbed Mary's hair, pulling it from its coil to dry more quickly. He loved her thick dark tresses. He loved everything about her. He couldn't remember a time when he had not adored her. Even the small exertion of rubbing brought on another bout of coughing. Mary's eyelids lifted.

'I'll be all right, Billy. Get out of your wet clothes. Please. . . .'

'I will.'

Billy had barely pulled off his clothes before the fire and rubbed himself dry, when a long low moan escaped Mary's lips despite her efforts to stifle it.

'Is it the babe, Mary? Is it coming?' Billy asked anxiously, yanking up his trousers impatiently as he hurried to her side. Her face was pale and he saw it was damp with sweat.

'I fear you'll need to be getting Mistress Cummins, Billy.' She broke off as another pain racked her body, and yet the pain was not the same as it had been with Andrew. Had she injured the babe when she fell? Her face paled. 'Oh, Billy, what if I've killed our babe?' Her eyes were wide with anxiety. Billy stroked her brow with his long gentle fingers.

'The bairn will be fine, lass,' he soothed. 'I'll go for Mistress Cummins.' He would not acknowledge his own exhaustion, even to himself. He pulled on his coat again and closed the door quietly behind him.

He suffered several bouts of coughing as he hurried the half-mile or so into the village and along the muddy road to the cottage of the woman who took charge of all the births, and deaths, in the village and beyond. He prayed she would be at home. He prayed even more fervently that Mary would be all right. He did not give a thought to his own precarious health or the effect the drenching rain might have.

Chapter Two

Mistress Cummins frowned and wagged her grey head in dismay when she saw Billy Scott out on such a wet evening. She knew his family history well, having laid some of them into their coffins. She shook her head sharply as though brushing aside an unwelcome spectre.

'Was there no one else ye could send, lad? You'll be soaked to the skin by the time we get ye back home, and I darena think what that will do for your chest.' She reached for her cloak and the bag she kept ready for calls such as this. She had passed her half-century but as she strode along she knew she was in far better health than the young man beside her.

The second time they had to stop, he urged her to go on without him.

'Mary fell,' he gasped, 'out on the merse. I think it started the babe.'

'A-ah, I see. . . .' She frowned. 'All right, I'll get along to your cottage. Take your time, Billy.' She sensed he would be better left to make his own pace. She didn't know he had already spent the day fishing.

She had been in the cottage a good ten minutes before Billy dragged himself through the door. She knew by the way he leaned against it that he was more in need of her attention than his wife.

She filled a bowl with water from the kettle and added cold water from the bucket, which Mary had filled from the village pump earlier in the day. She carried it to the stone slab in the corner of the room.

'Now get ye out o'your wet clothes and get warmed up, lad, or you'll catch your death. I've seen plenty o'naked men so dinna mind me. I'll make ye a hot drink and a bite to eat. Is there a bed doon the ben?'

'There's the sofa.' The little cottage, like most of the others, consisted of a but and a ben with a thick, thatched roof. They lived and slept in one end, but the far room, the ben, Mary kept with pride. She had furnished it with his mother's horsehair sofa and a polished chest which had belonged to her own mother, as well as two bright rag rugs which they had made together during the first winter of their marriage. Now they were planning to make it into a room for the children. They planned to have several, for it saddened them that neither of them had living siblings.

Mistress Cummins eyed him shrewdly and sighed. He had always been a shy laddie.

'You make haste, now. I'll busy myself in there and find ye a blanket or two frae Mary's chest. Ye look ready to drop. Food and a sleep will put some life into ye.'

'But Mary. . . ?'

'She'll be all the better when she can stop worrying about you.'

'Mistress Cummins is right, Billy,' Mary called weakly from the box bed. 'The pains have eased. I'll be fine in a wee while. You get warm and dry.'

'Aye, be quick and get out o' your wet clothes, laddie!' Mistress Cummins urged again, bustling away into the other room. She was a hardy woman but the room struck chill in spite of the fine spell of weather, which had just deserted them. Most of the cottages near the shore were inclined to be damp and the small windows did not let in much sunshine. Tonight the rain was finding its way down the wide chimney onto the hearth, bringing spots of black soot with it. She was sure Billy's weak chest would be the worse for this night's work.

The following morning, it was her own patient who was causing her more concern than Billy. She was tired herself and she knew Mary was exhausted. All night, the pains kept coming but they seemed to be leading nowhere. Things were not as straightforward as Agnes Cummins had expected. She suspected the fall had set the baby on its way before the passages were ready.

Lucy Hughes looked in from next door.

'I'm pleased to see ye, lass. Could you send one of your bairns to fetch my Polly? I was at a birthing on the other side o' the glen before Billy came for me. Polly will sit with Mary for an hour or two while I snatch a wee rest. I'll be needed later.'

'You think it's going to be a long haul, then?' Lucy asked in concern. Agnes Cummins nodded gravely, but she put a finger to her lips, nodding warningly towards the box bed.

'I'll take wee Andrew to my ain hoose for now,' Lucy offered, 'but when Billy wakens ye'll not be wanting him under your feet either. Send him off to the dominie's house. He can take the wee laddie with him. Then I'll come in and sit wi' Mary while ye take your rest.'

Agnes bit her lip, hesitating. Lucy was not the cleanest of women, but she was always willing to help. Her own daughter, Polly, had plenty to do with five bairns of her own. Reluctantly she agreed.

'Just an hour will see me right. 'Twas a big day yesterday and I hadna expected to be up all night as well.'

Billy had spent a restless night shivering and tossing on the hard sofa, his thoughts on Mary. He dressed and went into the other room.

'Nothing yet,' Mrs Cummins greeted him wearily. 'Mary is resting a bit now. I've made ye some porridge. Will ye take wee Andrew to see his grandfather?'

'But Mr McWhan will be teaching in the schoolroom. . . .'

'Aye, but his housekeeper will likely be there. She would make ye both a bite o' dinner. It would get Andrew out o' the way, ye understand. He's playing next door but I fear it will be nightfall again before I've any news.' Billy's face paled at her words. She was experienced enough to attend the women in the big houses dotted around the area. He had faith in her judgement.

'So long?' he whispered fearfully, trying to read the expression in her eyes.

'Long enough, I'd say.'

'Then I must let Mr Cole know I'll not be in to work. I've no appointments for suit fittings today. I think he'll understand.'

'I'm sure he will. He's a good man. But I know how it is, laddie: no work, no pay and we all need a wee pickle silver.'

Billy nodded and glanced longingly towards the alcove and the bed he and Mary had shared since they were married.

The day seemed to go on forever. Billy paced the dominie's house and garden and tried to keep his young son occupied. Mary's father had insisted he would walk back with them after school was over. He promised to give Andrew a ride home on his horse. Billy knew Mr McWhan loved his daughter dearly. Mary was all he had left. They were drawn together in their anxiety for her.

When they reached the little cottage, Lucy Hughes met them at the door, her face unusually pale. She ushered them firmly away.

'Mistress Cummins says not to come back for at least another hour or two.'

Billy opened his mouth to protest but the dominie said quickly, 'We'll call in on Mr Cole.' He had seen the anxious look on Lucy's face. 'Send any news to his house.'

'Can't I see Mary?' Billy pleaded. He had suffered several bouts of violent coughing during the day and he felt wretched and exhausted. Worry about his beloved wife was draining what little energy he had left.

'Better not.' Lucy shook her head. The dominie took his arm and turned him from his own cottage door.

Mrs Cole, the tailor's wife, was a motherly soul and she knew the dominie well. She washed Andrew and improvized a night-shirt for him. Before she had finished telling him a story he was sound asleep.

'He can stay here tonight,' she said. Her husband agreed and Billy accepted his employer's offer gratefully.

Mary's baby was born late that evening, a sturdy wee girl with a lusty cry. Mistress Cummins's concern was for Mary.

'If ye dinna mind, Dominie, I would feel easier if ye would call on Doctor Carr on your way back to the schoolhouse. Tell him,' she looked uncertainly at Billy's white face, 'I'll stay with her tonight. Ask him to come first thing.' Her eyes met those of the dominie. He nodded silently, his own face drawn with worry. He knew Mistress Cummins would never ask for the doctor unless she had a serious concern.

The following evening, Lucy Hughes was trying to persuade Andrew to snuggle down in his crib, but the little boy sensed there was something wrong. There were so many people in his house. His mother was tossing wildly in the alcove bed, never speaking to him. She was not cuddling the new baby either. It kept crying and crying until Andrew felt like crying too. He wanted to cuddle it in his crib but Mistress Cummins said it was too small. Grandfather McWhan had come again, but he had no stories tonight. His face looked stern and white. Andrew trembled with fear.

Doctor Carr was talking to Mistress Cummins. He shared her fears of the birthing fever. It claimed the lives of many a healthy young mother, but rarely one who had been attended by Agnes Cummins. Billy was huddled beside the fire, shivering and coughing, paying the price for the soaking two days ago.

Mary's father could not settle in his own house. He had ridden down as soon as school was out, anxious for news. He knew the slightest chill could make Billy ill. Tonight two bright-pink patches on his cheekbones accentuated the hollows of his thin face. Doctor Carr understood his concern as he watched Billy, head in his hands, trying not to cough.

'Mary has developed a fever,' he told them gravely. He swallowed hard and reached his decision. 'She is unable to feed the baby.' Billy's head jerked up. 'Ye need to be in bed yourself,' the doctor said gruffly. 'Dinna worry about the babe. I know a young woman who has lost her own infant. She will mother your bairn and give you and Mary peace until you both get your strength back.'

Billy stared up at the doctor, his eyes burning. 'No,' he gasped hoarsely. 'No.' He looked towards the alcove bed but Mary did not even hear the doctor's suggestion.

'She's too ill to know, laddie,' Dr Carr shook his head sadly. 'It's for the best – for all of you. Have you anybody to care for wee Andrew?'

'I'll look after the wee fellow,' Lucy volunteered.

'Who is the woman who would nurse the babe, Archie?' Dominie McWhan asked.

'Peggy Baird. She was a pupil of yours once. She lives in one of the cottages at Crillion Keep. Her mother is cook there for young Josiah Saunders.'

'Ah yes, I remember Peggy well. She stayed with us at the schoolhouse during the winter terms.' The dominie nodded in relief. 'She and Mary were friends. Her mother is a fine woman – clean and respectable.'

'Aye. She was widowed young, but she married again. Her husband is Jacob McLauchlan, coachman at Crillion Keep. They have a young son. A bit late in life maybe, but they count him as a real blessing. He's a fine wee laddie, young Fingal. He's about the same age as your grandson.'

'Yes, I remember now. So Peggy, the wee lad's half-sister, will nurse the babe?'

'Aye. She adores bairns. Young Fingal spends a lot of his time with her when his own mother is up at the Big House, but Peggy is taking it hard, losing her own bairn.'

The dominie nodded and looked at his son-in-law. There was no response.

'Billy, have I your permission to take the babe there?' Doctor Carr asked, frowning at Billy's bowed head. 'Peggy Baird will take good care of her.'

'I don't know,' he muttered. 'I can't go on without Mary. I can't. . . .'

'We'll get you to bed, and I'll give you a draft to ease your cough and help you sleep. We're not going to lose your wife if Mistress Cummins and I can help it,' Doctor Carr added with determination. He was a good doctor, considerably younger than Dominie McWhan. 'You get to bed and get well yourself so you can help when Mary needs you.'

Dominie McWhan was deeply troubled during the weeks which followed his granddaughter's birth. He never neglected the welfare of his young pupils, but as soon as school was over, he divided his evenings between his granddaughter at the Bairds' cottage and his daughter's. They were at opposite ends of the parish.

'Mary is putting up a valiant fight,' Doctor Carr assured him. 'Mistress Cummins is determined she will not slip away from us.'

Silently they all acknowledged that Billy's chance of a long life was slim. Mary's survival was vital but her recovery was slow. Billy never complained, but as she regained her strength Mary realized how ill he had become. He needed her. He was her main concern. She was the only one who could help him in his fight for life. She remembered little of her baby's birth and showed no yearning to see her. It was her father who insisted on taking her in his pony and trap to visit baby Janet at the Bairds' cottage. She was a beautiful baby with wide, smoky-blue eyes and thickly fringed lashes, but Mary felt no urge to hold the little one in her arms. She didn't feel any maternal tug at her heart. When Janet snuggled into Peggy, searching for milk, Mary felt no pang of jealousy. The dominie was concerned. It was unnatural. He knew his daughter was a loving mother with strong emotions.

'Surely you want to take the bairn home now, Mary?'

'I could not feed her,' she said dully, 'and Billy needs all the care I can give him. He needs me, Father.' She turned her gaze to Peggy. 'You will care for her?'

'Of course I will,' Peggy said softly, cradling the baby closer. 'I think 'twill break my heart when Janet has to leave us. I reckon it might break Fingal's too,' she added in a husky whisper. Mary nodded. She felt drained, permanently exhausted. In her heart she knew she would not have her beloved husband for long. Their time together was precious and she vowed to give him all the care and attention she could. There would be time enough to care for her daughter. As she put Janet to her breast later that evening, Peggy turned to her husband, her gentle face troubled.

'I think, subconsciously, Mary Scott blames this wee mite for her husband's illness. She didn't show any motherly feelings towards her.'

'She canna blame the babe,' Donald said, looking down tenderly on his wife's bowed head as she suckled the babe. 'Billy went fishing and got drenched. Rumour has it Mary went to meet him and tripped on the merse, bringing on the birth of the baby.'

'Aye, this wee mite is as innocent as the dawn, but Mary seems indifferent.'

Weeks passed into months, and Janet Maria Scott continued to spend them in the loving care of Peggy Baird. The family was close and affectionate and four-year-old Fingal was delighted with the tiny mite who had come to stay with his elder sister and had made her smile again. He spent his time bobbing between his mother's cottage and the house next door. Even young Mr Saunders, now the owner of the estate, called to visit. He brought the baby a silver spoon engraved with her name – just like the one he had given Fingal. His mother kept it in a cabinet and he was not allowed to use it.

Mary scarcely left Billy's side as month followed month, but in spite of her tender ministrations his strength ebbed away. Janet Scott never knew the earnest young man who had been her father, nor was she ever to catch more than a glimpse of the merry, carefree girl who had been his wife.

Mary accepted her loss as God's will, but the light had gone from her life. Only her promise to Billy that she would give his young son the best education possible gave her a reason to go on living. She was numb with grief. Her father took charge, acting as he believed best. He persuaded her to give up her rented cottage near the shore and move back to her childhood home at the schoolhouse. She obeyed without argument or enthusiasm. Her options were few with two fatherless children and little money. It was to be a long time before she realized the folly of giving up her own home.

Her father was not a man of wealth but he had a secure home and a regular income of one hundred pounds a year, four times what most labouring men earned. Mary knew he had been a benefactor to several boys whose parents could not afford to continue their education. Occasionally, he had managed to persuade his fellow elders to contribute towards fees and one of his students had gone to university in Edinburgh; the parish looked after its own. Collections in the parish box sufficed to keep the poorest from starvation without the English Parliament's plan to introduce the Poor Laws to Scotland. Mary shuddered at the thought of depending on the Poor Box and agreed to take over the running of the schoolhouse from her father's elderly housekeeper.

In winter, those families who could afford it paid the schoolmaster to board their children during the week. In summer, they walked several miles to school each morning from distant parts of the parish. Mary seized every opportunity to earn whatever she could and keep up the meagre savings in the Trustee Savings Bank in accordance with Billy's dream to educate their son. Mr Cole, the tailor, offered her a few hours' work. He knew she had helped Billy with the orders for lengths of tweed and thread, buttons and buckles. She had a neat hand and a good head for figures. On winter evenings, she spent hours spinning and weaving the locally grown flax to make fine linen.

During their second winter at the schoolhouse, Fingal McLauchlan became one of the young boarders. He was the same age as Andrew and the two quickly became friends. They both regarded Janet as a younger sister and were happy to entertain her when lessons finished for the day. She was a lively toddler and Mary was grateful for their help.

Dominie McWhan often gave extra lessons to his young grandson in the evenings and Fingal joined in eagerly.

'They're both bright laddies,' he declared proudly.

'Father, they are only five years old!' Mary reminded him.

'I can recognize a diamond long before it's polished,' he insisted. 'Fingal now, he's already strong in character, as well as in body. I've noticed how he protects Andrew when older boys would bully him.'

'Aye, he's a kindly laddie,' Mary agreed, thinking how gently he treated Janet.

As time passed, a close friendship developed between the two boys, but it did not prevent a healthy competition, something the dominie encouraged for their mutual benefit.

'I can just about afford to pay the fees for Andrew to go to university,' Dominie McWhan told Mary when the boys approached their fourteenth birthday. 'Fingal is preparing to leave and follow in his father's and grandfather's footsteps as coachman at Crillion Keep but it's a waste of his ability and hard work. He is better than Andrew at the English and Latin, though Andrew has the edge with the mathematics and science.'

'Are you thinking both boys should go to the university, Father? You know the McLauchlans could never afford it, and they would never accept charity.'

'I know that, lassie.' The dominie sighed. 'The laddie has more than his share of pride and independence already. But. . . .'

'What's worrying you, Father?'

'Andrew being away from home. He's a delicate laddie. I'd feel happier if he had a good friend beside him when he leaves us. His cough gets worse every winter.'

A chill of fear struck Mary but she replied sharply, 'Well you can't send Fingal as a nursemaid.'

A fortnight later, Dominie McWhan was sitting in church when his eye fell upon Josiah Saunders. Josiah was not a son of the parish. He had inherited the small estate and the house at Crillion Keep from his great-uncle. He was in his early twenties but he looked older due to a weak heart which had kept him in poor health since boyhood. He was a reserved man who kept his own council, but the dominie respected him as a man of integrity, with a fine intelligence and he was exceptionally well read. There were some who resented him. He had declined an invitation to become an elder of the kirk, but the Reverend Drummond, the doctor and the dominie knew he contributed to the parish Poor Box more regularly, and more generously, than most of the elders who considered themselves staunch pillars of the kirk. His workers considered him a fair employer, compassionate, even generous, when they or their families were ill. This aroused jealousy and resentment in his mean-spirited stepsister, Mrs Eliza Ross.

It occurred to the dominie that Josiah might be responsible for Fingal carrying on at school after the usual leaving age of twelve. Would his largesse stretch to financing a university education for Fingal McLauchlan, only son of his own coachman?

The dominie sighed. It had taken a lot of persuasion on his part to get the fees from his fellow elders to send young Charlie Nichol to university but now that he was soon to be ordained as a minister, they all claimed it had been their greatest pleasure to help him on his way.

Chapter Three

Two days later, Dominie McWhan rode to Crillion Keep to put the case of Fingal's education before Josiah. He found his task easier than he had anticipated. Josiah already knew his coachman's son was intelligent, as well as being polite, kind and helpful to his parents and to his half-sister, Peggy. After some pertinent questions regarding the dominie's opinion of Fingal's ability and aspirations, Josiah agreed to finance the boy's education.

'The only problem will be overcoming Jacob's pride. I respect the independent spirit of my head coachman so I must insist on remaining an anonymous benefactor.'

'Then I shall devise a plan to offer a bursary for which any pupil in the school can compete,' the dominie suggested. 'I shall ask the Reverend Drummond, as minister of the parish, to judge the competition but I shall ensure the examination will have an emphasis on English and Latin. Fingal excels in these subjects. Andrew will do well in mathematics.'

If his plan succeeded, the boys would attend university together, subject to the approval of Fingal's parents. They were a modest couple who had never considered the possibility of their son attending university. They believed Fingal had little hope of winning a bursary, especially in competition with the dominie's own grandson, so their consent was easily won.

Fingal was excited at the prospect of competing for the bursary. If he should win, it would mean the attainment of his dreams. Andrew knew his grandfather was prepared to pay his own fees, hoping he would follow in his footsteps and become a dominie too. He was kind and generous and already he taught himself and his sister without payment. Janet was eager to learn. She was well ahead of many pupils considerably older. She was patient too and loved to help the younger children. Andrew knew university fees would drain his family's resources and his grandfather was becoming an old man. So both he and Fingal worked hard, absorbing all the knowledge the dominie could cram into them.

'Extra learning is never lost. It will give you an advantage when you start at the university,' he told them.

The Reverend Drummond was scrupulously fair in his assessments. He praised Andrew for his excellence in mathematics and science, but it was Fingal who gained the bursary.

Mary hid her disappointment, but as daughter of the dominie she had received more schooling than any of the other women in the parish. She asked if she might see the examination papers.

'You arranged for Fingal to win, Father,' she said shrewdly, after studying them.

'The examination was fairly and independently marked.'

'I'm sure the Reverend Drummond would never be anything but fair,' Mary nodded, 'but the dominie who set the examination knew which of his students would win.'

Her father shrugged, neither agreeing nor denying.

'You'll see, my dear. We shall be glad Andrew will have a friend with him.'

'I am hoping that the air of the east coast will clear his chest,' Mary said. She was always defensive when her father mentioned Andrew's lack of stamina, or his cough.

'It's a pity girls don't attend university,' her father observed, moving her thoughts away from her son. In his heart he knew Mary was more obsessed with giving Andrew a good education than he was himself. She paid scant attention to her ten-year-old daughter.

'Girls? You mean Janet?'

'Aye, I mean Janet. She shows every sign of being as clever as Andrew, and she is bursting with good health and energy.' He looked out of the window to where his granddaughter was swinging dangerously on a branch of the old apple tree. His eyes softened at the picture she made with her round rosy cheeks and curly chestnut hair. She reminded him of his late wife, especially when she smiled in the impish way she had. She had the same smoky-blue eyes as her brother, though, inherited from their father. Lovely eyes they were, with their thick fringe of dark lashes and that steady, measuring gaze. It was unusual in one so young and it could be disconcerting. He sighed.

'I hope she doesn't get too badly hurt by life. She is as honest as the day, and expects everybody else to be the same.'

'She'll have a lot to learn, then,' Mary said grimly.

She herself had been let down twice recently by people she had trusted. She had often helped Billy and she had learned a lot about drafting and cutting patterns and sewing garments. Recently Mr Cole had begun to depend on her to write out his orders because his wife's memory and her eyesight were failing rapidly after she suffered a turn which had rendered her unconscious for three days. He had recommended Mary to some of the ladies from the larger houses when they required garments made or alterations done. She was grateful to him but two so-called ladies had unjustly accused her of not making dresses to their instructions. They had taken the dresses but refused to pay a single farthing for all the work she had put in. The two women were friends and she knew it was a plot to cheat her out of her earnings. One of them was Mrs Eliza Ross, stepsister of her father's friend Josiah Saunders, but she resolved she would never sew for either of them again.

Mary's mouth set in a tight line, remembering how hard she had worked to finish the dresses on time, and in excellent order, knowing they were for a dinner being held at one of the large estates. She would never forget Billy's resolve to save a few farthings every week to put in the parish savings bank for Andrew's education. The university fees would be a drain on her father's income and there would be books and food to buy. She was determined Andrew must not neglect his health. She had been bitterly disappointed when he did not win the bursary, but it made her even keener to take on extra work and save whenever she could.

Her hopes for an improvement in her son's health were futile. The cough did not improve but as the dominie had predicted, Fingal was a loyal and much-needed friend.

Both boys worked hard at their studies, conscious that they owed a debt to those who had assisted them. As time went on, Andrew found it difficult to summon the energy to learn all he wished to learn. Fingal was troubled. During their second winter they returned home for the break. They were fortunate to get a lift in a carriage, driven by the father of a fellow student, but it brought them only as far as the northern boundary of their home county of Dumfries. They walked the remaining thirty miles.

At the first opportunity, the dominie called on the McLauchlans. Janet had begged to ride up behind him on his big horse. She never missed a chance to visit Peggy Baird and her mother, Maggie McLauchlan. There was always a warm welcome for her even though Peggy had two children of her own now. Angus was two years younger than herself, and Beth, a little girl of four. Unknown to Janet, Peggy had lost two more babies and she cherished all children with a spontaneous and generous love Mary Scott seemed unable to show her daughter.

Janet loved to see the two young Bairds, reading them stories and pretending to teach them as her grandfather taught his pupils. As for Fingal, he had always been like another brother to her, although she was a little in awe of him now. He wore a suit and grew whiskers like her grandfather, but he did not grow a beard; he shaved that away every day. Her grandfather sent her off to find the younger children. He wanted Fingal's opinion on his grandson's health.

'I want the truth, laddie,' the old man said. 'Andrew has scarce been out of his bed since he arrived home, though even in bed his books are at his side. He is tired. He looks ill.'

Fingal regarded his old dominie anxiously. He liked and respected Mr McWhan. He owed the dominie a debt he could never repay and he was reluctant to tell him of his deep concern for Andrew.

'The truth, laddie?' the dominie prompted.

'It takes all Andrew's energy to study. Sometimes I fear he is too tired to eat, but I insist.' He smiled ruefully. 'He accuses me of fussing like a broody hen.'

'And the cough? It is no better?'

Fingal shook his head slowly. Then he looked the dominie in the eye. 'I fear it is getting worse, sir. But Andrew will never give in. He has set his heart on winning the highest award the university can offer. He wants you to be proud of him.'

'I am proud of him. I am proud of you both, laddie, but I would not wish either of you to risk your health for the sake o' book learning.'

'Have you heard of a man called Mr Telford? Mr Thomas Telford from near the town of Langholm?'

'I have heard of him,' the dominie said slowly. 'A shepherd's laddie who has turned himself into a builder?'

'He has learned much from books himself, sir. He is planning to build a canal all the way across Scotland from east to west. Andrew reads everything he can find about him. He says Mr Telford must be a great engineer. His ambition is to become an engineer himself and do work like he does. Mr Telford has used cast iron in some of his constructions. Andrew wants to understand how it is done. He – he has a vision of building bridges over great rivers – bridges to carry steam engines like the Puffing Billy.'

'Andrew? The laddie will never be strong enough to be a builder. Doesn't he want to teach? To pass on his knowledge to his fellow men?'

'I don't think that is his dream, sir.' Fingal bit his lip, knowing the dominie would be disappointed, and knowing in his heart that his friend would never have the health and strength to achieve his ambitions.

'He – er ... he dreams of steam engines which will carry people.'

'Never! It is an impossible dream.'

'Perhaps. He says wherever there are roads and towns they will need iron tracks. Like the ones Mr Stephenson made two or three years ago. Do you really believe such a thing is impossible, sir?'

'The rich people will always ride in comfort, in carriages drawn by fine horses. The rest of us must go on horseback, or walk on our own feet. It is but a youthful dream of Andrew's. When he settles down he will be a good teacher. And you, laddie? Do you want to be a teacher?'

'You think I am able?'

'Assuredly, my boy. You have a fine mind for learning, and great patience. The Reverend Drummond tells me the Academy at Dumfries is a good school. Maybe you will be selected as a teacher there one day.'

'Or – or maybe I could be apprenticed to a lawyer?'

'You were always good at the Latin.' The dominie smiled. 'I had not thought I was educating a man of the law when I was teaching you. I shall be proud of you, Fingal, whatever you decide.'

A few months later, Fingal recalled his conversation with Dominie McWhan when Andrew came to him, white-faced and distraught, holding out the single sheet of paper.

'It is from Mother. It came by messenger.'

Upset though they were, neither of the young men realized the full importance of the news.

Dominie McWhan had eaten his evening meal with Mary and Janet as usual, before retiring to the small room where he prepared the lessons for his pupils, marked their exercises, or read his favourite books. Two hours later, Mary carried in the drink of hot milk she had prepared, just as he liked it with a dash of pepper. She thought he had fallen asleep at his desk. She laid a hand on his shoulder, an affectionate smile lifting the corners of her mouth.

'You work too hard, Fath. . . .' The milk slopped onto the tray. 'Father! No! Oh no!' Mary stared, numb with shock. This was no ordinary sleep. This was the long sleep of death! She looked down at the bowed white head. 'Oh, Father. . . .' A sob rose in her throat. She trembled violently. She could scarcely think what to do.

Janet slept dreamlessly. She knew nothing of the night's grief and turmoil.

'Grandfather can't be dead! He wouldn't . . . he couldn't – just die. . . . No! No, I don't believe you,' she sobbed when Mary broke the news the following morning.

It was true. The pillar of their existence had gone for ever. The pattern of their lives had changed from the moment the good dominie breathed his last breath.

It was several days later before Mary sat down to write a letter to Andrew, in Edinburgh. As she had intended, the funeral was already over. She was determined that nothing must disturb her son's studies, or further drain his energy.

A new dominie was appointed to take over the schoolroom. Isaac Todd was unmarried. It suited him well to take over the household when he realized the old dominie's daughter had little option but to agree to whatever terms he chose to impose.

Mary's initial response was one of immense relief. She had worked hard to keep the school and the dominie's house clean and tidy, making sure the winter boarders were fed and warm, and that day pupils dried their feet and sodden clogs before the iron stove. In summer, they drank water with the hunk of bread and scrap of cheese which most of them brought for the midday break, but in winter Mary made each of the children a hot drink. She had expected the routine would continue but she had reckoned without the mean nature of the man who was now her employer, a man whose desire was to rule everyone in his power with an iron hand. Gone was the kindly father who had been her friend and protector since the day she was born, the man who had given her strength to carry on when Billy's death had snatched away her happiness, who had supported her children, educated them and loved them.

Isaac Todd had a lean, narrow face with protruding pale blue eyes and a high forehead. His thin brown hair was already receding. He paid Mary a pittance and expected a slave in return. She had to pay fees for Janet's lessons now, in addition to finding the money for Andrew's studies at the university. Her father had managed to save a little money in the parish savings bank but she knew it would not be enough for Andrew to finish his course. Dominie McWhan had not expected to die before his grandson had completed his education. He had paid the university fees from his own earnings.

Mary had managed to save a small amount in the parish bank

too, mainly because it had been Billy's most earnest wish. There would never be enough, but she was determined Andrew must finish his education. It had been his father's dream; her beloved Billy's dying wish.

'I intend to stay up later and weave more flax, and perhaps Mr Cole will send me more work,' she confided to Peggy Baird when her old friend called on her.

'If only I could help,' Peggy sympathized. 'We are all so grateful to your father for the help he gave Fingal. I know my stepfather would help if he could.'

'You helped us when Billy died. You cared for Janet, aye and loved her as though she was your own bairn, Peggy. She will always look upon you as a second mother. My father knew that. He wanted to show gratitude for all you did for us. If he could repay your family a little by helping Fingal, then so much the better. Anyway Fingal is a kind laddie and clever too. He was more than worthy of tutoring.'

'Aye, we're all proud o' him, but he's a modest laddie. He always enquires for you, and for Janet. I believe he thinks she's more of a sister to him than I am.' She smiled. 'But of course I'm old enough to be his mother and he spent so many happy hours with you all when he was staying at the schoolhouse.'

None of Mary's plans came to fruition. Isaac Todd made sure she had no spare time to weave the linen cloth. At night, she fell into bed exhausted.

'Mistress Scott, you will remember I am giving you a home. Your brat eats as much as two children. Why is she so skinny when she eats so much? Is she ill?' His brow darkened. 'I heard your husband died of the consumption.'

'Janet has excellent health.' Mary hastened to assure him.

'And she is nearly twelve, you say?'

'Yes, she—'

'Then she is old enough to work. You must tell Mistress Sharp I shall not require her services this winter. The girl must earn her own keep. I shall be taking four extra pupils. They will lodge with us for the winter term. They are farmers' sons. They can only be spared from their labours during winter.'

'But the two rooms are full already.'

'You and your brat can move into the small attic.'

'But Mr Todd, there is so much extra washing and cooking when the children stay here all week.' Mary's voice rose in dismay. 'Mistress Sharp is a widow. She works at the salt pits in summer. She needs the work here. She needs money to feed her children. All the boarders pay for—'

'You heard me, Mistress Scott. If the position is not to your liking you must find another.'

Janet had overheard this conversation. She already did her best to help her mother. Dominie Todd expected her to clean the schoolroom, wash the slates and mix the ink. In the winter the iron boiler was lit each day. There were buckets of coal to carry from the bottom of the schoolyard. Grandfather had chosen some of the older boys to do these tasks after school. He always gave the work to those from poor families to help them pay their fees. The schoolhouse had to be cleaned daily. There was the extra washing and ironing which the dominie insisted upon, as well as cooking, cleaning and washing for the weekly boarders. Mr Todd ate alone in the dining room. He expected to be treated like a gentlemen. All his linen had to be starched and ironed to perfection, his boots polished and his stockings darned.

Hatred for the new dominie was growing daily in Janet's young heart. He picked on her in school. He asked her the most difficult questions, often from lessons they had not yet done. When she could not answer, he caned her. She had discovered he was not nearly so quick at arithmetic as her grandfather had been, and as he had taught her to be. When she had answered the mathematics questions swiftly and correctly, he called her impertinent. He caned her for that too. It had been hard to hold back the tears when he was so unjust, but she was proud. She was determined not to let him see she was upset by his treatment of her.

Molly Foster, who sat next to her, was sympathetic and kind. She was older than Janet but she often had to miss school to help her mother so Janet had been in the habit of helping her catch up with her lessons. Then a whole week came when Molly did not come to school with her two younger brothers.

'Molly Foster will no longer attend school,' the dominie informed her with a sneer. Janet looked at him. So she was to be denied even the small pleasure of a sympathetic smile or a friendly chat. She was sure it had given the dominie some kind of cruel pleasure to impart this news. 'You will sit next to Fred and help him with his lessons.' Fred Bridges was a fat bully, he smelled and even her grandfather had been unable to teach him. He only stayed at school because his father was a man of influence in the parish and an elder of the kirk. Janet's heart sank but she knew worse was to come when the dominie went on, 'I shall hold you responsible. If either of you do not finish your lessons you will both be punished.' Janet stared up at him in dismay. Behind her she heard the two Foster boys murmur in sympathy.

The Fosters lived on a farm several miles away at the north edge of the parish. Their land straggled the boundary of the adjoining parish so they could have attended the school there, but their mother had insisted they should attend her grandfather's classes. During the week they lodged with their Grandmother Fortescue on the outskirts of Rowanbank village. Janet knew there were three younger Fosters at home. After school, the boys confided that their father had ordered Molly to stay at home to help their mother.

'Our Molly loves school, an' learning, but Ma's going to have another bairn.'

'Aye, our Molly wis greetin' when Father said she couldna come to school wi' us no more.'

'Ma said she ought to have a chance to learn her lessons, but Pa started to shout,' Joe Foster said. 'He threw the oil lamp at Ma. He says our Molly has learned enough rubbish frae the old dominie. He needs her to work on the farm and help in the dairy.'

'Tell Molly I'm sorry and I shall miss her,' Janet said, blinking back tears.

Fred Bridges was not only stupid, he was lazy. Janet began to dread each day and the cruel beatings the dominie administered with apparent pleasure. She dare not confide in her mother. It would add to her anxiety.

During one of the coldest nights of the winter, Janet was

wakened from sleep by the shuddering of her mother's body close to her own. It was bitterly cold in the attic just beneath the roof. They huddled together for warmth, but it was not cold which made Mary Scott's thin shoulders tremble. She was near to breaking point and she was trying hard to stifle her sobs. Janet was dismayed. Her mother rarely showed her feelings. Janet cuddled closer, hugging the thin body.

'What is it, Mama?' she whispered. 'Has – has something happened?'

'No, no, lassie. Go to sleep. Don't worry.'

'But why are you crying, Mama?' She clung to her mother in sudden fear. 'You're n-not going to die too, are you, Mama?'

'N-no! No, lassie. It's Andrew. I don't want him to leave his studies, but I've no more money left to pay the fees. There's no pleasing Mr Todd. If a dish gets broken, he takes it from my wages, even when it's one of his pupils. He – he seems to want to make us suffer, yet we have done him no harm.'

'He is jealous of Grandfather,' Janet said with a wisdom beyond her years. Even as she uttered the words, she knew she had stumbled on the truth. She did not understand why Mr Todd should be jealous of a person who was dead, she simply knew he was, and he was making her mother miserable. 'I hate him!' she whispered vehemently. 'Don't cry, Mama. Please don't cry.'

'I just wish your grandfather had let Andrew have Mr Saunders's bursary, instead of arranging for Fingal to get it.' As soon as the words were out Mary realized she had broken her promise to her father.

'But Fingal won the bursary, Mama.'

'I was not meant to know,' she whispered. 'You must keep it a secret.'

'But Fingal did win, didn't he?'

'I promised your grandfather I would not tell anyone. Mr Saunders funded the bursary but your grandfather asked him. The McLauchlans are proud. They would not have accepted charity. Your grandfather set the examination in Fingal's favour. I guessed what he had done when I saw the papers. He didn't deny it and Fingal is very clever. He deserved a chance and he has been

Andrew's best friend ever since they started school together. He is strong and loyal. We knew he would look after Andrew. I canna grudge him his opportunity. If only. . . .' She stifled another shuddering sob.

'Tell me what I can do, Mama. How can I help?'

Mary was silent for a while.

Should she tell her daughter she could not afford to pay the fees the dominie was demanding for her schooling? Janet loved her lessons, or at least she had until Mr Todd became the dominie. Her grandfather had been proud of her. He had been convinced Janet was just as clever as Andrew and Fingal.

At length she said desperately, 'Tomorrow, after school, I would like you to t-take a letter to Mr Cole. He – he's my only hope. If – if he could lend me enough to pay Andrew's fees I know we could repay him when Andrew finishes university and finds an apprenticeship. Perhaps the Reverend Drummond will help him find work in a bank. Andrew is good at arithmetic and all things with figures. I will tell Mr Cole that, if you could take the letter for me, lassie?'

'I will go,' Janet promised.

'It will make you late for supper. Mr Todd will be angry, but I'll set you something aside up here. I'll hide it beneath the bed.'

Janet shivered in the darkness. Dominie Todd took pleasure in beating his pupils, but she sensed he wanted to beat her more than the rest.

This was borne out the following evening. It was a long walk down into the old village, across the fields and past the building where the savings bank committee met, then along to the far end where Mr Cole lived and worked. She had to wait until Mr Cole read her mother's letter and wrote a reply. On the way home, she met Lucy Hughes, who had been her mother's neighbour. She was a kindly, chatty woman and Janet did not like to be rude and hurry on, especially when her mother had always spoken well of Lucy as a helpful and kindly neighbour. So she was even further delayed.

Janet was cold and desperately hungry by the time she reached home again. She knew the dominie would have eaten his meal ages ago. He was obsessed by punctuality. Fearfully she crept round the back of the schoolhouse and in through the wash house, hoping to get in without passing the room where he dined and read and enjoyed a glass, or more, of whisky. He must have been listening for her. As soon as she appeared in the kitchen he came across the passage and entered by the opposite door. His pale eyes were alarmingly bright and staring. Janet shuddered.

'Well, miss, and where have you been?' Out of the corner of her eye, she saw her mother give a quick shake of her head, but she knew instinctively that she must not let the dominie know the reason for her errand. He would find a way of preventing her mother doing any extra work. He was always devising unnecessary tasks to take up her time and energy, almost as though he guessed her plans and took delight in thwarting them.

'When I ask where you have been, I expect an answer, girl!' he thundered, his pale eyes bulging, his face growing puce with anger. Janet shivered but she answered civilly.

'I went for a walk. I – I met a friend. I forgot how late it is, s-sir.'

'Where did you go? Who did you meet? How dare you be late for meals in my house?'

Janet hung her head. She knew whatever she said he would punish her in some way. She saw her mother, white-faced and trembling, wringing her hands. When she dared to utter a word of defence, Isaac Todd rounded on her in fury.

'The brat is ruined. It is my duty to teach her to be prompt and mannerly when she lives in my house.' He reached through the door, then swung to face them. He was grasping the cane. He had it ready. He had intended to use it.

'No!' Mary gasped. 'She is my child. I told her to go to. . . .'

'In my house I make the rules. She will have nothing tonight except a beating. Nothing to eat! Do you hear me?' Mary had expected this and prepared, but she had not expected him to beat her daughter. She was not in school now.

'A-a drink of milk. . . ?' She played for time, trying to think. 'The bairn must have a drink.'

'Nothing.' He advanced on Janet brandishing the cane, cutting through the air. 'Nothing except this!' Mary rushed to intercept.

Swift as a flash he struck at her, catching her across her face and shoulder, raising an angry stripe across the tender flesh of her cheek. The pain brought tears to Mary's eyes, but it brought hatred to her heart, and anger to her brain. Before she could prevent him he had grabbed Janet and was laying the cane about her, uncaring where it struck. He was almost demented in his determination to be master of them both and Mary guessed he was well primed with whisky too. She stared around wildly. The poker lay on the hearth. She grabbed it and brought it down with all her strength. Fortunately for Isaac Todd, it hit his forearm and not his head. The cane fell from his grasp. Mary seized it. She faced him defiantly, pushing Janet behind her.

'Go to our room, Janet.' She spoke over her shoulder, her eyes fixed on the dominie. 'Fold all your clothes into a bundle. We are leaving this house.' Teeth gritted, she outstared the sallow-faced man. He stood, clasping his throbbing arm, trying to flex his fingers. His bulbous eyes glittered with venom.

'You are not fit to teach my child, or any other.' Mary did not try to hide her contempt and loathing.

'And where do you think you will go, madam?' he sneered. 'You have no money. You have no relatives. That I have learned. You have a son to educate, a sickly fellow by all accounts.' Mary stared at him. So that was it? He had made enquiries about her. He believed she was at his mercy, that she would do whatever he asked.

'I would rather sleep in the hedgerow than spend another night under the same roof as you. You are a fiend.'

'You cannot go. You have a duty to do. A duty to the school, to the children!'

'Find another slave.' Mary backed carefully towards the door, her eyes bright with anger, the whiplash burning in her cheek. She still held the cane in one hand and the poker in the other. Anger made her vibrant and beautiful. For the first time, the dominie saw her as a desirable woman.

'Come, come now,' he wheedled, wincing as he held out his throbbing arm. 'You cannot leave me in the lurch. Surely we can—'

'Don't come one step nearer.' Mary raised the poker. He knew she would strike him. She had courage. He had seen the same proud defiance in her child's eyes. He wanted to conquer them both, to be master.

'I cannot let you—'

'We shall be out of this house as soon as I have packed our clothes. Do not come near either of us, or I shall not be responsible for my actions.' Mary's voice was calmer now, firm and strong. She stepped through the door and closed it, breathing deeply.

She had no idea where she would go, or what they were going to do, but she felt a surge of relief. Whatever happened she was glad. Glad she was free of the mean and evil man who had thought to take her father's place. Only now did she recognize the fear and oppression he had brought to her, and to her daughter.

In the tiny attic bedroom, she found Janet stifling sobs as she folded their clothes. Mary took Janet's hands in hers. She felt the ridges, some with broken skin. The dominie must have caned her daily. This time he had struck blindly, uncontrollably. Wherever the cane fell it had pleased him.

'I-I'm s-sorry, Mama,' Janet gulped.

'You have nothing to be sorry for, my lassie.' Mary folded her in her arms and brushed her lips across the small, bruised face. Then she bent and drew a plate of bread and butter and a cup of milk from beneath the bed. 'Eat this; it will give you strength, Janet. I don't know where we can go, or where we shall sleep.'

'I hate him,' Janet sobbed. 'Why did grandfather have to die?'

'His time had come. It was God's will.' Mary felt panic rising. She really was alone. But nothing would induce her to stay under the same roof as that devil.

Chapter Four

It was very dark when Mary and Janet left the schoolhouse. Each had a pack strapped to their backs and carried another in their arms. Mary had insisted they must bring the blankets and anything they could carry from their room, as well as their clothes and spare boots.

'Will he accuse us of stealing?' Janet shuddered with fear. She was suffering from shock. The dominie had caned her regularly but it had always been with cold precision. Tonight there had been a demon in him. The Devil had entered his brain. The pain of her bruised body would heal but she would never forget the evil glitter in the dominie's eyes.

'We are not stealing.' Mary spoke with new firmness. 'I sold him all the contents of the schoolhouse and he paid a mere token of their worth.'

'Even grandfather's books? Did he buy them too?' Janet asked wistfully.

'Everything. He considered the house and everything in it was his. But I do not sell my soul to the Devil,' she added, half under her breath. Janet saw her clutch her Bible closer to her breast. The big Bible which had belonged to her father's family had been too heavy to carry; it lay in the tiny attic room.

'Grandfather promised I could read all his books one day,' she said sadly. 'How shall I ever learn all the things he promised to teach me now, Mama?'

Mary was silent. Her daughter's schooldays had ended – gone

for ever. Even if they had not quarrelled with Todd, she could not have continued to pay the school fees.

Automatically, Mary turned her steps towards the old village where she had lived with Billy in the few idyllic years of her marriage, but Janet tugged at her sleeve.

'Couldn't we go to Crillion Keep? Mama Baird will help us.' Janet reverted to the name she had used for Peggy. Mary hesitated.

'We could sleep in the stable?' Janet pleaded. 'Like Jesus did.'

'We can ask, lassie,' Mary agreed. 'For tonight anyway. I –I'm not clear in my head. I don't know what we shall do.'

'But you are n-not sorry we've left the dominie, Mama?' Janet asked anxiously. 'I never want to see him again,' she added vehemently.

'Whatever happens we shall never go back,' Mary promised.

It was a long walk whichever way they went and Peggy Baird's cottage was in darkness by the time Mary and Janet dragged their weary limbs up the path. The McLauchlans' cottage was equally dark.

'They are all abed,' Mary whispered. 'I dinna like to disturb them. Do you know where the stables are, lassie?'

'Yes, we passed them. Look, Mama, that dark shape at the other side of the track down there.'

'Then we'll spend the night there.'

Janet led the way, weary enough to lie down and sleep in the hedge after her earlier journey to Mr Cole's. When they reached the stable all the stalls were occupied with horses.

'There is a hayloft up above. Mr McLauchlan goes up the ladder.'

'We'll go up there, then. It should be warmer.'

Huddled together in the sweet scented hay, both Mary and Janet slept, too exhausted to think, or to plan.

Mary woke first to the sound of a stable boy starting his duties for the day. She crept down the ladder and almost frightened the lad out of his wits.

'We arrived last night. Mr and Mrs Baird had gone to bed. I did not wish to disturb them,' she explained, half afraid he might attack her with the fork he was holding. He lowered it and nodded dumbly. 'Are they awake yet?' He nodded again and Mary squeezed past him out into the fresh morning air. She did her best to tidy her hair, aware that she must look like a vagrant.

She was astonished to see Fingal McLauchlan walking towards her. He was in serious conversation with Donald Baird, Peggy's husband.

'Fingal! What are you doing home? Why are you not at the university?' A thought occurred to her. 'Andrew? Is he with you? Has he gone to the schoolhouse?'

'Hello, Mrs Scott!' Fingal's surprise equalled her own. 'No, Andrew is not with me. My father is ill. I – I was afraid he might die without me seeing him again. As Dominie McWhan did,' he added in a low voice. 'I must return to Edinburgh tomorrow.'

'I see. I – I'm sorry. I did not know your father was ill.' She looked at Donald Baird. 'We – we came to see Peggy. You were abed when we arrived last night. We slept in the loft. I – we must not trouble either of you further.'

'Wait!' It was clear to Donald Baird that Mistress Scott was distraught. 'You must see Peggy, now that you are here.'

'We?' Fingal asked swiftly. 'You are not alone?'

'Janet is with me,' Mary said more calmly, pulling herself together with an effort. 'She is still asleep. In the loft. But tell me, Fingal, what news of Andrew? Is he well? The cough?'

'It troubles him still,' Fingal admitted reluctantly. 'Otherwise he is – he is as always. He works at his books long into the night. Shall I give him a message, a letter perhaps?'

'A letter. . . .' Despair dulled Mary's gaze. 'We do not even have a quill.'

'See Peggy, now, Mistress Scott,' Donald Baird said gently. 'She will find you all you need.' And learn whatever troubles you, he thought silently. He shook his head. Troubles never seemed to come alone. Fingal had done right to make the journey from Edinburgh for he was sure Jacob was dying. His father-in-law had been a good friend to him and to Peggy.

'Perhaps I had better waken Janet and tell her where I am first. . . .' Mary said.

'I will tell her,' Fingal said quickly. 'We are on our way to the stables. Today I am helping Donald in place of my father.' Mary nodded. Fingal's father was head coachman and Donald Baird worked with him as second coachman. Fingal's young face was anxious and Mary could guess the reason. His parents lived in a tied cottage, which went with his father's job. True, Maggie McLauchlan also worked as cook and housekeeper but would she be allowed to stay in the coachman's cottage?

Fingal climbed the ladder to the loft and found Janet sleeping still. Exhaustion from the two long walks of the previous day, combined with shock and pain, had taken their toll. Rays of early-morning light came through the small window near the floor of the loft. It caught the wild profusion of chestnut curls spread around Janet's head. She was lying on her back, fully clothed and half-covered with hay but her arm was flung above her head. Along the open palm and fingers Fingal saw the wounds. Caning? Caning for Janet? He frowned. She had been the dominie's granddaughter through and through. He recalled how bright and intelligent she had been, how far ahead of the other children. She had needed no extra help or favouritism. She had loved learning.

True, she was a child of high spirits and determination. He half smiled as he remembered how often she had followed him and Andrew on their boyish pursuits, how she had fallen in the burn when they went to gather frogspawn. She had even climbed to the top of the old tree where he and Andrew had their secret meeting place. They had told her it was a wishing tree and she had insisted on making her wish. She had refused to tell them what it was in case telling spoiled the magic of the tree.

As he gazed down at her he realized her face was paler and thinner than he remembered. Fear struck his heart. Surely Janet had not developed the same racking cough which troubled Andrew? Consumption. He would not say the word aloud. He could not bear to lose both of his friends, and Janet was closer than a friend: she was almost a sister to him. Yet as he looked down onto her sleeping face, his boy's heart stirred with tenderness and something more than the feelings of a brother. She was so young, so innocent. Janet stirred and turned her head. Fingal gasped. Across her cheek were two angry lines, one of them running right down her neck and disappearing beneath the neck of her dress, torn when the dominie had grabbed her. There were three more stripes across her other arm. She opened her eyes as he moved closer. He watched them widen as he came into her line of vision.

'Fingal! Is it really you? I wished and wished you were here last night.' Her delight and trust warmed him. He reached down to help her to her feet. As soon as she moved, the pain and the horror of the previous evening returned. Fingal saw her wince.

'What has happened, Janet? Who has hurt you so?'

'The – the dominie. I took a message for Mama. I was late for supper. He – he was so angry, Fingal.'

He could see the disbelief in her eyes as the memory came rushing back.

'He even hit Mama.' She bit back a sob.

'Oh, Janet, my lassie.' Fingal drew her tenderly into his arms and she clung to him, sobbing against his father's dusty waistcoat which he had donned to help Donald in the stables. Anger flared in Fingal's young heart.

'I have heard of dominies who like to use the cane too freely. Some of the fellows at university tell tales of cruelty – but to beat you, a girl? And so cruelly. . . .'

'He – he's horrid. I hate him. Mama says we are never going back.'

'I see . . . I'm glad you are not returning to the house of such a man, but—'

'Fingal?' Donald Baird's voice came from the stable below. 'Is the wee maid all right? Have you wakened her?'

'Yes. We're coming down. Can you help her, Donald? She has been badly beaten.'

'Beaten?' Donald reached up two muscular arms and lowered Janet gently to the floor of the stable. He watched her move her stiff limbs and try to flex her shoulders. 'Beaten?' he repeated. 'Who has done such a thing, lassie?'

'The dominie,' Fingal told his brother-in-law grimly.

'So it's true! Angus and Beth say he takes pleasure in using the cane. We thought they must deserve it. They told us he caned Miss Janet every day. We did not believe them.'

'It's true,' whispered Janet. 'And I tried so hard.'

'I'm sure you did my lamb,' Donald's voice was gruff. 'No wonder our two bairns say they will walk to school through the snow rather than stay in the dominie's house.'

'You only have to look at Janet. See her face. She was not even in school. She had been obeying her mother's instructions to go on an errand.'

'The letter!' Janet gasped in dismay. 'I forgot to give Mama the reply from Mr Cole.' She pulled a thick white envelope from her pinafore pocket.

'Your mother is with Peggy, lassie. You take her up to the cottage, Fingal. We'll be getting on with the horses.'

'How is Andrew?' Janet asked as they walked side by side.

'He has the cough still, but he is working hard at his studies. Most of the students believe he will get the trophy for the best mathematics student next year. He works so hard. . . .' He hesitated, then added, 'Sometimes Janet, I fear for his health. I believe he would forget to eat if I did not insist.'

'You are a good friend to him.' Janet stopped and seized his hand. 'We are grateful to you, Fingal.'

'I hope I shall always be a good friend, to both of you, Janet. You are as dear to me as my own family. You will promise to tell me if ever you are in trouble? If ever you need my help? If only I could take care of you. One day. . . .' He broke off and bit his lip. 'I hate to think of the dominie caning you so,' he said vehemently. 'I would like to – to. . . .'

'No one can help with that. He – he takes pleasure in caning all of us. B-but he seemed to have a grudge against me.'

'I would like to give him a caning. . . .'

Janet looked up at him and he caught a glimpse of her old, impish smile.

'I wish you could. You are certainly as big as he is now. I think you could cane him very well. Has Andrew grown as tall as you?'

'No. He is very thin. . . . I do worry about him, Janet, but I don't like to trouble your Mama, especially now when she has more trouble than ever.' He pushed the door of his sister's cottage open for her to enter.

Mary and Peggy broke off their conversation.

'Come in, lassie, and have some porridge,' Peggy greeted Janet warmly. 'Oh, my bairn! What has that monster done to you? Your poor face. . . .' Peggy turned Janet's face to the light, and then examined her scarred hands, shaking her head in disbelief. 'You could never have deserved such caning! You were never a bad wee bairn.' Janet did not answer. There was nothing to say and she was ravenous for the plate of steaming porridge Peggy set before her with a bowl of cream.

'Now, you two,' Peggy turned to Angus and Beth, 'it is time you were on your way or you will be late for school.' Six-year-old Beth sidled up to Janet and put her hand in hers.

'Can't I stay here with Janet today? She could help me with my numbers.'

'No, Beth, you cannot stay at home today, but it is Saturday tomorrow and you will be at home then. Now off you go.'

'You said you had a letter for your mother, Janet,' Fingal reminded her.

'Oh yes! I forgot about Mr Cole's letter last night, Mama.'

'No wonder, lassie. So did I.' Mary took the letter and slit open the envelope.

'I wonder what Mr Cole means by this,' she said aloud. 'He says he has a proposition to put before me now that his wife is so frail. He says he will speak to me after the kirk on Sunday. He goes on about the little room at the back of the tailor's shop being little more than a cupboard but he assumes Janet will be lodging in the schoolhouse for the winter with the other pupils.'

'No! No, Mama.'

'No!' Fingal moved swiftly to put a protective arm around her shoulders, his young face filled with concern.

'I couldn't send you back, lassie, even if I wanted to.' Mary spoke wearily. 'I can't afford to pay the dominie's fees. I can't make head nor tail o' Mr Cole's letter.'

'Well, it's only two days until the Sabbath, Mary,' Peggy Baird said. 'You could bide here until you have talked with him. I wouldn't be surprised if he's wanting you to keep house for him and look after his wife.'

'Do you think we could stay here in the stables until then?'

'We're pleased to help. You could share the bairns' bed. Mother would have given you a bed but Fingal is sleeping in the bedroom. He'll stay with her again tonight. When he is not here I stay with Father at night. Mother doesn't want to leave Mr Saunders in the lurch. She worked at Crillion Keep before he inherited it and he kept her on as housekeeper. Mrs Mossy is a good cleaner but she is a hopeless cook.'

'I didn't realize your father was so bad, Peggy. Maybe I can help while I am here? I could give your mother a rest. I'm used to nursing after – after caring for Billy.'

'Would you do that?' Peggy's eyes brightened. 'I remember Doctor Carr saying how well you cared for Billy. I don't know when Mother last had a proper sleep. Father canna help himself and he's a heavy man to lift.'

'I'll go over to the cottage, then. It will be a relief to know I can help.'

'Eat up some breakfast first then, Mary. You look tired to death.'

Janet had already washed her hands and face in the pail of water Fingal had drawn from the well. It was stingingly cold but it banished the sleep from her eyes and made her feel alert and alive. The exhaustion of the previous evening vanished when she had eaten the large bowl of porridge.

'It looks to me as though you're both fading away. Did the dominie no' feed ye well?'

'He's the meanest, most miserable man you could ever imagine,' Mary declared.

'Can I go and help Fingal at the stables now?' Janet asked eagerly.

'Aye, away ye go, lassie,' Peggy said fondly. 'He was aye pleased to have your company and ye'll take his mind off his own worries. He'll need to return to Edinburgh tomorrow.'

'How will he get back?' Mary asked.

'Joe Nairn, the carrier, has promised to lift him to the crossroads when he takes a load o' wood over to The Place. He said he'd ask one o' the carters to take Andrew as far as Moffat and maybe he'll be lucky and get a lift or two for the rest o' the journey.' She sighed. 'He's a good laddie, but he's worried about my stepfather and mother being in the Coachman's Cottage. He is going to talk to Mr Saunders when he and Donald have finished the horses.'

Fingal was concerned for his mother and he made his way up to the big house to discuss the situation with Josiah Saunders.

'I know the cottage is tied and intended for the head coachman,' Fingal explained, 'but Mother was born there when her father was coachman. It would upset her to move. I could train as undercoachman with Donald if you will allow us to stay in the cottage, sir?'

'Ah, Fingal, you have only one more year to do at university. Would you throw it all away to become a coachman?'

'If it means allowing my mother to keep her home, sir, and if you will employ me?'

'You're a good son, Fingal. I know how hard you have worked, and it would be a waste to throw away your education. One day I hope to offer you more than work as my coachman. I value your mother's care of me and my household as much as I value my coachmen's care of my horses. Donald tells me young Mark Wright is a good worker and he is careful when driving the pony and trap. He assures me the two of them should manage very well. Mark's father is horseman at Home Farm so he is happy to live at home with his parents and walk across the field to work each morning. So you see you have no need to worry. You must continue your studies.' He asked a few more questions about Fingal's time at university before they parted. Fingal's heart was lighter than he had thought possible considering the state of his father's health.

Janet felt sad and alone when Fingal left for his journey back to Edinburgh. She struggled to hold back her tears. Fingal returned her hug, then bent his head and kissed her cheek, muttering fervently, 'I wish we were older. I wish I could take care of you, Janet.'

As Mary and Janet entered the kirk on Sunday morning, Mr Cole caught Mary's eye and gave a polite nod. He watched her follow

Peggy and her family into their seat, instead of taking the seat she had always occupied with her father and her husband. Dominie Todd sat there alone, his expression grim, his mouth a thin line. He knew he did not have the respect Dominie McWhan had commanded from young and old alike and he resented the dead man's continuing influence. Gossip spread rapidly in the small community and other members of the congregation were quick to notice Mary Scott and her daughter had relinquished her family's pew.

'The rumours must be true,' whispered one to another. Janet was too innocent to grasp the significance of the change of seats but she sensed that everyone was looking at them. The wheals from Dominie Todd's cane still showed bright pink on their faces. She shivered and glanced across at him

She was pleased when she saw Molly Foster and three of her brothers. She knew there were more young Fosters who must be at home with their mother. Janet guessed the man must be their father. His stare made her feel uncomfortable. She tried to catch Molly's eye but the older girl kept her head bowed, her eyes downcast. Janet thought she looked pale and unhappy. She raised her eyes and found Mr Foster looking at her strangely as though he was assessing her in some way. It reminded her of the way her grandfather had looked at the two pigs which he had kept in the pigsty behind the schoolhouse. He had looked that way when he was deciding whether one of them was ready for Mr McPhee, the butcher. She shuddered and lowered her own gaze.

The Reverend Peter Drummond was a good man and a fine preacher but Mary Scott kept her eyes lowered. She knew he, like everyone else, had noticed she was not in the family pew she had occupied every Sabbath since she was a small child. All the congregation would know her disagreement with the dominie was a serious matter when she would not share the same pew.

Josiah Saunders also noticed and concluded the disagreement at the schoolhouse must be as serious as Mistress McLauchlan had reported, but he had no idea how dire the situation had become for Mary Scott and twelve-year-old Janet. He was not a man who mixed in society and he abhorred the sort of idle gossip which his stepsister Eliza and her ilk relished. When Dominie McWhan had arranged for Fingal to win the bursary to attend university, he had assured Josiah he would finance his grandson's education himself, and his granddaughter's too if he was spared long enough. So it did not occur to Josiah that those fees had ceased with the dominie's death. His own concern was for his housekeeper, Maggie McLauchlan, whom he valued and respected. In spite of Fingal's reassurance that her home was safe, she had looked exhausted and deeply troubled since her husband had suffered a stroke ten days ago.

Although he was only thirty-two, he had known since he was a boy that his own health was precarious, but he had learned to accept the old doctor's advice to make the best of each day and he had already survived years longer than had been expected. He had been surprised when his great-uncle, on his mother's side, had died and left him the small mansion house of Crillion Keep, along with the surrounding land. It was not a large estate, but it gave him a secure living and amply provided for his needs. In the letter his Great-Uncle Cedric had left for him, he had bade him enjoy each day which God might grant him and if it gave him satisfaction to ease the burdens of those who needed help then he must follow his heart. There was one proviso: neither Eliza Ross, nor her offspring, were to benefit from the Crillion estate. The old man had been shrewd enough to assess his stepsister's avarice, just as he had known of his own yearning for knowledge and his ambition to pass on his learning had he not been thwarted by ill health.

Josiah understood his uncle's wishes because they both remembered Eliza quarrelling bitterly with his father when she could no longer drain his coffers. Josiah's own mother had died shortly after his birth. When he was four years old, his father had married a widow with a fourteen-year-old daughter, Eliza. Looking back, he realized she had been jealous of him from the first day she arrived in his home. She had resented the kindness and affection her mother had shown towards him.

As the congregation filed out of the little kirk, Mr Cole caught Mary's eye and indicated his wish to speak with her outside. She drew Janet to one side, reluctant to answer the questions she knew many of the parishioners were longing to ask, and she was thankful Mr Cole did not delay in seeking her out.

'I see 'tis true, then?' he greeted her, lifting his bowler hat politely as he reached her and Janet. 'You've left your position at the schoolhouse, Mistress Scott?'

'Ye-es,' Mary heard her own voice quaver alarmingly.

'Well, well,' Mr Cole was saying, 'I do believe God has answered my prayers, then. The dominie's loss will be my gain. As I explained in my letter, my wife is growing increasingly frail. She needs care, help in the house and with the meals, you understand?' He broke off, frowning at the large, ruddy-faced man who was hovering close by. He was not one of his customers but Cole had seen him in church from time to time. He had a vague recollection that the man lived at the north end of the parish, maybe even in the next parish. There had been some talk about him amongst the elders but this was not the time to dwell on gossip. The tailor turned his attention back to Mary with a questioning glance.

'Well, would you consider a full-time situation in my home, Mistress Scott?'

'I would be glad of it, Mr Cole but Janet—'

'Good, good, I know how neat and correct you are with the ledgers too. I shall be glad of your help with the orders for a few hours each week. You will eat with us but unfortunately I can only offer you the small room at the back for your accommodation. . . .' He looked towards Janet apologetically. 'Your daughter will be staying at the schoolhouse, no doubt, and—'

'No!' Janet was almost as surprised as Mr Cole when the words burst from her of their own accord. 'No,' Janet repeated, 'I do not want to attend the dominie's school.'

'I see. But. . . .' A look of consternation came into the tailor's crinkly eyes.

'Pardon me, ma'am, for interrupting.' They all turned. 'I'm Foster from Braeheights Farm. Ye'll ken ma bairns attend the school. My lads told me you had both left the schoolhouse Thursday night, without warning. They thought your bairn wouldna be going back to school. She was a friend tae my ain lassie, so I'm offering her a wee job up at the farm. She'll have a roof and enough to eat. Molly would like the company.' He glanced behind him. They all looked at Molly then. She was hanging back, glowering at the ground as though her life depended on it.

'Molly? We know Molly well,' Mary said eagerly. 'So you're her father?'

'That's right, ma'am. Our Molly works at home now. There's plenty to do with the bairns and the animals. Your lassie needs a place and we could use another wee maid.'

'Why er . . . well yes, I suppose. . . .' Mary frowned uncertainly. In the dim recesses of her mind she had visualized teaching Janet herself. She had not considered them living apart, or Janet earning her living, not yet. But Andrew's future must come first.

'Got on well together at school, our Molly and your wee lass,' Mr Foster went on in a jocular tone. Janet was looking at Molly, wondering why the older girl refused to meet her eyes, why she was so intent on scuffing the earth with her best Sunday boots. 'You'd like to come and live with us, wouldn't you, lassie?' Janet looked past him to Molly. Just for an instant she saw Molly raise her eyes and look at her intently. She was astonished to see a swift shake of her head, before her chin sank once more onto her skinny chest. Mr Foster caught Janet's startled glance and turned his head towards Molly, a fierce frown drawing his bushy brows together. 'She's having a bit o' a sulk. She'll be happier if she has a wee friend up at the farm for company.' He moved close to Molly's side, his large hand grasping her shoulder in an iron grip. She seemed to cringe. 'Won't you? Tell them you'd like your wee friend frae the schoolroom to keep ye company.' His grip tightened and Molly glanced up briefly.

'Aye, I'd like that,' she muttered, and lowered her head.

'Well, Mistress Scott, what do ye say? I havena all day to wait. The lads stay with their grandmother in the village on schooldays so I could take your lass back to the farm with Molly and me in the trap now. Molly can find her an apron or two. I'll be back next week to collect her ain things.'

Mary bit her lip and looked at Janet. They only had the few

clothes they had managed to carry away the night they left the schoolhouse.

'It would save the wee maid a long walk up to our place. It's a fair distance, even wi' the pony and trap. The wife was brought up in this parish, see, and she likes the bairns to come back for the school and the kirk. Ye'll need tae make your mind up,' he added brusquely.

Janet's eyes filled with tears but she looked at her mother bravely. She knew in her heart there was no choice. Mr Cole had no room for her and she could not stay with Peggy Baird indefinitely. She was homeless. 'I'll g-go with Molly,' she whispered.

Mary hugged her close. 'You're a good bairn, Janet,' she whispered. 'I'll make it up to you when Andrew comes home. He'll get a fine job and we'll buy you all the books you want.'

'Yes, Mama.'

'Here, lassie.' Mary pulled off her own cloak. 'Take this. Ye'll need it more than me.'

'B-but, Mama. . . .' She looked up at her mother's thin, pale face, at her shoulders already hunched and shivering in the cold air.

'I'll get a lift with Mr Cole in his trap,' Mary whispered hoarsely. 'I'll be there long before you reach the farm. Anyway, you might need it to warm you in your bed. . . .'

Janet nodded, unable to speak now over the hard lump in her throat. Mr Foster ushered her impatiently towards his waiting trap. Janet looked back once, but her mother had already turned to accompany the tailor to his home.

Josiah Saunders was not in the habit of lingering to gossip after the kirk as many of the congregation did but as he stared out of the window of his coach he was surprised to see Mary Scott being driven away in one direction by Mr Cole while the child, Janet, was being driven off in the opposite direction in the pony and trap belonging to the man Foster. He did not know the man personally. He frowned, trying to recall what he had heard about him. He was sure it was nothing to the man's credit. He knew he came from one of the outlying farms near the parish boundary, maybe even from the next parish. He leaned out of the window and beckoned Donald Baird.

'Why is Mistress Scott driving off with Mr Cole and leaving her child with that man in the pony and trap?'

'Mistress Scott needs the work, sir, and Mr Cole needs a woman to keep his books and help his wife who is ailing. He hasna room for wee Janet.' In spite of his best efforts, Donald Baird's voice was gruff with emotion. They all cared deeply for the wee lass they had fostered as their own when she was a babe, and rumours abounded about Foster from Braeheights Farm.

'But surely the girl should still be at school. I recall Dominie McWhan had great hopes for her education.'

'Aye, I'm sure he was right, but Mistress Scott canna afford to pay the school fees now that the old dominie isna there.'

'The school fees? Then I will pay the fees for the girl to complete her education,' Josiah said immediately. 'We must go after the child and bring her back.'

''Tis not only the fees, sir. Miss Janet doesna want to go back to Dominie Todd's school. He caned her cruelly. I saw the marks he has left on the lassie myself. My own bairns say he enjoys using the cane but they were troubled by the way he picked on Miss Janet, poor lamb. They say he invented reasons every day to cane her. If she answered the questions first he caned her for being impertinent. If she got a question wrong, he caned her for being idle. He made her carry all the coal for the school and he forbade the other bairns to help her. We only heard this yesterday.'

'But this is preposterous! The dominie is supposed to command respect from both pupils and parents. I shall speak to him myself.'

'No! No, please, sir. Frae what I hear, he's a spiteful, mean kind o' man. He would guess who had told you and take it out on Angus and Beth, our own two bairns.'

'I see. I had not considered he would make other innocent children pay,' Josiah said thoughtfully. 'All right, drive me home, Donald. I shall not speak to the dominie myself but I shall have a word with the Reverend Drummond and make sure he is aware of conditions at the school. He has already expressed concern about the number of boys who are not attending school regularly. The situation should not continue. Meanwhile we must hope the people at the farm treat Miss Janet kindly.'

'Mistress Foster was a decent, kindly young woman before she married Foster,' Donald Baird said. 'She used to live on the outskirts o' Rowanbank Village. Her mother is Mrs Fortescue and she still has a cottage on the road to the shore. We rarely see Mrs Foster now. She seems to have a bairn every year.'

Chapter Five

At first, Janet looked around with interest as she perched beside Molly in the trap. They wended their way around narrow tracks and roads she had never seen before. Gradually, she became aware of the biting cold and huddled more closely into her mother's cloak, glad of its warmth now, even though it was far too long for her. Beside her Molly sat as silent as a stranger, indeed they might have been strangers, so different was she from the chattering, carefree schoolfriend of a few weeks earlier. As the road rose more steeply, the pony walked slower and slower. Every now and then, Mr Foster shouted and wielded the whip, making Janet flinch and huddle closer to Molly, but Molly seemed to be too miserable and forlorn to offer any comfort to her one-time friend.

After the chill of the wind, Janet appreciated the warmth and noise of the big, flag-floored kitchen at Braeheights. There was a baby crawling around the floor and a toddler trying to climb onto a stool. He was only slightly bigger than his younger sibling and she learned later there was only ten months between them. An older boy stared solemnly at her. Then she saw Mistress Foster gazing at her in dismay. She looked at her husband, her eyes full of questions.

'I've brought ye a maid,' he growled. 'She's the old dominie's granddaughter so that should please ye, ye and your education.'

'A maid? The dominie's wee lass canna be our maid! And she's only a bairn forbye. How old are ye, lassie?'

'Twelve. And a half,' she added hastily. 'Nearly. . . .'

'Just a bairn,' she said sadly, 'not even as big as our Molly. . . .' She glanced at her daughter and noted her wan face; her eyes dull and downcast. Her own heart sank within her. Surely he had not been at Molly next? Her gaze moved to her husband. He wouldn't – would he. . . ? An idea occurred as she stared at the two young girls. A determined glint came into her eyes. She turned to Janet.

'We'll see how you get on, lassie. Ye can sleep with our Molly. At least ye'll be company for each other, and maybe ye'll—'

'No!' Foster snarled. 'She'll sleep in the maids' room. Where the maids always sleep. Through there.' He looked at Janet and jerked his head to a door at the far side of the kitchen beneath the slope of the staircase, which led to rooms above. His wife scowled at him but she could not hold his hard stare. Her shoulders slumped. She guessed the truth. Her heart ached for her eldest child. 'Show her then, Molly. Where's your bundle, lass? Have ye left it in the trap?'

'N-no, ma'am. I came straight from the kirk. . . .' She looked at Mr Foster for help.

'Molly can lend her some aprons. I'll collect her ain things on Friday when I fetch the lads frae your mother's.'

'I see. . . .' Mrs Foster pursed her lips and turned towards her husband, hands on hips. Janet saw her swollen stomach and stared at the misshapen figure with sympathy. She did not understand then that Mistress Foster was soon to deliver yet another child to Braeheights Farm.

In the tiny room both Molly and Janet could hear the ensuing exchange.

'What possessed ye tae bring a lassie like that here? She's just a bairn—'

'Whisht, woman! She'll grow. Anyway, frae what I hear she'd nowhere else to go. She'll be grateful for her food and a roof over her head, more grateful than your little madam—' he added through gritted teeth.

'Molly's a good lass, or she was until . . . until. . . .' She swallowed the words with an effort. 'Are ye never satisfied? It was bad enough ye taking auld Abe's lassie, then the maid frae o'er Dumfries way. Now ye're trying to make my ain bairn into a – into a—'

'Maid!' Foster bellowed. 'You needed a maid, you said. Now you've got twae. I'll have nae more grumbling, or refusing me my rights. Where's the dinner, woman? I could eat a horse after the drive down to the kirk and back.'

'But . . . you canna expect a lass like that to do farm work! Even if she'd been full grown. . . .'

'If she wants tae eat she'll work all right, and everything else she's asked tae dae, or my name's no' Wull Foster. There's rumours going round the parish that the new dominie put the lassie and her mother out into the road, though naebody seemed tae ken the reason. Miserable-looking critter he is. The lass will be better off under my roof.'

'Will she?' Mistress Foster muttered. 'I wonder.'

In the small maid's room off the kitchen, Janet had listened to this exchange with alarm, unable to understand the innuendoes, the half-finished sentences. Her heart was heavy. She turned to Molly, her eyes full of unshed tears.

'Your mama doesn't want me here, does she? What am I to do? Where. . . ?'

'Of course she wants ye,' Molly assured her quickly. 'Ma's a good woman but Faither . . .' She looked at Janet's innocent young face despairingly, knowing the friend of her schooldays would never understand the torment she was suffering under this roof, the hatred that was growing in her heart for the man who called himself her father. Her mouth snapped shut and she frowned fiercely. 'It's just that ye're so small, Janet, and the work is hard up here for a woman – milking and churning, cleaning o' the byre, lighting up the boiler every day to wash clothes for the bairns, and Mother having another one any day. . . .'

'Another baby? You're getting another baby here at the farm?' Janet clasped her hands together, her blue eyes shining. 'How lovely!' she breathed.

'Ye'll not be saying that if ye've tae rock it tae sleep half the night, aye and still be up when he calls us for the milking at the crack o' dawn, and before the dawn in winter. It's a hard life up here, Janet. Is there no' other place ye could go?'

'You don't want me here, Molly? I-I thought you were my

friend.' Janet's eyes misted with tears.

'Oh, I do want ye, I do, b-but,' she lowered her voice to a hoarse, vehement whisper, 'I'd run away maself if it wasna for Mother needing me sae badly.'

'You'd run away? From your own home? Your own parents?' Janet remembered Mr Foster shouting at the pony and whipping it with the lash. She shuddered. 'Your father wouldn't beat us any worse than the dominie did, would he?'

'I. . . .' Molly looked at her young friend searchingly, then she shrugged. 'There's worse things than beating, Janet. I pray tae God ye'll never find out.'

'I shall work hard, I promise. And we shall be together like we used to be in the classroom, and when we ate our pieces at noon. We could go on with the reading. . . .'

'We've no books here! Well, only the Bible.'

'No books? None at all?' Janet saw Molly's brow darken and she said hastily, 'Well I could help ye learn to read with the Bible and then you could read any books you like one day.'

'We'll see,' Molly said tiredly. 'Mother would like that, but I dinna think either o' us will get much time for anything but work.'

Molly's words proved only too true. Janet didn't think she had ever been so tired in her whole life, but at least there was usually enough to eat. That was something to be thankful for after the miserable table the dominie had allowed her and her mother. The pupils who boarded at the schoolhouse hadn't fared much better either. She wondered how her mother was managing at Mr Cole's. Did she have enough to eat? Was she warm there, and happy? Every night before she went to sleep, she remembered her mother in her prayers, and Andrew too, as her mother had taught her. Always she prayed he was in good health and that his studies were going well. She longed for the day when he would come home and they would all live together again. Perhaps Andrew would be appointed as the dominie and they would all return to the schoolhouse and they would be happy again as they had been with her grandfather. Tired though she was by the end of the day she never forgot to add Fingal McLauchlan's name when she asked God for His blessing.

When the new baby was born, Janet loved him from the moment she set eyes on his crumpled little face and tiny clenched fists. Mrs Foster named him Peter and Janet never tired of rocking his crib with her foot as she stood at the large stone slab, peeling potatoes for the midday meal, and carrots and turnips to make barley broth. Or rubbing the soiled washing on the rubbing board until her knuckles bled. As she worked, she sang in an effort to soothe the baby. Her voice was low and sweet as she sang the hymns her mother had taught her, until Mr Foster came in and bellowed at her.

'Hod yer whisht, lassie, if ye canna sing anything else!'

'Leave the lassie be,' Mrs Foster protested. 'Can ye no see the twa wee bairns are listening tae? At least she keeps them quiet.' It was true that Adam and John, the two youngest boys, little more than babies themselves, attached themselves to Janet like two shadows.

'Ye're not very big, lassie, and I didna think ye'd be much use for work when I first saw ye,' Mrs Foster confessed, 'but I dinna think I could have managed without ye, especially now himsel' takes Molly tae work outside every day.'

'I like your wee boys, Mrs Foster,' Janet smiled.

'Aye, ye're a good, patient lassie with them. Even Joe listens tae ye.' Tis a pity he canna attend the school again come the summer. He aye enjoyed learning, not like Mark and Luke. They have aye had a bit o' the Devil in them.'

'The boys are not going back?' Janet asked in surprise. The Foster brothers were younger than herself. 'They're only ten.'

'Mark's eleven. His father wants them home to help on the farm, he says.' She sighed wearily. 'Old Jake will be going to the hiring come May. Foster thinks 'tis time the laddies started to earn their keep.'

'Oh.' Janet frowned. 'Do they want to leave school?'

'Och, they'll no' be minding. They dinna like the new dominie. Your grandfather was a fine man, lassie. Well respected i' the parish tae, he was. Helped many a poor body with the fees if their bairns wanted tae learn. Ye're a wee bitty like him, I was thinking when I saw ye chalking the letters on the slate for Joe tae learn. He wouldna have listened tae any other body.'

'Yes.' Janet sighed almost as heavily as Mrs Foster. 'I'd love to teach little children. . . . Mama says when Andrew finishes at the university he'll get a fine job of work and earn enough money to have a house of our own again, and she says I shall be able to read as many books as I like. If. . . .'

'Aye, if!' Mrs Foster said bitterly. 'It's a little word, lassie, but it makes a world o' difference. I wouldna count on that brother o' yours over much, frae what I've heard. Frail creature he is, they say. Just like his father. But look ye, lassie. We havena time tae dream. Will ye hang that great basket o' washing on the line for me and see if the first load is getting dry. Then if ye'll gather some sticks for the fire. . . .'

It was as Molly had warned her, Janet realized. There was always another task waiting to be done. As fast as one got finished, it came round again in a never-ending circle.

When the end of the May term arrived, Janet did not receive any wages although she had been at Braeheights Farm eight months. She had been unable to give her mother anything to put in the savings bank. Janet knew how much it meant to her mama to save money for Andrew's education. She listened to her mother asking Mr Foster about her wages but she was dismayed and near to tears when the big man answered gruffly, 'She hasna earned any yet. I keep her in food, provide her aprons and clogs, and a warm bed at night. What more d'ye want, woman? Shall I send her back tae ye?' he asked slyly. Mary Scott looked up at Mr Foster and bit her lip. She looked down into Janet's anxious face and her eyes, bright with tears. She shook her head mutely and whispered, 'You'll have to work a bit harder, lassie. I need the money for Andrew's books.'

As winter came round again, Janet worried. Her mother insisted they must save all they could in the parish savings bank. She said it had been her father's dying wish to put money into the bank so that Andrew could have an education.

Mr Foster did not allow them to attend the kirk every Sunday, so her meetings with her mother were brief and irregular and there was never enough time to talk. Mr Cole was usually anxious to return to his ailing wife, taking her mother with him, but Peggy Baird always had a warm smile of welcome for Janet. She wished she could have time to talk with the child she had fostered as a babe. Sometimes she had news of Fingal but Mr Foster always wanted to usher Janet away back to Braeheights. He didn't give her time to talk.

Other members of the congregation had little to say to Mr Foster, she noticed. Like his farm, he too seemed to exist on the fringes. Janet guessed he did not share his wife's respect for the Sabbath, or for the minister, and it was only his fear of dying and being burned in hell which brought him to the kirk at all. After the service, he always hurried his brood to the trap, impatient to return home and eat a hot dinner.

At the end of November Janet heard her mother asking Mr Foster about her wages again. She was dismayed when the big man growled, 'Wages! What wages?'

'It is the end of the November term. Surely Janet has earned some wages by now?'

'She's still a bairn.'

'She's thirteen. And a half.'

'I told ye before, I give her food, and a warm bed at night. What more d'ye want, woman? D'ye want tae take her back wi' ye?' Mary Scott looked into Mr Foster's hard grey eyes. Shaking her head she looked at Janet's anxious face, seeing her tears of hurt and humiliation. She had worked so hard and had done her best to please everyone. Janet couldn't remember when her mother had last hugged her with warmth and affection, so when she bent to her now Janet realized it was only so that she could whisper, 'You'll have to work a bit harder, lassie. I need the money for Andrew. He's doing well. We shall be proud of him.'

'Yes, Mama.' Janet bit back a sob. She didn't know how she could work any harder, or what more she could do to please Mr and Mrs Foster so that she could earn some money like the other workers at Braeheights Farm. She felt a stirring of resentment. She tried so hard but her mother only had thoughts for Andrew.

In Edinburgh, Fingal continued his self-imposed task of

keeping a watchful eye on Andrew. Secretly, Janet wished he could help her as he did her brother but he was too far away, and anyway what could he do? He had no money of his own. He knew nothing of women's work, or how hard life was at Braeheights Farm, not only for herself but for Mrs Foster and Molly too.

Janet loved Mrs Foster's children but when another baby boy was born in the spring of 1824, she realized it was just as Molly had warned her. Another round had begun, rocking the crib, feeding and bathing, washing, ironing and mending. She had overheard the midwife telling Mr Foster he was going to kill his wife if he didn't give her a rest from having babies. Molly heard her warning too and her shoulders slumped when she heard her father's growled reply.

Janet had noticed how often Molly's eyes were red and puffy as though she had wept far into the night. Did Molly know her mother's life could be in danger because of all the babies she had to feed? Was that the reason she seemed so withdrawn and moody, so unlike the friend Janet had known at school?

Ten days later, Mrs Foster was out of bed and going about her daily tasks once more and Mr Foster whisked Molly off to the byre and the dairy again.

'Aye, and 'tis time you were helping with the milking and the pigs,' he growled, eyeing Janet closely. 'You're a woman grown now.'

Janet blushed to the roots of her hair. Could Mr Foster have overheard Molly explaining about the monthly bleeding and how it happened to all girls when they became women? She had been terrified at the first sight of blood but Mrs Foster had patted her kindly and shown her what to do. She had said it was not a matter to be discussed with men and boys, so how could Mr Foster know she had become a woman? Surely he could not have been spying on her when she went down to the closet? Her cheeks flamed at the thought. There were two doors to the rickety wooden shed, one for people to use the toilet, and the other, larger door at the opposite end, for cleaning it out twice a year. Sometimes she thought she had heard the hinges of the other door creaking while she was sitting in private on the wooden bench, but she had never seen anyone around when she came out of the closet. She looked up and caught Mrs Foster's eyes upon her.

'I need the lassie in the house to help me. Can't you see there's more to do than ever with another bairn to look after? Is it not enough that you've taken Molly to work outside?'

'If I say she'll learn to milk a cow, that's what she'll do. Her mother's aye asking when I'm going to pay her some wages. She'll need to earn them first.'

'She does earn them! I couldna manage without her.' But Mr Foster's gaze was fixed on Janet, noting her slender waist and the way her dress had grown tight over her budding breasts. His eyes narrowed.

'She's taller than Molly now, and she eats as much as the lads. I'll teach her to milk myself.'

Janet shivered. She had seen Molly milking the cows, sitting on her small stool with her head tucked close into the animal's flank.

'Aren't you frightened? Won't they kick you?' she had asked fearfully.

'They're all right, once they get used tae ye, and the feel o' your hands,' Molly had told her calmly. 'There's worse things than milking cows,' she added grimly.

A few days later, Mr Foster led Janet to the byre and set her on the stool. The cow fidgeted uneasily and Janet jumped nervously.

'Steady now, steady,' Mr Foster said softly, but Janet realized he was speaking to her and not the cow, and his big rough hand was on her shoulder, pressing her down onto the stool. Then his fingers were on her neck, stroking it as he guided her head against the warm flank of the cow. He bent over her and she could feel his hot breath against her cheek as he showed her what to do. As soon as Joe finished milking his own cow, he came to her. Mr Foster straightened immediately. He glowered at his son.

'I'm just showing the lassie how tae milk a cow. She's never been near one before. She's nervous as a fawn.' That was the longest speech Janet had heard Mr Foster utter to any of his sons. Usually he did no more than growl out an order.

'We'll see she's all right,' Joe muttered through tight lips. He was a year younger than herself but since he had left the schoolroom and worked on the farm, Janet felt he seemed years older than her in experience. When his father had left the byre, Janet heard Joe speaking to Molly, his voice low. A little while later when she had finished milking her first cow and was wondering what she should do next, Molly came to stand beside her, holding her own stool in one hand.

'The cows'll d'ye no harm, Janet. You milk old Roany next. She's quiet as a lamb. And . . . and Janet, if Father asks ye, just tell him you're getting on fine. We'll help ye, Joe and me. Dinna go with him to the stable, or the hay loft or – or anywhere else on your ain. . . .' She broke off and bit her lip, her colour high one second and ebbing the next so that her skin seemed as pale as death. Janet frowned at her.

'She doesna ken what ye're trying tae tell her!' Joe said impatiently and got up from the cow he was milking. He came to them and put his face close to Janet's. 'Ye ken nowt o' things yet, for all your learning frae the dominie's books.'

'I pray she'll never learn, then,' Molly muttered, while Janet's eyes moved from one to the other in bewilderment.

'Listen,' Joe said, as though reaching a decision. 'D'ye remember the time ye had tae help me take the sow over tae Lowbreer Farm, Janet?'

'Yes, I remember. . . .'

'And Mr Kerr was busy and he told us to put her in the pen beside his boar?'

'Y-yes.' Janet frowned. Then she shuddered. 'She squealed and squealed. I thought the boar was hurting her.'

'Aye, because he – he. . . .' Joe bit his lip now and looked at Molly for help but Molly's face was white, her lips pinched. Her eyes had a sunken look as though they could only focus on something inside her head. 'The boar jumped on the sow and shoved his – his thing into her,' Joe finished in a rush.

'Ye-es, I remember,' Janet said slowly, shuddering as she recalled the incident. 'He wouldn't let her go but when Mr Kerr came he laughed and laughed because I wanted to rescue poor Aggie from his nasty old boar. He said she would think it was worth all the trouble when she got her piglets. . . .'

'Aye, well that's what animals do. S-some men act like that – like animals.' He looked searchingly at Janet and saw her bewildered frown. He scuffed the earth floor with his clog and kept his eyes lowered. 'So dinna let Father get ye on your ain or he'll dae the same to you!' he said in a rush and swung away, his face red with embarrassment as he curried down against the flank of a cow. Janet blinked, unable to take in the meaning of Joe's awkward phrases. He couldn't mean what she thought he meant, could he? The blood rushed to her cheeks and she turned to Molly. Her friend gave a brief, unhappy nod and turned away.

Janet's work in the byre and the dairy did not last long. The baby was called Ezra and he was only two months old when Mrs Foster took ill again. Every morning she was sick.

'She's started even sooner this time,' Molly muttered unhappily as she and Janet heard her mother retching in the washhouse. Baby Ezra was hungry and fretful and between him and Peter, as well as their mischievous brothers, Janet had more to do than she could manage. Sometimes Molly stayed indoors to help with the washing and Janet enjoyed it when they worked together.

One day when the wind was sending the fluffy white clouds scudding across the sky and the sun was shining, Mrs Foster decided some of the blankets should have their annual wash.

'We'll do them, Mama,' Molly told her. 'You rock the cradle and rest. We'll give them a good poshing i' the tub.'

'Aye, ye're good lassies,' Mrs Foster sighed wearily. 'Light the fire under the boiler, Janet, then the water will be hot enough.'

Janet felt it was almost like old times as she and Molly kicked off their clogs and peeled off their woollen stockings. Together they stood in the tub, holding their skirts high above the water as they tramped the thick blankets, wriggling their toes and enjoying the squelch of the wool and water under their feet. Suddenly Molly stopped laughing. Her eyes narrowed. Her face grew hard as stone. Janet followed her gaze to the doorway and saw Mr Foster leaning against it. How long had he been there? Watching them through his narrowed eyes. There was a strange expression on his face and Janet shuddered. Suddenly she became aware that

Molly had dropped her skirts, right down into the water, but she was still holding hers high above her knees and it was on her long white legs that Mr Foster's eyes were fixed.

Mrs Foster's health seemed to get rapidly worse instead of improving as it usually did. The sickness continued and her hands and feet had begun to swell. She was constantly tired and she had stopped putting Ezra to her breast. Molly's moods of brooding silence returned. Every morning, her face looked pale and drawn, her eyes red and puffy.

Molly's small room was directly above her own at the top of the stairs. The older Foster boys also shared the loft but Molly's bed was partitioned from theirs with a curtain. Mr and Mrs Foster and the two youngest children slept in a small room on the other side of the kitchen. Sometimes during the night, Janet was awakened by creaking on the wooden steps up to the loft. Sometimes strange noises seemed to be just above her head. Twice she was sure she heard Molly sobbing but when she asked her Molly snapped sharply. 'Ye must have been dreaming.'

Early one morning Mrs Foster sent Janet to the byre for warm milk from the cow. It was to feed baby Ezra. He had been particularly wakeful and cross during the night.

Neither Joe nor Molly had heard her approach and Janet was dismayed to overhear Joe speaking angrily.

'If only I was strong enough I'd come through and. . . .'

'Och, Joey. Ye should close your eyes, and your ears. He'd hurt ye for sure if—'

'He's an evil brute. I wish he wasna our father. I'll kill him one o' these nights. . . .'

'No! Dinna say that Joe. Ma needs ye. She needs both o' us. If it wasna for her I'd be gone frae here—'

Janet coughed and they both peered past their cows to stare at her in surprise.

Many Sundays passed but no one from Braeheights Farm was allowed to attend the kirk. Janet longed to see her mother and Peggy Baird. She yearned for news of her brother Andrew and Fingal McLaughlan. One Sunday, she asked whether she could go to the kirk and take some of the younger children.

'I'm sure I could manage the pony and trap now,' she ventured.

Mr Foster went red with rage. 'No one takes the trap except me, young madam. Say your prayers at night and that'll suffice.'

As the weeks passed, Mrs Foster seemed to get more and more swollen everywhere. Even her thin face was so puffed up her eyes were hardly visible. Baby Ezra seemed to know his mama was not well and he whimpered constantly.

'Ye wouldna think he was nearly six months old, such a puny wee thing he is,' his mother lamented wearily.

She always insisted the older members of the household should be bathed in the tub in the wash house once a week and it was Janet's job to boil the water in readiness for Mr Foster, then Joe and Luke and Mark on Friday nights. Mrs Foster, then herself and Molly bathed on Saturdays. Usually they looked forward to the luxury of sitting in the big wooden tub together, each washing the other's hair. Recently Molly had been more moody and miserable than ever and not even the bathing ritual could lift her spirits. It was while she was rubbing Molly's hair one Saturday night that Janet noticed her stomach was growing quite rounded in comparison to her own flat front. She was almost a head taller than Molly now, but neither of them had ever been fat. They worked too hard for that.

Once again none of them attended the kirk on the Sabbath but on Monday morning the Reverend Drummond sent Tom Friar, one of his young protégés, with a message for Janet. Her mother wished her to visit. She was filled with excitement.

'Andrew must be home at last!' she breathed, her blue eyes shining.

'I dinna ken the reason, miss, but the minister said I was to take ye back with me. We're to go across the fields. He'll meet ye with the pony and trap when we reach the road.'

'Perhaps Andrew has found work already! Peggy told me he has won one of the highest awards at the university. Fingal sent her a letter.'

'But, ye'll be back by tomorrow, lassie?' Mrs Foster asked anxiously. 'I dinna ken how we shall manage without ye now.' Janet paused in her eagerness to set out. She looked into the pale, weary face. Mrs Foster seemed an old woman, but Janet remembered she had allowed her to stay, had given her food and found work for her to do when she had nowhere else to go. Her own happy anticipation abated for a moment.

'I will come back. I will stay until you can hire another maid to take my place,' she promised.

'Ye're a good bairn. Fetch your cloak, lassie. It's a bonnie day but it could change by night.' She looked searchingly at the solemn-faced lad. 'I hope the news is as good as she thinks it's going to be,' she said.

He shook his head. 'I dinna think it's good, mistress,' he muttered. 'The Reverend Drummond is going tae drive Miss Janet down to Rowanbank himself.'

Chapter Six

Janet remembered Tam Friar well. He had been at her grandfather's school and he was two years older than her.

'So you work at the manse now, Tam?' she asked as they crossed the fields together.

'Aye, he's a good man, Reverend Drummond. Some o' the families would starve if it wasna for him. Some o' them are breaking stones to improve the road, but we all ken he's paying frae his ain pocket so they can hold their heads up and buy victuals to feed their bairns. Last winter he ordered grain from his brothers in Liverpool. He had it brought in the wee boats to Rowanbank so that we wouldna starve after the bad harvest.'

He led her through a wood, careful not to let the brambles scratch her face. He still thought of her as the dominie's young granddaughter, but from what he had seen when he arrived at Braeheights Farm she was probably no better off than himself.

'And what do you do at the manse, Tam?'

'Whatever there is,' he said simply. 'Sometimes it's the stables, sometimes I help the minister in the garden. I like that best of all. I wish – I wish. . . .' He shook his head impatiently. 'What's the point o' wishing? We're lucky if we've food in our bellies.'

Janet was tired and she was glad when Tam said they would stop for a drink when they reached a burn.

'It's further than I thought,' she confided. 'I've never been across the fields before. Mr Foster drives us to the kirk in the pony and trap and we go through a village called Molden.'

'Aye, it's queer Foster coming all the way down to Rowanbank Kirk, but I heard that Mrs Foster's mother keeps the Foster lads, the ones who go to school during the week.'

'Some of Braeheights land is in Rowanbank Parish too.'

'It's still a long way, though, even cutting across country. It must be a fair step for the pony – there and back.'

'It is. Mr Foster doesn't bring us every Sunday though.' Janet sighed. 'I miss not coming to the kirk. I miss not being able to see Mama and Peggy Baird, and – and everyone. I can't wait to get there. Have we much further to go, Tam?'

'No. We're in luck today. The burn's low. I'll place some stones and help ye across. If it was winter we'd have to walk a lot further to get across.'

'I see. I'm glad you're here, to guide me. I'm quite lost. Oh, look! Look! I can see the road now we're over the hill. Isn't that the minister with his pony and trap? Down by that gate on the road below?'

'Aye, it is that.'

'It's such a long time since I had a proper talk with Mama,' Janet sighed. 'It will be wonderful if we can all live together again like we used to do.'

Tam gave her a pitying glance but it was downhill now and she was already running ahead. At fourteen, she was neither child nor woman but at that moment she felt as she had at eight years old, running after Andrew and Fingal, carefree and secure in her world. Janet longed to see her mother and Andrew. She hoped Fingal might be home too.

The minister greeted her kindly, taking her hand in his, feeling the work-roughened palm. He looked down at her fingers, small and chapped, the nails broken. He shook his head, wondering what his old friend the dominie would have thought to see his beloved grandchild reduced to this. He allowed himself a momentary feeling of exasperation as he recalled Mary Scott, so devoted to her son, so eager to give him everything she could, yet barely aware of her daughter's existence. Surely as a mother she should have arranged a better place than Braeheights Farm for her only daughter – and yet the child did not look unhappy, or ill-thriven as so many of his parishioners did. He sighed. There was only so much he could do to help them all. He looked into Janet's face, bright with anticipation, her eyes alight and eager, a smile of gratitude on her lips as he helped her into the trap and seated her beside him. His heart sank at the news he was about to impart. He looked down at Tam Friar, who was awaiting his orders respectfully.

'Jump onto the step, laddie, and hold on tight. I'll drop you off before we turn off the road and down to Rowanbank.'

As they passed the long track leading to Peggy Baird's cottage and Crillion Keep, Janet peered longingly through the gently swaying trees, but she could not see the houses and there was no sign of any familiar figures.

'Has Fingal McLauchlan returned with Andrew, sir?' she ventured timidly.

The minister gave his kindly smile. 'Not yet, child. He has to stay in Edinburgh for a few weeks longer until he finishes his apprenticeship. He has been a good and loyal friend, Andrew tells me. . . .'

'You have seen Andrew? Spoken with him?' she asked eagerly. 'Has he got a posting? I am so looking forward to seeing Mama. We shall all be together again at last. . . .'

'Ah – ahem, maybe. . . .' The minister cleared his throat, aware of Tam hanging onto the back of the trap. He didn't want to tell her that it was Andrew who had asked for her so urgently, pleaded with him to bring his sister to see him while he still had breath to talk with her. Surely Mary could have sent a message to her somehow, a warning. . . . He would wait until he had dropped Tam off on the other side of the hamlet of Crillion.

'I hear Mrs Foster is not keeping in good health? Will she manage today?' he asked, to take her attention.

'Molly will help her until I return, I think. I have promised I will not come to live with Mama until she has hired another maid.'

'You have told her you are leaving Braeheights Farm?' The minister sounded alarmed and Janet looked at him in surprise. He frowned. 'Molly was not at the kirk with you the last time you came with Foster and his laddies,' he said with an effort.

'No, Molly has been sickly lately,' Janet told him innocently.

'Sickly? I see. . . .' His frown deepened. 'Does she need Doctor Carr?'

'She would not hear of it when I asked. She said I had made the porridge too salty. I had not. Since then she always says she has eaten it too greedily – though Molly is never greedy,' Janet added thoughtfully. 'Some days she scarcely eats at all.'

'I see. . . .' He hoped his thoughts were unworthy. He knew Molly's grandmother well, and he remembered her sadness the day her daughter had married Wull Foster. Already she had seen three small grandsons buried in the kirkyard.

'There's the Meeting House!' Janet exclaimed, her eyes alight at the sight of the familiar building. 'Do many attend the peoples' bank?' she asked wistfully.

'Why, yes. . . .' He turned his questioning glance on her. Then his expression softened. 'Of course, no doubt your mother needs your wages to support Andrew at present.' It was more a statement than a question and he was surprised to see tears spring to her eyes before she bowed her head to hide them.

'I have not earned any wages yet,' she confessed. 'Master Foster told Mama it cost him enough feeding me and giving me a bed. He says he treats me as one of his own family while she is unable to provide a roof for me. B-but I had my fourteenth birthday three weeks ago. I work as hard as I can, really I do. Mistress Foster said she would speak to Mr Foster and tell him. She is kind to me but she is so busy with babies. She needs me, and Molly is my friend b-but I think I ought to have gone to the hiring fair at the May term. He did not give me even a groat for the Sabbath. . . .' But would she have had the courage to find her way to the hiring fairs to stand in a line with other maids and men, waiting like cattle to be bought? She had asked herself this many times since her birthday.

All thoughts of the Fosters left them both as the tailor's neat little cottage came into view. It was already an hour past noon and he knew he would find Mary Scott sitting beside her son in the peace of the tailor's small garden. Luke Cole was a good man and he knew Mary would work long into the night to compensate for the precious few hours she could spend with her son. She worked when Andrew returned to the house of her old neighbour and friend, Lucy Hughes, who had offered him a bed now that her own family were away in service.

The Reverend Drummond helped Janet alight from the trap and took her arm to guide her round to the back of the cottage.

'I think we shall find them enjoying the sunshine.'

'Shall we?' Janet blinked in surprise. They passed two young men sitting at a wooden table at the back of the cottage busily stitching dark woollen cloth to make a suit for one of the gentlemen of the parish. The minister greeted them pleasantly.

'It is warmer and lighter for them to work outside on such a day as this,' he explained to Janet. Further away, half shielded by a rickety fence, clothed by a budding rambler rose, two figures sat on a wooden bench. Above them. a blackbird trilled sweetly in the summer air. The two heads were close together, the one so fair and curly, the other dark like her own. Janet felt a fleeting pang of envy until Andrew glanced up and saw them approaching. A look of joy lit his thin, pale face and he would have risen to welcome them, but her mother laid a hand on his arm, pressing him back. Her face showed astonishment and Janet realized it could not have been her mother who had sent for her after all. She felt a shaft of disappointment, but it was nothing to the cold hand of fear which gripped her heart at the sight of her brother's thin face and emaciated body. She bent to embrace him, eager to have his reassurance that he was well, but he held out his hands, taking hers, gently holding her at a distance.

'Let me look at you, little sister,' he said softly. 'How you have grown! You are so pretty, so slender and graceful. . . .' His thin fingers gently rubbed her palms, but just as he felt their roughness, so she felt the bones of his, held together by the white skin which covered them. There was no spare flesh on Andrew. She stifled a shiver and looked anxiously into her mother's face, searching for some sign of reassurance. All their hopes had rested on Andrew. He was here at last, but he seemed as insubstantial as a shadow.

Mary Scott rose, her eyes questioning as she looked from the minister to Janet.

'Andrew expressed a wish to see his sister,' the Reverend Drummond said quietly. 'I arranged it.'

'I should have thought of it,' Mary said with remorse.

Yes, so you should, the minister echoed silently, but he knew she had thoughts for no one but Andrew. Did she realize she would not have him much longer? He sighed and declined her offer of a drink of ale or some cool buttermilk.

'Nothing, thank you, Mary. I have some visits to make in the village. I shall have refreshment enough, but Janet must be very hungry. She has done a morning's work at Braeheights Farm before setting out on the long walk down to the road. I'm sure Mistress Cole will not begrudge your daughter a little food.' If there was a trace of reproof in his tone Mary did not notice. She gazed distractedly at her son.

'Yes, Mama, do get Janet something to eat. See, I have my book of poems to keep me company until you return, and I enjoy lifting my face to the sun.'

'Can I not stay with Andrew, Mama?' Janet pleaded. 'I could eat here, in the garden. I must set out again all too soon.'

'I shall take you back to Braeheights Farm tomorrow, lassie,' the minister intervened. 'Tonight you will sleep at the manse. My wife will be pleased to make a bed for you, never fear.'

'Oh thank you, sir! Thank you so much. I am not sure I could find my way back across the fields if darkness fell. We seemed to take so many twists and turns.'

'Don't you worry about that, child. Just enjoy your time with Andrew. I'm sure the two of you have plenty to talk about. Mary, I'll walk with you to the house,' he said, taking her arm and leading her firmly away.

Janet's head buzzed with questions but the first thing which came to her tongue was to enquire after Fingal McLauchlan.

'Fingal?' Andrew threw back his head and laughed. 'How close you two have remained in spite of the distance and time which has separated you. Whenever I receive a letter from Mother, Fingal always asks for news of you before anyone else. But yes, he is well, and soon he will be leaving Edinburgh and taking up a post in Annan. He has been like a brother to me, Janet. I could not have had a better friend.'

'He is like a brother to me too,' Janet nodded. 'I am glad he cared for you so well, Andrew, but it troubles me to see you looking so frail.'

'Ah yes.' Shadows darkened his blue eyes. 'That is why I asked the Reverend Drummond to arrange this meeting, Janet.' He looked at her gravely. 'Will you make me a promise, dearest sister?'

'If I can, Andrew. You know I would do anything to help you if I could. . . .'

'It is not for myself I ask, Janet. It is for mother.' He turned the full force of his clear grey eyes on her then and they seemed to burn into her soul. She shivered without knowing why. He took her hand in his long fingers and held it gently. 'I have not long to live on this earth, Janet. I. . . .'

'No! No, Andrew, please don't say things like that.'

'But I must. I must, little sister. I had dreamed of giving you a better life, the life you deserve, with books to read and pretty things to wear. . . .'

'I don't need such things, Andrew,' Janet protested, forgetting all the times she had longed for her grandfather's collection of books, and just half an hour to have the pleasure of reading them.

'Perhaps not, but it is Mother who worries me. She had such faith in my ability to provide for both of you. I have let her down, Janet.

'No! No, you have not. Peggy Baird told me how well you had done in your studies.'

'Oh, yes, but now. . . .' He gave a small frown. 'Please, Janet, give me your word, before Mother returns. Promise me that you will care for her when I am gone. . .? You will always tend her needs above all else?'

'Oh, Andrew, I hate to hear you speak so. Soon you will—'

'No. I am like our father, frail and useless. Promise me, Janet. . .?' He caught her other hand in his. She felt she could crush them both as easily as the shell of the skylark's tiny eggs. In her heart she knew Andrew was speaking the truth, knew too he had accepted that death was just around the corner.

'I promise, Andrew,' she whispered hoarsely. 'I will care for Mother if ever she needs me. . . .' She squeezed his fingers gently but she could not stop the tears which filled her eyes and rolled down her cheeks. She saw his eyes were bright too, and over-moist.

'What are you two talking about? What have you done to upset him, Janet?' her mother demanded sharply, when she was close enough to see the emotion on Andrew's face, the lines of strain as he struggled to summon a smile.

'We have much to talk about, Mama,' he managed cheerfully, 'and I am not the least upset. We were – we were laughing about Fingal staying with us at the schoolhouse.'

Janet would have enjoyed her brief stay at the manse and the kindly ministrations of Mrs Drummond, if her heart had not felt so heavy with sorrow. The following morning she was astonished when the Reverend Drummond presented her with a card bearing her full name of Janet Mairi Scott.

'This is from the savings bank, my dear. It is in your name and I have taken the opportunity of putting in one shilling. It is my gift to you. Now. . . .' he held up a hand to silence Janet's surprised protest. 'You know I encourage all my parishioners to save what little they can. Thrift and independence . . . your grandfather, and your father, approved of these qualities.'

'But I must earn money myself, especially now. . . .' The minister nodded, knowing she was thinking of her brother and the hopes and dreams her mother had invested in him.

'You will earn money. I shall see to that,' he said firmly. 'Now do you think you could ride behind me if I take you back to Braeheights Farm on my horse? Doddi is a sturdy beast. He carries me all the way to Dumfries and home again when I go to edit my newspaper. I'm sure he will not notice your light weight. It would be much quicker than the trap and I wish to speak with Mistress Foster and her husband. After her next baby has been born, and Mistress Foster has regained her strength, if you wish to leave Braeheights Farm, I will keep my ears open for a more suitable posting for you, but until then. . . .' He shook his head sadly. 'It is a pity, a great pity, that your education was cut so short.'

'Andrew gave me a book to read,' she told him eagerly. 'I shall treasure it, for there are no books at Braeheights Farm except the family Bible. He said this was one of his favourite books. It was a gift from Fingal McLaughlan. He saved up all his spare farthings to buy it for Andrew. It is a book of poems by a man called Robert Burns.'

'Indeed? May I see?' The minister took the leather-bound book and turned it over in his hands. 'I met Mr Burns once at my father's house when I was a young man, and he was well acquainted with my wife's family.'

'He must have been a clever man. Andrew says he died at a young age. Was he a good man?'

'My own father considered him a genius. You will enjoy reading his poetry, child. It was thoughtful of young Fingal to purchase such a gift.'

Barely four weeks later, Janet returned to the village of Rowanbank to attend Andrew's funeral. She had no suitable clothes for a funeral and her mother had not written or made any mention of what she should wear. It was Mrs Foster who offered to lend her own best black skirt and shawl. The skirt was too long and too wide, for Hannah Foster had been sturdier when it had been purchased several years previously.

'Maybe ye could tack up the bottom and take out the stitches when ye come back, lassie. We will pin the waist. It is the best we can do.'

'Thank you, Mistress Foster,' Janet said huskily, struggling to swallow the lump in her throat and hold back her tears. Surely her own mother should have thought of what she could wear.

This time, Wull Foster drove her to the funeral himself in the pony and trap. He was determined she would spend no more nights at the manse. He intended to see she returned to Braeheights Farm as soon as her brother's funeral was over.

Fingal was at the funeral with his mother and Peggy and Donald Baird. Peggy shook her head in dismay when she saw Janet dressed in Mistress Foster's skirt and shawl with the shabby black hat almost swamping her pale face. She looked like a bairn at Halloween, dressed up as a witch. She hugged her close and her own tears mingled with Janet's. When she drew away Fingal took Janet's hands in his.

'If only I could care for you and take you away from that place where you work so hard, Janet. The Reverend Drummond told me it is no life for a girl like you up at the farm. It is not what your grandfather would have wanted for you. It grieved Andrew that he was unable to provide a better life for you and your mother.'

'I know,' Janet whispered over the lump in her throat. Fingal put one arm around her shoulders and she leaned closer, finding comfort from his warmth and strength.

'If only I had enough money to rent a cottage for you, instead of living in lodgings.' He looked down at her bowed head tenderly. 'Even if I earned enough to provide food and clothes. . . .' Fingal muttered. 'I ought to have been a dominie as your grandfather hoped Andrew would be.'

'Please do not worry about me, Fingal. One day you will be a lawyer with enough money for all your needs. That is what Mr Saunders told your mother and Mama Peggy. They are very proud of your education.'

'I know, but it has taken so long, and I am still only earning the wages of a clerk.' He had to release her when the funeral service began in Mr Cole's small cottage.

The churchyard was more than a mile from the village and Fingal wished he could have stayed with Janet but he knew he should feel honoured to be asked to take one of the cords, which would lower his friend into his grave. Mary Scott and Janet had no male relations of their own to ask, so Mr Cole and some of the elders would hold cords too. Usually the women stayed at home while the men attended to the burial, but the Scotts had no home and Mary Scott seemed barely aware of what was going on around her and oblivious to her white-faced daughter's sorrow as the coffin was borne away.

Wull Foster was impatient to get Janet back into his pony and trap and he could hardly wait for the coffin to be placed onto the horse-drawn hearse.

'Give Miss Janet a little time alone with her mother, and

her friends. Allow them to comfort each other,' the Reverend Drummond intervened brusquely before he turned to follow the other men and the coffin on its last journey.

Wull Foster's only response was a scowl but Janet knew the minister was one of the few men he held in awe. She remembered how disgruntled he had been the morning the minister had accompanied her back to Braeheights Farm and ordered that she must be paid the wages which were due to her. Wull Foster had made relatively little fuss in the minister's presence, but he had been furious when he discovered the Reverend Drummond had taken charge of the money, intending to lodge it in the village savings bank on Janet's behalf.

Foster had known then that the minister was a shrewd judge of men and that he had guessed his intention of taking the money back at the first opportunity once the minister had gone on his way.

Mary Scott seemed remote from grief. She had had time to see the approach of Andrew's death, but Janet sensed that her mother's spirit, her reason for living, had gone with his death. Janet wished with all her heart that she could stay with her mother, but there was neither room nor work for her at the tailor's cottage.

''Tis time we were on our way,' Wull Foster insisted, grasping Janet's arm. 'Ye've spoken tae your mither.'

'B-but. . . .' Peggy came then and hugged her tightly, reluctant to let her return to Braeheights at all and especially so soon.

'Fingal will be sorry you have gone,' she whispered. 'He had hoped to talk with you, Janet.' Both Peggy and her husband, Donald, assured her of a warm welcome if she could visit them on her day off, but there never seemed to be any time for leisure.

It was on the return journey to the farm that Janet felt her first real fear of Wull Foster. He had insisted she should sit up at the front beside him on the bench seat. Usually she sat on one of the side benches of the trap with Molly or the boys on their way to church.

The summer evening was calm and warm but as soon as they had left the cottages behind and started on the lonely track up the hill to Braeheights Farm, Foster reached out an arm and pulled her close to him, almost suffocating her against his chest. He had taken her by surprise and for a moment she had to cling to him to keep her balance on the narrow seat. When she tried to pull away his arm tightened.

'I ken ye'll be needing comfort, lassie. Never fear, I'll look after ye.'

'No! No, I'm fine. Please let me go. . . .'

'There now, there's no need to take on so. Ye're safe enough wi' me, I tell ye.' But Janet didn't feel safe. Hadn't Joe warned her never to go anywhere alone with his father? Today she had had no choice. She struggled to be free but instead of releasing her, he relinquished the reins, knowing the pony would continue up the familiar track. He pushed his wife's hat from her head, heedless as it rolled onto the dusty floor of the trap. He began to stroke her hair with his free hand while the arm tightened around her shoulders. The more she struggled, the tighter he held her. He thrust his hand inside her shawl and his rough fingers fondled her small breast through the cotton of her shift and her blouse. Her heart raced in panic.

'Let me go! Let go of me!' she shouted furiously. He saw the fire in her eyes and the twin patches of angry colour in her cheeks and he laughed aloud.

'My, my, I can see ye've got spirit. I like a woman wi' some fight in her.' Janet managed to pull one arm free and she began to beat against him but it was like hitting a log of wood, so little effect did her small fist have on him. His only reaction was to squeeze painfully at her breast so that she gasped and tears sprang to her eyes. 'That's better now,' he growled hoarsely. 'Ye'll find it does no good to fight wi' me. It's a fine evening for a roll in the hedgerow.'

Chapter Seven

A loud whoop from the hedge startled the pony and almost jerked Foster and Janet from the seat. A moment later, Joe and Luke appeared on the other side of the hedge.

'What the devil! What d'ye think ye're doing?' their father bellowed.

'Catching rabbits for a stew,' Joe called, holding up two furry bodies. 'Tis a lovely evening. Would ye no like tae walk with us across the field, Miss Janet? The air would be good for ye after – well, after everything.'

'Yes! Yes, I'd like that.' Janet stood up with relief. Wull Foster had little option but to draw the pony to a halt and let her down, but his face was purple with rage.

Janet never discovered whether Joe had been in the fields beside the track by accident that evening, or whether he guessed what tricks his father might try, but she was filled with gratitude. The boys never forgot she was the old dominie's granddaughter. They treated her with respect and called her Miss Janet, but that evening she could have hugged them in her relief.

Instead of improving, Mrs Foster's health seemed to be getting steadily worse and Janet believed Molly's listless and tearful state must be due to her mother's condition and the extra burden of work which fell to both of them. There was a tension in the household and Mr Foster's presence only increased it. Janet hated the way he watched every move she made as she served his meals or washed the floor. She wanted to tell him to go away. He seemed to think his wife should shake off her ill health as if it was a cold. As for Molly, his eyes glittered angrily whenever he saw her drooping shoulders and her drawn face.

Towards the end of September, the mellow autumn weather gave way to lashing rain accompanied by high winds.

'This will bring the tides up frae the Solway Firth,' Wull Foster muttered. 'There'll be floods before 'tis over.' There were often storms and floods in the autumn and spring so no one paid attention to him, or so it seemed.

The storm was still raging during the following night and Janet was wakened by the creaks and groans of the sturdy farmhouse. The door to her own small chamber had never latched securely and a sudden draught blew it further ajar, making the old hinges creak. She was sure the gust must have been caused by someone opening the back door but she was afraid to get up and check in case she met Mr Foster. She hated the way he eyed her, as though his eyes could see through her clothes. She snuggled down and went to sleep, exhausted as always by the day's work.

Early the next morning, Janet had raked out the cinders and lit the fire in the big black range when Joe put his head around the outer door. The wind still howled and smoke came belching out of the chimney, making her eyes sting.

'Our Molly hasna come oot tae the milking, Janet. Can ye come and give us a hand? Please. . . ?' Joe always tried to speak politely to her but his accent was stronger when he was excited or upset. He looked dreadfully pale, almost ill himself, and the look of pleading in his dark eyes tore at Janet's heart. He tackled a man's work on the farm and, although he was almost as tall as his father now, he was even younger than herself, not yet fourteen. His young face looked strained and weary.

'I'll just set the water over the fire to boil, ready for the porridge, then I'll come out to the byre.' She frowned as she took in his red-rimmed eyes. The pallor of his face seemed to accentuate the hollows beneath his cheekbones. 'Are you all right, Joe. . . ?'

'Aye,' he snapped. Janet frowned. Joe always treated her kindly and rarely snapped at anyone except his father. Something was bothering him, however much he denied it.

The porridge was not ready when Wull Foster came into the kitchen after attending to his horses. He swore loudly, thumped the table with his spoon and demanded his breakfast immediately. Janet's eyes grew bright with anger but she clamped her small teeth against her lower lip and bent over the fire, stirring the blackened pan, willing the porridge to cook more quickly. Still the wind howled in the chimney, blowing the fire back at her instead of drawing up the flames and kindling the embers to the glowing red she needed to cook.

It was Luke who spoke up. 'Janet helped us with the milking. She canna be in twae places at once.'

'And why did ye need her at the milking? Where's your lazy bitch of a sister?'

Luke scowled back at his father.

'Well? Answer me! Is she still in her bed?'

'I-I think Molly must be sick again, Mr Foster,' Janet said. 'I will take her a dish of porridge when it is ready. Maybe she will feel better then.' Janet hated when the family quarrelled; it reminded her of Dominie Todd and the last scene in her grandfather's house.

'Good God! Trying her mother's tricks, is she? Eating in bed! Acting like ladies!' he thundered in disgust. He scraped his chair back on the flagged floor and pushed himself to his feet. Hastily Janet ladled a bowl of steaming porridge and set it before him.

'Y-yours is ready now. I'll just bring a jug of milk from the dairy. . . .'

'Here's the milk.' Joe came into the kitchen carrying the large tin jug. He set it down in front of his father with a thump so that some of it sloshed over the side. His father swore at him. Joe straightened, drawing himself to his full height, his eyes glittering.

'Ye ken fine what's wrong.' He outstared his father, his face full of contempt. 'Ye've done the same to our Molly as ye did tae the other maids and they. . . .' Before he could finish, his father lashed out with the back of his hand. He caught Joe a stinging blow against the side of his head, sending him reeling across the kitchen. Janet gasped and ran to Joe but he regained his feet instantly. He rushed towards the table. But stopped just out of his father's reach.

'If you ever raise your hand to me again,' he said through gritted teeth, 'I'll swing for ye.'

'You'll. . . ?' Wull Foster gave an explosive guffaw. 'You and how many men, lad? Wait till ye've grown a bit afore ye start threatening me. Now get your porridge down ye. There's work to be done after the storm. And you,' he raised his eyes to Janet, 'get up the stairs and tell that lazy bitch I want her down here and ready to work. Now!'

Janet bit her lip but when she had ladled the rest of the porridge she climbed the wooden steps to the small loft room where Molly slept. There was a hump in the bed and Janet moved to give her friend a gentle shake. The hump was a pillow stuffed under the blankets. There was no sign of Molly. Janet returned to the kitchen.

'M-Molly isn't there.'

'Not there? Where is she, then?' Wull Foster growled. 'If she's not in her bed why wasn't she at the milking?' He looked from Joe to Janet, to Luke and to Mark. They all looked back in silence.

'She'll be in beside the other two brats. Adam! John!' he bellowed loudly.

'We're coming, Da,' two small boys chorused.

'Molly was not in with them,' Janet said quietly. 'I looked.' She felt anxious and uneasy. 'I'll take some porridge in to Mrs Foster.'

Janet hoped Molly might have crept in beside her mother, or that Mrs Foster would know where she was. Her uneasiness increased when she saw the look of fear and despair which leapt into the older woman's eyes when she heard Molly had left the house.

'I-I thought I heard the door open during the night,' she said in a low voice. 'Do you think Molly would go outside? To the closet, maybe?' But why had she not returned?

'She's gone. Ma poor bairn.' Mrs Foster's words were no more than a whisper. Janet was not sure whether she had heard properly, or whether she was meant to hear at all. Mrs Foster pushed away her porridge and began to weep, rocking backwards and forwards as though she was in pain.

All thoughts of mending the hinges on the stable door, or the hole in the cart-shed roof, or clearing up the debris left by the storm, were cast aside. Wull Foster set his four oldest sons to search for Molly while he himself paced up and down the yard, and in and out of the house, like a caged lion. He blustered and uttered dire threats for when he set eyes on Molly. Janet was left to soothe the babies and try to coax Mrs Foster to eat a morsel of food. There were the daily chores of washing and cleaning, peeling potatoes, making beds and emptying chamber pots. Mrs Foster dragged herself around the house like a large, rudderless ship, unable to concentrate, even on the needs of her youngest child.

Janet could not dispel her uneasiness. Was it Molly who had opened the door and crept out into the night? Where could she have gone? Janet felt that Mrs Foster and Joe both knew why Molly had gone, even if they were not sure where.

'Could Molly have gone to her grandmother's?' she suggested tentatively when the boys and their father came in at midday for bowls of the hot thick soup she had prepared. There was no bread or plain scone. Mrs Foster had not felt well enough to bake any and she had been too busy trying to do all the other household tasks and attend to the demands of the younger Fosters.

'I'll harness the pony and get off down to her grandmother's!' Wull Foster declared. 'Why didn't ye think o' it before? I expect that's where the brat is hiding. Causing all this trouble. . . .' But Janet saw the expression on Joe's face and her heart sank. She guessed Joe knew they would not find Molly there. But she had to be somewhere. Why had she run away when her mother needed her so badly? They all needed her. Janet felt near to tears with exhaustion and anxiety by the time she went to bed.

It was nothing compared to the weariness which claimed her in the days and nights to follow as she struggled to cope with the never-ending chores, and still no sign of Molly.

Mrs Foster was doing her best to help with the daily tasks but it was obvious to everyone except her husband that she was ill. Each day she seemed worse. What little spirit she had shown before had been quenched since Molly left.

'Has Mr Foster told the minister?' Janet ventured. 'Perhaps

some of the elders would help. . . ? Spread the word. . . ?'

'Oh no, lassie! Dinna mention this to the minister. There's shame enough. . . .' Hannah Foster broke off and bit her lip, but as she turned away Janet saw tears squeezing from her puffy eyes.

'I've never felt this bad before,' she gasped a few minutes later. She was struggling to catch her breath after picking up a small nightgown she had dropped.

'Pull yoursel' together, woman!' Wull Foster stood in the doorway between the kitchen and the wash house. 'If your face gets any fatter we'll never see your eyes,' he taunted. 'Ye're lying in bed o'er long. There's no good fretting o'er the wee bitch, I tell ye. She'll come running back home when she's hungry. . . .'

'You talk about ma poor bairn as though she's a stray dog!' his wife flared with unexpected spirit. Janet looked from one to the other, scooped up the baby and made for the door to the yard, but not before she had heard Wull Foster's growled retort.

'She's less use than a stray dog! Get on wi' your work. There's nae wonder ye canna get your feet into your clogs. Ye canna even get intae mine!' He glared down at his wife's swollen feet clad in thick woollen socks.

Molly Foster did not come home to plead for a crust of bread, or anything else. Three weeks after she had left Braeheights Farm, a man came to the house, asking to speak to Mr Foster. The two men talked, then left the farm together. There was tension in the house. Even the baby sensed it. Joe's face was white and pinched. Janet heard him speaking in a low voice.

'D'ye think they've found her, Ma?'

'I pray it wasna her. Not like that. . . . Please God not like that. . . .'

It was the following morning when Joe came to join Janet as she was hanging washing in the cold October wind.

'They've found our Molly's body,' he said in a strained voice.

'Body? Oh no!' Janet spun to face him. 'Oh no, Joe. . . .'

'Aye.' He nodded dully. 'Aye, 'twas her. The man . . . yesterday. He took *him*.' His lip curled in contempt and Janet knew he meant his father. 'He . . . he identified her. She must have walked miles the night o' the storm. . . .' His voice choked and he gulped down the knot of emotion. 'She must have jumped in the river. . . .'

'Jumped? Into the river. . . ?' Janet stared at Joe's white face in horror.

'A fisherman found her. Swept against the roots o' a tree. L-left by the flood.'

'No! I c-can't believe. . . .' Janet began to cry. She couldn't help it. Joe moved towards her and patted her awkwardly. He had cried half the night himself but he would never admit it to anyone but Luke.

Janet turned into the circle of his thin arm and sobbed. 'There must be a mistake. . . ?' she pleaded.

'She said she . . . she'd do it. But she didna ken how. . . .' He shuddered. 'I didna think she'd go for the river. . . . She was aye feart o' the water.'

'B-but why. . . ? Why. . . ?' Janet shook her head in bewilderment.

''Twas his fault. One day I'll . . . I'll do for him!' Joe said, his young jaw clenched, his teeth gritted in anger. ''Twas him gave her the bairn.'

'B-bairn?' Janet drew back and stared up into Joe's white face. Molly's sickness, her moods of black despair, her swelling stomach. . . . Still Janet stared into Joe's face, wide eyed with shock, realizing at last. . . . She shuddered, remembering how Wull Foster had grabbed at her on the way back from Andrew's funeral. Now she understood the change in Molly from her happy, carefree schoolfriend. Now she understood why she had wanted to run away.

Later that night Janet wrote a letter to the minister, asking him to find her a place to live and to work, anywhere away from Braeheights Farm and Mr Foster. She knew it was no use writing to her mother. Mary Scott was a shadow of her former self since Andrew's death. Her reason for living had gone the day Andrew was laid to rest beside their father. Janet's thoughts went round and round in circles; she was alone. It was true, Mrs Foster and the little ones needed her. The thought weighed her down with guilt. But she knew the truth about Molly now. She shivered. Fingal had been right. She must get away from here.

Janet planned to give her letter to the Reverend Drummond when they went to the kirk but she discovered Wull Foster had no intention of letting any of them attend the kirk until the wagging tongues found someone else to talk about. She was dismayed. She tucked her letter beneath her mattress and resolved to go to the kirk herself. She would walk there. The winter days were short and cold now, but desperation fuelled her determination. Surely she could find her way over the fields and through the wood in the daylight? Perhaps Fingal would accompany her part of the way back? Did he come home for the Sabbath? If only she could see him, he would pass her letter to the Reverend Drummond.

Long before another Sabbath day dawned Janet's plans to leave Braeheights Farm were thrust aside. It was dark and cold in the farm kitchen. Wull Foster, accompanied by Joe and Luke, had gone out to begin the morning feeding and milking. Mrs Foster called urgently to Janet. She had not yet kindled the range and she shivered in the frosty air.

Janet's first thoughts were that Mrs Foster had at last given way to the grief of Molly's death. She had not wept since Molly's body had been found. She had remained pale and silent, withdrawn, even from her babies. Now she huddled on the straw mattress, curled into a ball, her whole body shaking as though with violent sobs, yet she made no sound. Janet almost jumped out of her skin when Mrs Foster uttered a sudden scream of agony. Young though she was Janet knew it was a scream of pain and fear. She had heard such a scream once before when Joe took her to check the rabbit traps.

'It's the babe!' she gasped. 'Tell Joe . . . run for Mistress McClure. . . .' The pain came again and with it Mistress Foster's whole body seemed to contort, her skin grew damp and waxy. Janet gathered up her skirts and ran out of the house and into the darkness of the muddy yard. A strong arm shot out and seized her around her waist, swinging her off her feet. Wull Foster had stepped out of the darkness of the stable door as she passed.

'Coming tae find me were ye, lassie?' He leered with satisfaction. Janet could not see his face in the darkness but she hated his arm, holding her tightly against his hard body. 'We'll just gang intae the stable. . . .'

'No! Joe!' she yelled instinctively at the top of her voice. 'Let me go. . . .' she panted. 'Mrs Foster needs the midwife. The babe is coming. Joe!'

A square of yellow light appeared in the darkness. Joe was standing in the byre doorway, the storm lantern swinging behind him from a nail.

'Oh, Joe,' Janet almost sobbed in relief as his father released his grip on her. 'Y-your mother wants you to get Mistress McClure. . . .'

'What? Now. . . ?

'Yes. She says the baby is coming.'

'The bairn isna due until February,' Wull Foster muttered. 'That's three months away. Tell her—' he broke off as he saw Joe clench his fists and stride towards them.

'Your mother is in terrible pain, Joe. Please. . . .'

'I'll go.' He tugged her arm and pulled her with him towards the house, his young face grim. Once there, he took only the briefest look into his mother's room. His face was white and young as he turned to Janet. 'I'll gang richt away.' Janet saw the fear in his eyes. Joe loved his mother. It was for her sake he stayed at Braeheights Farm.

She busied herself kindling the fire and filling the big black pot and the kettle and setting them to boil. She knew little of the birthing of babies. Molly had always attended her mother, along with the midwife, but every time Mistress McClure had visited Braeheights Farm she had demanded large quantities of hot water. Then Janet went back to the bedroom and lifted the two sleeping infants from the crib they shared. It amazed her that they slept undisturbed while their mother stifled her screams of pain and the bed creaked with her writhing. Mrs Foster was barely aware of either her or the bairns, Janet thought, as she carried them up to the loft and tucked them up in the space Joe and Luke had vacated earlier.

'Cuddle up to your wee brothers,' she whispered to the other young Fosters. 'Mark, you'd best get up and dress. Joe has had to leave the milking. Luke will need you.' Mark grumbled but he did as she asked. Of all the Foster boys, he was growing most like his father. He was big and sturdy for his age and he hated school and welcomed any excuse for staying at home.

Joe returned with Mistress McClure in the trap. She praised Janet for getting the fire lit and the hot water ready, little realizing that Janet performed these tasks, and many more before dawn, every morning.

Two hours later, she asked Mr Foster to send for the doctor.

'Pay ten shillings and sixpence for a birthing? She should ken what tae dae by now!'

'This is no ordinary bairn. . . .'

Wull Foster drained his mug of tea and strode out of the kitchen, ignoring all Mistress McClure's protests. Janet looked after him anxiously. Didn't he care if his wife died? she wondered.

The late November day was fading fast and Mistress McClure asked Janet to light a lamp, that she might see better. Her plump face was drawn and tired but darkness had descended completely before Hannah Foster found any relief from the dreaded pain. Mistress McClure had delivered twins. They were far too early, and both were dead.

'God knows there's plenty o' weans up here at Braeheights Farm without wishing for any more,' Mistress McClure said wearily as she sipped the hot mug of tea which Janet had prepared for her. 'They were lassies, though, and they might have brought the poor woman a bit o' comfort after sae many laddies, especially now Molly's gone.' The older woman eyed Janet speculatively, revived by the welcome drink of tea. Not many places gave her their precious tea, and when they did it had usually been dregs from the day before. 'Did ye ever hear exactly what happened?' she asked curiously. 'With Molly. . . ?' Janet shook her head, refusing to be drawn into gossip.

'There wasna a proper funeral, I was told. They never asked me to do the laying out, and I do most folks frae Molden and this end o' Rowanbank parish.'

Janet was just about to change the subject and ask Mrs McClure if she would pass on her letter to the Reverend Drummond when the woman went on gravely, 'I just hope I dinna end up laying out the poor lassie's mother. It'll be touch an' go for the next few days.

Even if she pulls through, it'll be many a long day before she's on her feet again. She'll need a lot o' care. Who else comes to help i' the hoose, lassie?'

'Nobody,' Janet said, staring at her, wide-eyed with shock. 'You d-don't think Mistress Foster might – might die?' she said in a hushed voice.

'It wouldna surprise me, lassie. She must have been ill long before the birth to be in such a state. Getting rid o' the babes early is the best thing could have happened for her, her being sae swollen everywhere. But it's more than that. I've been at the birth o' all her bairns and I've never seen Hannah Foster sae weary o' life as she is now. If ye ask me she's lost the will tae live noo her lassie's dead. Och, but I shouldna be talking like this tae ye. Ye're little more than a bairn yourself. A fine bairn ye are, though. There's shame on that miserable creature, Foster. He should have got another woman in tae help with the washing and cleaning with all these wee mouths tae feed.'

'B-but what should I do, for Mistress Foster, I mean?' Janet asked fearfully. 'I-I didn't mean to stay here, not now that Molly. . . . But if Mistress Foster is so ill. . . ?'

'She's ill all right, but dinna ye worry, lassie. I'll be back in the morning and I'll give Foster a bit o' ma mind. He'll need to get a woman in tae help ye. Mean wretch that he is. There's only one thing he's good for. . . .'

Janet made up her mind then.

'I-I've written a letter for the Reverend Drummond,' she said breathlessly. 'C-could you give it to him? Please, Mrs McClure? B-but would you tell him how things are with Mistress Foster? Tell him I must stay with her until – until she is well or at least until Mr Foster gets someone to take care of her. . . .' She pulled the letter from the pocket of her pinafore. It was crumpled now and she smoothed it out slowly, still undecided whether she should send it until Mistress Foster recovered, but this might be her only chance to get the letter away from Braeheights Farm. Supposing Mrs Foster were to die. . . ?

'It's not often I see the Reverend Drummond, lassie,' Mrs McClure said, taking the letter. 'Molden is my kirk, ye see. It's nearer for me. But I'll give it to him when I see him.' She glanced at the envelope. 'My, but this is bonnie writing, lassie!' She tucked the letter safely into her bag.

'It would have been much better with a proper quill,' Janet said wistfully. 'My grandfather taught me to write,' she added with pride. There was never any opportunity to write since she came to Braeheights Farm. She had borrowed the bottle of ink, which Mistress Foster kept on the high mantle above the kitchen range, but she had had to make do with a feather from a hen. She knew that a crow's feather would have been harder and better, but even if she had had one, she had no way of preparing it properly with hot sand and a sharp knife, as her grandfather had shown her. As it was, Mark Foster had seen her replacing the ink bottle the next morning. She wondered whether he had told his father for she had noticed the ink had been removed.

'I was forgetting the old dominie was your grandfather.' Mistress McClure was shaking her head. 'He was a fine man. He'll be turning in his grave, I shouldna wonder, if he kens ye're working as a maid for a man like Foster. I'll see the minister gets the letter, never fear.'

'What's that about a letter?'

They both jumped, startled by the sound of Wull Foster's deep voice. They had not heard him come into the kitchen. He must have come through the wash house. Mistress McClure flushed, but she faced him squarely.

'Ye're just the man I'm waiting to see. Your wife will need a lot o' care if she's tae pull through this time, Wull Foster. There's o'er much for this lassie tae manage. I'll come back in the morning, but that's all I can promise. . . .'

'Never mind yer blethers, woman! Where's that letter?' he thundered impatiently.

'I havena any letter for ye. . . .'

'I didna say the letter was for me. Our Mark said ye'd used the ink.' He glared accusingly at Janet. 'If there's any letters tae be written in this hoose, I'll be writing them. Now hand o'er the letter she gave ye.' Mrs McClure clutched her bag and stepped back but before she could leave the house Wull Foster snatched the bag from her and opened it. He saw the envelope immediately and pulled it out. 'I'll show ye where that belongs.' He strode to the fire and shoved the letter into the flames. Janet felt tears well in her eyes. It would be impossible to write another. She bit her lip. Mrs McClure looked from one to the other, her mouth compressed. She had neither liking nor respect for Wull Foster. She knew well enough why Hannah Foster had married such a man, but she was far too good for him.

'Ye dinna deserve a lassie like Miss Janet in your hoose, Wull Foster. There's far o'er much work for one pair o' hands wi' all these bairns tae wash for and to feed, even without a sick woman tae tend, so. . . .'

'You mind your ain business, woman! Now get yoursel' awa' home and nag at yer ain wee bit o' a man.'

'My Billy might be a wee man but he's worth ten o' your sort, Wull Foster,' Mrs McClure flared angrily. 'And if your ain wife dies ye'll never get another in this parish!'

'Get awa' oot my hoose!' Wull Foster growled.

True to her word, Mistress McClure returned to Braeheights Farm the following morning and attended her patient, though her efforts at coaxing Hannah Foster to eat were unsuccessful.

'I dinnae think she'll take the birthing fever,' she said to Janet, 'but it'll take a good while afore she gets o'er this. She needs chicken broth and plenty o' milk, if he'll let her have it. . . .'

'I'll see she gets milk,' Joe announced sturdily, 'whatever he says. I'll dae anything for Ma, Mistress McClure.' He looked and sounded young and vulnerable despite his tweed cap and clogs. She remembered it was only thirteen or fourteen years since she had delivered him into the world. Her face softened.

'Well, wring the neck o' one o' them old hens out there, then, laddie, then get the feathers plucked off if ye really want tae help.' She turned to Janet. 'D'ye ken how tae make a pot o' soup, lassie?'

'Of course Janet can make soup,' Joe gave a mocking laugh. 'She's done all the cooking since Ma's been bad.'

'Aye, I see.' Mrs McClure frowned thoughtfully, then she seemed to make up her mind. 'I've asked around to see if any o' the women would come up to lend a hand until your Ma's on her feet again.

There's only Lily Bloddret. . . .' She shook her head in the way Janet was beginning to recognize. It meant that she was troubled. 'I wouldna send her up here wi' so many young lads about if there was anybody else. . . . But there isna,' she finished briskly, and tossed her head. 'Tell your father I want to see him, will ye, laddie?'

Wull Foster argued and blustered, telling her that the boys would help Janet until his wife was on her feet again.

'Help? They're no more than bairns. They're all needing their mother, including young Joe, fine laddie though he is. Either ye get Lily Bloddret or somebody else tae help in the hoose or I'm taking the lassie away wi' me. Now.' She faced him squarely, hands on her ample hips, feet apart. He frowned and blustered but in the end he agreed that she should send Lily Bloddret up to the farm.

'Her ain hoose is no more than a hovel. She'll manage fine on the hearth if ye give her a blanket or twae. Dinna be having her sleeping up them stairs, mind, not with the laddies just a few feet away frae her.'

'A-ah, I see. Like that, is she?' His eyes gleamed speculatively.

'Aye, she is, but I'm warning ye, Wull Foster, she'll be giving ye more than ye want, or bargain for, if ye mess wi' Lily Bloddret. She's wandered the length and breadth o' the country, and been in many a port. Come the spring she'll take tae the road again, I shouldn't wonder. I guarantee she'll hae left a packet o' sorrow behind for any man fool enough tae seek his pleasure at her door.'

Mistress McClure gathered up her bag but before she left, she warned Hannah Foster what kind of woman she was sending to help.

'She's the only woman free and willing to come up here tae Braeheights Farm,' she said in troubled tones, 'but yon lassie canna manage all this work on her own.' Hannah Foster made no response. She lay in the big bed, white-faced, eyes closed, her hands folded across her breast as though preparing for death. 'I hope ye're listening, Hannah? I wouldna have any man near me if he'd been with Lily Bloddret and her ilk,' she said urgently. Still Hannah Foster made no response. Even opening her eyes seemed too great an effort. Mrs McClure frowned and shook her head anxiously.

Back in the kitchen, she took Janet's arm.

'Listen carefully, lassie. The woman I'm sending up is a good enough worker, but she's – she's. . . .' She looked into Janet's wide-eyed innocent face and wondered whether it would be better to leave the girl to manage as best she could, rather than have a woman of the roads up here. She glanced around the big farm kitchen, she glimpsed the washing basket piled high with washing waiting to be hung and another pile on the wash house floor. Two of the toddlers crawled over her feet and the youngest began to cry in his crib by the fire. 'Lily Bloddret isna the kind o' woman for decent company, but there's nobody else. Set her to do the washing and scrubbing, but whatever ye do, lassie, dinna let her near your mistress. Make sure you prepare all the food and you take hers in to her yourself.'

'Yes, Mistress McClure. I'll do my best,' Janet promised, bending to lift the baby from the crib and hush him. She pushed back a tendril of hair which had escaped from her cap. Mistress McClure shook her head. 'This is no place for a lassie like you.' She lowered her voice and leaned close to Janet. 'If I should see the Reverend Drummond shall I give him a message instead o' the letter, lassie?'

'Oh yes, please.'

'*Whisht.*' She held her finger to her lips and looked towards Mark and his younger brother standing at the door of the wash house. She leaned closer and Janet whispered in her ear.

'Tell him I must stay here until Mistress Foster is on her feet again, b-but say I would be obliged if he could help me find a new position.' She looked up into Mistress McClure's face. 'He-he did say he would help me if he could. . . .'

'Aye, and I'm sure he meant it, lassie. I'll tell him. But I reckon it'll take Hannah Foster a good six months or more before she's back to her old self. . . . If she ever is,' she added, more to herself than to Janet.

Chapter Eight

Lily Bloddret arrived at the farm two days later with a pathetically small bundle. She had the darkest hair Janet had ever seen and her eyebrows and lashes were black too. Janet realized that if the woman bothered to keep herself clean, she would be beautiful. Her green eyes seemed to have a constant sparkle and she flashed them at Wull Foster from the moment she set eyes on him, and even at the boys. Joe regarded her curiously but he had met Mistress McClure on her way down the track and she had told him plainly what kind of woman Lily was and the sort of trouble he was likely to get if he had anything to do with her. She had instructed him to pass her warning on to his father and his brothers, though Joe couldn't see himself or them satisfying a woman like Lily Bloddret.

It felt strange to Janet to be telling a woman so much older than herself what she had to do, but Lily nodded and smiled, swayed her ample hips and sallied forth to tackle the tasks she was set. She did everything Janet asked, but she was not as thorough or as clean as Janet had been brought up to be and she understood now why Mistress McClure had insisted she should do the cooking herself. Although it took her most of the morning cleaning and peeling vegetables to feed so many hungry mouths, she enjoyed the satisfaction of preparing a tasty pot of broth or a pan of stew, as Hannah Foster had shown her. She had been quick to learn and she had an instinct for cooking, inherited from the grandmother she had never known.

Except for the presence of Wull Foster and the way he eyed her, Janet felt life at Braeheights was bearable. Hannah Foster was always grateful for everything she did to tempt her appetite and build up her strength and slowly she began to improve. She knew that as soon as her husband saw her on her feet again and in her clothes he would be back to making his demands, in spite of Mistress McClure's warning that she should bear no more children.

It was true, Wull Foster was restless and frustrated. In his opinion, he had a useless wife, but under his own roof he had a young, spirited girl on the threshold of womanhood and he meant to teach her what it was like to be a woman. Meanwhile, he was fully aware of the constant temptation Lily presented to any red-blooded man. He knew she could satisfy even his lust but he was mindful of the midwife's warnings. He took to going down to the nearest inn on the outskirts of Molden. There were always wenches there, and if he got too drunk, the pony knew the way home and brought him back. Many a night it was left to Joe to wait for his father's return and unyoke the pony from the trap and feed the weary animal. Lily longed for a man like Wull Foster to satisfy her yearnings but so far he had resisted all her wiles. Meanwhile she was glad to have a roof over her head and enough to eat each day, as well as a bed beside the dying fire instead of under a hedgerow. She bided her time and sure enough, as winter settled over the land, Wull Foster lost the urge to venture forth and brave the elements after a hard day's work outside.

Janet's small room was off the kitchen so she heard the scuffles and grunts taking place and she knew that Wull Foster had succumbed to Lily's attractions. She shuddered as she imagined what they must do. Lily hummed now as she went about her work and her generous hips swayed even more than before.

Hannah Foster knew her husband had not chosen to sleep in the loft out of consideration for her, nor even because of Mrs McClure's warnings about her health. She guessed he was spending the nights with Lily Bloddret. She no longer cared about his infidelity but she did worry about the diseases he might bring to her when the woman moved on. Mrs McClure had told her it would take a long time to regain her former energy after the excessive loss of blood she had suffered, but nothing had prepared her for the feeling of perpetual exhaustion. She kept to her bedroom when her husband was likely to come into the house. If he did not see her he would neither growl orders nor make his demands.

Janet guessed how she felt in spite of her youthful innocence. She kindled the bedroom fire each morning to make her mistress as warm and comfortable as she could. Hannah did her best to ease the burden of the young girl who worked so hard and so cheerfully for a mere pittance. She took to ironing the clothes in her room, heating the flat irons on the bedroom fire. She did the mending and darning, much to Janet's great relief for it was never-ending, and by night she was always exhausted and ready to fall into bed.

Janet knew Mrs Foster was doing her best and she was always ready to advise when Janet encountered a problem with the cooking or any other task. Joe often crept into his mother's bedroom for a chat when he knew his father was occupied outside. His brothers rarely did more than put their head around the door to call goodnight. Their father didn't even manage that since he had taken to joining Lily on the rag rug in front of the fire.

Janet longed to see her mother and Peggy Baird. She wondered whether Fingal came home often at the weekends. None of them had been to the kirk since Molly's death. There had been no word from the Reverend Drummond but Janet didn't know whether Mistress McClure had managed to pass on her message. Even if she had, the minister could not procure jobs out of the sky for all his parishioners. Janet knew she was fortunate to have a roof over her head and enough food to eat. Even so she hated the way Wull Foster watched her, and she took care not to go into the yard if he was there alone. Even going out to the privy was difficult if he was around the buildings. For such a large man he seemed to move with stealthy silence.

Christmas came and went but still Janet heard nothing from her mother. Slowly Hannah Foster felt her strength returning, though she had no desire to draw her husband's attention to the fact. She crept around like a mouse in her own home, Janet thought, but Lily Bloddret was aware that the mistress was gradually taking command of her household again. It was she who made her wash the boys' shirts again when their collars and cuffs had not been rubbed on the ridged rubbing board, or made her scald the milk jugs and cans when the milk went sour in midwinter.

An unexpected spell of good weather at the end of February cheered all their spirits. Lily Bloddret sang at the top of her voice as she rubbed at the washing, then as she hung it on the line to dry beneath the high white clouds floating slowly across the blue of the sky. She made no mention of her urge to set out on her travels again, though, so it was a shock to Janet when she went out to the orchard with a second big basket of clothes intending to bring in the first lot and help Lily hang the rest. There was no sign of her. Janet hung the clothes herself then went to see if Lily was in the closet, wondering whether she was ill. Still no sign of her. Janet returned to the wash house, and then to the kitchen.

'I can't find Lily anywhere,' she said to Mrs Foster.

'I noticed her bundle was not in its usual place beside the big press,' Hannah replied. 'I thought she had decided to wash her clothes since it is such a lovely day.'

'She never washes them,' Janet said. 'She says a bit of dirt keeps out the wind.' She went to look beside the press herself. 'The two blankets you gave her have disappeared too.'

'Perhaps she has decided it is time to set out on the roads again.' Hannah sighed wearily. 'I have heard of people who get the wanderlust and canna settle in one place for long. Mistress McClure warned us that Lily Bloddret was like that. She is a foolish woman if she thinks a couple of days of fine weather in February mean spring has come. I have no doubt we shall pay for this with cold March winds and possibly floods.' She gave an involuntary shudder and they both remembered Molly.

Two of the younger boys still wetted the bed frequently and Janet sighed. 'I had better make sure she made the beds before she left.'

Lily had not. Something in the spring-like morning had called to her and she had simply tied a string around her bundle and gone. The meal was barely ready when Wull Foster and his sons came in for their dinner.

'It will not be long,' Janet said. 'Lily has left us without warning. It has made me late with the cooking.'

'What?' Wull Foster bellowed. 'Gone? She can't have gone. She was happy here. She had made up her mind to stay!' He sounded like a spoiled child who had been thwarted, Janet thought. Nevertheless, she was wary of his swift temper, and so were the boys. They ate in silence and went back out to work as soon as they had cleared their plates. Wull Foster slurped up his gravy, pushed back his chair and strode into the bedroom where his wife was finishing her own meal from a tray. She was almost hidden by the two wooden clothes horses already hung with freshly ironed clothes. Foster pushed one aside, knocking it to the floor and the shirts and clothes with it, oblivious of the work and care it had taken to get them cleaned and ironed.

'What are ye doing hiding in here, woman? Are ye still pretending tae be poorly? What have ye done wi Lily? Did you send her away – you wi' your lady's airs and graces?' he snarled, reaching down to grasp Hannah's shoulder and yank her to her feet.

'Of course I have not sent her away. I was content to let her stay as long as she wished to bide here.'

'Then why has she gone? Tell me that!' He heaved Hannah's slight body across the room with such force that she almost lost her balance and Janet saw her wince and the tears spring to her eyes, as her shoulder caught the doorpost with a resounding crack.

'I-I don't know why she has gone. Mistress McClure warned us she did not stay in one place for long. Maybe the spring day made her restless. Maybe she will be back by night.'

'Maybe? Maybe my arse!' He kicked a small wooden stool out of his way and went to the big press in the kitchen. 'Her bundle has gone. Ye ken fine she'll no be back.' Janet went on quietly washing the pile of dishes, shrinking inwardly, hoping he would not notice her. He was frightening when he flew into one of his rages. Although she had remained wary and tense when he was anywhere near, she realized now that the winter had passed in relative peace while Lily Bloddret had kept him happy – or as happy as a man of his nature would ever be. His eyes narrowed and his lip curled as he looked at his wife.

'Well ye'll regret getting rid o' Lily Bloddret,' he bellowed. 'I'll make sure you carry out your marriage vows whatever the McClure woman thinks. "Love, honour and obey"; aye, I'll see ye obey at least,' he sneered. He was about to stride across the kitchen when his eye fell on Janet washing the dishes with her wooden bowl on the stone slab in the corner. 'Aye, and as for you, young miss, it's time you learned what it is to be a real woman. What life is all about. Ye've been here long enough now.' He made a rumbling sound which was half gloating laugh and half a bellow of frustrated anger as he headed out into the farmyard.

'Oh, lassie,' Hannah whispered, coming across to where Janet was working. 'There'll be no pacifying him until he gets Lily out o' his head. Make sure ye lock your bedroom door when ye go to bed at night.'

'The door does not have a lock,' Janet said, all her fears rising in her so that her voice ended in a squeak of fear.

'Then I will ask Joe to bring a lock next time he is down at the store. He will fix it for ye. Meanwhile wedge it as best ye can for he can be a beast of a man. Although he is my own husband, there's no denying it.' It was the first time Hannah Foster had spoken so frankly to Janet, speaking to her as to another woman and no longer as a child, but this only added to Janet's fears, both real and imagined. She shuddered in silence. Would Joe protect her if his father tried to – to. . . . What exactly she didn't know, except that she didn't want him near enough to touch her.

That evening, Wull Foster set out for the inn as soon as he had finished his meal.

'Here we go again,' Joe groaned as he struggled to make himself comfortable on the old settle, which lay in one corner of the kitchen. 'I'd best wait to tend the pony or he'll leave it in harness all night and without a drink or a bite to eat.'

'Surely he would not do that, Joe,' Janet protested. 'Your father always cares for the horses. You told me so yourself.'

'Aye, he knows we depend on the horses for all the farm work, but when he's drunk he doesna remember how much we need poor old Tommy.'

'I see.' Janet tried to suppress a yawn. 'Well I'm going to bed. I

– your mother said she would ask you to bring a lock for my door.'

'Aye, she did ask but they didn't have one at the store. Mr Jacobs has promised to order one for us, though. I'll fix it for ye, Janet, never fear.' His young face looked tired and troubled. 'It will be Mother who will suffer this night,' he muttered almost under his breath, 'unless he finds Lily and brings her back.'

'Surely she was foolish to take to the roads so early in the year?' Janet said. 'Everyone knows there's still half the winter to come – either snow or rain.'

'Ye'd think so but folks like Lily Bloddret dinna stop to consider tomorrow, or what the weather might do.'

'She took the bread that was left and a lump of cheese, but that would not last her long.'

'I suppose she's used to finding food for herself. Ye gang tae bed, Miss Janet. Ye look tired out. And dinna worry. He'll not trouble ye when he knows I'm still up and about tending to Tommy.' He shook his head despairingly. 'Poor Mother,' he muttered softly.

Wull Foster asked every man who came into the inn if they had seen Lily.

'Aye, I saw her just before noon,' Geordie Smith grinned. 'Singing like a wee linty, she was. I asked her where she was going but she shook her head and laughed. "Off to find ma fortune," says she.'

'Where was she headed?' Wull Foster asked.

'Doon through Molden and on the road tae Dumfries. There's no use worrying about Lily Bloddret: she knows all the roads for miles around, aye and beyond. But I did warn her there's the worst o' the winter tae come yet, so she might turn around and come back, at least as far as that old shack she stayed in afore ye took her in at Braeheights.'

'Where is the shack?' Wull demanded. Geordie looked from him to Jim Sparks, the innkeeper, and it was he who answered.

'Why, 'tis no more than a broken-doon hen hoose, next tae the burn on auld Bowman's bit o'land. A good March wind will blow it doon in minutes. I dinna think she'll go back there. Anyway, how is your ain wife these days, Wull? Mistress McClure said she was a very sick woman the last time she was up at your place.'

'Och, she's fine.'

'Glad tae hear that. Sent Lily on her way, did she then?' Sparks asked innocently, but with a sly wink at the rest of his customers. Wull Foster slurped at his drink and chose not to answer.

Hannah Foster remembered Mrs McClure's warnings about the troubles a woman like Lily Bloddret could bring, but no amount of feigning sleep or trying to reason with her husband would make him see reason and she was forced to submit to his brutal demands.

After a few unseasonably mild days, the weather turned bitterly cold again. Each night since Lily left, Wull Foster had gone to the inn but no one there had seen anything of her since she left Braeheights. Even the sauciest of the girls who hung around refused to have anything to do with Wull Foster when they knew he had been with Wandering Lily. This added to his frustration and it was his wife who suffered. Joe, coming in from tending the pony, heard his mother's muffled sobbing and his young fists clenched, but he knew he had neither the strength nor the right to stand up to his father, even for his mother's sake. Janet now had a bolt on her bedroom door but Joe admitted he was disappointed that it was such a slender affair and the door was so warped he had only managed to fix it near the top where the door met the frame.

Janet grew increasingly tense and nervous – jumping whenever she heard Wull Foster's voice. She took care to keep the table between them when she served his meal for even in his wife's presence he did not hesitate to touch her.

Then came a morning when Janet wakened to find the whole world transformed.

'The snow looks so beautiful,' she said to Hannah when she returned from the log shed with her basket piled high. 'It is a pity we have to spoil the perfection.'

'Aye, beautiful it might be,' Hannah sighed, 'but it makes a lot of extra work watering the animals and trudging through it to feed them. There will not be many hens laying either if it stays as cold as this.'

'No, I didn't collect many eggs yesterday. They were all too busy fluffing out their feathers to keep warm.'

'Was the snow still falling when you were out?'

'Yes, but it's already quite deep and it is getting worse.'

'So Joe will not be able to take the pony and trap to the store today, think ye?'

'I doubt it, but we are fairly well stocked except for paraffin, which Joe uses for the storm lanterns he uses in the byre when he's milking.'

'Aye we shall have to make do with tallow candles inside until he can bring more for the lamps. There'll be no trip to the inn for himself tonight either,' she muttered, more to herself than to Janet. Even his own wife dreaded Mr Foster staying at home on winter evenings. A shiver of fear shook Janet's slender frame. If only she could be sure of locking him from her own small room.

'I wonder where Lily Bloddret is now and where she will find shelter?'

'I don't know, lassie, but she was a foolish woman to take off so early in the year. She could starve to death beneath the hedge and no one would know.'

It was still snowing on and off when Foster and his sons came in for their dinner. They were cold, hungry and bad-tempered but the meal was ready and Janet served them ample portions of potato and cabbage with a little of the fat pork from the pig which was hanging from the iron hooks in the pantry. Hannah had made a suet pudding and some jam sauce.

The snow was deep by evening and a cold wind was beginning to blow small drifts against the buildings and hedges. Janet was glad to step in the footprints which Joe had left when she made her last visit to the privy. Even so, the hems of her dress and her mother's old cloak were powdered with snow and clinging wet and cold about her ankles by the time she returned to the house. Janet was thankful to get to her room, cold though it was, with its tiny, ill-fitting window with bits of old duster stuffed in gaps to keep out the draught. She pulled on her thick flannel nightgown which covered her toes and warmed her feet if she curled up small. Her prayers before sleeping were always for her mother and Fingal. She often read a poem from his book before going to sleep.

Tonight it was too cold to keep her hands above the blanket and she had only a small stub of candle left. It was a bitter night. She got up again and groped for her thick woollen drawers and her socks, pulling them on in the darkness, then spreading her damp cloak over the bed. She fell into an exhausted sleep as soon as she was warm.

She never forgot to slide Joe's flimsy snib into place and wedge the small trunk between the door and her bed. The trunk had belonged to Molly, and Joe had carried it downstairs, along with Molly's pitifully few clothes, her treasured hairbrush and a small mirror. She hadn't even had a room to sleep in, only a curtain across a corner of the loft, screening her from the boys.

'I reckon she'd want ye to have these,' he had said gruffly over the ache of grief in his chest. Janet's room was so small she often knocked her shins on the edge of the chest, but since Mrs Foster's warning she had been doubly glad of it to use as a wedge between her door and the bed. She had witnessed Foster's strength, and his fury, so she knew it would not keep him out for long, but at least it would warn her of his presence.

Janet had been deeply asleep when a thump on her door disturbed her. She yawned and blinked in the darkness, turned over and prepared to sleep again. Another thump and loud curses brought her wide awake, her heart thumping with fear.

'What have ye done to this bloody door?' Foster growled. 'Open it up, you silly wee bitch.'

Janet began to tremble. She clutched her blankets close to her chest. 'G-go away,' she called nervously. 'I shall scream for Joe if y-you don't g-go away.'

'Joe?' Foster gave a guffaw. 'Come on now, do as I say and open the door. 'Tis time ye earned your keep and learned how to pleasure a man.'

Fear propelled Janet from her bed. She pushed her fists into her boots and hammered against the small window. It was her only chance of escape. There were gaps at the bottom and side but the top was firmly wedged. Even if she opened it she would struggle to squeeze through, but Foster would not be able to follow her. The swollen frame would not budge but the four slender struts holding the glass were rotten. Two of them broke, shattering the glass and making a jagged cut along Janet's arm. She was oblivious to the pain as she heard Foster burst the latch at the top of the door. His sheer strength would move the trunk, and the bed, enough for him to squeeze into her room. She grabbed her cloak from the bed. Fingal's book fell at her feet. She picked it up and stuffed it in one of her boots. She threw them both out of the window. She heard Foster grunting as he heaved against her door.

'Open it up, you bitch. You'll pay for this.'

Desperation made her squeeze through the small aperture head first, ignoring the cuts from the glass splinters left in the frame. There was nothing she could do to steady herself. Her window opened onto the sloping roof of the wash house, which had been built as a lean-to. Everything was covered in snow and Janet could not stop herself from sliding head first down the roof and onto the ground. A hundred fleeting thoughts crowded her mind in those desperate seconds. Even if she broke her neck it was better than her fate in Foster's hands.

'Oh, Fingal,' she sobbed beneath her breath. She remembered Molly. She had drowned herself because of the fiend who was her father. She landed in a heap of snow, spluttering but with no more than a bruised hip bone from a boulder hidden beneath the snow. She groped for her boots and shoved her wet feet into them, clutching her poetry book as though her life depended on it. She dare not stop to do up her laces in case Foster came out with his lantern. She tucked them in, pulled her cloak round her and ran. To reach the track to Molden she needed to go through the farmyard. Foster might seize her as she passed the door. Tom Friar had taken her across the fields to the Crillion road. She ran that way, stumbling in the darkness, hampered by drifts of snow. She passed the privy and scrambled through the hedge into the field beyond. Her blood seemed to freeze when she heard Foster's furious roar from her window.

'Come back here! You stupid bitch. D'ye hear me? Ye'll freeze to death. Come back inside, you silly wench. I'll warm ye.'

There was only a silver sliver of moon and Janet prayed he could not see her as she cowered against the hedge. Then she heard him bellow again.

'All right, stay out there. Ye'll be glad to come back.' Did he mean he would not pursue her? Janet didn't believe he would give up easily. Was he waiting for her to crawl back into the house? Or was he already pulling on his clothes to haul her back again? She had to run as far and as fast as she could.

Swearing to himself Foster regarded the broken window and vowed to board it up in the morning. She would not get away from him that way again. He had known she had spirit. He was going to enjoy mastering this one.

The hedge hid Janet from view but the snow was deeper where it had blown off the fields. It would be easier to see her in the open field but the night was dark and speed was what mattered. She dare not imagine what Foster would do to her if he caught her, but her heart almost failed her as she remembered the long distance to the road, even in daylight with Tommy to guide her. Flurries of snow kept falling and her cloak was already damp and heavy. She ran on, holding her side when she developed a stitch, determined to keep going. She scrambled through another hedge. How many fields had she crossed with Tommy?

Sometime later, she saw the side of a wood loom into view. They had definitely passed a wood. She breathed a sigh of relief. She must be heading in the right direction. It would be more sheltered in the wood, beneath the trees.

'I must stop and lace up my boots,' she muttered to herself, 'and catch my breath.' She had nearly lost one of her boots several times and she knew there were blisters on her heels. She crouched against the trunk of a sturdy tree. Her fingers throbbed with cold and it seemed to take forever to lace her boots tightly. Her toes were numb with cold. She was beginning to get her breath back when she heard the snapping of a twig.

Janet did not wait to discover whether it was a fox, or Foster. She ran on as fast as the undergrowth allowed. She reached another hedge and knew she had not come this way with Tom. Still her only desire was to put as much distance between herself and Braeheights as possible. No one would hear her scream here, and no one would find her starved to death beneath a hedgerow.

She pushed her way through the hedge, oblivious to the scratches from the thorns. Her strength was waning now and the deepening snow hampered her. Fortunately the field was sloping downhill. She came to another hedge, and another field. Janet lost count of the fields; she was lost. She was freezing cold and exhausted. Instinct told her Foster would have caught her by now if he had pursued her as far as the wood. She was tempted to curl up in a ball and wait until daylight. She thought of Fingal: he would never give up. Without warning she almost stumbled into the burn. The banks were covered in snow and it was difficult to tell how wide it was. Relief warmed her temporarily. At least she was heading in the right direction even if she had arrived at a different part of the burn.

She put a boot tentatively onto the ice-covered water but it shattered, not yet thick enough to bear her weight. She must jump and hope she would reach the other side. She did her best but one foot went into the water before she managed to crawl up the side of the burn. Her feet were so numb already she was barely aware of the freezing water. She paused to ease the pain in her side, but she had to summon her strength and keep moving.

It was several hours later before Janet saw the road down to Crillion Keep. All thoughts of reaching her mother had long since vanished. She plodded up the familiar road like a homing pigeon, putting one foot before the other by sheer force of will. At last the dark shape of the stables loomed into view. She could go no further. She had not the strength to climb the ladder to the hayloft. She fell onto the small pile of hay at the bottom as oblivion claimed her.

It was Mark Wright, the undercoachman, who found her.

'Mr Baird! There's a body in the stable,' he shouted hysterically. 'C-come and see.'

'Is't a tramp, laddie? It was a rough night. He'll do ye no harm.'

'N-no. 'Tis a lassie an' I think she's dead.'

'Surely not!' Donald Baird hurried from the coach house and followed the shivering youth into the stable next door. 'Oh my God!' Donald fell to his knees and touched Janet's cold cheek with a gentle finger. 'It's Janet! Oh, lassie, whatever can have driven ye tae this on such a night?' he muttered, his voice gruff with emotion. 'Open the door wide, laddie. I'll carry her to my wife.'

'Is she dead, Mr Baird?'

'She's not far off,' Donald said grimly. 'You be getting on with the horses, laddie.'

As he approached the cottages, he met Maggie McLauchlan, his mother-in-law, coming out of hers, on her way to the Keep to start cooking breakfast.

'Whatever has happened?' she gasped.

'It's Janet. She was in the stables. She's near frozen to death.'

'Carry her into my house. Peggy will be upset and the bairns. . . .' She pushed her door open. 'I'll need to light the fire. Will ye go and tell Mr Saunders what has happened and I'll come as soon as I can. I must get her out o' her wet clothes and rub some warmth into her.' Donald was relieved to leave Janet in the capable hands of his mother-in-law, though he feared there was little hope for her and his kindly heart was heavy with sorrow.

'Janet Scott? The dominie's granddaughter?' Josiah Saunders echoed incredulously. 'You found the child in the stable?'

'Aye, sir. She's no a child now but I doubt if she'll survive this night's freezing.'

'Bring her up here. There is no time to lose and Mrs Mossy already has the fires burning here. Ask Mrs McLauchlan to come as quickly as she can. We shall attend the girl here. There is water boiling in the kitchen and a fire in the small sitting room.' No one questioned Josiah Saunders when he issued orders. An unconscious Janet was carried into Crillion Keep and laid on a thick rug before the fire in Josiah's own sitting room.

'She lives, but only just,' Maggie McLauchlan whispered hoarsely in answer to his question.

'This is the warmest room in the house. She must stay in here.'

'But this is your own room, sir. You dine in here when you are alone.

'The child's need is greater than mine. Do as I say and tell me what else we might do to revive her.'

Janet stirred but did not regain consciousness as Maggie McLauchlan towelled her damp hair and gently bathed her face and hands in warm water. She tried to rub warmth and life into her limbs. She had been amazed to find Janet was dressed only in her nightgown beneath her sodden cloak. It was clear she had made a sudden flight and she pondered anew what could have possessed her to flee from Braeheights on a night like this. Had she heard how frail her mother's health was? Was she on her way to see her? But no, she would not set out at night, in the snow, dressed in her nightgown.

'Her poor feet are raw frae the blisters,' Mrs Mossy said, interrupting her conjectures. She was gently drying first one foot and then the other, to restore Janet's circulation as Mistress McLauchlan had bade her. 'D'ye think she'll live?'

'I pray she will. I've never seen Mr Saunders so distressed, but he and the old dominie were good friends.'

'Aye, they passed many an evening together talking about books and playing that game on a board,' Mrs Mossy said.

'Dear God, the bairn is beginning to shake,' Maggie said. 'Pass me more blankets.' She clasped Janet in her motherly arms, hugging her, willing the heat from her own body to suffuse Janet's with warmth and life. 'Why, oh why, does she not open her eyes?'

'Can I come in?' Josiah called through the closed door.

'Aye, we have rolled her in a blanket for now. When it is daylight I will bring one o' my own nightgowns for her. It will be too big but it will do for now.'

'I'll get her own nightgown washed and dried as soon as I can,' Mrs Mossy said. She was a kind-hearted woman and she didn't like to see suffering in man or beast.

'I have asked Donald and the gardener to bring my own bed in here for her,' Josiah Saunders said. 'Will you have one of the other beds brought downstairs and aired for me before tonight, Mrs Mossy?'

'Y-yes, sir, if ye're sure you should give the lassie your bed, and – and this room. It has always been the warmest and your favourite, especially in winter.'

'I shall survive. I am not so sure about the child. We must do all we can. I shall ask Donald to bring the doctor when we can get through the snow. Why is she shaking?'

'I d-don't know. I think it is the circulation returning to her limbs. She has not opened her eyes or spoken a word yet.'

'And you are trying to instill the warmth from your own body into hers?'

'Yes, sir. I – I don't know what else to do until we can get her into bed and warm it with a shelf frae the oven.'

'Then I will sit before the fire and hold her close while you supervise the making of a bed for her.'

Maggie McLauchlan's eyes widened. 'Y-You sir? Are ye sure? I-I mean she's not exactly a bairn now. She is nearly sixteen. I shall never forget Janet's birth. She brought such comfort and joy tae Peggy after she had lost her own babe. The poor wee lamb, her mother lavished all her care on Andrew. Since he died Mary Scott is more in need o' care herself, frae what I hear.'

'That is true. Mr Cole is at his wits' end to know what to do about her. He was telling me about his predicament the last evening we spent together. His own wife is an invalid. He cannot care for two of them.'

'Aye, I heard he doesna ken which way to turn, but it grieves me to think o' Mary Scott, the dominie's only daughter, ending up in the poorhouse. I wondered if the lassie had heard o' her mother's plight. She must be sorely troubled to leave in her nightgown.'

'She was dressed in her night clothes?' Josiah stared at Mistress McLauchlan, then his eyes flashed with anger. 'I heard vile gossip about the man Foster when his own daughter died. Surely Mistress Scott would not have allowed her daughter to stay there if there was any truth? Can you pass the child to me?' He seated himself in his large armchair before the fire and held open his arms.

'There was nowhere else for the bairn to go when Mary Scott went to work for Mr Cole. Janet was good friends with Molly Foster so we all hoped she would be happy at Braeheights. Hannah Foster was always a kindly woman, but they say Foster himself is a brute of a man.' She placed Janet in his arms cocooned in her blankets.

'I shall do my best to get her warm and keep her safe while you and Mrs Mossy make a bed for her. Maybe you could arrange to stay here for a few nights, until she recovers. or until we can get someone to nurse her?'

'Aye, I can stay, sir. Peggy will help to nurse Janet. She has aye had a tender heart for the lassie.'

'I'll do what I can to help,' Mrs Mossy offered.

'Thank you,' Josiah Saunders said with genuine gratitude. 'The dominie was a good friend to me from the first week I came to Crillion Keep. I shall do everything I can to help his granddaughter. I wish I had known she was unhappy, or in danger. We rarely saw her at the kirk in recent months.'

'No. Foster hardly ever brought any o' his brood to the kirk after they found the body o' young Molly,' Maggie McClauchlan said darkly. 'There's some reckon he was responsible for her death.'

'What is this? Where did it come from?' He lifted a small leather-bound book from a table beside the fire.

'It belongs to Janet. She was clutching it as though her life depended on it when Donald carried her in frae the stables. Fingal gave it to her brother, Andrew. He must have passed it on to Janet before he died. She always loved reading.'

'Yes, I remember the dominie telling me she was as intelligent as any of the boys he had ever taught. Well there are plenty of books here for her to read if only we can make sure she survives, and I pray to God we can.'

There were several days and nights when both he and Mistress McClauchlan doubted whether that was possible. Janet drifted in and out of consciousness for the next ten days, alternatively burning with fever, then shivering as though with ague.

As soon as the snow had begun to thaw, Josiah sent Donald Baird to bring Doctor Carr.

He shook his white head. 'You're doing all that I could do, Josiah, you and Mistress McLauchlan. I brought the lassie into the world. I'd hate to see her leave it before her time.'

'So would I, so would I,' Josiah said heavily. 'If I had known she was so unhappy at Braeheights I would have made a place for her here. When I came to Crillion Keep I was glad of her grandfather's help to guide me through the tangled threads of local society, the gentlemen and the supposedly righteous elders of the kirk.'

The old doctor cocked an eyebrow at his cynical tone and accepted a tot of best French brandy.

'I am an elder of the kirk. Some of them are good men but a few are hypocrites. I'm sure the Reverend Drummond must have told you some of us try to be good Christians. I hear he often spends an evening here with you, especially since Dominie McWhan's death.'

'Yes, he does, but I prefer to judge for myself now that I know them better. Mr Cole, now, he is genuine; almost a saint, I think. He is making a suit for me but he is extremely worried about his wife since Mistress Scott has become an added burden rather than a help to him. He is reluctant to ask her to leave when she has no one to care for her.'

'Mary Scott lived for Andrew. Her reason for living died with him.'

'But she has a daughter!' He glanced towards the bed where Janet was tossing feverishly. 'Even if she did not realize the danger she was in at Braeheights, surely she must have known how hard her life was.'

'Mary Scott put everything out of her mind when her laddie died. I don't think she has long in this world but that is no consolation to Luke Cole in his present circumstances and I see no solution.'

'No.' Josiah stared into the fire in contemplation, then he looked at the doctor. 'If her daughter survives I may be able to provide a solution.'

'You, Josiah? How so?' But Josiah would not be drawn further, even by the good doctor, discreet though he knew the old man to be. Josiah was startled by his next question. Had the doctor guessed what was in his mind?

'Does your sister know you're nursing a young woman back to health?' Archie Carr raised a quizzical eyebrow. 'I know she disapproves of your acts of charity.'

'Whatever I do it is none of Eliza's business. It is better if she does not hear. On the occasions she has visited the Keep she has caused trouble. I almost lost the good services of Maggie

McLauchlan and Jacob, a fine cook and the best horseman I ever knew.'

'Aye, you were fortunate to inherit your uncle's staff as well as his estate. He was a good judge of men and they respected him, as they do you now, if I may say so, Josiah. I heard the manager at the Home Farm trudged through the snow himself to bring fresh eggs and milk and make sure you have all you need.'

'He did indeed. Hugh Bell is a fine man and I shall not forget.'

'Aye, be thankful you don't share the same blood as Eliza, despite her claim to be your sister.'

Chapter Nine

Fingal was concerned about his mother with the harsh winter weather, so he hired a horse to ride to Crillion Keep on the first Saturday afternoon the roads were passable. Maggie was not at home so he called on Peggy next door.

'Mother is staying up at the Big Hoose.' She explained about Janet being so ill and Mr Saunders insisting she stay at the Keep. 'He has been wonderfully generous and kind. Mother and I have taken turns at nursing her.'

'Janet is here?' He could barely wait for Peggy to give him the details of Janet's flight from Braeheights.

Maggie saw Fingal pass the kitchen window on his way to the back door of the Keep. She opened the door before he could knock, delighted as always to see her only son.

'I'm fine, laddie,' she assured him as she drew him through into the large kitchen. 'I've told ye often not to worry about me when I have Peggy and Donald so close, and Mr Saunders is a most considerate employer. Did Peggy tell you we have a visitor here, though? I reckon ye'll want to see her, though she will na ken ye,' she warned. 'She's still very ill with the fever.'

'How can this be? How did Janet come to be here?'

'Peggy has aye been a second mother to the lassie. Where else could she go? Anyway I dinna think she had the strength to go any further. I thank God she reached the stable.' She explained how Donald had carried her here, almost frozen to death.

'Why did she come at night, in the snow? Why is she here, at the Keep?'

'Mr Saunders thought it best and I am glad. We can keep her warmer here. He and Mrs Mossy watch over her during the day. Peggy and I take turns to stay with her at night. She drifts in and out o' the fever. The only word she's uttered that I can catch, is your name, Fingal. She was clutching the wee book you gave to Andrew. She didna want to let it go.'

'I must see her,' he said urgently. 'So many Sundays I have journeyed all the way to attend our own wee kirk but Janet has never been there. What can be wrong, Mother?'

'I fear she must have run away frae Mr Foster. Nothing else would drive her out wearing only her nightgown on such a night.'

'You think he has harmed her?' Fingal asked, a muscle pulsing in his lean jaw.

'We don't know, laddie. She must have been badly frightened to flee like that. It's obvious she hadn't planned to do it.'

'I'll kill him if he has—'

'Hush, hush, son. Don't say such things,' Maggie McLauchlan said in alarm.

Fingal was dismayed when he saw Janet's slight figure tossing and turning restlessly beneath the blankets. Josiah Saunders watched the concern, compassion – and was it love in his troubled gaze?

'I fear she is worse today,' he said quietly, 'but Doctor Carr warned us this might happen. He said it would be the beginning of the end.'

'Oh dear God, surely she can't die? So young? Not Janet. . . .'

'You care deeply for her, Fingal?'

'You must know I do. She was like a younger sister to me. And more. . . .' he added in a choked whisper.

'Then you will not return to your lodgings tonight? Tomorrow is the Sabbath. Tell your mother I have requested you eat here with us. She cannot be in two places.'

'Thank you, sir.'

'Your mother and your sister will watch over her tonight.'

Janet's fever increased alarmingly. She tossed aside the bedclothes and shouted unintelligible words, almost screams at times.

Peggy and Maggie stayed with her, willing the fever to break, each exhausted but unwilling to leave.

'The doctor said we must keep her warm, but her brow burns like a furnace as soon as I have wiped it with a cooling cloth,' Maggie McLauchlan said in a troubled voice. She was worried and weary.

'It is the delirium which worries me,' Peggy murmured brokenly. 'She raves like a madwoman. It is as though all the demons in hell are chasing her.'

'She has grown worse, and weaker. I fear we're going to lose her,' Maggie said. 'Mr Saunders said we must call him if she reached a crisis during the night. I fear the time has come.'

'Oh, Mother, surely not,' Peggy wept. 'Janet is as dear to me as my own bairns.'

'I know. It is because you suckled her as an infant and she brought you comfort. I believe Fingal loves her too. He did not want to bide at the cottage tonight but I persuaded him to sleep so that he might help watch over her during the day while we rest.' She sighed heavily as Janet threw off the eiderdown again and gabbled incoherently.

'I will waken Mr Saunders. I fear the end is near.'

Josiah did not wait to dress but pulled on his woollen robe and slippers and followed Mrs McLauchlan back to the sick room. His heart had been heavy with dread when he went to bed and now his fears were confirmed.

He knelt beside the bed and helped Peggy Baird to hold Janet's thrashing limbs and keep her covered with the blankets as Doctor Carr had advised, while Maggie bathed her burning forehead and cheeks and hands with a cooling cloth. They fought together until the first streaks of the winter dawn began to peep through the side of the curtains. Then, as though all the strength had drained from her exhausted body, Janet shuddered several times and lay still, her body drenched, her long hair dark and damp with sweat.

'She breathes still,' Josiah said and took her hand in his, stroking her wrist gently as he felt for her pulse. He began to talk to her in a low voice. Peggy Baird realized he was reciting poetry. Janet showed no response but neither did she struggle any more. She lay white and still upon the bed.

'I think we should bathe her and put on a dry nightgown and sheets,' Maggie McLauchlan said, following her instincts. Almost as though recognizing her voice, Janet's head turned slightly and for a moment she opened her eyes and actually looked at the two women. But then her eyelids fluttered as though the effort of lifting them was too great.

'The wildness has gone!' Peggy said. 'Is the crisis past? And ma bairn still lives?'

'I think you are right,' Josiah said. 'We must thank God. I will go and dress now while you wash and change her so that she may sleep naturally at last. Then I shall watch over her from my chair before the fire. You have both done well to nurse the child so diligently. Now you need rest.'

Although Janet was too weak to speak to him, indeed almost too weak to lift her eyelids, Fingal felt the faint pressure of her fingers in his own when he spoke to her. He uttered prayers of thankfulness as his mother assured him she had reached a crisis as the doctor had predicted, and she had come through it.

'She will need time, a long time, before she is well and strong again. Mr Saunders says she will need good food and plenty of rest so she should stay here.'

'Here at Crillion Keep?' Fingal asked in surprise.

'Yes.' His mother chewed her lower lip thoughtfully. 'Where else can she go, except with us? Mr Saunders is a kind man and he has the room here and he knows Peggy and I will do all we can for her. I don't know what he has in mind but he told the doctor he would have found work for her here if he had known the granddaughter of his old friend was so unhappy and living in fear up at Braeheights. We – we don't know what that devil Foster may have done to make her flee in the dead of night. Fingal, we must trust Mr Saunders's judgement.'

'I don't like it but there is no place for Janet with her mother. I wish I did not have to leave today, but I need my work more than ever now. I must save enough money to rent a house instead of lodgings and then. . . .'

'And then?' Maggie asked.

'Then I will take care of her. I have nothing to offer yet, but one day I shall have more, and I. . . .' He looked at his mother, his blue eyes pleading for understanding.

'You love the lassie, Fingal?'

'I think I always have.'

'She is so young still. And what if Foster has given her a child?'

'A child? You think it is possible?'

'We don't know.'

'Whatever happens I shall always love her.' But could he love another man's child, he pondered, especially the spawn of a devil like Foster was reputed to be?

His horse had been well fed and rested and Fingal decided to make a two-mile detour to call on Mary Scott on his way back to the town of Annan. He wanted to tell her that Janet was still frail and in need of her care.

It was Mr Cole himself who opened the door in answer to his knock early on Sunday afternoon. He explained his mission but the tailor stared at him in dismay.

'You must come through and speak with Mistress Scott, Master McLauchlan, but you will see she is not in a fit state to care for herself, even less for her daughter; or my wife,' he added almost to himself.

Fingal had seen the look of despair in the tailor's eyes. When he came face to face with the woman who had been almost a mother to him during his years at the dominie's schoolhouse with Andrew and Janet, he understood the tailor's dilemma. There was no sign of the active young woman who had fed and cared for the winter boarders so diligently. He barely recognized the skeleton who stood before him, with her haggard face and wispy grey hair. She was around the same age as his half-sister, Peggy, but she looked old enough to be his grandmother.

On the other side of the fireplace sat Mr Cole's wife, rocking silently to and fro in her chair, clutching her arms around her thin body as though she was cold, although the room was hot and she was warmly dressed. Her eyes were vacant and she never uttered a sound, apparently lost in a world of her own.

Mary Scott buried her head in her hands and began to weep silently.

'If only Andrew had been spared,' she whispered brokenly. 'He would have cared for us, for Janet and for me. What am I to do? I can no longer do the work I came here to do. I am a burden to Mr Cole but I have nowhere to go.'

Fingal looked helplessly at the dapper little tailor in his best Sunday suit. He was an elder of the kirk and he attended every Sunday. Fingal's parents believed he was one of the most genuine men in the parish and anyone with a less kindly heart would have dismissed Mrs Scott. He bit his lower lip.

'I am so sorry to have disturbed you all on the Sabbath,' Fingal apologized, moving backwards toward the door, recognizing an impossible situation, knowing he could do nothing to help. 'I thought you would be glad to have news that your daughter has survived the fever, Mistress Scott, but I see you have problems of your own. Do not worry about Janet. My mother and sister will take care of her until she regains her strength.'

'Thank you, Fingal,' Mary Scott said listlessly.

As he followed the tailor out of the small cottage and into the crisp cold air, Mr Cole wagged his white head.

'I wish I was in a position to offer help,' Fingal said sincerely, 'but I am still a clerk in training and the pay is low until I am a fully-fledged lawyer. Sometimes I wish I had taken the dominie's advice and become a teacher. I owe him, and Mistress Scott, a debt I cannot repay,' he said unhappily.

'I understand, young man, and I know your intentions are good, but the problem is not yours. I wanted to send word to Miss Janet but she rarely attends the kirk these days.'

'No, I think Foster was responsible for her absence,' Fingal said grimly. 'I am sorry to have troubled you, Mr Cole.'

'But what will happen to the child?' Mr Cole asked with genuine concern. 'Her father was a fine tailor and a hard worker when he was in good health. The dominie was a good friend to many of us.'

'Mr Saunders regarded Dominie McWhan as a good friend too and he seems willing to allow Janet to stay at Crillion Keep for now. Her mother's plight is more serious, I think.'

'You are right, young man. I don't know how long I can go on supporting two invalid women. The Reverend Drummond assures me the Lord works in mysterious ways and my prayers will be answered. I pray He may not take too long.'

The following day, the housekeeper from one of the large houses on the outskirts of the village called to collect the suit Mr Cole had been making for her master, an elderly bachelor. Her husband was also employed as coachman and gardener and he had driven her down in the pony and trap.

'It was Mary Scott who wrapped up the parcel and wrote the receipt when I handed over the money,' Mrs McBain told her husband. 'She looks like a ghost. I'm sure a puff of wind would blow her away. She barely had the energy to tie the string. She doesn't have the same look as her husband and son did but I'm sure she doesna have long for this world.'

'Did ye tell her what we heard at the kirk yesterday?'

'No, but I asked how her lassie was keeping. She gave a sorrowful sigh and leaned on the table as though she hadna the strength to stand. She said she hadna seen Janet but Fingal McLauchlan told her Janet had been close to death with a fever but his mother and sister are nursing her at Crillion Keep, so 'tis true she must be biding there. Mary's eyes filled with tears and she muttered. "I can only thank God for Mr Saunders's generous heart for I canna look after my own bairn." She turned away frae me but I heard her whisper, "Only God knows what will become of us." My heart felt sore for her because she was always a pleasant, kind young woman when she looked after the schoolhouse for the old dominie.'

'Aye, our ain bairns liked her well when they attended the school. I'm wondering what Mr Saunders's sister will say if she hears her brother is giving a home to the dominie's granddaughter. Nae doubt he'll be paying Mistress McLauchlan to nurse her, and from what I hear, Mrs Ross grudges every penny her brother spends on his good deeds.'

'Aye, and she'll take out her spite on your sister-in-law and the rest o' the maids who work for her. Poor Maisie, I dinna envy her working for that vicious-tongued woman.'

'Maisie has worked for the Ross family since she was thirteen, long before Mr Ross married that she-cat. Maisie said his first wife was a gentle, sweet-natured woman.'

'I'll bet he regrets his second choice, then,' his wife said darkly, 'but she's given him a son. Some say the boy is as sly and spiteful as his mother.'

'It's hard to believe she's Mr Saunders's sister.'

'They're not kin by blood. Her mother married his father.'

Two evenings later, Benjamin McBain was at the Meeting Rooms to pay his sixpence into the savings bank in the presence of the minister and two of his elders. Ben saw several men he knew and as usual they fell to exchanging news. He told them it was true young Janet Scott had run away from Braeheights and was being cared for at Crillion Keep. These bits of innocent gossip usually spread like goosedown in the wind.

So it was that early on Friday afternoon Donald Baird hurried to warn Josiah that the Rosses' carriage had turned into the long drive to Crillion Keep. Josiah groaned aloud. He thought for a moment, then he sought Maggie McLauchlan.

'Get a large white handkerchief and tie it in a triangle around your mouth and nose. Ask Mrs Mossy to do the same and tell her to wait with Janet beside her bed. I shall answer the door myself and I shall tell Mrs Ross we have a patient with a fever, which is like to be infectious. You may enter the hall when you hear me speaking. Let Mrs Ross see you in your mask, then scurry away out of sight. She does not like illness of any kind, especially if her son is with her. I hope that will keep her from entering the house. If she insists on peering into the room, I shall warn Janet to snuggle beneath the blankets and pretend to have a fever or a spasm of violent coughing. I think she can do that without pretence,' he added with a frown. 'Her illness has left a rattle in her chest. Doctor Carr says it may take six months or more before she can get rid of it. Today we shall make use of it.' His eyes twinkled and he gave Mrs McLauchlan a grin like a mischievous boy. 'We must act as though we are at a playhouse. Will you do that for me, for Miss Janet's sake?'

'Aye, sir. We'll try our best.' She hurried out to find Mrs Mossy and to tell Donald, so that she could prepare him to tell the same story to the coachman.

'What's this, Josiah! Answering the door yourself? Keeping guests waiting?'

'We have not had many guests, invited, or otherwise.' He paused watching a flush mount Eliza's sallow skin as she drew up her bosom in indignation. 'No one wants to catch an infectious disease. We are at pains to prevent—'

'Oh, I'm sorry, sir,' Maggie McClauchlan mumbled behind a large white handkerchief. 'I couldna get to the door any quicker. I-I must get back to the sick room. Excuse me, ma'am.' She scurried away before Eliza could ask her any questions. Josiah bit back a smile as he watched his sister's eyes grow round. He knew Mrs McLauchlan had opened the door of Janet's room when they heard a deep chesty cough, slightly more prolonged than usual, he fancied. Eliza stared at him and edged backwards onto a lower step.

'So it is true! You do have that girl staying here? You are a fool! You with your weak heart, taking that waif into your own home? The fever could kill you if it brings a cough like that!'

'The girl is too young to die for want of warmth and food. But, Eliza,' his eyes were mocking, 'I'm sure you will not grieve, if the fever should carry me away. You have wished me dead many times since I inherited my great-uncle's estate.' Eliza became aware of the irony in his expression. Even as a young boy, he had been able to see right through her motives. He had often made her squirm with his clear-eyed honesty. Even as a sickly child, death had held no fear for him. His stoicism had found him a tender place in her own mother's heart, something she had never achieved herself, even though she was kin by blood, rather than by marriage as he was.

Josiah watched the expressions chasing over her face. He had never seen a vestige of tenderness there. Not that he expected any for himself. He had learned there was only one love in Eliza's life and that was for herself.

'Is Henry with you? He must be cold waiting in the coach. You are welcome to come in and take refreshment, but the risk must be on your own head. Mistress McLauchlan and Mistress Mossy attend our patient before their other duties.'

'I shall not enter,' Eliza snapped. 'You are a fool to waste your inheritance. I have heard rumours of your generosity, even though you would keep them secret from me and my son. It is our inheritance you are wasting.' She ignored Josiah's raised eyebrows. 'What reason had you to take this chit into your home? Don't tell me she is the granddaughter of that old fool of a dominie!'

'The dominie was nobody's fool and he was a good friend to me. I forbid you to criticize him,' Josiah interrupted sternly.

'The dominie would have done better if he'd provided for his own daughter,' Eliza sneered. 'They tell me she's ready for the poorhouse if death doesn't claim her first. Be careful you don't end up paying for two funerals as well as your own, dear brother.'

'If I do, it will be nobody's concern but my own.'

'Of course it will, you stupid man. It will be my concern if you squander your money on every waif in the parish. I am your only relative. It is my due to inherit when you are gone. I must consider my son.'

'Surely his father will provide for his own son?' Josiah asked mildly. He liked the Right Honourable Edward Ross, but he had long suspected he was not as wealthy as Eliza had anticipated, or perhaps he had learned to keep a firm hand on his purse strings. 'But this is not the place to stand and talk,' Josiah said briskly. 'Unless you and Henry wish to enter and risk taking home the coughing disease then I must bid you good day.'

'And good day to you, you stubborn, foolish shadow of a man,' Eliza spat venomously. 'If I hear the girl has recovered I shall return to make you see sense and get her away, her and her stupid mother.'

Josiah shut the door with a sigh of relief.

Janet was worried that she was causing strife between Mr Saunders and his sister and as soon as she heard the coach drive away, she climbed out of bed. She must get her strength back so that she was able to work. She did not realize how ill she had been, nor the effects her illness had had. Her feet touched the floor, but when she tried to stand, her legs buckled beneath her. Both Maggie McLauchlan and Josiah heard the tumble and hurried across the wide hall. Tears sprang to Janet's eyes.

'I am a burden to you all,' she whispered hoarsely. 'I do not want to cause strife between you and your sister, sir.' She looked up at Josiah, her blue eyes pleading and wide with anxiety.

'You are not the cause of any trouble, my dear. There has never been anything else but strife between my sister and myself. We are very different by nature. Now I will let Mistress McLauchlan help you back into bed. If you are feeling better tomorrow, you can sit for a little while in a chair before the fire and each day you may do a little more, but you must understand you have been near to death and we must build up your strength gradually.'

'But I am a burden to everyone. Perhaps my mother. . . ? Could I send word to her? Maybe she will care for me?'

Maggie's heart ached at the sight of Janet's anxious young face.

'We shall not worry your mother for a while, Janet,' Josiah said. 'She has not been well herself and Mr Cole has no spare room. Here we have plenty of rooms and there is a way in which you can repay me if you will agree to stay. First we must let Mistress McLauchlan tuck you back into bed and we shall devise a plan to increase your movements each day.' His housekeeper looked up at him with relief and a warm smile creased her kindly face.

'Janet was aye an independent wee soul, even as a bairn,' she said to him later when they were away from the sickroom. 'I don't know how you will keep her here when she grows stronger, but I don't know where she will find work until the Hiring Fairs at the end of May.'

'I have a plan,' Josiah said reassuringly. 'We must convince her that I have long wanted to restore order to the library and catalogue the books in there. It is partly true, ever since I first came to Crillion Keep, even before the death of Great-Uncle William. I think Janet may enjoy helping in return for a roof over her head and plenty of good food. What do you think, Mistress McLauchlan?'

'Oh, sir, that would be a splendid idea – if you mean it? Janet loves books. It grieved her terribly when they had to leave her grandfather's books behind the night they ran away from the schoolhouse and that horrible dominie. She clings to the wee book she brought with her as though it is a lifeline, yet she does not even possess a bible of her own.'

'Good. Dominie McWhan had great plans to tutor her so that she could teach the younger children and the girls in his school. He did not anticipate such a short stay on God's earth. Maybe we can help,' Josiah said with satisfaction.

'Ye're a good man, sir,' Maggie answered with feeling. 'But she is an intelligent lassie, as well as fiercely independent. She would soon suspect if she thought you had only made up work for her,' Maggie warned.

'Leave it with me. As soon as she is strong enough to climb the stairs to the smallest bedroom on the first floor, we shall use this room as a day room again. I shall explain that I want to rearrange many of the books from the library. If Janet wishes to help you in her spare time and perhaps learn to cook, then I have no objections. You know I have never believed in formality.'

'Thank you, sir.' Maggie beamed at him. 'I think Janet may be a good wee housewife already. Mistress Foster was a genteel woman before she married Wull Foster and I believe she taught her own daughter and Janet how to cook and wash and clean, especially when she had no energy to do the work herself. The Reverend Drummond spoke highly of her but he knew her before she married.'

'Then we must allow Janet to find her place with us a Crillion Keep. A useful helper but not a slave to anyone, ever again.'

'We have another problem if Janet is staying here when she is up and about. I have almost finished knitting her a large shawl to cover her nightclothes. It will do while she stays here in the small dining room, but she had nothing but her nightdress with her. She must have left her clothes behind at Braeheights in her hurry to escape.'

'Ah, now that is a matter I had not considered, and it will soon become urgent.'

'Peggy or I would have given her a dress and underclothes, but she is much smaller than either of us, and she's so slender since the fever.'

'And you have both done more than I could have asked of you already, Mrs McClauchlan. I know Peggy is good with her needle and sometimes takes in sewing. Please tell her I will pay her if she will make whatever Janet requires in the way of underclothes. Do we have any suitable material here in the house, cotton or flannel perhaps?'

'I think we could find material from the linen cupboard, sir, and Peggy would be pleased to sew when they are for Janet.'

'Nevertheless I shall pay her for her work. You have both done more than could be expected of you.'

'We love the lassie. We're thankful our prayers have been answered.'

'You're true Christians, Maggie McLauchlan.' He smiled and Maggie thought how much younger he looked when he lost the furrows in his brow and his lean face relaxed. 'As to the dresses, if you will write down Janet's measurements I shall ask Donald to take them down to Mr Cole's. I will write him a letter asking him to make three suitable dresses and deliver them to me himself as soon as he has them ready. I would like to see him anyway and hear how he is coping with Mrs Scott and his wife. I shall ask him to dine with us if he can be spared. He was a very troubled man when last we spoke together.'

Each day, Janet's muscles strengthened as she persevered with the exercises which Josiah planned for her. She wondered how he knew about such things when he asked Peggy to massage her legs each day with some kind of oil. He seemed to read her thoughts.

'You may wonder how I can advise,' he said with a smile. 'When I was a boy I was very ill and the fever left me with a heart defect, so my father and my stepmother thought it wise to keep me in bed. They did not realize they were making me a worse invalid. My muscles wasted away, as yours are doing now. Fortunately, our old family doctor became ill himself and his nephew took his place. He was young and I shall bless him for ever. Not only did he recommend I should begin to take exercise every day, but that I should increase my activities. My parents were fearful and disapproved of his advice but we became good friends. If I had been kept immobile much longer I should probably never have walked again. He taught me to make the most of each day,' he grinned boyishly, 'rather than let life pass me by thinking I was postponing death by staying in bed.'

'I understand,' Janet said. 'I am dismayed to find my own legs are so weak. They look like twigs which might snap at any time. I was so strong before I – before I ran away.' She shuddered, remembering that awful night. 'Where is he now, your friend the doctor?' she asked, not wanting to dwell on her own ordeal.

He was silent, his brow creased and Janet hastily apologized for asking questions.

'M-my grandfather often told me I never stopped asking questions. I am sorry.'

'Don't be sorry for taking an interest in other people, Janet,' Josiah said gently. 'I rarely talk about my friends, but Doctor John was an exceptional man. He had once told me he would like to go to Edinburgh to work amongst the poor. He wanted to treat those who could not afford a doctor, and those whose ignorance of hygiene often caused their illnesses. There are many who cannot afford nourishing food, or keep their houses free from damp and cold, children die before they know what life is about. Have you heard of cholera? He believed it was a disease of the stomach and bowels caused by drinking foul water. He had many dreams, but not many people listened.'

'But you did,' Janet remarked softly.

'Yes, I used to wish I had the physical strength to become a doctor like him so that I could help people too.' Janet waited quietly. He began to speak again, slowly, his voice low, as though he was thinking his thoughts aloud. 'When my great-uncle told me he intended making me his heir, he said he hoped I would put my inheritance to good use for the sake of my own health and for the needs of others. It occurred to me that Doctor John was one person I could help to achieve his dreams. I gave him money to set up a clinic in one of the poorest areas of Edinburgh and for a few years I paid him enough for his food and clothes. Gradually the clinic has become known. He did not confine his knowledge to helping only the poor. Word spread and now he has a few wealthy patrons who appreciate his skill and the sons of two of them now share his dreams and assist in the clinic. It will take many men like Doctor John, and many generations, before the world can be a better place to live.' He sighed, 'Now, Miss Janet, that is enough of my life. When you are strong enough, I am hoping you will help me to sort out my library. Your grandfather always said you had a great love of books as a child, and a thirst for knowledge. Did you know he hoped to make you a teacher like himself one day?'

'He often let me help the little ones to learn their letters. We – we had to leave all his books behind. I longed to be able to read them, but there was no time at Braeheights, even if I had had them. I would have liked to teach the boys to read, but their father considered education a waste of time. He-he said they must learn to work, and so must I.' She shuddered and colour flooded her pale cheeks as she remembered Mr Foster had made time for his own pleasures with Lily Bloddret. Josiah saw the remembered horror in her eyes and he wondered exactly what the man Foster had done to make her flee from his house on a winter's night.

Within the week, Mr Cole arrived in person to deliver three dresses for Janet and, as Josiah had suggested, he told her that her mother had helped to make them for her.

'You will recognize her stitching on the bodice and sleeves,' he said. He was shocked at the sight of her pale face and thin figure. He had known her since she was a child with a merry smile and chestnut curls bouncing around her rosy cheeks. Her smoky-blue eyes, so like her father and her brother, seemed too large for her thin face now. Two of the dresses were in russet wool for everyday wear but to Janet, who had only ever worn clothes cut down from her mother's dresses, or loaned from Mrs Foster or Molly, they were truly beautiful and she could have hugged the elderly tailor.

'The other is for church when you are well enough to attend again,' Mr Cole told her. Janet unwrapped the third dress and gasped in delight at the emerald-green woollen gown with a matching cloak and a muff, warmly lined with rabbit fur.

'I have never had such beautiful clothes in my life,' she breathed. A look of anxiety clouded her gaze. 'Could my mother afford to send these for me?' she asked doubtfully.'

'You will recognize her stitching on the bodice of the green dress,' Mr Cole said, catching Josiah's warning shake of the head, and tactfully avoiding a direct answer to her question, for he was an elder of the kirk and he never lied.

'Then I must strive to get well soon so that I might thank my mother in person.'

'Mr Cole is dining with me today, Janet. Perhaps you would like to write a letter to your mother? I understand she is not well enough to leave the house or to attend the kirk.'

'A letter would please her,' the old tailor said with his kindly smile.

When they were alone together Mr Cole turned to Josiah. 'It is true Mary added stitches to the cuffs of Janet's dresses but even that took all her strength. She seems barely aware she has a daughter. Each day I wonder if she will have the strength to rise from her bed and I wonder what I shall do when that day comes.'

'That is why I hoped you would deliver the dresses in person. I intend to keep Janet here at Crillion Keep. I know she can read and write. I can find plenty of light work for her but she has a proud and independent spirit. We must tread carefully. I have plenty of empty rooms so I intend to persuade her to bring her mother here where she can care for her, with help from Peggy Baird when she needs it. I believe Peggy and Mary were friends when they attended the dominie's school as young girls.'

'You would do that, Josiah? You would take Mary in too?' Mr Cole stared at him incredulously, then with dawning relief. 'The expense and trouble of caring for another. . . .'

'Is as nothing to me. I have no family and the dominie was a good friend to me.'

'Aye, and to me, and many another,' Mr Cole nodded. 'But your sister? Everyone in the area has heard of her fury because you are caring for Janet here.'

'I no longer consider Eliza a member of my family. We share no blood ties. Her mother was good to me as a child, but my father provided well for both of them. My fortune is not large but if I can spread a little happiness then it will be well spent.'

Chapter Ten

Two weeks later, the Ross coach came up the long drive once more. This time, both Eliza and her son alighted almost before the coachman could open the door and let down the step. Mrs McLauchlan and Mrs Mossy saw them through the kitchen window and it was clear from Mrs Ross's demeanour that her arrival spelled trouble. They could never have dreamt of the far-reaching consequences her arrogance and greed would precipitate.

Maggie McLauchlan straightened her cap and smoothed down her white apron. Both were spotless as usual. She hurried to open the door but almost before she could step back Eliza swept past her, her expression haughty and her beady eyes glittering. Her son followed in her wake and from his expression, Maggie guessed he was anticipating a quarrel with as much glee as other men derived from a cockfight or bouts in the boxing rings.

'I'll tell Mr Saunders you're here, ma'am,' Maggie said.

'I don't know why he can't employ a butler and a footman to attend to the door.'

'It's no trouble ma'am. I will tell—'

'You needn't bother. I shall find him in that cramped little room near your kitchens, no doubt. He always did prefer the company of servants,' she added contemptuously.

Maggie hurried back to her own domain, knowing that for once Mrs Ross would find Mr Saunders's favourite room empty. It had surprised them all when he had vacated it to give Janet a warmer and more convenient bedroom during her illness and the most convenient for herself, popping in and out from the main kitchen. He was always considerate.

Three days ago, Janet had moved upstairs to a bedroom of her own and the fires had been lit in the long library. Billy Nairn, the carrier's son, was always willing to assist indoors or out when required, especially if there was a chance of seeing Lizzy Semple, the young maid. Josiah had instructed him to move two of the big leather chairs and a table nearer the fire at one end of the library. Maggie didn't know what he intended to do but she knew Janet shared his interest in books and she looked happier than Maggie had seen her since she was a young girl at school.

The only cloud on her horizon at the moment was her mother's health. Since Mr Cole's visit, Janet realized her mother must be very ill. Maybe that was the reason she had never contacted her at Braeheights. She confided her anxiety to Maggie.

'We must have faith, lassie, and the Lord will provide.' It was the only comfort or advice she had felt able to offer. 'We are all thankful you have been spared, Janet. Your health and strength are improving every day.'

It was true. Peggy had helped her wash her thick hair and it had sprung back into shining curls. Janet had regained the strength to brush it daily again. Even in the woollen working dress, she looked trim and neat with the snowy white apron she had sewn herself. Mr Saunders had surprised them all when he told her to remove her cap, declaring it was a pity to cover such lovely hair. Instead, Janet had tied her hair back with one of the ribbons Peggy had given her but that only served to emphasize her fine features. It was plain to see she would be a lovely young woman when her health was fully restored and the hollows beneath her delicate cheekbones filled out. There were still faint blue shadows beneath her eyes but they seemed to emphasize her clear gaze.

Josiah Saunders noticed all the improvements and decided the time had come to occupy Janet's time and thoughts before she grew restless and anxious to find work.

Twice Fingal hired a horse to visit Crillion Keep and both times he had stayed overnight. He also noticed Janet's return to health.

'She is almost like the girl I remember from our schooldays,' he said to Maggie, 'but what will become of her, Mother? I wish I was earning enough money to look after her and protect her from men like Foster.'

'Mr Saunders doesna seem in any hurry for her to leave,' Maggie reassured him. 'I think he plans to find her some light work here, at Crillion Keep.' She had thought Fingal would be pleased at the news but he had scowled and fallen silent.

'What sort of work?' he demanded abruptly.

'I don't know, laddie. We don't have many workers for a house this size but all the rooms in the tower are closed up and the furniture is under dust covers. Peggy and me – well, we're grateful he is willing to keep the lassie here where she is safe and warm and getting some good food inside her. She's lucky to be alive. You should be thankful for that and pleased that Mr Saunders has a kind heart.'

'I am grateful for that,' Fingal said, 'but it depends what else he has in his heart,' he muttered to himself; but Maggie heard. She frowned. It was becoming more apparent to her that Fingal's feelings were no longer schoolboy affection for a fellow pupil. He had always had a tenderness for Janet but she suspected he was falling in love now she was almost a young woman.

'There's plenty of time, laddie. She's but a lassie yet.'

'She will be sixteen in a few weeks. Mr Saunders may look older but he is only fourteen years older than me.'

'That makes him about thirty-six then, but what of it, Fingal? He's an ailing man. Age doesna matter.'

'Och, I don't know,' he said impatiently. 'Maybe I was imagining things when Janet was so ill. He watched over her with such tenderness. . . .'

'That's because he has a kind heart. We all thought Janet was going to die and he felt he should have offered her help earlier. If he had known how bad things were for her at Braeheights, he would have brought her here. He said so. As it is, we don't know what lasting harm Wull Foster might have done.' She frowned, thinking over the discussion she had had with Peggy. There had been no sign of Janet's monthly courses.

'What do you mean, Mother?'

'What if Foster has given her a child?'

'Janet? No! Surely he didna. . . ?'

'It is too early to know and it's not your problem. We must wait and see. Right now she is getting well and Mr Saunders doesn't want her to take any risks. That's all.'

'Dear God, I hope she's all right. I-I'll kill Wull Foster if he has harmed Janet!'

'Don't talk like that, Fingal!'

'But – but. . . .' He sighed. 'Sometimes I wish I had taken Dominie McWhan's advice. I would be a dominie by now. It will be years before I become a lawyer and earn enough to keep a house and a wife.'

Maggie met Mrs Ross as she flounced out of the small dining room.

'Josiah is not in there! Why didn't you tell me?'

'I think you'll find him in the library, ma'am. Shall I . . .'

'I know where the library is! Come, Henry, we'll find our own way. We shall be staying until I have restored some sense into my brother and some order into this house – and that means sending unwanted paupers on their way. Tell Mrs Mossy to prepare two rooms. We shall dine in the dining room from now on. It is time someone took charge and brought some civilization to this place.'

'Yes, ma'am.' Maggie McLauchlan's eyes had widened in surprise, but they narrowed angrily at the veiled criticism. 'I'm sure Mr Saunders will tell me if he is not pleased with the way I run his household,' she said coldly and hurried away without waiting for a reply. What sort of trouble would there be before Mrs Ross departed? she wondered. She called for young Lizzy to help her in the kitchen.

'There will be two extra for meals from now on,' she said. 'I shall need you to prepare more vegetables while I devise an extra course for luncheon. Will you ask Mrs Mossy to light the fire and set the table in the main dining room? Ask her to make sure everything is without fault from Mrs Ross's critical eyes.'

Lizzy rolled her eyes. 'Oh Lordy, is she staying? That means big trouble, doesn't it, Mrs Mac?'

'It seems like it,' Maggie said grimly, 'but just remember, lassie, if it's bad for us it's worse for Mr Saunders. Only God knows what will happen to Janet, poor lamb. That woman wants her out of here. I'm sure that's why she's invited herself to stay without warning.'

Eliza marched into the library, closely followed by a smirking Henry. Janet and Josiah both looked up, startled by the intrusion. They had been examining the spines of several leather-bound volumes and Janet was holding the duster she had been using to wipe each book before replacing it on the shelves in the order Josiah instructed. Before they began, he had selected several books which he recommended for her own reading.

'Later you can arrange them on one of the lower shelves, Janet. You can come in here whenever you feel like reading and they will be yours. We shall add to them as we sort through my collections.'

'Oh, Mr Saunders, I-I don't know how to thank you.' Janet's eyes were bright with gratitude and unshed tears.

'There, there, my dear. I should have been lost without my books, even as a young boy, and I know how much you enjoy reading too. I understand how deprived you have felt during your time at Braeheights. Now we shall make up for that as your grandfather intended. Maybe one day you will be able to share your knowledge by teaching other young girls.'

'That would be wonderful,' Janet breathed, overwhelmed by his generosity. Her eyes were alight with joy and Eliza was astonished and angered by the cosy tableau when she stepped into the room. It fuelled her resentment.

'It would seem I have not come a moment too soon, dear brother!' Her eyes were venomous slits. 'The fever could not have been so bad when the chit has made such a remarkable recovery,' she sneered. 'I believe it was no more than an excuse to prevent me entering the house, but I'm here now – to stay.'

'Good morning, Eliza, Henry,' Josiah said mildly, although he was seething inwardly at Eliza's unexpected arrival. His dark brows had risen, his mouth tightened, and Eliza knew he was annoyed and not at all pleased to see her.

'You, girl, you should not be in here. You look perfectly healthy to me. It is time you were on the road and looking for work. . . .'

'Eliza!' Josiah pushed himself to his feet to confront her. She ignored him and continued to glare at Janet. 'Right now there is work for you in the kitchen.' She jerked her head towards the door. Trembling Janet rose to her feet.

'Stay where you are, Janet,' Josiah said quickly and pressed her shoulder, pushing her back onto her chair. Her eyes darted fearfully from one to the other and her heartbeat quickened. What would she do if she was put out now? It was weeks to go before the hiring fairs.

'I said go!' Eliza snarled angrily. 'I wish to speak to my brother in private. I have told the old woman we shall be staying, so you can help prepare two of the best bedrooms. Make sure you light the fires.' Janet glanced at Josiah Saunder's white face and saw the pulse beating in his jaw, just below his ear. She could see he was angry and she bit her lip.

'I don't want to be the cause of any trouble,' she said, her voice barely more than a whisper. 'I will help Mrs McLauchlan in the kitchen.'

'Very well, my dear,' Josiah said, struggling to control his anger. 'You may tell her there will be two extra for luncheon and—'

'I have already given instructions and told her we shall eat in the dining room.'

'A moment, Janet.' He held up his hand, his expression grim. 'You may order your own staff as you please, Eliza, but you will remember I give the instructions in my own home. Janet please tell Mrs McLauchlan we shall eat in the small dining room and you will dine with us as usual.'

'Y-yes, sir,' Janet said nervously, giving a small bob before she scurried towards the door without daring to glance in Mrs Ross's direction. She was so intent on making her escape she did not notice Henry's foot shoot out as she was passing. She tripped, but he failed to catch her and pull her close against him, as he had intended. Instead she collided with a side table, knocking one of the lovely, coloured-glass oil lamps crashing to the floor in a thousand pieces.

'You clumsy idiot,' Eliza stormed. 'See what you have done! You will pay for that from your wages. That is if you ever earn any.'

'I-I'm s-sorry Sir.' Janet looked across at Josiah, struggling to hold back her tears. It had been a beautiful lamp and there was a matching one on the table at the other end of the long leather settee.

'It was not your fault, Janet. Wait a moment.' He turned a stern face towards Henry. 'Sticking your foot out is a childish prank. If anyone pays for the lamp it will be you. Now, Janet, please ask Mrs Mossy to come in and clear up the glass and you can also tell her there will be no need for fires in the bedrooms, or for extra beds. Our guests will not be staying overnight.'

Janet heard Mrs Ross gasp indignantly and closed the door hurriedly behind her. She was thankful to escape.

Josiah ignored Eliza's furious protests and turned to his nephew. 'I recall you enjoyed playing mean tricks when you were a boy,' he said with contempt. 'You were fortunate Janet was not badly cut from the glass. I would have expected you to be more of a man now you are – what age? Twenty-two, if I remember correctly.' Henry glowered at the floor. His uncle might be an invalid but he had always been sharp-eyed, and sharp-tongued too if he didn't approve of a fellow. Today he had accompanied his mother because she had ordered him to do so, but he knew she was planning a confrontation with his Uncle Josiah. She was determined to get rid of the girl. He had looked forward to witnessing a scene and seeing his uncle cowed. Few people outfaced his mother. Now here she was, gasping like a stranded fish while his uncle calmly ignored her demands to stay for a week or more to put his house in order.

Eliza revelled in gossip and she had regular sources who kept her informed on all manner of subjects, but particularly anything concerning Crillion Keep and its occupants. She had learned that the dominie's granddaughter was recovering quickly since their last visit when she was supposedly at death's door. Today she had come with every intention of making sure the girl packed her bags and got on her way, with or without his uncle's agreement. News that the old tailor had recently made a visit to the Keep and had stayed to dine with Josiah had agitated her even more. It was common knowledge Mary Scott was employed by Mr Cole and that she was becoming increasingly frail and in need of nursing herself. She had no place to go and Eliza knew her brother's philanthropic nature well.

Unfortunately this visit had got off to a bad start and it was clear Josiah did not want them to stay. His lack of hospitality only increased Eliza's determination and her temper. During the arguments which followed Janet's exit, Josiah realized that Eliza fully expected to move into Crillion Keep and take over completely at the first sign of his health deteriorating. He had no fear of death but he had an unwelcome vision of being under Eliza's command. He had not the slightest doubt she would overlook the loyalty and good services of his workers and replace them with those who would do her bidding irrespective of his own needs or wishes. The prospect filled him with horror. He had always known she was greedy and bossy but until this outburst he had not realized the full extent of her ambitions.

Janet helped Mrs McLauchlan prepare the luncheon in the kitchens but she begged to be excused from dining with Josiah and his guests. She trembled at the thought of having to eat with Mrs Ross's gimlet eyes fixed upon her.

'The lassie isna feeling so well, sir,' Maggie said in a low voice when she took in the soup. 'She asks to be excused. All of a tremble, she is.'

'Very well, Mrs McLauchlan, I understand her nerves may be upset by her fall.' He nodded. 'See that she eats something nourishing in the kitchen then, please.'

'That's where she should be eating, if there was any need for her to be here at all,' Eliza snapped, fully intending Maggie should overhear. Josiah's mouth tightened and a new determination to deal with his personal affairs hardened. He could not afford to delay. No man knew what tomorrow might bring and his health had always been precarious.

Maggie McLauchlan had been surprised herself when Josiah first insisted Janet should dine with him each day even though she knew he preferred informality, except on the rare occasions when he had guests. He said he wanted to make sure Janet ate decent meals and built up her strength, but Janet was intelligent and eager to learn and it had soon become clear that he enjoyed her youthful company. Conversation between them flowed easily. Sometimes Maggie heard him talking about books he had read, or quoting poems, and occasionally he laughed out loud. It occurred to Maggie that there had never been much laughter at Crillion Keep and it cheered her to hear it. She mentioned this to Fingal on his next visit but he scowled and didn't seem as pleased as she had expected. She knew he had no reason to be jealous of Janet because he had often been invited to dine with Mr Saunders himself when he came home on a visit from university, and sometimes since he had been training as a lawyer's clerk. They also shared a love of books and discussed things well beyond her own understanding.

The day of Eliza's visit, Josiah had gone straight to bed as soon as they had left. Their discussions had been extremely heated and he had felt his heart racing, and sometimes it appeared not to beat at all, leaving him breathless. He felt drained of energy and completely exhausted the following day and he was thankful he had forbidden them to stay, but he still did some serious thinking. He decided he must make a will without delay. On the Saturday morning, he asked Maggie McLauchlan whether Janet showed any signs of being with child.

'She isna sick in the mornings as many women are,' Maggie said slowly, 'and she doesna have strange whims when it comes to food either but. . . .' She faltered into silence, her cheeks flushed with embarrassment. She had never talked to a man, even her own husband, about the ways of women and their monthly courses. It was beyond her to explain such things to Josiah Saunders.

'You are still uncertain?'

'Aye, I am. Her woman's rhythms have not returned to normal.'

She had mentioned the subject to Janet for the second time, asking her if she needed cloths for her monthly times.

'No thank you, Mrs McLauchlan,' Janet had been matter of fact.

'Did you have cloths to wash when you were at Braeheights, lassie?' Maggie persisted anxiously.

'Yes.' She blushed, remembering how Mr Foster had seemed to know when she started the horrid monthly bleeding. 'Mrs Foster explained it was women's business but it was difficult with so many boys and Mr Foster in the house,' she added.

'But you have not needed them since you came here?'

'No.' She grimaced. 'I don't like that part of being a woman.'

'Did Mrs Foster tell ye they stopped when she was expecting a baby?'

'Molly told me. That's how she knew as soon as her mother was having another baby. It made her sad.' Janet looked so sad herself at the mention of Molly that Maggie felt bound to change the subject. She discussed the subject with Peggy.

'Maybe Janet needs to regain her strength before her monthly cycle returns,' Peggy suggested, 'but I will ask Donald if he can explain about such things to Mr Saunders. She is growing into a beautiful young woman,' Peggy smiled. 'I hope she does not cause Fingal too much heartache. Young love can be a painful experience and he has always had a special tenderness for Janet.'

'It will be a heartache for everybody if Janet is carrying a bairn sired by Wull Foster, and she may not even realize it.'

Peggy mentioned the subject to Donald. 'I imagine Janet must understand about the birds and bees after living at Braeheights,' was his opinion. 'Mr Saunders certainly knows about such things, Peggy. He reads books. I expect he's concerned for Janet's future and she does seem incredibly innocent still, I must confess. None of us would like to see her going out into the world if she's expecting a bairn with no man to support her.'

'It would be terrible,' Peggy agreed, 'but I canna see what Mr Saunders can do. Even if he could help her, we all know he doesna expect to live a long life. What would happen to Janet if he wasn't here?'

'It will be heaven help all of us if Mrs Ross and her miserable, rat-faced son take over,' Donald declared grimly.

'Aye, it would,' Peggy said with a shudder.

On Sunday morning, Josiah came into the small dining room dressed for church.

'Do you feel well enough to accompany us today, Janet? We shall all be going, Fingal too, though he intends to continue back to his own lodgings afterwards.'

'I would like to go. It is a long time since I have been to the kirk. Perhaps I shall see my mother if her health has improved.'

Josiah shook his head and opened his mouth to reply, but he said nothing when Janet continued wistfully, 'She has not replied to my letter but perhaps she did not know of anyone coming this way to deliver it.'

Janet expected to sit with Maggie McLachlan and Peggy so she was surprised when Mr Saunders took her arm and escorted her to his own pew, beckoning Fingal to sit with them. She was pleased she had worn the green dress and matching cloak which Mr Cole had delivered and she blushed shyly when she caught Fingal's admiring gaze. Although she had little opportunity to speak with him, he stood close beside her and she could feel the warmth of his arm against her own and she loved the sound of his rich tenor voice when they sang the hymns they had both learned as children and sang in her grandfather's school as well as in church. She looked across and was relieved to see a different dominie in the pew where her family used to sit. There was no sign of the horrible Dominie Todd. She was disappointed to see her mother was not there, but she thought perhaps Mrs Cole could not be left alone. She tried to look further back for any sign of the Fosters and she felt a pang of relief to see Mr Foster was not there. She felt Fingal's hand brush her arm and realized her attention had wandered and everyone else had bowed their heads in prayer.

When the service was over, Fingal did not seem in any hurry to lead them from the pew and Janet wished she could read the unspoken message in his dark-brown eyes.

Then Josiah leaned forward and spoke quietly. 'I would like a word with the Reverend Drummond and Mr Cole, Fingal. Perhaps you would see Janet to my coach and wait with her until I come, please?'

'Yes, of course, sir.'

Josiah nodded his head and smiled. 'How many times must I tell you, Fingal, there is no call to address me with such deference. You are an educated young man with a good position in the town. We all look forward to your visits and I am happy to count you among my friends.'

'I, yes, sir . . . I mean yes, Mr Saunders.' Fingal murmured.

'I look forward to you visiting your mother too, Fingal,' Janet said softly.

'Do you, Janet? I thought perhaps you had forgotten me when you never replied to my letters while you were at Braeheights.'

'Letters?' Her eyes clouded and she frowned. 'I did not receive any letters. But I could not have replied. I tried to send a letter to the Reverend Drummond once, but Mr Foster snatched it and threw it in the fire. He took away the ink and my quill.'

'He is a bully and a brute. I left the letters with Mrs Foster's mother, who lives near the village. She promised to give them to her grandson to take to you. I expect Foster discovered them and destroyed them too.'

'I sent a letter to Mama with Mr Cole but she has not replied. I so hoped to see her today at church.'

'You thought she would be here, Janet?' Fingal stared at her in dismay. 'Did Mr Saunders, or my mother, not tell you how ill she is?'

'I thought she would be getting better and she always liked going to church. Perhaps she could not leave Mrs Cole?'

'Dear Janet,' Fingal frowned and drew her hand from her muff so that he could hold it in both of his. 'Your mother . . . she is more in need of nursing than Mrs Cole herself. Mr Cole can't bear the thought of asking her to leave his house because she has nowhere to go, except the poorhouse.'

Janet gasped.

'He is a good man but he was at his wits' end to know what to do the last time I saw him. He has great respect for your mother and your grandfather was his friend. He is hoping Mr Saunders might help him find a solution.'

'Oh, Fingal! Can this be true?' Janet stared up at him in horror, her blue eyes, so darkly fringed and so like his dearest friend, Andrew's. He longed to take her in his arms and comfort her, but already people were watching them curiously.

'If only I had enough money to rent a house of my own,' he groaned. 'If only I could offer you a place to bring your mother so that we might care for her together.'

Janet looked into his face and saw the distress and sincerity there. 'Dear Fingal, I know you would help if you could but you did so much for Andrew, I cannot ask for more. It is my place to care for my own mother.' She put a hand over her eyes to brush away the tears, wondering what she could do. She shivered. Watching the shadows chase across her expressive face it took all Fingal's control not to draw her close and comfort her, but he saw Mr Saunders striding towards them, a half-smile lifting the corners of his mouth as though his talk with the Reverend Drummond had given him satisfaction. Fingal sighed and drew away, straightening his shoulders, preparing to say goodbye. He needed to take charge of his horse, which Donald was holding ready for him while trying to soothe the coach horses.

Josiah Saunders looked shrewdly at Janet. Her eyes, wide with anxiety, seemed to swamp her small face. He was sure she was paler than when they had set out for church earlier that morning.

'Has attendance at church tired you out, Janet? Perhaps you are not yet so strong as we thought. After all, you were very ill, and so long without food.'

'Please do not be concerned. I am well enough, thank you, sir. I-I do not wish to be more of a trouble than I have been already.'

As they ate their luncheon together, he broached the subject again after watching Janet toying absently with her soup instead of enjoying it with her usual relish.

'Is the soup not to your liking today, my dear?'

'Oh yes, yes, thank you. It is delicious as it always is.'

'Then may I ask what troubles you? Maybe I can help?'

'No one can help and you have been kind and generous already.' Her eyes filled with unexpected tears and she swiped them away impatiently. 'I did not mean to take advantage of your kindness, but I don't know where I shall find work and a place to live until the Hiring Fairs. I have a card for the savings bank but I earned so little money and I ran away without my wages. It is two months until the Hiring Fairs. I can't wait so long.'

'Are you so desperate to leave Crillion Keep, Janet? I thought you were beginning to enjoy living here amongst your friends and having books to read again and an opportunity to continue learning. There are many subjects I would like to share with you, things your grandfather would have taught you.'

'I do love reading your books. I have been so happy here, but I do not want to be a burden or cause more trouble between you and your family or—'

'Don't you think you should let me deal with my family?'

'Well yes, I suppose so but—'

'Then let me assure you I have already made my plans for Eliza and her son, well almost. The Reverend Drummond will be calling tomorrow to sign some papers for me. They will make my wishes very clear to Eliza and Henry.'

'I am glad if you have managed to make peace,' Janet said quietly.

'Ah, I did not say that exactly. Eliza does not understand the meaning of peace. Wherever she is there is strife, but forget about that. You have troubles of your own?' he asked gently, thinking she might tell him she was with child.

'Yes.' Her voice was barely more than a whisper. Josiah waited patiently. 'I hoped to see my mother today. Fingal knew. He – he told me the truth, that she is – is dying. I need to help her, to be with her. I want to care for her but I don't see how I can manage.' She pressed her fingers to her temples. 'I can't think what to do. Fingal said he would help me if he could, but he is working hard to become a lawyer. He says he sometimes thinks he should become a dominie instead, as Grandfather hoped he would.'

'There is always a way, Janet. Do not despair, my dear. Fingal is a good man and sincere, but he is young, no more than twenty years, I believe.'

'He and Andrew were the same age, four years older than I am.'

'I had intended waiting for the Reverend Drummond's arrival tomorrow. I thought he would offer you some reassurance but I think we must have a serious talk now. If you are finished eating, my dear, we shall adjourn to the library and talk without interruption. I have a suggestion to make, which I hope you will consider carefully. I had hoped to give you time to get used to me and to being in my home, but I fear the situation requires urgent action, for your mother's sake and for Mr Cole's.' His face looked grave and strained and Janet's heart raced with anxiety.

She added more logs to the fire and swept the hearth, as she had done many times a day at Braeheights.

'You're a good girl, Janet, and very capable,' he said, watching her with affection and respect. 'Peggy Baird tells me you will soon be sixteen?'

'Yes, a week on Wednesday.'

'Your grandfather would have been proud of you. He would have welcomed your help as a pupil teacher with the younger girls. I want to teach you all the things your grandfather would have taught you, had he been spared, so that you may be able to teach some of the poorer children in the parish one day.'

'I can't see how that could ever be,' she said wistfully, shaking her head.

'Life is full of surprises. If I had thought it possible I would live as long as I have I might have become a dominie myself and taught some of the children in our cities. But enough of my own daydreams. Do you trust me, Janet?'

'Of course I do. I think God guided my footsteps here when – when . . .'

'When you ran away from Braeheights?'

'Yes. I only wanted to escape from Mr Foster.' She shuddered. 'He frightened me.'

'So if I tell you I would never – not ever – ask you to do any of the things Wull Foster wanted you to do, would you believe me? Whatever the circumstances?'

Janet turned to look at him then, her eyes wide and puzzled. He was nothing like Mr Foster.

'Of course I believe you. You saved my life, and cared for me, even though I can never repay you.'

'You have repaid us all by recovering, Janet, but please believe me when I say I shall never ask you to do anything which would hurt you, or make you afraid. I want you to marry me and take my name.' Janet opened her mouth in surprise but he waved her to listen. 'I have several reasons for asking this but the most urgent one is not for my sake, or for yours. It is for the sake of your mother and to relieve Mr Cole of his burden. As my wife you could bring your mother here and nurse her yourself. Mr Cole will then have room again to hire a nurse for his wife so that he can continue to earn his living in his tailor's shop. Do you understand?'

'I-I, yes, I think so. I know it is my duty to care for Mama. I promised Andrew I would look after her. But . . .'

'She will have a place here with you. You will be able to nurse her and stay with her. Peggy will help if you need her. You will be glad to spend the remaining time together?'

'Oh yes, more than anything. . . .' Janet's eyes shone with gratitude.

'That is good, but we must also consider your own good name. Too many people are quick to gossip. My health may be as precarious as that of an old man but I am still young enough to arouse evil speculations when I share my home with a beautiful young woman – which is what you will become on your birthday. If you agree to marry me you will always have security and protection, and not only you, but the people we both regard as friends as well as employees.'

'Oh. Y-you mean if. . . .'

'If you bear my name, that is all marriage need involve, but it must be legal. You and your mother will have the two adjoining rooms, which used to be occupied by the nursemaid when there were children here. Do you understand what I am saying, Janet? You will be my wife in name. I ask nothing more, except your companionship and to share in your eagerness to learn. Do you understand?'

'Y-yes, I think so,' Janet said, but her head was whirling. Why should Mr Saunders bother to give her his name in marriage if he didn't expect the things Mr Foster demanded from his wife? She looked at him earnestly. Her heart told her she could trust him. But surely marriage was a serious thing, and for life? Her heart plummeted. What would Fingal think to such a proposition?

'Couldn't Mama and I just stay here until – until. . . ?'

'No. It is essential that I guard your reputation and my own, my dear, as your grandfather would have expected of me. Apart from your mother's need of care, I have plans of my own. I shall enjoy helping you learn all the things you missed when you went to work at only twelve years old. I shall look forward to discussing books and poetry and learning of the latest inventions with you, just as I enjoy the company of Fingal McLauchlan and as I enjoyed your grandfather's companionship. I think he would have approved of my proposal and it would have been a great relief to him to know his daughter and his granddaughter had food and shelter and were safe, as you will be as my wife, in my home.'

Janet knew she should be grateful, and she was. So why did her thoughts go winging back to Fingal? He could not help them. Mr Saunders was being generous and kind, so why did her heart feel so heavy? She bit her lower lip then raised her gaze to his.

'C-can I have time to-to think about it?' She saw the flash of disappointment in his eyes before he lowered his lids.

'You can, my dear, but I do not think Mr Cole can keep your mother much longer. His own wife needs constant care, and so does your mother.'

'C-can I tell you in one week?' What she wanted was to tell Fingal first and hear what he had to say.

'Very well. You will give me your decision next Sunday afternoon?' He thought perhaps she wanted to pray for guidance in church.

'Yes,' Janet whispered. Fingal had said he would see her again next weekend. What would he think if she became wife to Mr Saunders? Her heart ached. Could he find a better solution to her problems, and her mother's? In her heart, she knew he couldn't. It was true, she longed to explore the books in Mr Saunders library and to learn the things her grandfather had taught to Andrew and Fingal, but she longed to do such things with Fingal.

The Reverend Drummond came the following morning and he and Mr Saunders were closeted in the small room next to the library, which Josiah called his office. He had a big desk in there with drawers which locked, as well as a tall cupboard with locked doors where he kept papers relating to the Home Farm and the two tenanted farms and various private papers. He had told Janet this when Maggie McLauchlan had asked her to dust in there.

Just before lunch, Doctor Carr rode up on his chestnut mare.

'Thank you for coming, Archie.' Josiah greeted him with a smile, which wiped ten years from his lean face. 'If you will witness my signature and add yours to the documents the Reverend Drummond and I have prepared we shall dine without delay.'

A little while later, Josiah put the papers in two envelopes and sealed them with wax before locking them in the drawer of his desk. Afterwards, the three men had lunch in the small dining room and Josiah insisted Janet should join them. She felt shy in their presence, especially knowing what she ought to do for the sake of her Mama, as well for the Bairds and everyone here who treated her with such kindness. But in her heart it was not Josiah Saunders she longed for to share her future.

She had confided in Maggie McLauchlan about Mr Saunders's proposal of marriage. Maggie's first reaction had been one of shocked surprise.

'How can that be? He has always said his health was too uncertain to take a wife and have children,' she declared. 'He said he would never risk leaving a child of his without a father, as he had been without a mother.' Then Maggie frowned and looked shrewdly at Janet. Did he think the lassie was carrying Foster's bastard? Was he trying to protect her and to give her child a name? She seemed well and content but there had been no sign of her monthly bleeding.

'He-he said people would gossip if I stay here and look after Mama when I am an unmarried girl and he is not an old man, even though his health is poor. He said if I marry him, I shall have the protection of his name and a home, and people who are my friends here will have security. I think he means everyone at Crillion Keep.'

'Ah, now I see!' Maggie McLauchlan exclaimed as understanding dawned. She put her hands on her hips and smiled as she did when one of her pies had turned out extra well. 'He is a wise man! And a clever one. Do you see, Janet? When Mr Saunders dies, Mrs Ross and that miserable son of hers expect to inherit everything here. That's why she keeps coming, trying to tell him what he must do. If it was left to her, none of us would be safe. She would probably put us out on the road and hire new workers and pay them less. God only knows what her son would do. Already he gambles, I hear. If Mr Saunders makes you his wife, Janet, they cannot control everything. Mr Saunders will see to that and I think wives have some rights to inherit. He knows you would be honest and kind and fair, as your grandfather was. He trusts you, ma bairn. Now I understand. You will be safe if you marry Mr Josiah Saunders, and so shall we. He is considering the future for all of us.'

Still Janet waited for the weekend and Fingal's visit. She needed to know if he too thought she should marry Josiah Saunders.

As soon as Fingal arrived at his mother's cottage late on Saturday evening, Maggie told him of Josiah's proposal. She knew Fingal would be upset. She was convinced Mr Saunders was doing his best to protect them all from his sister's greedy scheming but she wanted to prepare Fingal.

'Surely Janet has not agreed to marry him? She would never marry for money.'

'She would marry to give her mother a place to stay,' Maggie said. 'She tells me she made a promise to Andrew to care for their mother.'

'But she may only live a few weeks, or months at most. Marriage . . . it is for life.'

'If Mary Scott is dying it is all the more reason why Janet would want to bring her here. She would never forgive herself if her mother dies in the poorhouse when she could have prevented it. Can you offer Janet a better solution, son?'

'I can offer her love.'

'Aye,' Maggie sighed, 'but love doesna provide a place to bide or food in our bellies. Think about it, Fingal. Mr Saunders told her she would have security as his wife, and so would the folks she counts as friends. I'm sure she has waited to tell you herself. Don't upset the lassie, Fingal. Let her do her duty, for all our sakes, but especially for her mother.'

'Her mother didn't consider Janet when she sent her to Braeheights when she was only twelve years old. She wanted money for Andrew's education, but she didn't consider the danger

Janet might encounter from a brute like Foster. Maybe you never heard the rumours that he got his own daughter with child? Molly drowned herself to hide her shame.'

'I heard stories,' Maggie said quietly. 'It was no excuse for his evil doings but Molly was not Foster's own bairn. I expect he resented her. Her real father was a young soldier with the local volunteers when Napoleon and his French army were threatening to invade our shores. He was killed soon after he joined. The Fortescues were a respectable family and the rumour was Hannah married Foster to avoid facing the elders in the kirk and bringing shame to her parents. For all I know, Janet could be in the same condition as Molly. Even if you could offer her and her mother a home, could you take the bairn of such a man, give it your name and love it?'

'You think Janet is. . . ?'

'I don't know. She doesn't show the usual signs but it's hard to tell.'

'Surely she must know? She can't still be innocent after seeing Mrs Foster producing a babe every year.'

'I only know about the nature o' women and I'm worried about the lassie. If you're going to persuade her to refuse Mr Saunders's offer, when you canna offer her anything yourself, then you'd be better not to see her. At least that way she'll reach her own decision.'

Fingal's mouth tightened. He longed to see Janet, to tell her he loved her, to ask her to wait for him, but that would make him as selfish and single-minded as Mrs Scott had been over Andrew. His mother was a wise woman and she had a great affection for Janet.

He didn't sleep much that night. At dawn, he rose and lit the fire and cut himself a thick slice of bread while he waited for the kettle to boil, then he wrote a note for his mother.

'It is against my will but I am taking your advice, Mother. I am leaving now because I cannot see Janet without trying to persuade her not to marry Mr Saunders and I know he can give her everything she and her mother need right now. I cannot go to

kirk today and not speak with her, so it is better if I leave now. I may not return for some time. I have had an offer to continue my apprenticeship in Edinburgh with more opportunities. I intended to refuse it but I shall consider it now as I feel there will be little to keep me here unless you need me. If you do, please send a letter with Donald to my lodgings in Annan.'

Fingal's heart was heavy as he saddled his horse and rode away.

Janet had waited all week to discuss her situation with Fingal and she was bitterly disappointed when she did not see him. Maggie McLauchlan's heart quailed when she saw her disappointment and the unhappiness in her clear gaze. She had already made Fingal unhappy. Perhaps she should not have interfered, but she trusted Josiah Saunders to act in the best interests of those around him, not least to relieve Mr Cole from the burden of Mary Scott. She prayed she had acted wisely.

Chapter Eleven

At Josiah's request, the Reverend Drummond arranged a discreet morning marriage service, in the village church which Janet had attended all her life.

'I agree, it may give the lassie comfort to receive a blessing,' the minister said.

Doctor Carr declared he was privileged to give away the bride and, with his usual consideration, Josiah asked Peggy Baird to attend Janet. Peggy's loving kindness proved a great support to Janet. Afterwards, they returned to Crillion Keep where Maggie had prepared an excellent meal.

Dr Carr and the Reverend Drummond joined them, as well as Peggy and Donald Baird. The meal was over and the minister was thanking God for the food and asking His blessing on the newly married couple, when Mr Cole drove up as close as he could get to the front steps of Crillion Keep.

'He has brought your mother to stay with us, as I promised, my dear,' Josiah said. The look of gratitude in his young wife's eyes was all the thanks Josiah needed. Janet flew outside and embraced her mother with joy, but Mary seemed barely aware of her, or that she had come to live at Crillion Keep. Janet was dismayed at her haggard face and thin body.

Maggie and Peggy were equally shocked at Mary's appearance. She was a ghost of the brisk and capable young woman they had known. She had to pause twice for breath while climbing the five steps to the door, aided by the stone balustrade and Mr Cole. Janet felt like weeping, even though Josiah had warned her of her mother's frailty, but even he was shocked. He agreed with Mr Cole that Mary Scott would not be with them long and he was doubly glad he had brought her here. At least he had given Janet a little time with her mother but he guessed Mary Scott craved nothing more than to join her husband and her son. She had barely acknowledged Janet, and he saw the tears mist her lovely eyes before she turned quickly away. His heart ached for her.

He had already asked Mrs Mossy and Lizzy Semple to prepare the room adjoining Janet's. If they thought this a strange arrangement for a new bride, they did not comment. Only Maggie knew of Mr Saunders's promise to Janet and she was relieved that he intended to keep it, at least for now. Josiah sent for young Mark Wright to help Donald carry Mary up to the bedroom. When Janet had seen her settled into bed as obediently as a child she returned to Josiah's side.

'My mother really is dying, isn't she?' she asked in a croaky whisper, doing her best to hold back tears.

'I'm afraid so, my dear, but don't be upset, we are—'

'But she should not be your burden.'

'She will not be a burden. This is your home now and she is with you, and the people who have always been her friends. We shall all help.' His expression was grave.

'How can I ever thank you? You have done so much and I can never repay you.'

'My dear Janet, you are my wife now.'

'But I do not deserve your kindness and generosity,' Janet said.

'You will more than repay me with your companionship, especially if you help me with my library. Peggy Baird will help you nurse your mother if you need her. One day you will find a way to repay kindness, not necessarily to me, but there are always others who need help and I know you will give it.'

During her first two days at Crillion Keep, Mary Scott made an effort to rise and dress but it was clear to everyone that climbing the stairs back to her room was like climbing a mountain. Josiah suggested Janet should take her meals to her room on a tray to conserve her strength. Mary thanked him and proffered a gentle smile but Janet knew that keeping to her room was the beginning of the end for her mother. Peggy tried to comfort her.

'Doctor Carr says she is tired and breathless, because her blood is thin,' she said. 'Mr Saunders suggests we should feed her calf's liver and the best beef.'

'She has no appetite for food, even though your mother has prepared it with such care,' Janet said, struggling to hold back her tears.

'At least she is warm and comfortable. She is not in pain and she is among friends. We must be thankful Mr Saunders is a true Christian.'

'I don't know how I can ever repay him,' Janet said.

'You are repaying him by agreeing to be his wife. You love books and learning as much as he does. He read to you while you were ill. Your eagerness to learn has given him a new interest in life. In fact, you have brought a ray of hope and sunshine to all of us, lassie.'

Surprisingly, the days stretched into weeks and then months. Mary Scott had days when she was more alert and cheerful and she talked to Janet of the past, of her own girlhood and of Janet's father and her love for him. Sometimes, Janet read to her from the book of poems which Fingal had bought, or from *The Cottage Fireside* and other books Josiah recommended from his collections.

When Mrs Ross paid a visit, supposedly to see if her brother was in good health, Josiah was surprised to find she had not heard the news of his marriage but he saw no reason to enlighten her. She stayed to lunch but he did not encourage her to linger once the horses were rested enough for the return journey. Janet avoided her by taking her meal with her mother in her room, sitting before the window so they could look out on the fine summer's day and watch the birds darting in and out of the trees and bushes in the garden below, and see the ripening corn in the fields beyond. Everyone was praying for a good harvest; several bad ones had driven the poorer people in the parish to the verge of starvation.

As the time passed, Janet herself regained her former healthy colour and rounded figure and the natural rhythms of her body returned to normal. Maggie MacLauchlan had never been so relieved as she was to see the blood-stained cloths soaking in the laundry.

'Of course I knew she could not be having a bairn after all this time,' she said to Peggy. 'But I'm glad she has returned to normal.'

'I'm pleased to see her filling out,' Peggy said. 'She was like a living skeleton after the fever. I expect nature has its own way of healing.'

'We still don't know whether Foster had his way with her. She must have been badly frightened to risk dying in the snow rather than staying at Braeheights.'

'We'll just be thankful she is in a safe place now,' Peggy said firmly. She would have liked to add 'and happy' but she sensed Janet was not completely happy and she suspected her brother Fingal was the reason. He had moved back to Edinburgh. It was a long journey to come home, but she had expected he would have returned for a visit by now.

Towards the end of September, Mary Scott seemed more like the mother Janet remembered. She even asked if Josiah would come up and spend a little time with her. Josiah rarely ascended the stairs but in spite of his racing heart he made the effort and spent an hour in conversation with Mary. He was smiling when he descended the stairs again and Janet met him in the hall.

'Mama is so bright today, isn't she?' she asked, her eyes shining. 'Perhaps God has answered my prayers after all and she is getting well again.'

'We can only hope so, my dear. Whatever happens, she is very proud of you. One day she hopes you will be able to teach girls to read and write as she would have liked to do herself. I believe she did work as a pupil teacher and help teach the younger children before she married. She told me what a happy household it was then.'

'It was happy when Andrew and Fingal were there too. I shared their adventures and they helped me with my lessons.' Janet sighed. 'Fingal must enjoy life in the city now.'

'He must live where his work is.'

'I suppose so,' Janet nodded. 'Mrs McLauchlan had a letter

telling her that he sometimes travels to other towns now, dealing with clients for his employer.'

'That means they trust him and they know he has the knowledge and initiative to deal with problems on his own. He is doing well. We should be proud of him.'

'I suppose so,' Janet said.

The following morning, Janet's spirits rose. There was a hint of frost in the air but the day promised to be fine and sunny again. She washed in the basin of cold water and dressed quickly before hurrying into her mother's room, hoping she was in the same lively spirits as the previous day. She might even be persuaded to venture downstairs for an hour.

Mary Scott had slipped away during the night, and Janet found her with a small smile tilting the corners of her mouth and a hand outstretched as though in greeting, but it was not to anyone in this world. Janet couldn't believe it. She ran from the room and downstairs, tears streaming down her face as she tried to stifle the sobs which rose in her throat. Josiah was on his way in to breakfast and she ran into his arms and sobbed as though her heart would break. Maggie McLauchlan came from the kitchens carrying a hot, covered dish for breakfast. Over Janet's head he nodded in response to her questioning eyes.

Janet didn't expect many people would attend her mother's funeral and she protested at the amount of food Josiah instructed Maggie McLauchlan to prepare. She felt lost and alone without her mother needing her attention, so she was glad to stay in the warmth of the kitchen and bake apple pies and girdle cakes.

'Hannah Foster taught you well, lassie,' Maggie McLauchlan said with approval.

'I can't believe anyone will come to eat all the food we are preparing.'

'I'm obeying Mr Saunders's orders. He has arranged everything with the minister.'

'But the minister does not think people should spend precious savings on a wake. My mother told me some people feel it is their duty to the dead, but the Reverend Drummond says their duty is to feed the families rather than see them starve afterwards.'

'It is true the poor people of the parish have more need of food themselves than many of those who attend the funeral and eat their precious provisions. That is one of the reasons he encourages us all to save what little we can in his savings bank. He says it will not make any difference to the way God takes our loved ones into His kingdom but many people think they must hold a wake as one last sacrifice for their loved ones.'

'My mother and I have no money for a wake,' Janet protested.

'It is what Mr Saunders wants and he is your husband and master now. He is trying to be kind for your sake, Janet.'

Maggie did not tell her Mr Saunders had written to Fingal and despatched Donald to catch the mail coach at the inn when it travelled along the north road. They were not sure he would receive the letter in time, or be free to come, but Maggie was sure he would try.

Janet was overwhelmed by the number of people who came to pay their last respects but she knew at least two had an ulterior motive when she saw Mrs Ross and her son Henry glowering at her. She gave an involuntary shudder. She wondered why Mr Ross never accompanied them. Then she caught sight of Fingal. In spite of her grief, her heart lightened and she smiled at him. In that moment Fingal knew it had been worth the haste and the overnight journey in the mail coach. The irony was, he could afford to rent a house now as well as keep a wife. He was doing well since his move back to the city but Mary Scott had lasted longer than anyone had anticipated and he would have been deeply in debt if he had been responsible for keeping her and Janet, even if they could have made the journey to Edinburgh. He sighed. Janet was beautiful.

Josiah was pleased Fingal had come, even though he had guessed the reason for his long absence. When the men returned from the graveside and assembled at Crillion Keep for the refreshments, he sought him out.

'I hope you will stay a while, Fingal, although I know your mother will be looking forward to some time with you too. Until people leave I should be grateful if you would stay close to Janet if others demand my attention. Mrs Ross has a vicious tongue. Although Janet appears calm, I know her control is fragile, her grief thinly veiled. She is young and needs our protection. Henry is sly and as spiteful as his mother.'

Fingal watched Janet move quietly amongst people, thanking those she knew for their attendance. Clad from head to toe in a black dress, black veiled hat and gloves, the pallor of her fine features was emphasized but he was pleased to see her thick chestnut curls had resumed their lustre and were trying hard to spring free from her hat. He remembered how they had danced down her back when she was a girl, chasing him and Andrew. People had begun to depart and the dining room was emptying now. Across the room, Doctor Carr waylaid Mr Saunders. Fingal watched Mrs Ross head for Janet but there was nothing she could do to avoid the woman, unless she scampered for the kitchens like a rabbit down a hole. Even then, Fingal guessed Mrs Ross would have followed for she had a determined set to her thin mouth and her narrow eyes glittered with venom. Unobtrusively he moved closer.

'Well Miss you've had more than your money's worth out of my brother, you and your pathetic mother,' she sneered. 'There is no reason for you to stay any longer. It's time to pack your bags and get out of here.'

Both Fingal and Janet looked up sharply and he heard Janet's indrawn breath, but behind Mrs Ross, the Reverend Drummond gave a wry smile and a small shake of his head as he laid a finger over his lips. Janet's eyes widened. Fingal saw her wring her hands together, feeling the thin gold band of her wedding ring beneath her black silk glove. She looked up again at the minister saw him close one eye in a deliberate wink. Fingal wanted to laugh out loud. It seemed the parish grapevine had been more lax than he would have believed when Mrs Ross had not heard her brother and Janet were married. He watched as Janet chewed her lip and cleared her throat.

'Mr Saunders has been very kind to my mother and myself and I shall always be grateful for the months we have been able to spend together. I owe him a great debt, which I can never repay. You can be sure I shall do whatever he asks of me, Ma'am.' Janet's voice was soft but her tone was firm. The minister gave a nod of satisfaction before he turned away to join the good doctor and

Josiah, but Eliza Ross snorted in derision.

'I'm telling you what is best for him, whether he knows it or not. It's time to pack your bags and get out.' She eyed Janet's slender figure in her black dress and her eyes narrowed again. 'You have done well enough out of him. No doubt he paid for the dress you are wearing. Now go and—'

'Indeed I did, Eliza. As I have told you many times I give trade to the local tradesmen whenever possible. You will not find a better tailor than Mr Cole if you travel the length and breadth of the country, as you seem to do. Charity begins at home.'

'Then it is time you remembered that, dear brother. Henry could use a monthly allowance. You are his uncle, after all.'

'He has a father to provide for him. Many young men are not so fortunate and have to make their own way in the world.'

'You're nothing but a miserly sinner! You—'

'I try not to be either miserly or a sinner,' Josiah said evenly. 'Now I think it is time you were leaving if you wish to be home before dark. The days are getting shorter now.'

Janet stepped back and collided with Fingal. He steadied her and gripped her elbow, guiding her away into the hall and then into the library.

'Out of sight out of mind,' he said with his old smile. 'I gather Mrs Ross has not heard you are now Mrs Saunders.'

'Apparently not. The last time she was here Josiah did not encourage her to stay long. I stayed out of her way.'

'I should think even the angels would quarrel with a woman like that,' Fingal said. 'I have not had an opportunity to talk with my mother yet. I travelled down on the mail coach overnight. Tell me, Janet, did your mother suffer any pain?'

'No, she died in her sleep. She had been so much brighter the day before. I-I thought she was getting better. It was a shock.' Her eyes filled with tears. 'Everyone has been so kind, Fingal. Doctor Carr said she could never have recovered. He has seen people like Mama before. He says it is not due to grief, but something takes away all the goodness from their blood. Her skin was like thin white parchment.'

'But she did not have the coughing as Andrew did, Janet?'

Fingal asked anxiously.

'No. All she wanted was to sleep.'

'Thank God for that. I should not have gone away as I did without talking to you, but I could not wish you well when you were marrying another man. It was selfish of me when I had nothing to offer.'

'I understand, Fingal,' Janet said quietly and laid a hand on his arm. He put his hand on top of hers, holding it there, feeling the delicate bone structure through her glove. 'I cannot regret what I have done for my mother's sake. She lived longer than Doctor Carr had expected. He said it was because Josiah had given her the best food possible and I – I gave her the love and care she needed.' She drew her hand away from his to dash away her tears.

'I do understand, Janet, even while I regret I could do nothing. Is – is Mr Saunders good to you?'

'Oh, yes. He is kind and generous. He has put ten pounds in my bank book in the Reverend Drummond's bank. He says it is for a rainy day, although he hopes all my days will have sunshine from now on. We both know life is not like that,' she added sadly. 'Best of all, he is teaching me many of the things I would have learned from Grandfather and he says I can read any of the books in his library.' Her eyes shone. 'You don't know how wonderful that is after having only the Bible to read at Braeheights, at least until Andrew gave me the book of poems which you bought for him.'

'I knew he did not have long to live and that he would pass on the book to you, Janet. Andrew always preferred mathematics to poetry. He would have made a fine engineer.'

Josiah joined them in the library when he had seen a disgruntled Eliza take her leave with a very sulky Henry. Apparently Henry had hoped to stay at Crillion Keep for some weeks until his father recovered from their latest quarrel concerning Henry's extravagance.

'That is the last of them away,' he said with a sigh, seating himself in one of the large leather armchairs beside the fire. 'You will join us for dinner, Fingal. I would like to hear about your work now you have moved to Edinburgh. I asked your mother to join us too but she refused.' He smiled. 'She says she would not feel comfortable eating in my company since I am her employer, but she says she will have time to talk to you this evening when she gets back to her own fireside.'

'Thank you, sir. If my mother is happy with the arrangement I shall be pleased to join you, for I must leave on the morning coach and return to Edinburgh and there will be no other opportunity to catch up on the local news. Has Mr Bell from Home Farm fully recovered?'

'He has indeed and his son Thomas was hoping he might have an opportunity to catch up with you.'

'Do you remember Thomas, Janet? He was at school with Andrew and me.'

'Yes, but I did not know him well. He only boarded with us in the winter.'

'He always knew much more about nature and the seasons than we did, and the moon and stars too.'

'He loves the land,' Josiah said. 'He will be a good manager one day if he follows in his father's footsteps, as I hope he will. I was fortunate to inherit so many loyal families from my great-uncle, including your parents, Fingal, and now your sister and Donald. I knew little about farming the land.'

Fingal had the strangest feeling that Mr Saunders was giving him some sort of hidden message but he couldn't think how this conversation applied to him, other than giving news of old friends, but then Josiah continued, 'Someday there will be no such thing as class. There is no reason why a hard-working, honest woman who is also an excellent cook, as your mother is – there should be no reason for her to be ill at ease with someone like me. Education should be for everyone, and especially for girls from poorer families. The changes will not happen in my lifetime, nor in yours perhaps, but I see changes ahead.'

'I have heard there are rumblings and disagreements amongst the clergy too,' Fingal remarked thoughtfully.

'So I believe. Many of them disagree with being dependent on the local laird for their living. I believe the Reverend Drummond sees trouble ahead on that score.'

Janet was very tired after the strains of the day and she was happy to sit quietly and listen to the deep voices in pleasant conversation. She loved the library with its wall of book-filled shelves. Above the fireplace, a semicircle of daggers was neatly arranged in order of size and on either side hung two pairs of swords in beautifully decorated scabbards. Josiah said he believed they had belonged to his ancestors but when she said she preferred the paintings of the cows and sheep and the pretty girls beside a stream, which were hung on either side of the long window, he had laughed and told her he had bought them himself and he preferred them too.

'Isn't that right, Janet?'

She jumped and looked up startled. 'I-I'm sorry I was not listening,' she stammered, coming out of her reverie.

'I expect you are exhausted my dear,' Josiah said gently. 'I was telling Fingal how happy we should be to receive a letter from him occasionally, especially if he includes a sheet for his mother. I'm sure she misses your visits now you have moved back to Edinburgh.'

'Well, if you're sure you don't mind paying to receive what little news I might have, sir, I would be happy to write. Can I expect a reply?' He grinned. 'Andrew and I guarded our pennies closely when we were at university so we did not get letters, but I can afford to pay to receive a letter now and I would be pleased to hear news of my family and friends.'

'Then that is settled. Janet enjoys writing. She is a great help with my ledgers. I'm sure you would be happy to write to an old friend, wouldn't you, my dear?' He turned to Fingal. 'Perhaps your mother will add a few lines of her own too.'

'Yes, I would be happy to write you a letter,' Janet said. 'When I was at Braeheights I longed for a letter but nobody ever received one. Mr Foster would have sent them away rather than pay to accept their delivery.' Her tone was faintly bitter and both men realized this was unusual for Janet and belied some of the yearning she must have felt for news of Andrew and her mother, especially when Foster refused to allow her to attend church.

They ate their evening meal together and Fingal recounted

anecdotes about his work.

'Now that the senior partner knows he can trust me, he sends me to the distant cases because I am a single man without the responsibility of a wife and family. Unfortunately it has stirred some jealousy with one of the other young lawyers who has been there a year longer than I have, but he is not very conscientious, and sometimes not very honest. This troubled me at first, but I have learned that Mr Crosby, the senior partner in the firm, is a shrewd judge of character. He knows everything that goes on in his offices.'

'I'm sure it pays to be honest in the long run, Fingal,' Josiah agreed. 'You have done well. Dominie McWhan always said you would go far when you got the scholarship to go on to university. He would have been proud of you, as we all are.'

As she lay in bed that night, Janet felt it had been one of the saddest days of her life and yet it had ended with peace and contentment in the company of Josiah and Fingal. She had been happy listening to them talk. If only Fingal did not have to leave so soon, or stay so far away. She had no idea when they would see him again and it saddened her when she rose the following morning and heard that he had already left.

Chapter Twelve

Janet had been helping the two gardeners make a herb garden with wedges of sage, thyme, mint, lavender and a low hedge of rosemary. She had left spaces where she could plant parsley and other tender herbs in the spring. It was not far from the kitchen and that pleased Maggie McLauchlan too, but as winter approached she was happy staying indoors.

'I have a surprise for you, Janet,' Josiah said one day when he came to find her in the library. He held out a small oblong box and when she slid open the lid she was astonished.

'Are these the writing pens with metal nibs you were telling me about?' she asked, lifting one slender wooden rod from the box and gently stroking the back of the shiny end.

'Yes. You will never need to sharpen a quill again with these. Each one has a different end so I bought two shafts and four nibs. You can practise with them all until you find the one which suits you best.'

'That's wonderful!' Janet stood up and faced him. 'I don't know how to thank you. You are so thoughtful.' She stood on tiptoe and kissed his cheek.

'Thank you, my dear.' Josiah's voice was husky, then he chuckled softly. 'You may not thank me when you make blots on the page. It takes time to get used to the new nibs so I would suggest you practise before you reply to Fingal's letter. I know how neat you are. And this is for you too.' He lifted a stand from a box. It was a heavy brass stand with an inkwell at each end with hinged brass lids. In the middle was a tray for resting pens. 'One for black and one for blue ink,' he said. 'They are similar to the one I have on my desk. You can keep yours in here. I am pleased you enjoy using the library.'

'I think it is the loveliest room in the house,' Janet said.

'Yes, I think I might agree with you since you have come to Crillion Keep, my dear. Your presence makes it welcoming and the fire burns more brightly now it is in use every day. We are gradually getting the books into order too.' He sighed. 'Crillion Keep is far too large for one man, or even one family, unless he had a large number of children and staff. It would be ideal as a school for all the parish children.'

'A school?' Janet echoed.

'I would have dearly liked to be a dominie like your grandfather and inspired children to learn as he did. The tower was already shut up when I came to live here. The furniture is covered in dust sheets but the windows are never opened nor fires lit. No doubt everything will smell of mould. Maybe one day it will be put to good use again. There are four floors as well as stairs up to the roof. I have never managed to climb further than the first floor. When summer comes again you must go and explore and tell me all you have found. There may be pictures you would like to hang in this part of the house.'

'I would love to explore and then describe the rooms to you.'

'When it is warmer, then. Already it is cold whenever we leave the fire.'

'It is,' Janet agreed. She knew Josiah felt the cold much worse than most people. Doctor Carr had mentioned something about poor circulation and the heart being like a pump, which didn't always work very well. Josiah's bedroom was directly across the hall from the library. It had once been used as a sitting room and it was rather too large to be cosy, although Mrs Mossy always kept the fire burning, even in summer. It was Janet who suggested moving the large screen from the main dining room to keep the draughts at bay when Josiah was washing and dressing or preparing for bed. He had been full of praise for her thoughtfulness and declared it a great improvement, especially as he valued his independence and refused to have a valet or a butler, despite Eliza's hectoring.

It was the middle of December when one of the Rosses' footmen rode up to Crillion Keep with a letter from Eliza requesting that Josiah should come to visit her in her sickbed. She had the influenza and was feeling down in spirits. It was Mrs Mossy who brought the letter to the library where Janet and Josiah were discussing the philosophies of Adam Smith with Doctor Carr, who had come to lunch. Now that she knew the old doctor better Janet realized he made these monthly visits to observe and check up on her husband's health rather than because he was in need of a good meal, although he always ate with relish and praised Mrs McLauchlan's cooking.

Josiah read Eliza's letter aloud the second time, his astonishment evident.

'Mrs Mossy, will you see the man gets some refreshment please. I shall speak to him shortly. Perhaps you could ask if Mrs Ross is very ill and confined to bed all day?' He waited until Mrs Mossy had left the room, then turned to look at Doctor Carr. 'My company always causes Eliza aggravation. Could it be that she is seriously ill?'

'Whatever her reason this is not the time of year for you to be away from home, Josiah,' Doctor Carr said firmly. 'Perhaps she wants to pass on the influenza and kill you off,' he joked. 'Is she badly in need of your fortune, my friend?'

'That could be the reason,' Josiah said, but he was serious. 'She asks for an allowance for Henry every time she comes but we have not seen her since Mrs Scott's funeral. We did not part on the best of terms, but then we rarely do. Eliza constantly tries to organize me and my household.' His face broke into a smile, wiping away several years. 'Did you know her private grapevine failed her for once? She had not heard that Janet is my wife. Perhaps she has heard recently and wants to rage at me.'

'Your marriage was such a quiet affair it could almost have been a secret. I have been surprised at the number of people who are not aware you have taken a wife, Josiah. The Reverend Drummond and I have enjoyed many a chuckle at their surprise but we saw no reason to inform them.' He broke off as Mrs Mossy returned.

'The footman says Mrs Ross stayed in her room for a week but her health is much improved. He spoke to her this morning.'

'In that case I shall write a note for the man to take in reply,' Josiah said.

'Donald will be glad ye're not venturing frae home for he smells snow in the air.'

'Well, Donald is rarely wrong about the weather. Will you tell Mrs McLauchlan we shall be ready to eat in half an hour? I will bring my reply for the footman shortly.'

Donald was right about the weather and Janet was pleased Josiah had not left his own home where they could all look after him. He inspired loyalty and respect from those around him.

'I have never been so spoiled in my life,' he said to Janet with a chuckle, one cold morning at the end of February. 'Mrs McLauchlan cooks all my favourite dishes, Mrs Mossy keeps the fires going to keep away the chills, and even young Lizzy does her best to please, making sure I have a hot stone pig in my bed at night and hot water to wash each morning. She plumps up my pillows and mattress to make sure I shall sleep soundly, and now, Janet, I have you for a cheerful companion. I believe some of your youth and enthusiasm has rubbed off on me.'

'But I do nothing to earn the luxury you have given me.'

'My dear, you have done more than you will ever know since that snowy night when you struggled here more dead than alive.'

Janet shuddered at the memory. 'I have been so fortunate,' she said, her voice little more than a whisper.

'No, I am the one who is fortunate. I have enjoyed sharing my books and my knowledge with you, Janet, but there is little more I can teach you. We might practise our Latin and French a little more but I have been wondering if you would like to help me with the ledgers in my office? Would you like to learn about the costs of running the Home Farm, and this house, paying the wages every six months and keeping stock of things? Mrs McLauchlan tells me there is little she can teach you about cooking or running a house after your time at Braeheights.'

'It was a very busy household. I would like to learn everything you are willing to teach me,' Janet said eagerly, her eyes shining. 'Mama said Mr Cole told her my father was the best keeper of ledgers he had ever had, as well as being a good tailor.'

'Yes, it is true. Mr Cole told me that himself. He said he could trust your father to keep stock of the materials and threads and to order more at the best prices. Life seems cruel to take away young men with so much to offer.' He sighed. 'I wish I had known your father, Janet. But tomorrow I will start to teach you how to manage Crillion Keep and everything attached to it, the cottages which are let, the cost of repairs and those needing maintenance.'

'I shall look forward to that.'

The following morning, when Janet tapped at Josiah's office door he called her in immediately and surprised her by presenting her with a polished wooden box.

'This is one of the few things I have which belonged to my mother and I would like you to have it, Janet.' He opened it to reveal a writing slope covered in dark red leather. It had a narrow, lidded partition to hold pens and pencils and a heavy glass inkwell at either end with silver screw-top lids.

'It's beautiful,' Janet breathed, 'but I can't accept it when you treasure it so much.'

'Who better to have it than my wife, Janet? Eliza commandeered my mother's possessions, her silver-backed brushes and perfume bottles, and she disposed of the things she did not want. Fortunately my father kept this writing box in his own office. He said my mother was very fond of writing.'

'Once again I don't know how to thank you.'

'There is no need to thank me. See here beneath the slope is a supply of paper and envelopes, and sealing wax. You will be able to use it when you reply to Fingal's letters. I am pleased he has retained an interest in everything that goes on around Crillion Keep. At the bottom there is a secret drawer. If you feel beneath the pen box there is a tiny catch. Press it down and the drawer will open at the side. Perhaps it will be a good place to keep your savings bank card.'

'That's amazing!' Janet's eyes shone with pleasure.

'Speaking of the bank it is time to add a little more to both our accounts.'

'I couldn't take any more after everything you have done for me, all the clothes. . . .'

'My dear Janet, it is a pleasure to give to you, but in the case of the bank it is wise to have something set aside and the Reverend Drummond appreciates our support. Also you may be glad to have money in your own name if it should take longer to settle my affairs than I anticipate when I am not here to protect you.'

'Oh please don't – don't think about such things,' Janet pleaded, her eyes shocked.

'Very well, but leave your bank card with me for now and I shall add a contribution for both of us. Now shall we look at the way I keep the ledger for this household for a start? Draw up your chair, my dear.'

Janet enjoyed studying Josiah's methods of keeping his ledgers. He was methodical and each ledger was kept for a different purpose. They began with Crillion Keep and how it was run, then moved on to Home Farm, which had many more items of income and expenses, and lastly there was the ledger for the two tenanted farms and the woodlands which were part of Josiah's estate.

'It is so much more interesting when the figures relate to real people and items,' Janet said the third week she helped Josiah. Her eyes were shining and he saw the eagerness in her young face. His expression softened.

'I couldn't have wished for a more apt or eager pupil, my dear. On Friday morning Mr Bell will be making his weekly visit. Why don't you join us and then you will understand the figures even better as we discuss the week's work.'

Janet listened attentively while Mr Bell explained about the repairs needed to a barn roof and about the well where one of the workers drew water for his household.

'The bucket is leaking and the rope is badly worn.'

'Then we must have it renewed. Order a new bucket and a stout rope from the store in town and add it to my account.' He turned to Janet. 'Now you will understand what the items are and why they were needed when you enter them in the ledger,' he said with a smile. Then, to Mr Bell, 'Janet is assisting me with my ledgers and very efficient she is proving too. Next week if the weather is kind I will visit Home Farm instead of you having to come to see me. Can you ride a pony, Janet?'

'No,' she said, disappointment clouding her blue eyes.

'No matter. We shall take the pony and trap.'

'That will be splendid,' Mr Bell said. 'My wife and daughter will be pleased to see you Miss Jan . . . er sorry, I, er, I mean Mrs S-Saunders.'

'I expect you have known my wife since she was a child,' Josiah said comfortably.

'My son remembers her at school, and the old dominie taught me too. He was a fine man and a good teacher. Unfortunately our lassie came along too late and she suffered at the hands o' that man Todd.' Janet nodded in sympathy and couldn't suppress a shudder. 'We were glad when the minister and the elders insisted he move on. Evie likes Dominie Mason but he's getting old, I hear, and she says he sometimes falls asleep over his books in the afternoons.'

'Yes, it is a big responsibility being a dominie, shaping the future of the children, and therefore the future of our country. I'm glad Tom benefited from the teaching of Dominie McWhan. Now he has you to instruct him regarding the care of the animals, Hugh. He will make a good manager for Home Farm one day.'

'I hope you're right, sir,' Hugh Bell said fervently. He and his wife had often pondered what their future would hold if Josiah Saunders died and things were in the hands of his avaricious sister and her sly son. They had considered looking for a new place but Hugh's family had been at Home Farm for three generations and Hugh himself had begun managing the farm in the time of Josiah's great-uncle. They had been astonished when Donald Blair told them of Mr Saunders's marriage to the granddaughter of the old dominie. Young though she was, it cheered Hugh Bell considerably to hear she was taking an interest and that Mr Saunders was encouraging her and planning to bring her to the farm.

Janet knew how very fortunate she had been when her instincts had led her to Crillion Keep the night she had fled form

Braeheights, but she could never have dreamed of becoming the wife of Josiah Saunders, or that he would be so kind to her and ask so little in return. She knew he had begun to regard her with affection. He was not old enough to have been her father but she had begun to regard him with the same love she would have felt for her brother Andrew. There was just one small cloud on her horizon and that was the distance between herself and Fingal, and it was not only the distance in miles. She replied regularly to his letters and she knew he was interested in her accounts of all that was going on in the lives of the people she knew or came into contact with, such as her visits to Home Farm with Josiah and the warm welcome she always received from Mrs Bell and young Evie. Indeed she had started helping Evie with her arithmetic and English, setting her exercises to do ready for her next visit, and the girl was keen to learn.

'Her mother tells me she is enjoying school and getting on well with her lessons now,' she wrote in one of her letters to Fingal.

In his next letter she could visualize Fingal smiling as he wrote in reply, 'I remember you sitting your doll and Andrew's stuffed toy dog on seats and trying to teach them their letters. Your grandfather thought you were born to teach. I remember he encouraged you to help the youngest children when they were learning to read.'

There were so many things she would have liked to write to Fingal but she was always aware that Josiah was free to read her letters and his replies. Indeed she sensed a certain polite reserve in most of Fingal's letters to her and she knew he could not forget she was a married woman now. It pleased Maggie McLauchlan when Fingal sent a letter. As Josiah had suggested he enclosed a page for her. She did not write much in return but she always sent him a note.

'I shall leave you to tell him all the news, lassie,' she said to Janet. 'I should really call you Mrs Saunders now,' she added apologetically.

'Oh no, please don't do that. I've known you and Peggy all my life and I would have died if you had not cared for me.'

'Aye, we-ell, I'm glad you came to us, my lamb. It's hard to think of you as Mrs Saunders of Crillion Keep when we've known you since you were a babe in arms.'

'You are the nearest I have to family of my own now,' Janet said softly. 'I don't want you to change.'

'You'll always have a place in our hearts, Janet. You can be sure of that.'

It was true Maggie left the daily details to Janet but one thing she did tell Fingal herself, and which Janet had modestly omitted to mention, was that Beth, and even Angus, had begun asking Janet to help them with their lessons since Evie Bell had told them how Janet explained things and made them interesting.

Except for a private ache in her heart and a yearning to see and talk to Fingal, Janet felt her life had never been so settled.

Her contentment was shattered one sunny day when the Rosses' coach arrived and Mrs Ross stepped out. She had come alone.

Maggie McLauchlan opened the door to her and brought her into the library expecting to find both Janet and Mr Saunders there. Janet was alone, curled up in one of the leather chairs immersed in a new book which Fingal had sent. The title was *Sense and Sensibility* and it was written by a woman called Jane Austen, who had died a few years ago. She didn't look up. She thought Josiah had decided to join her instead of retiring to his room as he often did for an hour after lunch.

Eliza Ross stood in the open doorway of the library, her eyes popping in disbelief.

'Why is that girl still here?' she screeched. 'It is months since her mother died. I told her to move on then! And what. . . ?' She marched into the room and grabbed a startled Janet by the shoulder, shaking her vigorously. 'And what is a chit like you doing in here? It is bad enough that my brother has allowed you to stay so long, but he will hear about this, idling away your time like a lady with his books. You are downright—'

'But madam . . . er, Mistress Ross. . . .' Maggie McLauchlan tried to interrupt her tirade and explain Janet's position but she was beyond listening as she hauled Janet from her chair, snatched the book from her hand and hurled it at the fire. Her treatment of her precious book affected Janet far more than being roughly shaken herself. She darted out of Eliza's clutch and snatched her book from the flames, which were beginning to lick up from the recently placed logs. Janet beat it on the rug to make sure the charred edges of the pages would not smoulder, then she turned to face Eliza, her blue eyes blazing.

'How dare you treat a book with so little respect?' she demanded furiously.

'Even more importantly, Eliza, how dare you come into my home and speak to my wife like this?' Eliza turned to face Josiah, her mouth opening and shutting like a fish, as Maggie told Peggy and Donald later. 'I thought her eyes were going to pop out of her head.'

Eliza stared at Josiah in disbelief. She turned back to glare at Janet. 'Your wife? I don't believe it! You always said you would never marry. You weren't expected to live past twenty. . . .'

'I have defied the doctors' predictions and my own. Janet is my wife.' He moved toward the fireplace and laid an arm around Janet's shoulders. Both Eliza and Josiah were tall and slim and fully head and shoulders taller than Janet.

'I have never heard of your marriage. You could not be so stupid. She looks no more than a child, but she's a brazen hussy. . . .'

'Eliza!' Josiah warned sternly. He looked down into Janet's face. She was standing very close beneath his arm and she could feel his heart racing much too fast. He smiled at her. 'Don't worry, my dear. I have no intention of allowing Eliza's vile tongue to upset me any more. If you need proof of our marriage you will have to ask the Reverend Drummond since he married us in church. Did your usual gossips fail to inform you?'

'You're a fool, Josiah. You've been taken in by a money-grasping maid,' Eliza sneered.

Josiah squeezed Janet's shoulder reassuringly. 'Is that what you came here to tell me?'

'Of course not. I didn't know. I ought to have come sooner.'

'We have been married since the day Mary Scott came to stay with us so you are a long way behind, for once.'

'You mean you were already married at her funeral and you never breathed a word?'

'I didn't consider it necessary, though I was surprised you had not heard.' It was a long time since Josiah had felt such satisfaction in his dealings with Eliza. 'So to what do we owe this visit today?'

'I wish to speak to you. In private,' she added, glowering at Janet. 'You could at least offer me some refreshment too.'

'It is two o'clock.'

'I had to leave before lunch and it took a while to get here. The horses are getting too old. I keep telling Ross it is time he bought fresh stock.'

'I will go and make a tea tray,' Janet offered. 'Would you like sandwiches, as well as scones and cakes, Mrs Ross?'

'Yes, I would.'

Josiah's mouth tightened in disapproval at her ungracious manner. 'Thank you, Janet, my dear,' he said, giving her shoulder another gentle squeeze. 'Will you bring it into the office, please? That is the best place if Eliza has business to discuss, but I warn you now, Eliza, if you have come to ask again for an allowance for Henry then you have come in vain. I hear he is a frequent visitor to the cockfights and to the gaming in Annan, as well as developing a liking for drink.'

'I am not asking you for an allowance,' Eliza said, pursing her mouth tightly.

Janet was pleased to make her escape and when she took the tray of food into Josiah's office, followed by Maggie with the tea and crockery, she made sure there were only two cups.

'I am going to get my shawl and go for a walk into the woods for a while,' she said to Maggie when they had closed the office door firmly behind them.

'Quite right, lassie. You'll not be wanting to keep company with that she-dragon more than you can help.' Maggie clapped her hand to her mouth. 'Oh dear, I beg pardon, Janet, I shouldna say such things to you.'

'Never mind,' Janet smiled, 'you have guessed my intention is to escape until I see the coach departing. Please leave the wash house door unlocked though. If I need to come in I will use the back stairs to my room.'

Maggie nodded her understanding and wished she didn't have such a dark feeling of foreboding. Mrs Ross had certainly been furious to learn Mr Saunders was married.

Janet was relieved when she saw the Ross coach departing less than two hours later. When they retired to the library after their evening meal, Josiah seemed vaguely troubled as he confided the reason for Eliza's visit.

'Eliza wanted, nay demanded, my help to save Henry from joining the army.'

'Does he want to join the army?' Janet asked in surprise. Her impression of Henry was that he was a bully and a coward, but she would never hurt Josiah by saying so.

'No, he does not want to do anything which might involve effort,' Josiah said grimly. 'His father is a decent man and I agree the discipline of army life might make a man of Henry so I refused to intervene. Eliza spoiled him and he has grown into a self-indulgent young man. He has been gambling for serious sums and his father has refused to pay off his debts. He intends to buy him a commission in the army.'

'I see,' Janet said after some thought. 'I suppose Henry will still have to pay his debts but he is fortunate his father is not banishing him without a penny.'

'If he is honourable he will pay his debts but Henry is not honourable. He will wriggle out of them like the worm he is, if he can,' Josiah said with contempt. 'Eliza wants me to pay off his debts so that his father might relent about sending him to the army. She left in a fury when I refused.'

'Ah,' Janet said, 'now I understand.' She knew her husband well enough now to know he disliked quarrels of any kind and Eliza Ross was the nearest he had to family. She went to kneel beside his chair and took his twisting hands in her own small, strong fingers. 'You have done what you consider best for Henry. You have tried to be fair. I believe you have helped him several times already so you must not feel troubled,' she said gently. Josiah looked down into her upturned face and saw the earnest expression in her wide-eyed gaze. Young though she was, she had coped with the hardships of life with courage and honesty and hard work.

'You have a wisdom beyond your years, Janet. My mistake was in giving in to Eliza's demands on Henry's behalf in the early days. I shall write a letter and send it with Donald to Edward Ross tomorrow. I shall assure him of my full support and promise I will not interfere whatever he decides regarding Henry's future. He does not need it of course, but he is aware Eliza has tried to involve me in Henry's life. It is time that young man stood on his own feet. It is a pity he did not have several siblings to teach him to share.'

Janet was content during the next few weeks. Evie Bell was an eager pupil and making excellent progress as her confidence increased.

'I can understand now why my grandfather enjoyed his work so much and why he seemed to have such endless patience with Andrew and Fingal. Although they enjoyed different subjects they were both keen to learn whatever he could teach them.'

'In that case, Janet, you should understand how much pleasure you have given me in allowing me to guide your taste in books. As for anything to do with numbers, I believe you are teaching me since you began to deal with the ledgers. However ill I might be, I have no fear now of things falling behind.'

'But I enjoy sharing your interest, and even the problems which some of your tenants present,' Janet assured him.

'Yes, and they seem to like your visits when you accompany me. As for Mrs Bell and Evie, I think they would be very disappointed if you did not accompany me each week.'

'The enjoyment is mutual,' Janet said with a smile.

It was ten-year-old Beth, Peggy's little girl, who told Janet that the younger boys from Braeheights had begun attending school.

'They stay with their grandmother, Mrs Fortescue, during the week and their big brother Joe collects them on Fridays. Mr Foster had an accident and his leg is – is cripped.'

'Crippled?' Janet prompted gently

'Yes, that's it. So Joe is allowed to bring them to school now.'

'I see. I wonder how Mr Foster did that?' Janet mused.

'Adam says he tried to move a cow from the bull's shed so the bull knocked him down and trampled on him and broke his knee and his other leg. The doctor says it will take months to heal and he'll never be able to bend his knee again.'

'Oh dear. Poor Mrs Foster. I wonder how they are managing.'

'Angus and me – well we thought you would be glad because our mother said Mr Foster was nasty to you.'

'I certainly didn't like him but Mrs Foster was kind to me, and so was Joe and – and Molly.' Her voice trembled when she thought of Molly. Perhaps Mr Foster had got what he deserved. 'I wonder how they will manage the farm?'

'Adam says Joe is the farmer now and their mother sings while she is working and they are happy. They have a big strong man to help Joe. His wife helps in the house.'

Janet told Josiah and Maggie McLauchlan what she had heard about the Fosters.

'Pity the bull didna finish him off all together, if you ask me,' Maggie said bluntly, 'but at least it sounds as though Hannah is happier. I hear Joe is a hard-working, capable lad.'

'He is. I'm sure he'll manage, with help.'

'It is true the Lord works in mysterious ways,' Josiah said. 'I am pleased Mrs Foster is able to manage the farm and her family. If you wish to invite the Foster boys to visit they are welcome to come here after school with Beth and Angus. Donald tells me he is nearly fourteen and he will be leaving soon. He wants to be a blacksmith. Perhaps you would like to make a special tea for the four of them? The young Fosters could stay here overnight and I shall instruct Donald to take all four of them to school the following morning as a treat.'

'Oh, they would love that!' Janet said eagerly, her eyes shining. 'I could make them a caramel custard for a pudding. It was their mother's favourite food when she was – if she was feeling ill.'

'I think the children are not the only ones who will enjoy it, my dear,' Josiah said with an indulgent smile. 'I suggest you invite them for Thursday evening and perhaps you would write a note for them to give their grandmother so that she knows where they are.'

'Thank you Josiah. You think of everything.'

'I like to see you happy, Janet, and it takes so little to give you pleasure.' She smiled at him and hurried away to tell Maggie McLauchlan.

'I would enjoy preparing a meal for them so please don't think I want you to do extra work,' she said.

'Eh, lassie, I wouldna mind. Mr Saunders is right though, the bairns will enjoy a treat and I know you like cooking and baking so I will leave the kitchen to you on Thursday.'

So Janet got out her precious writing box and wrote a letter for Beth to give to the Foster boys. 'Tell them I shall need a reply from their grandmother so that I know they have remembered to give her the letter. I don't want her to be worried when they don't return from school on Thursday.'

'I will give it to Adam and I will make sure he does not forget. It will be lovely to have a tea party at Crillion Keep and Granny says you are going to feed us in Mr Saunders's favourite wee dining room so we have to be good and mind our manners.'

'I'm sure you will do that,' Janet laughed. 'And Beth, if you would like a girl for company you can invite Evie Bell to join us if you like. The days are much longer now so I could ask your father if he will take her home in the pony and trap later that evening.'

'Oh, I'd love that,' Beth said eagerly.

The small tea party went well and Josiah guessed Janet had enjoyed preparing it as much as the youngsters. Janet knew he enjoyed her caramel custards with the sweet golden sauce and beautifully smooth egg custard but he was pleased and touched to find she had made one specially for him.

A few weeks later, Janet felt she should have guessed life could not go on so happily but her heart sank when the Ross coach drove up to Crillion Keep again. This time it was clear Mrs Ross and her son had come to stay because she had brought her own maid and a great deal of luggage. The moment she alighted she informed Mrs McLauchlan that she required accommodation for her coachman and her maid as well as herself and Henry. She and Joshua were getting ready to drive to Home Farm in the pony and trap. They both enjoyed these little jaunts and their discussions with the Bells and seeing round the animals. Mrs Bell always made a special afternoon tea for them but Janet knew they would not be going today when she heard Josiah demanding to know the meaning of Eliza's invasion of his home.

'It is your own fault,' she stated sullenly. 'You refused to help with Henry's debts. Now Edward is insisting he must leave for the army next week. You wrote him a letter giving him your support so he will not think of us hiding here when he returns to find we have gone. So, dear brother,' she sneered, 'you with your Christian principles can scarcely put us out into the road. We shall stay until Edward changes his mind about the army. My poor boy could be sent to foreign lands.'

'Most young men would relish such a project,' Josiah said. 'I would have gone if my health had permitted it.'

'But Henry could be killed!'

'Not necessarily. Knowing Henry he will take care of his own skin even if they do engage in battle.'

'He's not going, I tell you!' Eliza snapped. 'I have already told McLauchlan she must have rooms prepared for us and for my maid and the coachman. He cannot return or Edward would demand to know where he had taken us.'

'I see,' Josiah said, his eyes narrowing thoughtfully. 'I am sure you can make yourselves comfortable. I have some business to attend before I join you and I shall need to hire extra staff since you are inconsiderate enough to double my household without any warning.' He rang the small silver bell on the hall table and when Lizzy Semple came hurrying through the green baize door at the far end of the passage he beckoned her closer.

'You may go and find Donald and tell him I shall not be needing the pony and trap to visit Home Farm today. Ask him to send Mark Wright to Mr Bell to tell him we shall visit as usual next week, then I need to see Donald in my office as soon as he is free, please.'

'Yes, sir, very good, sir,' Lizzy bobbed a clumsy little curtsy but Josiah knew it was for Eliza's benefit more than his and he hid a small smile.

'Oh, and Lizzy, we shall need extra help while we have visitors staying. I believe you have a sister? Do you think she would care to come in daily to help you and Mrs Mossy with the fires and the bedrooms and general cleaning, or Mrs McLauchlan might require help in the kitchen. Four extra people will mean more food to prepare.' He cast a glance at Eliza but she returned a stony glare.

'My sister has a baby, sir but I know she would be glad to earn some extra money,' Lizzy said tentatively.

'We don't want any screaming babies here!' Eliza snapped, stepping forward. 'You must order some of your tenants to help in the house, Josiah!'

'Oh, sir,' Eliza's face fell with disappointment. She knew her sister Emma would be glad of the work. 'I-I think our mother would look after the baby if it is only for a week or two.'

'It will not be longer than that, Lizzy,' Josiah said firmly, ignoring Eliza's indignant gasp. 'Take an hour off this afternoon. Call on your mother and sister, then let me know.'

'Emma's husband is Jim, the under-gardener, sir. I could ask him to go home at midday instead of eating his piece in the garden shed. He could ask Emma.'

'Very well, Lizzy.' He smiled kindly at the earnest young maid. 'You're a good girl. Most young women would have seized time off.'

'You're far too soft with your staff, Josiah,' Eliza said sharply. 'She's only a maid.'

'Excuse me, Eliza. I have things to attend in my office. I shall see you and Henry at lunch. Where is he, by the way?'

'He has already gone to his room. He was late home last night and I had to waken him earlier than usual to pack his clothes. The poor boy is exhausted.'

'He is scarcely a boy now he is in his twenties. A spell in the army with some discipline would do him a world of good.' He turned away before she could reply and went into his office. He knew Janet was waiting for him there and he gave her a wry smile as he sank into his own leather chair on the opposite side of the desk. He ran his fingers through his hair and sighed. The door had been ajar so Janet had heard most of the conversation.

'I'm afraid we shall have no peace for a while but the first thing

I shall do is write to Edward Ross and tell him his family arrived here without my invitation. I will send Donald with the letter in the morning. Edward is away from home until tomorrow.'

'I will help Mrs McLauchlan with the extra cooking,' Janet said.

'Oh no, my dear. I will not have you slaving after Eliza or Henry.'

'I enjoy cooking,' Janet said with a smile. 'It will irritate Mrs Ross less if I keep out of the way, especially if she thinks I am doing extra work on her account.'

'I shall leave it to you to do whatever makes you happiest, Janet, but don't tire yourself out, my dear, and you must eat with us. I need your support. I find it gets more difficult to remain civil to Eliza every time I see her, and as for Henry, he is the most aggravating and idle young man I ever knew.'

'I know.' Janet leaned across and patted his hand. She no longer felt so young and gauche with Josiah. He treated her like a favourite younger sister and they were at ease with each other. She gave him a sympathetic smile, though she would have preferred to eat her meal with Maggie McLauchlan.

'I have sent for Donald. I will ask him if Peggy can give her mother a hand in the kitchens too.'

'Very well but I will go there now,' Janet said. 'There will be four extra for lunch and no warning so I imagine Mrs McLauchlan will be getting flustered. I have noticed Henry has a good appetite for all he is still slim.'

'Very well, my dear. I will see you at lunchtime and we shall make the library our sanctuary afterwards. Neither Eliza nor Henry enjoy reading.'

'Thank you.' Janet smiled, glad of his understanding if she avoided the visitors.

When Donald came to see him he gave him the letter to be delivered to Mr Ross and asked if Peggy would help with the cooking.

'Another thing, Donald,' he frowned slightly then went on quickly, 'do you think you could find a bolt, or even two, from the joiner's shed and fix them on Janet's bedroom door, please?' Donald's head jerked up and his eyes widened. 'I hope the bolt will not be needed and I trust you will be discreet? Perhaps you could fix them while we eat lunch?'

'Aye, sir, I'll do that. But I – er, I hope there will not be trouble.'

'I hope not too but Janet is a very pretty young woman. Perhaps you could advise her to lock her door. I have no wish to frighten her so it is better if she thinks it was your idea to fix the bolts. I promised Janet she would be safe here but my bedroom is downstairs and I could not run to her aid if she needed me.'

'Aye,' Donald said slowly, ''tis best to be prepared. I'll see to it.'

Janet was surprised when Peggy told her later that afternoon that Donald had fixed a bolt to her bedroom door.

'There is a lock on the door already but I have never used it.'

'I'm not saying Master Henry is like that brute Foster, but ye're a bonny lassie and I reckon he has noticed. Promise me ye'll take care, Janet. A key can easily be removed and go missing. I've seen the way he prowls around. He's as stealthy as a cat.'

'Please thank Donald for me.' Janet hugged Peggy. 'I hope they will leave soon.'

'We all hope that,' Peggy agreed with feeling.

The first night of the Rosses' visit Janet was almost asleep when she remembered about the bolts. She didn't think she was in any danger. Henry had been pale-faced and ill-looking at both lunch and dinner. Even so, she got out of bed and groped her way to the door in the darkness.

The following day, Henry was more lively, having recovered from his hangover of the previous day, but Janet was tired after being busy in the kitchen helping Maggie and Peggy with the cooking. She retired early and remembered to bolt her door before she climbed into bed. She had worn one of her new dresses for dinner and she would have had to be blind not to notice the gleam in Henry's pale eyes or the wariness in Josiah's.

During the night, she thought she heard footsteps passing her door but she pulled the blankets over her head and was soon sound asleep again. The following night, she couldn't believe it when she noticed the key had been taken from the lock on the inside of her bedroom door. When she went to bed, she made sure she bolted her door securely and she offered a silent prayer of gratitude to Donald, and to Peggy for prompting him to fix the bolts, or so she thought. Later, when the old house was silent, she was sure she could hear someone outside her door. She sat up and lit the candle. She saw the doorknob turn slowly and silently, but the door did not open. She lay still barely daring to breathe. Someone muttered an oath. It had to be Henry since there was only him and his mother, besides herself, on this floor. Mrs Mossy and Lizzy slept in the servants' quarters and used the back stairs, while Maggie McLauchlan went home to her own cottage at night, as did Lizzy's sister, Emma, who had agreed to help out while the Ross family were here.

In spite of the bolts, Janet's heart was racing. Please, God, don't send any more trouble, she prayed silently. The only person she yearned for was Fingal and that could never be when she belonged to Josiah. It was a long time before she could sleep again and she felt jaded the following morning as she helped Maggie McLauchlan with the breakfasts.

'Mr Saunders has simple tastes but Mrs Ross and her son are never suited,' Maggie grumbled. 'They don't know what they want. If I cook kidneys they want fish and if I make fish they want mushrooms or scrambled eggs or the Lord knows what. It is a waste of good food when half the parish are near starving. According to Riley, their coachman, they are the same at home, but Mr Ross is easy-going and fair in his dealings so long as no one tries to cheat, or idle their time away. He says there's been tension for weeks with the quarrels between Mr Ross and his son.'

'You seem to have had a good talk with the coachman,' Janet said with a smile.

'Aye. I'm glad there's more than me doesna like Mrs Ross and her son.'

After her broken night, Janet felt too irritable to cope with the moods of their visitors so she sought refuge in the office; it was one room they never entered. She left the door slightly ajar so that Josiah knew where to find her. He had begun to leave most of the ledgers to her and she loved using the metal nibs he had given her. He kept a detailed diary of every event on his small estate. She guessed it was because his health had never allowed him to be as active at supervising as many of the gentlemen with large estates who employed managers. Janet admired the way he tried to be fair and just to all his workers.

'My grandfather would have said you were a true Christian,' Janet told him with a smile. 'He judged men by their actions rather than their words.'

'Your grandfather was a fine man himself and a good judge of people. I think Crillion Keep, and all those connected with it, will be safe in your hands, Janet, when my time comes.'

'Oh please, please don't think about dying,' Janet pleaded. 'Do you feel ill?'

'No, my dear. I can't remember when I felt so well, or so content, and I know that is due to your cheerful company and Mrs McLauchlan's care for my welfare. Nevertheless, it reassures me to know you will do your best to carry on here and treat everyone kindly and fairly, and with compassion when needed. I have great faith in you, my dear, young though you are. I hope you will choose wisely when you need a companion. We all need help.'

Janet was thinking about this conversation as she sat behind the big desk. She had just finished reading the last letter from Fingal for the fourth time. He wrote regularly if he could and his letters were the bright stars in Janet's world, although she never admitted it even to herself. Her reverie was disturbed by loud voices and the sound of quarrelling in the hallway. It was Mrs Ross and her son Henry.

'I'm bored to tears already and we've only been here a few days. What am I supposed to do all day?' There was a bang like someone kicking a wooden stair or the oak settle. 'Why can't you make the old skinflint pay off my debts, then we could go back home.'

'You sound like a sullen schoolboy!' his mother said. 'Even if I could persuade Josiah to pay your debts again, your father is determined to send you to the army. You must stay out of his way until he calms down after your last escapade. You could learn how to run the Crillion Estate. After all, it will be yours when Josiah dies.'

'Estate!' Henry gave a mocking laugh. 'It's no bigger than a pocket handkerchief. I shall sell it. No doubt Lord Swinbourne will be pleased to buy it since he owns nearly everything else around here. I hear he likes to dictate to people in his power.'

Janet could visualize Henry's sullen face. He did sound like a spoiled child. She heard him kick something again and hoped it was not the settle.

'For goodness' sake, Henry, why don't you borrow one of Josiah's horses and take yourself for a good gallop,' his mother snapped in exasperation.

'On my own? Anyway, he doesn't own a nag worth riding.'

'Well, go for a walk, then, to get rid of your ill temper.'

'A walk!' Henry sneered. 'I'm not in the nursery waiting for a walk with Nanny. I'm a man! I need some excitement. There isn't even a decent maid to seduce around here.'

'Josiah would soon send you packing if you attempted that sort of thing.'

'Would he?' Henry said in a low hiss. 'He has taken the pick of them himself and he's not even man enough to sleep in the same room with her.'

'Henry! I'm warning you,' Eliza snapped. 'You'll get both of us thrown out if you don't behave like a gentleman, then you'll have no option but to join the army.'

Janet heard her footsteps climbing the stairs. Henry muttered some response. Janet gave a sigh of relief when she heard him going outside, slamming the door behind him.

Henry's restlessness and ill nature seemed to fill the household with tension. Janet was glad when Josiah asked her to accompany him for their weekly visit to Home Farm.

'Where do you think you're going?' Henry demanded when he saw her dressed for outdoors on Friday morning.

'I am accompanying my husband to Home Farm for the weekly visit,' Janet answered civilly but her voice was cool, her expression wary.

'Am I invited to come too since you provide no other entertainment for guests in this establishment?'

Josiah appeared in the office door at that moment. He closed and locked it behind him, which was unusual. He had given Janet a key of her own but the door was rarely locked. Josiah slipped it into his waistcoat pocket before buttoning up his coat.

'You are not invited, Henry, because this is estate business and in any case there is no room in the trap for you. As to providing entertainment for guests, if you had waited to be invited then we would certainly have arranged entertainment for you. As it is. . . .' Josiah shrugged his shoulders and turned to Janet. 'Come, my dear, I think the Bells will be waiting for us. I told Mrs McLauchlan we should not be back for lunch today.'

Henry watched them go with narrowed eyes. His mouth set in a mean line. It was clear his precious uncle did not welcome his company and he had always been immune to both his charm and his complaints. How much longer was the sickly devil going to last? he wondered. Well, he would provide his own amusement and see how his uncle liked that. He turned and ran upstairs, but he did not go to his own room. He was intent on examining the door to see how Janet barred him from entering her room at nights. He did not notice Emma on the other side of the room where she was collecting the empty water ewer.

'Can I help you with anything, sir?' she asked politely, but her voice was icy as she watched him fingering the bolts on the back of the door. They had been well fixed and there were two of them. She was glad. She liked the young mistress. Maybe she should warn her, or tell Peggy Baird.

Peggy knew Donald had made a good job of fixing the bolts and all the doors were strong solid oak and would withstand the likes of Henry Ross, but she took the precaution of warning Janet about him snooping in her bedroom.

Chapter Thirteen

As usual, Janet enjoyed her visit to the Bells and Home Farm. Josiah always seemed younger and carefree as they bowled along in the pony and trap with the breeze in their faces and the sun on their backs. They were both smiling and happy when they entered the hall at Crillion Keep late that afternoon. Janet's fresh young skin had a bloom that no artifice could achieve. Henry was crossing the hall. How did a pathetic man like his uncle make a girl so happy?

He was missing the excitement of the cockfights and the company of his gambling friends. He seldom rose until noon, so he slept badly at night. After midnight, he crept along to Janet's door and turned the knob, hoping she had forgotten to use the bolts, but it held firmly. In frustration he heaved against it. Janet had been deeply asleep.

'Hello? Who is it? Is something wrong?' she called drowsily.

'Open the door before your husband hears,' Henry hissed. 'Consider his heart.'

'Go away!' Janet's pulse was racing. Henry heaved at the door again.

'Don't be a prim little bitch. I'll show you what you're missing!' His voice was growing more impatient and unconsciously louder. Janet was sure the bolts would hold secure but her heart raced. Then she heard another door open.

'What is all the noise about?' Eliza Ross demanded.

'Couldn't open the door. Must've got wrong room. . . .' Henry muttered. Janet listened to their sibilant whispers and shivered. It was a long time before she slept again.

Henry was even more restless the following day. The weekend stretched before him. Even a visit to the kirk on Sunday proved out of bounds because his mother didn't want to advertise their presence at Crillion Keep.

'There was no need to go to such lengths,' Josiah said dryly during Sunday lunch. 'Edward is aware you have taken refuge here.'

'Have you sent word to him?' Eliza demanded. 'Have you betrayed us?'

'Betrayed? Where else would you seek refuge, Eliza?' Josiah challenged. 'You have no friends who would hide you and your spoiled brat from his father.'

'You have a duty to protect us.'

'It is not my duty to keep Henry from a father who seeks only to guide him and make a man of him,' Josiah said, his voice hardening.

Janet saw the tension in her husband and the pulse throbbing visibly in his neck.

'Please don't quarrel,' she urged.

'Be quiet, girl! Answer me, Josiah. Have you sent word to Edward?'

'Do not order my wife to be quiet, Eliza.' Josiah's eyes flashed angrily. 'I have written to your husband and the sooner he comes the better pleased I shall be. Clearly he is no more eager for your company than I am.' It was unlike Josiah to be so blunt. Eliza gaped at him then turned her bile on Janet.

'This is your fault. He never said we were not welcome until you came.'

'Leave Janet out of this, Eliza,' Josiah ordered. 'If you are finished eating I shall retire to my room for a little peace.' He stood up and Janet followed him. Henry stood in the doorway and watched her. His eyes widened in speculation when she followed Josiah into his bedroom and quietly closed the door.

'You look exhausted, Josiah,' she said softly. He saw the anxiety in her eyes and summoned a smile as he stretched out on top of the bed.

'Eliza has always been exhausting,' he admitted, 'but I refuse to condone her behaviour. Henry needs discipline and the situation is creating tension in my household. I hope Edward comes to remove them soon.' Janet unlaced and removed his boots and lifted his legs more comfortably onto the bed. 'Thank you, my dear,' he said gratefully. She reached for the woollen blanket, which was kept folded over a chair, and spread it over him.

'Would you like me to read to you for a while until you relax?'

'Yes, please, I would like that. You are a most considerate young person, Janet.' He smiled at her. She drew up a chair and lifted the book from his bedside table and began to read. Gradually his eyelids drooped and she felt a wave of relief. Doctor Cameron had told her sleep was the best cure whenever her husband was upset or agitated.

She crept soundlessly from the room, careful not to fasten the door in case the click of the latch disturbed him. She crossed to the library and settled down to read her own book with a sigh of contentment. It was her favourite room in the whole house and it was one room both Henry and his mother avoided.

Josiah had seen how much she enjoyed the book by the late Jane Austen and he had bought her another called *Pride and Prejudice.* She was totally immersed in the story so she did not hear Henry Ross creep in as stealthily as a cat. She almost jumped out of her skin when he held his hands over her eyes.

'Who. . . ?' she gasped. 'Let me go! What do you want?'

'You know what I want after the times I've tried to enter your bedroom.' He slid one hand down her neck to her breast, squeezing none too gently.

'Stop it! Don't do that!'

'Don't pretend to be a prim little bitch with me.' Before Janet could move, he vaulted over the back of the heavy leather settee and seized her, knocking the book out of her hand as he pressed her back. She struggled, but he was stronger than he looked. He held her tightly and pressed his mouth hard against hers. She clamped her lips shut but his kiss was brutal. She tasted her own blood as he crushed her lips against her teeth. She couldn't get her breath. He moved to thrust his hand up her skirts and grope at her drawers. She screamed. Fear and desperation lent her the strength and she hit at his face with the hard edge of her hand. Fingal had once told her it hurt far more than a slap. Henry swore and swung one leg over her, pinioning her down, trapping one arm painfully beneath her. Panic gripped her and she screamed in desperation.

'Shut up, you bitch!' He slapped her face with his free hand and clamped one hand over her mouth as though he would suffocate her. 'It's time you learned what women are for.' She struggled to free her arm. 'Keep still, damn you!'

Janet's breath was coming in terrified gasps. He moved his hand from her mouth in an attempt at another brutal kiss, but she twisted her head this way and that, fighting him with all the strength she could muster. Her horror increased when she felt him tug at the strings of her drawers.

'Help!' she screamed. 'Peggy-y-y. Help me!'

Henry gave a sneering laugh.

'You might as well give in. I made sure both doors to the kitchen are shut. They will never hear you.'

Janet gave another piercing scream as his fingers touched the bare flesh of her thigh and he clawed at her stockings. 'Be quiet,' he hissed, wishing he had closed and locked the door behind him. 'Is it possible you're still a virgin? I've never had a virgin yet.' The thought seemed to spur him on with increasing brutality. Desperately Janet scratched at his cheek with all the strength she could muster. He felt the trickle of blood and cursed.

'I'll teach you a lesson you'll not forget, you little alley cat,' he hissed, tearing at his neckerchief. He wiped the blood from his cheek, then before Janet realized his intention, he jerked her forward, pushed her free hand behind her back and tied her wrists together. He shoved her down again and fell on top of her, panting with exertion and excitement. The pain in Janet's arms was excruciating, trapped beneath the weight of both their bodies, but she refused to let him see the tears of pain. He squeezed her cheeks together brutally and pushed his tongue into her mouth. She felt sick, but she bit his lip. His head jerked up. His eyes blazed and he slapped her hard. She sagged against the settee, but hate and revulsion boiled in her. She gathered her failing strength in one last desperate attempt to resist. Lifting her knee sharply she tried to punch him. Molly Foster had explained the best place to hurt a man. Her attempt was futile. He caught her leg and pushed it high.

'I see you're eager,' he sneered but Janet screamed in terror. 'Help! Dear God, help me!' she sobbed as she writhed and struggled and tried to roll him off her.

Neither of them heard Josiah enter, or saw him rush to the fireplace and snatch one of the daggers from its place above the high mantleshelf. He had never felt so angry in his life. His heart was pounding with fury as he lashed out at Henry. The short, sharp blade struck his shoulder and sliced deeply down his upper arm to the elbow. Henry yelled in shock as blood spread from the wound, falling onto Janet's dress, the settee and the floor.

In the doorway, young Lizzy Semple stared in horror. She had been bringing a basket of logs to mend the library fire when she heard Janet's screams and saw Mr Saunders hurrying across the hall. She had never seen him move so fast, or look so grim. Everything seemed to happen in a blinding flash. Henry Ross was on top of the young mistress, trying to force himself on her. She saw Mr Saunders grab the knife then there was blood, so much blood! Mr Saunders dropped the dagger and clasped his chest. His legs seemed to collapse beneath him. Lizzy dropped the basket of logs and ran for Mrs MacLauchlan.

Henry was clutching his arm and yelling like a stuck pig as he rolled away from Janet and onto his feet. Anger, emotion, the spurt of exertion – it had all been too much for Josiah. Janet sprang off the settee the moment she was free and threw herself to her knees beside her husband. She could not even reach out a hand to him and tears of frustration gathered as she struggled to free her wrists.

'My dear Janet. . . .' he whispered. They were the last words he would ever speak.

'No! Oh, no! Josiah, please don't die. Please don't die. . . .' She knelt beside him, laying her cheek against his blue lips. She was deaf to Henry's cries that he was bleeding to death. She didn't notice Mrs Ross enter the room.

'He tried to kill me!' Henry yelled at his mother. 'I'm bleeding to death. He tried to kill. . . .'

'Be quiet!' his mother hissed. 'You're a mess.' She jerked sharply at his breeches and fastened his buttons. 'Listen to me! She! *She* tried to kill you! *She* killed him, then she tried to kill you. Do you hear me, Henry?' She gave him a little shake. She stared intently into his face, willing her words to sink into his coward's brain. '*She* tried to kill you. Remember that.' Only then did she bend to tear the bottom off her cotton petticoat. Lizzy came running back with clean towels. She stopped on the threshold. The master was stretched out on the floor, white as a ghost, and Janet's hands were tied behind her back. Maggie McLauchlan almost collided with her. The bowl of water splashed the floor.

Maggie set the water beside Mrs Ross and went straight to Janet. She bent stiffly to kneel at Janet's side, her own face paling as she took in the full portent of the scene. She felt for the pulse in her master's neck but she knew his life had ebbed away.

'Untie me. Please,' Janet whispered hoarsely through her tears, turning her shoulder towards Maggie. For a moment, she stared stupidly at Janet's bound wrists, then swiftly she untied the silk neckerchief and thrust it in her pocket. One of Janet's hands was numb and bloodless and she could have cried with pain as the blood began to circulate again, but all her feeling was for the man who had given her his name. She bent closer to wipe away the tears, which had fallen onto his dear white face.

'I need a doctor! I'm bleeding to death!' Henry yelled hysterically. Janet and Maggie looked up. There did seem to be a lot of blood everywhere.

'Lizzy, ask Donald to bring Doctor Carr,' Maggie said and rose slowly to her feet, her stiff knees reminding her she was not so young and supple as she had been once. What would become of them all without the master? As she passed her, Mrs Ross clutched her shoulder with hard, bony fingers. She stared pointedly at the neckerchief in her apron pocket.

'If you and your family want to work you'll keep your mouth shut,' she hissed.

Maggie asked Riley, the Rosses' coachman, to help Peggy move Josiah's body to his bedroom. Janet followed them like a shadow and crouched beside the bed. It was there Doctor Carr found her. He had insisted on seeing Josiah first but he shook his grey head in sorrow. There was nothing he could do.

'He was a fine man, Janet, lassie. We shall all miss him. There's many a one who doesna know the good he did. Will you write a letter to Fingal McLauchlan while I attend that whining cur in there.' He jerked his head towards the library. 'Josiah had a great opinion of Fingal. I'm sure the laddie will want to be here for the funeral. I will tell the Reverend Drummond.' He wagged his head in despair. 'He will arrange everything.'

'Th-thank you,' Janet said in a choked voice.

'Go to Josiah's office now then, lassie. Write that letter.' Doctor Carr guided Janet firmly out of Josiah's room. 'I will see it catches the mail coach.'

'She's in shock,' he said to Maggie. 'I will leave something to make her sleep. Young Lizzy might need something too. Donald told me she had seen it all and run for you.' His mouth tightened. 'We've lost a good friend this day, all due to that – that spoiled brat behaving like an animal. Was Josiah in time, do you think?'

'Aye, Doctor, I believe so but he'd tied Janet's hands behind her back with this.' She drew Henry's neckerchief from her pinny pocket. 'He meant to master her, poor lassie.'

'It will do him no harm to suffer a bit now, then. The wound will likely need stitches. Bring me a bowl of clean water and a towel, will ye please, Maggie? Oh, and some brandy to clean the wound, and my needle and thread. It was the old dominie who told me to use spirits to cleanse the needle and thread. It will sting the young devil and no doubt make him squeal,' he added with relish.

The cut was long and deep but Doctor Carr had no sympathy for Henry. It would need a lot of stitches and he would have a scar for life. He wondered whether Josiah had meant to stab the lad to death. He had not been a violent man. He had been sorely provoked.

'Hold still, will ye!' he ordered Henry brusquely. 'And stop your whining.'

'You're hurting him,' Eliza protested. 'Can't you be more gentle? He's suffered enough. He could have been murdered.'

'Murdered? He must have done something wicked to deserve murder. . . .'

'She killed Josiah and she tried to kill Henry,' Eliza said venomously.

Doctor Carr looked up, his needle half in Henry's wound. 'She?' He raised his bushy white eyebrows and pressed a bit hard on Henry's wound, making him scream in protest.

'That – that bitch who married Josiah. She took all she could get and gave him nothing.'

Doctor Carr's mouth tightened. He had seen for himself the pleasure Janet had brought to Josiah's life. Their relationship had been more that of a brother and young sister or a favourite uncle and niece but there was no doubting the genuine affection which had developed between them. 'And how did Janet kill her husband, then?'

'She must have hit him and knocked him down. He was on the floor over there.' She pointed towards the hearth. 'She tried to stab Henry when he saw what she was doing, didn't she, my boy?'

'Ouch, you're hurting me,' Henry cried out and jerked his arm away.

'She stabbed you. Tell the doctor what she did, Henry!' Eliza persisted.

'Madam, I think we would get on faster if you would leave us alone. As for you, young man, I can't stitch your wound if you keep jerking your arm. Go now, Mistress Ross, and send Donald Baird in here immediately.'

'Why do you need him?' Eliza asked with a scowl.

'I need him. Go and tell him. I will call you when I am finished.' As soon as Eliza left the room the doctor turned to Henry. 'So how did you get the scratches on your cheek?'

'I – I er, I don't remember,' Henry stammered, feeling his cheek with his free hand and smearing it with blood.

'Don't remember, eh? Get scratched with a woman's nails regularly, do ye? Well let me tell you this, you whining brat, you tried to foist yourself on Josiah's wife and in so doing you roused his anger and *you* caused his death. You've lost the best friend you're ever likely to have.'

'Best friend? He was no friend to me. He wouldn't even pay my debts. . . . Ouch! You're hurting me, you. . . .' He broke off as Donald Baird came in.

'Right, Donald. This whining young pup will not keep still while I clean his wound, let alone stitch it. I want you to hold his wrist and put your other hand round his neck and make him stay still. Sit on him if you have to. We'll pull his arm over the side of the settee, then he can't see what's going on.' Donald looked sharply at the doctor. He had known him all his married life and he knew he was usually a kindly man, patient and gentle with the children, or anyone in pain, but today there was a frosty gleam in his eyes and a grim set to his face. Donald shivered and was thankful it was not his arm which was about to be stitched. Before he resumed his task, Doctor Carr locked the library door to make sure Eliza Ross could not return.

Henry howled like a baby and screeched obscenities between every stitch, and there were a lot of them. Doctor Carr took his time. Henry was sobbing like a schoolboy by the time they were finished.

'Right, we just need to bandage you up for several days, then you're done,' Doctor Carr said with satisfaction. He bent down and put his face close to Henry's. 'You're not so much of a big man, eh, for all ye were intent on raping another man's wife. I can't imagine what sort of a soldier you're going to make.'

Henry didn't answer. His face was white and he looked exhausted after his ordeal. Donald would have felt sorry for him but he knew the fellow had intended to make Janet suffer. He deserved his fate.

Before he departed, Doctor Carr went through to the kitchen to leave sleeping potions for Janet and Lizzy with Maggie McLauchlan.

'Mrs Ross is insinuating Janet killed Josiah, then tried to murder Henry,' he said slowly. 'We know that's not true, but you'd best warn Janet to be wary.'

'Murder! That's impossible. You think Mrs Ross might accuse Janet, Doctor?'

'If she can gain by it,' Doctor Carr said grimly. 'Josiah respected his brother-in-law but the Right Honourable Edward Ross does have friends in high places. Mrs Ross might try using them against Janet if she can. Josiah didn't trust her, I know that.'

'You think Janet could be in danger?' Peggy asked fearfully.

'I don't know, but I believe Mrs Eliza Ross is devious.' He sighed heavily. 'It's a sad day, this. We have all lost a good friend. We can only hope Josiah's wishes will be carried out. Now, I will see if Janet has written the letter to Fingal. We'll pray he gets here for the funeral. He will know the law and how to deal with malicious tongues.'

Eliza Ross was indignant when the Reverend Drummond refused to discuss the funeral arrangements with her instead of Janet. Doctor Carr had warned him of her wild accusations but he was dismayed to find Janet made no attempt to defend herself.

'I am responsible for Josiah's death. If only I had not screamed. . . .' He looked at her pale face with the dark circles beneath her eyes and tried to reason with her.

'Don't you see?' she said. 'He would not have jumped off his bed, or hurried into the library. He would not have reached for the dagger to – to defend me from that – that b-beast. J-Josiah collapsed onto the floor and I-I could not help him . . . I could not help. . . .' Tears welled in her eyes.

'Have you sent for Fingal McLauchlan, Janet?' the minister asked quietly.

'I have written. Doctor Carr took the letter. In his last letter, Fingal said he would be working in another town further north for a while. He may not get my letter in time.'

'He will come for the funeral, I'm sure of it. He will help you deal with Mrs Ross and her son,' he added firmly, his mouth tightening. 'Now, do you have the key to Josiah's desk, please? I know he kept his will in this top drawer. It is locked.'

'I do not have the key. He kept it in his waistcoat pocket on his watch chain.'

He knew Peggy and Maggie had washed and laid out Josiah's body but Peggy had told him Mrs Ross had snatched away his suit of clothes as fast as they could remove them. He rang for Eliza Ross now. 'Can I have the key to Josiah's desk please?' he asked.

Eliza glared at him. 'Why? You have no authority! My brother's affairs have nothing to do with you!'

'On the contrary I am the executor for his will, with Doctor Carr.'

'He didn't leave a will.'

The Reverend Drummond looked up sharply and saw twin patches of colour stain her sallow cheeks. He guessed he would not find the will in the locked drawer, or anywhere else, even if he had the key. 'Nevertheless I must search. There are ledgers relating to payments to be made to the workers.'

Eliza drew herself up and sniffed, but she realized she had no option but to give him the key.

When she had gone Emma came in with a basket of logs to mend the fire. 'Please, sir, Mrs McLauchlan said I was to ask you if you would like a tray of tea brought in and if you will be staying for the evening meal.'

'Thank her, Emma. I would enjoy a cup of tea and one of her scones with her raspberry jam, but I shall not be staying for a meal. I have much to do.' He sighed. He had not found Josiah's will in the desk drawer. 'Emma, do you know if anyone has been in this office since Mr Saunders died?'

'Only Mrs Ross, sir. Miss Jan. . . er, I mean Mrs Saunders often came in here with Mr Saunders. She helped with the ledgers for Home Farm, I think. She hasna been in since he died.'

'So only Mrs Ross has been in here?'

'Yes. She was burning papers,' Emma said. 'There were lots of blackened pieces in the grate this morning when I came in to light the fire.'

'I see. Do you know what sort of papers?'

'No, sir, I'm not very good at reading. There had been a big yellow envelope because part of it hadna burned. The papers were written by Mr Saunders. I know that because he had such lovely writing.'

'Indeed he did. Thank you, Emma.'

'Very good, sir. I will bring your tea now.'

The Reverend Drummond watched her go thoughtfully. It was true Josiah had had fine copperplate handwriting and he had painstakingly made a copy of his will. Neither he nor Doctor Carr had considered it necessary to take so much trouble for such a long document. One of the copies Josiah had entrusted to himself to lodge with a lawyer in Dumfries. He remembered thinking Josiah was being over cautious, but apparently he had had good reason. Certainly there was no sign of the will where it was supposed to be. He scratched his head, trying to remember what Josiah had said. He had certainly put one copy of the document in a big yellow envelope, along with two sealed letters which he had said were to be given to his wife, Janet, and to Fingal McLauchlan. He had closed the envelope with wax and his personal seal in two places.

His first duty as minister of the parish would be to see his good friend Josiah Saunders laid to rest in peace, but he would contact the lawyer and ask him to ride out to Crillion Keep and read Josiah's will in person to all those mentioned in it. He knew there were quite a few because Josiah had been a scrupulously fair and generous man. Eliza Ross and her son would get a shock.

Janet avoided both Mrs Ross and her son and prayed Fingal would get here in time for the funeral. When she went to bed, she relived the nightmare of Josiah's death, and still she blamed herself, deliberately shutting out the memory of Henry's marauding hands and evil intentions. Sleep evaded her, or if it came it was filled with nightmares.

On the morning of the funeral, Janet looked like a ghost clad from head to toe in black. Fingal had not come. Henry's arm had twice as many bandages as usual and he held it prominently in a sling fashioned by his mother. As soon as he had an audience he moaned about his wound, the pain and how he had nearly died. Maggie McLauchlan beckoned Janet in to the kitchen away from the other mourners who were still arriving.

'Donald thought you would like to see these two people, Janet, and they want to see you. I've put them in my wee room off the kitchen.'

'Has Fingal arrived?'

'No, not yet. Maybe he didn't get the letter in time. Come through here. . . .'

'Mrs Foster! And Joe!' Janet cried, her face lighting for a moment. She ran towards them and Mrs Foster opened her arms wide and hugged her, while Joe looked on shyly, twisting his hat in his hand. He was still a boy even though he did a man's work and carried the responsibility.

'I am so sorry, so very sorry, I left you in the lurch when I ran away,' Janet said.

'No, no, Janet, you're not the one who should be sorry. I was more grateful than you'll ever know when I heard you had survived yon winter's night and found refuge with your friends here.' She looked at Maggie. 'And now you have more grief, lassie, when you should be enjoying life.'

'It's a long drive from Braeheights so I've made Hannah and her laddie a cup of tea and a bite to eat,' Maggie interrupted, afraid too much sympathy might shatter Janet's fragile control.

'Oh, thank you, Mrs McLauchlan,' Joe said gratefully. 'I didna have time to eat my breakfast this morning.' He turned to Janet. 'Ye would hear about father's accident? His leg was broken in three places. His kneecap is twisted. That's why Ma and me were able to come. She really wanted to see you, Janet. We all missed you.'

'I've missed you and your brothers too, Joe,' Janet said. 'Is your father improving?'

'He'll never walk again without a stick the doctor says. He's dependent on Ma now so he has to do what we want. There's been no more babies since Ma nearly died. I'm thankful for that and so is Ma.'

'Yes, she looks well; quite lovely, in fact,' Janet said sincerely. She had noticed at once how different Mrs Foster looked to the tired, haggard woman she had been.

The Fosters went through to mix with the other mourners now the large hall was filling up. Afterwards there would be food and wine in the main dining room, which Maggie and her helpers had opened up and cleaned. Janet's heart was too heavy with sorrow to pay much attention. She simply saw a blur of faces and greeted people politely when they sought to shake her hand, or murmur sympathy. Then the prayers were over and Josiah was being driven away for the last time in the coach pulled by four shining black horses with the men following.

Janet felt a tug on her sleeve. She turned to see Hannah Foster looking anxious.

'Can we go somewhere private? I need to talk to you, Janet.'

'Come to my bedroom, then, but I must see that things are ready for the wake. . . .' She led the way up the stairs away from the crowd of women gathering in the large sitting room.

'It's Mrs Ross, Janet. She's spreading nasty rumours and saying you killed your husband and you tried to kill her son and he's badly wounded.'

'She has been saying such things ever since J-Josiah d-died,' Janet said wearily. 'Anyway, it was my fault he died, even though I didn't strike him dead. I screamed and he rushed to help me. We knew his heart was very weak. I should not have screamed for help.'

'So it is true what Donald Baird told us? Henry Ross tried to molest you?'

'Yes. He is a beast of a man!' Janet said through gritted teeth. 'I wish they would go home and leave us in peace, but Mrs Ross is planning to take over here.'

'That's what I need to tell you. Joe was standing on his own at the far end of that great hall. He wasn't hiding but Mrs Ross didn't see him beside the stone pillar. She was whispering to a man Joe thinks he is her husband because he said he would take her and their son home with him today. She said she was not leaving, and neither was Henry. She says they are staying because the Crillion estate should be theirs now her brother is dead. She told him you had killed your husband and tried to murder Henry and—'

'That's not true!'

'I know. She says the Reverend Drummond has to carry out the funeral for two young children so he will be unable to return here for the wake.'

'I know, but he has been a great comfort already.'

'Yes, but you don't understand, Janet. That woman has sent her coachman to Dumfries town to bring the constable. She says when he has heard her story he will take you to prison to be put on trial. The minister will not be here to speak up for you.'

'B-but I have done nothing wrong.'

'Joe said the man told her she was crazy, but she told him she had already sent for the constable and he would see she was right when you were taken away.'

Janet's face had turned ashen. She had never seen a constable or a prison. She had never been further than Braeheights. She shuddered at the thought of being locked up.

'If only Fingal had come! He would know what I should do. He would believe me.'

'We all believe you, lassie, but the constable will be a stranger. He will listen to that – that evil woman. Don't wait for the constable to come. Don't let him take you to prison to wait for a trial. Listen to me, Janet. Pack a bag now. Leave it outside the door of the laundry. Joe will pick it up and take it in the trap with us. As soon you've seen the mourners occupied with their food and drink you must slip away through the back. Joe says you can cut through the woods behind Crillion Keep to keep out of sight. We are going to stay the night with my mother. She lives on the edge of Rowanbank village. We'll pick you up at the far corner of the wood and take you with us. Mother will give you a bed for the night. Then we'll think what to do. Maybe you could go to my cousin over the border into England. You would be safe there until someone can convince the constable of your innocence. At least if you are free you can get Fingal McLauchlan to defend you!'

Janet had flopped down onto the bed and now she hid her face in her hands.

'Why, oh why did Josiah have to die? He was a good man,' she wept.

'I'm sure he was, Janet,' Hannah Foster said more gently, 'and he wouldn't want you to be locked in prison to await a trial for the trumped-up charges his sister intends to make. I want you to be safe until someone can help. Joe thinks Mrs Ross must be a wicked woman.'

'Mrs McLauchlan tried to warn me,' Janet said. 'She says the Ross family have influential friends, but we never thought she would send for the constable.'

'Please do as I say, lassie,' Hannah Foster pleaded. 'At least until we know whether the constable will act on the word of Mrs Ross. I must get back to the others now and so must you. After the men return you can slip away. I have never seen so many people. Mr Saunders must have been well respected in the parish.' She patted Janet's shoulder. 'Pack your bag now, Janet. We'll wait for you at the corner of the wood. Better not tell Mrs McLauchlan in case Mrs Ross blames her for helping you.'

Janet didn't want to run away when she had committed no crime, but would the constable believe her? Would he have to take her to prison while other men decided who to believe? She shivered and stuffed some of her things in a canvas bag. She longed to take her wooden writing box but it would take too much room; but she would take the pens Josiah had given her, and her bank book from the secret drawer. She gathered what coins she had.

After she had mingled a little while with the mourners, offering them the trays of food or drink, Janet slipped away. Once in the woods she felt the breeze and lifted her face to the sky, still visible in patches through the treetops. She found the path and followed it blindly. She didn't want to leave the place which had always been her refuge in time of trouble, even when she was a helpless baby, but what was there for her now with the venomous Mrs Ross in charge? Josiah had said she would always be secure and he had made her promise she would take care of his loyal workers too, but how could she do that now? He was dead and she had no influence with anybody.

Most of the mourners were leaving by the time the constable arrived, riding an elderly horse which Donald declared in need of a good feed and a rest. He didn't believe for a minute that the man could believe Janet guilty of hurting anyone but he was as surprised as everybody else when it seemed Janet had disappeared.

'It proves she is guilty when she is hiding,' Eliza Ross declared triumphantly. Even so she wondered why Janet had gone and if she knew she had sent for the constable.

'Did you tell her, Henry?' she demanded, rounding angrily on her son.

'Of course not! What do you think I am?'

'A fool. I will go and see if she has run away, or if she is just hiding until nightfall when she thinks the constable will have left.' Eliza poked around in Janet's bedroom. 'Her clothes are still there, and even her precious writing box,' she sneered. 'She wouldn't leave that. Josiah made her believe she was a scholar. She will be skulking somewhere in the lofts or outbuildings until you leave, my man. You had better stay the night.'

The constable was only too happy to get a bed and a sleep before embarking on the eight-mile ride back to town. In fact he didn't think his hired horse would carry him back tonight.

'McLauchlan,' Eliza called loudly, 'have the maid prepare a bed for the constable in the servants' quarters, and give him some bread and a drink of ale.' This was Eliza Ross's first mistake. The constable didn't like being despatched like a box of rubbish and he resented her superior manner. On the other hand, Maggie McLauchlan could see the man was hungry the way his eyes devoured the remains of the food from the funeral wake.

'I'll make you up a tray of food to take to your room,' she said in a low voice. 'Better not let her see you eating in here, even though half of this will probably go to the pigs. She will be expecting a cooked dinner tonight.'

'You don't seem to care much for your mistress?'

'We don't believe Mr Saunders meant her to be mistress here,' Maggie said bluntly. 'He promised we would all be secure in our jobs with Janet – er Mrs Saunders, his – his widow.' She sighed. 'The minister says he made a will but he can't find it in the house, even though he is an executor, whatever that means.'

'Well, I'm afraid I shall have to take the young widow away with me for trial when we do find her,' the constable said. 'It is not up to me to judge whether she is guilty or not, but why did she need to hide if she is innocent?'

'She must have heard you were coming. She's no match for a woman like Mrs Ross. She has warned all of us to keep our mouths shut or we shall lose our jobs.'

'I don't know what to think.' The constable shook his head. 'Mrs Ross made a good case for murder in her letter to the magistrates and running away smacks of guilt.'

'If Janet had stayed here you would have had her halfway to prison by now,' Maggie said sharply. 'But I'm surprised she didn't tell me she was going.' She wiped a hand over her brow. 'I hope she's safe, wherever she is.'

When she returned to her own cottage for the night, Maggie had half hoped to find Janet hiding in the box bed, waiting for her. She knew Donald had searched the loft above the stable and the sheds where the joiner and the gardener worked and even the blacksmith's forge and his barn. She had had a busy and upsetting day. She undressed and almost fell into bed in her exhaustion. Even so, sleep did not come easy. If only she was sure Janet was safe and warm somewhere.

A few hours later she was wakened by someone kindling the fire in the grate and pouring water from her big jug into the kettle. She drew the curtain aside and peeped out.

'Fingal! You've come! Oh, laddie, I am glad to see ye!' She sprang out of bed and hugged him tightly. Then she grabbed her shawl and pulled it around her. 'You look exhausted, Fingal?'

'I am. Janet's letter was waiting for me when I arrived back in Edinburgh yesterday morning. I set out again straight away but I knew I would be too late for the funeral. How is Janet?'

Maggie filled him in on all the events since Henry's attack on Janet to the arrival of the constable and Janet's disappearance. 'I could boil some eggs for ye in the kettle, Fingal, and I have some fresh bread I brought down from the kitchens. I might have guessed ye'd be here and hungry. You were always hungry when ye came home.'

'Thanks, Mother. I could eat a horse, but I could whip Henry Ross and throttle his devious, lying mother.'

'Oh, hush, laddie! Don't talk like that, it will get ye into trouble.'

'Tell me everything again, then, while I eat so that I have the story clear in my own head. After that I will sleep for an hour in the chair, then I shall waken the constable so that I can talk to him without Mrs Ross. I must try to convince him she has brought him here on a wild goose chase.'

'I don't think he'll be pleased to be wakened so early. Oh, I nearly forgot. The Reverend Drummond gave me a note for ye.

He was sure you would come.'

Fingal broke the seal and read the brief note. He frowned. 'He wants me to send word to him with Donald whatever time I arrive. He says something about a missing will and needing my help to deal with Mrs Ross and her son.'

'He hasna seen the constable. He arrived after the minister had left for the burial.'

'I will tell Donald on my way up to see the constable, then,' Fingal nodded. 'I wish I could think where Janet would go to feel safe. She has no one except us.'

'We'll both get some rest, then I'll come up to the house with you and cook a good breakfast for you and the constable. It might get him in a better mood to listen.'

Tired though he was, Fingal found it impossible to sleep and he was up at the crack of dawn bringing in water and boiling the kettle so that he could shave and make himself as presentable as possible. He had learned impressions were important when dealing with people in authority.

'I will serve your breakfast in the small dining room so you will not be interrupted,' Maggie said later, surveying him proudly. 'And I will introduce you as Mrs Saunders's lawyer so it sounds more official.'

Fingal grinned at her but he agreed.

His mother was right about the constable. Once he had eaten his porridge and started on a large platter of bacon, eggs and mushrooms, he seemed less irritable and more willing to listen. Besides which, he was impressed with the smart young man who had travelled all the way from Edinburgh to speak to him on Mrs Saunders's behalf. They were just finishing their meal when the Reverend Drummond arrived. Maggie brought him some breakfast too. The minister praised the young widow and proclaimed her innocence even more than her lawyer and it put the constable in a dilemma.

'It is not for me to decide whether she is guilty or not,' he said awkwardly. 'When the wife of the Right Honourable Edward Ross made such a serious charge I was ordered to take her in to stand trial before the magistrates.'

Fingal sighed in frustration.

'You must hear what young Lizzy has to say. Apparently she saw everything.'

'The young maid? She was too nervous to answer any questions last night.'

'Mrs Ross has threatened all the staff. They will lose their jobs if they talk to you.'

'Bring Lizzy in here, Fingal. I must convince her to tell the constable the truth,' the Reverend Drummond said decisively.

When she came into the office, Lizzy was trembling with nerves but the minister took her hands gently and placed one on the Bible on the desk.

'Now Lizzy, my dear child, do not be afraid. Even if you lose your job I will find work for you, I promise. But if you tell the constable everything you saw, you will help Mrs Saunders. You don't want to see her taken to prison and locked up, do you?'

'Oh no, no sir! She is not the one who is wicked. She couldn't get away frae Master Henry. He – he had tied her hands behind her back. He was laid on top of her. She screamed in terror.' Lizzy shuddered, then with a little encouragement she went on to tell the constable what she had seen. 'Then Mr Saunders dropped the wee dagger. His legs seemed to crumple. . . .' she began to cry. 'He d-died, sir! There on the floor in front of the fire. . . .'

'Wait a minute, Lizzy,' Fingal said. 'Do you mean Mr Saunders reached for one of the daggers hanging on the wall above the high mantleshelf in the library?'

'Yes. It – it made s-so much b-blood everywhere. . . .'

'Thank you, Lizzy. You can go now. You have done very well,' Fingal said and turned to the constable. 'Will you come with me to the library please, gentlemen? I will prove Mrs Saunders could not have tried to kill Henry Ross with a dagger, even though he deserved it, taking another man's wife against her will, under that man's own roof too.'

He led them to the fireplace in the library and pointed up at the semi-circle of daggers, flanked by the swords which adorned the walls. There was one dagger missing and it lay on the high mantleshelf now, waiting to be fixed back into place.

'Now, Constable Reynolds, there was a good fire in the grate on the day in question. Can you lean over the fender and reach the place where the dagger belongs? Please try.'

Puzzled, the constable obeyed. He could feel the heat from the fire and he had barely reached the first dagger, even less the space for the third one, still lying on the mantle.

'Now imagine you are a young woman in wide skirts and your height is about here.' He held a hand to the middle of his own chest and turned to the minister. 'Janet is about this height. Am I right?'

'Aye indeed. Now, why didn't Doctor Carr think to tell ye that last night, constable? There is no way Janet could have reached any of the knives. Anyway, Lizzy said her hands were tied behind her with Henry Ross's own neckerchief. Josiah Saunders was taller than I am. He would know the best dagger to choose. He had vowed to keep Janet safe. Seeing her molested in their own home would drive any man to fury.'

'But I understood he was murdered first. . . .'

'Murdered? Of course he was not murdered, man!' The Reverend Drummond stared at him incredulously. 'He had a weak heart. He had already lived years longer than the doctors had predicted. I can imagine his anger at seeing his young wife held captive by that – that scoundrel. . . . No wonder his heart gave way,' the minister finished. 'In an hour, Doctor Carr will be here to meet with the lawyer from Dumfries. He will vouch for Josiah's precarious health.' He caught Fingal's surprised glance. 'Mr Saunders left two copies of his will,' he explained. 'We thought he was being too cautious when he said he didn't trust Mrs Ross, or her son. It seems he was right. The copy he kept in his desk has disappeared. Burned, I suspect, but Mrs Ross does not know he sent the other copy to his lawyers in Dumfries. I despatched my man to inform Mr Glenlydon early this morning as soon as I heard you had arrived from Edinburgh, Fingal. Constable, if you care to wait for the reading of the will, I think you will discover Mrs Ross's motive in sending for you. She wanted Mr Saunders's widow removed because she hopes to inherit his estate herself.'

'Well, sir, I would have liked to judge the widow for myself but you all speak highly of her, and you present a good case for her innocence. Perhaps the magistrates will understand the reason why I have not returned with the prisoner if you, as minister of the parish, will write a letter vouching for Mrs Saunders's character and detailing the events. Also if Mr Glenlydon will confirm the contents of the will, and his belief in Mrs Saunders's innocence, when he has met her? He and his brother are well respected in the town.'

'Thank you.' Fingal gave a sigh of relief.

'If you don't mind, gentlemen, I think I shall get on my way,' the constable said. 'My ten years as a constable will end in three months but Mrs Ross is one of the most formidable women I have encountered. As for her son, he did not inspire my respect, even before I heard of his dastardly conduct.'

'I think you are wise, young man,' the minister said. 'I will write the letter now.'

It was almost midday when Eliza came down. When she discovered Janet had not been found and the constable had returned to town alone she flew into a rage. Her fury increased when she found the Reverend Drummond and Fingal McLauchlan in Josiah's office.

'How dare you make yourselves so familiar in here?' she demanded haughtily.

'We are awaiting the arrival of Doctor Carr with Mr Saunders's lawyer from Dumfries,' the Reverend Drummond informed her calmly. 'You may not recognize Fingal McLauchlan these days. Josiah had a high opinion of his abilities. He is a lawyer in Edinburgh now and he is prepared to act in defence of Mrs Saunders should you make any more scurrilous accusations.'

Eliza's face paled a little but she gave a scornful snort. 'Who is this lawyer from Dumfries? How do you know he is coming here? What has it to do with either of you?'

'Mr Glenlydon will read Mr Saunders's Last Will and Testament. I am one of the executors but that will not interest you.'

'An executor? There is no will . . . I am his sister and expect. . . .'

'You are welcome to stay and hear the reading if you wish,' the

Reverend Drummond went on blandly. 'As Josiah's wife, Janet will be the main beneficiary but as she is absent. . . .'

'Wife! She was not a proper wife. She married him for what she could get and I mean to see she gets what she deserves and that will be prison, if not the gallows.'

'It is a pity you have driven her from her home with your malicious gossip but Mr Glenlydon will be sure to convey her husband's wishes to her when we find her.'

'She is guilty or she would not have run away! And there is no will.' She went out and slammed the door behind her.

'I don't think the will can have anything to do with me,' Fingal said, 'unless it concerns my mother. I pray to God we shall find Janet soon. If only I knew where to look.'

'I can help you there, Fingal. Janet is safe and well, though still grieving for Josiah and the way he died.'

'You know where Janet is? Did you. . . ?'

'No, her departure had nothing to do with me but on reflection perhaps it was better that she was not here. The constable might have taken her to prison before we had a chance to convince him she could not reach the dagger to attack Henry Ross. It would not have been easy to get her out of prison immediately once she was there, even though we know she has probably never committed a crime in her life.'

'Then how do you know where she is hiding?'

'It was dawn when Donald came to tell me of your arrival. No one would expect to see me abroad so early. I met Janet waiting to catch the mail coach into England.'

'England? Dear heaven, I shall never find her there.' Fingal's face was white.

'She was with Joe Foster. He and his mother were at the funeral yesterday. He overheard Mrs Ross telling her husband she had sent for the constable to take Janet to prison. He couldn't bear the thought of her being locked up. He and his mother persuaded Janet to meet them later. They all spent the night with Hannah Foster's mother.'

'Thank God for that!' Fingal said fervently.

'Yes, we all need friends. Janet was to travel to England to stay with Hannah's cousin. I persuaded her to return to Mrs Fortescue's for one more night. I promised to send word if it was safe for her to return to Crillion Keep, or if she should go to England until we had proved her innocence. She gave me her bank book in case she needed money but she has great faith in you, Fingal. She seemed comforted when she knew you had come.'

'I thank God she is safe,' Fingal repeated. 'I must tell my mother and Peggy. They are very worried. We could not think where she could go.' Fingal stood up and took one of the minister's hands in both of his. 'Thank you, sir, for keeping Janet's secret and for being such a good friend to her.'

The Reverend Drummond eyed him quizzically and held on to his hands to detain him. 'Just a minute, Fingal. You love Janet. That's it isn't it? You love the girl.'

'I think I've always loved her,' Fingal admitted quietly, 'but I would never have betrayed Mr Saunders as Henry Ross tried to do. It was better for me to move away.'

'Josiah was wiser than I realized,' the minister mused. 'Yes, he was indeed. As you will see when you read the letter he left for you with his lawyer. I thank God he was shrewd enough to send a copy of his wishes to Dumfries. Ah, I believe that will be Mr Glenlydon now, and Doctor Carr.'

'I will tell my mother that Janet is safe, and ask her to send in some refreshments.'

'Very well. Perhaps we should move to the library where there is more room. I think curiosity will bring the Rosses to hear what the lawyer has to say.'

The Reverend Drummond smiled reassuringly at Maggie McLauchlan when she came in with a tea tray piled high with refreshments. She looked as though a weight had been lifted from her. Mrs Ross followed her in, looking haughty and making no effort to welcome the new arrivals. Henry followed, looking sullen and heavy-eyed. He had partaken freely of the wine and brandy available at the funeral and afterwards. His mother had assured him she had destroyed Josiah's will; now nothing seemed to be going to plan.

Mr Glenlydon took his time but eventually he stood up behind the table and began to read the will. Eliza gasped. She had known Josiah would have to leave something to his stupid wife but she had been too eager to destroy the will to study details.

He had left Janet sole ownership of a small house which she had often admired as she and Josiah rode to Home Farm in the pony and trap. In addition, she would have a yearly allowance to be paid from the estate income. There was also a letter addressed to her. The Bairds and Maggie McLauchlan were guaranteed occupancy of their respective cottages for the remainder of their lives. The lawyer looked over the top of his papers and held Eliza's gaze.

'To Mrs Eliza Ross he leaves one hundred sovereigns.'

'And Crillion Keep?'

'No. It is as I have stated, Mrs Ross. One hundred sovereigns is a considerable sum.'

'That will not pay my debts!' Henry hissed. 'Has he left me the Keep and estate?'

'You, young sir? What is your name?'

'You must know I am his nephew, Henry William Ross. I should be his sole heir.'

'Mr Saunders did not mention he had a nephew and he makes no mention of you in his will.' He looked enquiringly at the Reverend Drummond, who explained in a low voice that there was no blood relationship.

'I see. Then everything is in order. Apart from several bequests to his workers, Mr Saunders leaves the remainder of his estate, including Crillion Keep and Home Farm, plus the rented farms and cottages equally to his wife Janet, and to Mr Fingal McLauchlan.'

Fingal gasped aloud. 'Surely there is some mistake!'

'There is no mistake, young man. Here is a letter for you. The other one I shall give to Mrs Saunders when we can locate her. The letters detail the plans Mr Saunders hoped you would carry out between you, I believe, though I am not privy to the exact contents. You cannot be compelled to carry out the deceased's wishes but he trusted both of you to do what you considered best and were able to do. The Reverend Drummond tells me you are making a good career for yourself in Edinburgh, Mr McLauchlan, so I am sure Mr

Saunders would understand if you choose your own path.'

'This can't be true! You have got it all wrong!' Eliza Ross shrieked, standing up, almost hysterical with rage.

'Everything is as my client instructed, madam,' Mr Glenlydon said stiffly. 'I believe he left a copy of his will, presumably so that anyone who had any questions could read it for themselves. However, I understand someone had access to his private papers and destroyed the copy,' he added smoothly, giving Eliza a level look from beneath his dark eyebrows. He watched guilty colour rise to her cheeks before she gave a haughty sniff, turned on her heel and headed for the door, calling, 'Come, Henry. We leave for home today. Please tell Riley to have the coach ready.'

Chapter Fourteen

On the Reverend Drummond's advice, Fingal waited until the following morning before he took the pony and trap to bring Janet home to Crillion Keep. His only thoughts were to see she was safe and well. He had barely considered the terms of Josiah's will or the changes it might mean to his own destiny. His mother and Doctor Carr had warned him Janet blamed herself for the manner of Josiah's death and that she was taking it badly and scarcely eating.

'Mrs Ross and her evil aspersions would make matters worse,' Fingal said grimly. 'There is a different atmosphere already. Lizzy and her sister were creeping around like mice being stalked by a hungry cat.'

Fingal had not discussed Mr Saunders's will with anyone until he could talk to Janet but the Reverend Drummond had assured Maggie, Donald and Peggy that their homes and work were secure for their lifetime. That proved a big relief after the veiled threats cast by Mrs Ross.

When Fingal saw Janet's small, black-clad figure standing beside the elderly woman whom he remembered as Mrs Fortescue, he longed to seize her in his arms and promise to protect her for the rest of her life, but he knew he had to restrain himself while she was in mourning for her husband. Janet tried to pay Mrs Fortescue for giving her safe refuge but the old lady smiled and shook her head.

'I know you were a good friend to Molly and I believe my poor

Hannah might have died having that last baby if you had not been there to cook and care for her. I am the one in debt to you, lassie.'

'It was Mrs McClure, the midwife, who saved your daughter's life,' Janet said simply, but the old lady shook her grey head and hugged her.

'Hannah told me she couldn't have gone on without you, especially after Molly drowned herself. That brute Foster deserves to rot in hell. Now,' she said briskly and straightened upright, 'I'm glad everything will be all right for you at Crillion Keep, Janet. Will you come back to visit sometimes?'

'Of course I will, and thank you with all my heart,' Janet said sincerely.

'Aye, things are different up at Braeheights too now. No more bullying and blustering and spending his money on drink and women. Himself is dependent on Hannah and young Joe now. He'll be a cripple for life. Hannah has hired a cousin of Lily Bloddret to help in the house. She's a widow in her fifties and as different from Lily as chalk from cheese. That was the first time Hannah has spent the night under my roof since she married Foster, but she'll be back again now things have changed. She is sending the younger boys to stay with me so they can attend the school. They will all be coming to the kirk on Sundays too so you'll see Hannah then.'

Janet was quiet on the drive home to Crillion Keep but as they approached the long drive up to the house, she turned to Fingal.

'Are you sure it is safe for me to return?' She shuddered. 'I know Mrs Ross hates me but I never thought she would send for the constable to put me in prison. I thank God Joe overheard her plans and was able to warn me.'

'I'm thankful he did too,' Fingal said. 'I still can't believe what a convincing liar Mrs Ross is. It would not have been so easy to prove your innocence once you were in prison.' He felt her shiver beside him and he squeezed her hand. 'It's all in the past now, Janet. The Ross family will never trouble you again. Tomorrow Donald is going to drive both of us to Dumfries in the coach so that you can hear Mr Glenlydon read Mr Saunders's will. The Reverend Drummond asked him to come to Crillion Keep to read it yesterday. He wanted Mrs Ross to hear it because she could not argue with the lawyer and Mr Saunders's written word. They went home yesterday afternoon.'

'Thank you, God, for that,' Janet breathed fervently. 'I could not live in the same house with them whatever Josiah's last wishes.'

'He was wise enough to know that, Janet. Tomorrow you will hear his plans for your future. I hope you will be happy with the generous provisions he has made.'

He didn't tell her that Josiah Saunders had been equally generous to him. Was the Reverend Drummond right in thinking Josiah had believed Janet loved him, as he loved her? What if he was wrong? If they carried out the terms of his will they would be bound together for life, even if they were not man and wife. Fingal didn't think he could bear that – to see Janet every day, to work together side by side, to share their problems and their triumphs, but never be able to take her in his arms and love her.

Janet was up early and neatly dressed in black ready for the journey to Dumfries.

'I have never been as far from home as this,' she said in a low voice. 'Part of me feels excited, and that makes me feel guilty when Josiah is dead, but I am apprehensive too. You are sure the lawyer will not hand me over to the constable or the magistrate?'

'I am absolutely sure you are safe, Janet, and your husband was one of the wisest and kindest men I have met,' Fingal said sincerely. 'He would have been pleased to give you a little excitement. After we have visited the lawyer, we shall walk down the main street of the town. You will like that. Donald will take the horses to the inn so they will be fed and rested for the return journey and we shall meet him there to eat some refreshment.'

'Thank you, Fingal. You have thought of everything. I don't know how I would have managed without you.' Her expression grew sad. 'If only you did not have to go so far away for your work,' she added with a sigh. 'The Reverend Drummond says you have done well since you moved north again. When must you return to Edinburgh?'

'I shall be here for a few more days, then I must return and make plans for the future. Part of my success has been because

I am unmarried and free to travel to the more distant clients. Unfortunately, finding favour with the senior partner has caused jealousy with two of the clerks who are older than I am and who have been there longer.' He sighed heavily. 'Jealousy and greed cause so much unhappiness. I had no wish to usurp their places.'

'I am sure you work hard, Fingal. The Reverend Drummond says you are a credit to the parish and to Josiah and my grandfather.'

Fingal frowned, puzzled by her words. 'I hope I am a credit to your grandfather. He taught me so much about the world beyond our parish boundaries. Why does he think I am a credit to Josiah Saunders?'

'I suppose it is because you have worked hard and done so well. Josiah had faith in you when he awarded the scholarship to enable you to attend the university.'

Fingal's face went pale. He turned towards her. 'Did your husband tell you that?'

'Oh no! Josiah never mentioned any of his good deeds or the small kindnesses he did for those in need, but he often said he wished he had been a dominie like my grandfather. He believed knowledge was the route to many kinds of riches – and he didn't mean money.'

'Then how do you know it was Mr Saunders who paid for my time at university? I thought the scholarship was awarded by the elders, especially the laird. I thought it was probably due to the persuasion of your grandfather and the Reverend Drummond. I never knew. I could have thanked him so many times, and in so many ways.'

'Josiah was proud of your achievements, Fingal, and he respected you as a man. I believe he considered that enough reward,' Janet said softly. 'He had no respect for Henry Ross, or he would have helped him too.'

Fingal was deep in thought for the rest of the journey, mulling over her words. He realized now that he was already indebted to Mr Saunders. Without his help he would have become a coachman like his father and Donald. He was beginning to understand why Josiah Saunders wanted to leave education as his legacy for all the children of the parish, however poor they might be. How could he refuse to carry out his wishes? What would he do if Janet refused to share the duties which Josiah had delegated to both of them in the belief they loved each other? What if he had been wrong about Janet's feelings, or if the Reverend Drummond had misunderstood Josiah's meaning?

Janet was overwhelmed when she had listened to the lawyer reading Josiah's will.

'He has been so generous to me already,' she said, 'and now to leave me a house of my own. As for Crillion Keep,' she cast Fingal a puzzled glance, 'I do not understand why I should have a part of it as well.'

'You will, my dear, when you read the letter which my client left for you. I suggest you retire to a quiet room in the inn and read it in peace. If there is anything you would like to discuss, or anything for which you need my help, then I shall be here until 3.30 this afternoon. Your husband was a good client and it will give me pleasure to assist you.'

When she had read the letter, Janet realized that Josiah had fully understood, and even shared, her desire to teach the younger children of the parish, but he had known the task of organizing a school where children could board would be too great for her on her own.

'Did he write about setting up a school in the letter to you, Fingal?' she asked in troubled tones, 'even though he knows you are making a career for yourself as a lawyer?'

'He did,' Fingal admitted. 'I must say it was a shock.'

'Josiah knew how much I longed to teach. He encouraged me to help Evie Bell and Peggy's two children. He taught me so many things, which you and Andrew learned from Grandfather. Josiah knew so much. He said it was because books had been his companions when he was a boy and unable to do many of the things other boys did on account of his health. He has taught me more Latin and I can speak French fairly well.'

'My mother tells me he also instructed you in keeping the ledgers for running the household and Home Farm, as well as explaining about rents for all the cottages?'

'Yes, he did. I enjoyed keeping the ledgers and understanding the figures.'

'You are more like Andrew than I realized,' Fingal said. ' He could always beat me at mathematics and science.'

'Yes, but Grandfather said you could beat him at Latin and French and everything to do with English writers.'

'So the idea of setting up a school in Crillion Tower does not frighten you, Janet?'

'No, it is what Josiah wanted more than anything else.' She looked suddenly troubled. 'But I know I cannot do it alone and I shall understand if you decide to return to Edinburgh and your career as a lawyer.'

'I see. When your period of mourning is over I had planned to ask you to marry me. I had hoped to persuade you to come with me to Edinburgh.' He watched her expressive face.

'I couldn't do that, Fingal! Josiah was a good man and he was kind to me when I had no home and no one to help me. I must respect his wishes now.'

'I understand that, Janet.'

'Oh, Fingal, you'll never know how much I longed to hear you say you wanted to marry me when Josiah was waiting for my answer. But you went away.'

'I went because I had nothing to offer you then, except my love. That would not have provided a roof for us, or for your mother when she was so badly in need of care. You'll never know what it cost me to follow my mother's advice and leave you to make your own decision. I was sure Josiah Saunders would never treat you badly, but I wanted to care for you. Now I can afford to keep a wife and you will be free again after a year.'

'I do love you, Fingal. I think I have always loved you, but I cannot go to Edinburgh. I must try to carry out Josiah's wishes and help other children as he helped me. He believed we should all have the opportunity to learn.'

'Ah, Janet,' Fingal's eyes were shining and a wide smile lit his face. 'All I ever wanted was to hear you say you love me. I don't care where I live so long as we can be together. It is true I am enjoying my work and the progress I am making, but so long as we can work together, side by side, knowing that you love me, I will wait for you for ever.'

'Y-you mean you would come back to live at Crillion Keep? You would help me establish a school and you would teach the older boys, and the girls if they wanted to go on learning?' Janet's eyes were wide with hope.

'Of course I will, so long as we are together,' Fingal responded joyously. His expression sobered. 'I shall have to give fair notice to my employers. But perhaps it is a good thing if I am away from you while you are in mourning. Each week without you will seem like an eternity. I long to hold you in my arms and make you truly mine, Janet.'

'Oh, Fingal, that's wonderful! I'm sure Josiah will be sending us his blessing.'

'Now let us go and find Donald and eat. Then we will call again on Mr Glenlydon and tell him what we have decided to do.'

Fingal was in for another surprise when the lawyer had heard their plans.

'The Reverend Drummond hoped you would carry out my client's wishes together. He assured me that you are an intelligent and capable young woman, Mrs Saunders, and that you will organize the facilities for a school efficiently. He tells me there are many people in the parish who will be glad to work for you and assist you. However, it seems a pity to give up your career as a lawyer entirely, Mr McLauchlan. When you return from Edinburgh finally I suggest you contact me again. Perhaps we could come to some arrangement if you would like to work two days each week with me and my brother. We have already discussed this and he is agreeable. Your work would mainly be dealing with country clients on your side of the burgh. Many find it difficult to travel into town. I think you would find the work stimulating and the extra money would be useful no doubt, especially if you get a wife and family of your own.' He smiled and looked from one to the other. 'The Reverend Drummond told me it is no secret that Mr Saunders hoped the two of you would marry.'

*

A year later, Janet, and her childhood sweetheart were married in the village church. It was not a large wedding but Maggie McLauchlan and Peggy, with help from Mrs Bell and Evie, had made a feast at Crillion Keep for all those on the estate to wish them well. Also Mr Cole, who was now a widower, had insisted on making Janet a wedding dress in pale-blue silk as a gift. Hannah Foster and her brood of boys were there, along with Mrs Fortescue, as well as the Bell family and all their workers from Home Farm. Lizzy and Emma were beside themselves with excitement. They had cleaned the whole house under Mrs Mossy's supervision and brought in a vase of fresh flowers for the bedroom which the bride and groom would use. Fingal's niece, Beth, was Janet's bridesmaid. She smiled shyly at everyone, while her brother Angus stood stiffly in his best suit and starched collar and Peggy beamed proudly at her offspring.

'It is wonderful to be home at last and amongst so many friends,' Fingal said later that evening. 'But I thought I would never get my beautiful bride to myself,' he added softly, drawing Janet into his arms and lifting her onto the big feather mattress. He was almost certain Josiah had never consummated his marriage to Janet but he was less sure whether she had suffered at the brutal hands of Wull Foster the night she had run away from Braeheights. It was a subject he had avoided but he vowed he would be gentle and patient with her. He was rewarded with wonder and delight when he discovered his bride was his, and only his, and a passionately responsive and loving wife.

WORDS FAIL US

In Defence of Disfluency

JONTY CLAYPOLE

PROFILE BOOKS

wellcome collection

First published in Great Britain in 2021 by
Profile Books Ltd
29 Cloth Fair
London
EC1A 7JQ
www.profilebooks.com

Published in association with Wellcome Collection

wellcome collection

183 Euston Road
London NW1 2BE
www.wellcomecollection.org

1 3 5 7 9 10 8 6 4 2

Typeset in Sabon by MacGuru Ltd
Printed and bound in Great Britain by Clays Ltd, Elcograf S.p.A.

A CIP catalogue record for this book is available from the British Library.

ISBN 978 1 78816 171 8
eISBN 978 1 78283 508 0

FSC
www.fsc.org
MIX
Paper from responsible sources
FSC® C018072

For Constance
(Love at first stutter)

Contents

Introduction: The King and I

In the months prior to King George VI's coronation in 1937, a great deal of time, effort and resources went into anticipating, and therefore mitigating, the worrisome issue of his speech. George's impediment wasn't the charming, if somewhat affected, stutter fashionable with the aristocracy, but a juggernaut of blocks, repetitions and slurred sounds.

As a young prince, George had been unable to avoid public speaking engagements, which often left him feeling humiliated. According to friends, his stutter had rendered him 'intensely sensitive', and amounted at times to 'mental torture'.[1] His one consolation was that as the second son of King George V, he was never going to inherit the throne and the relentless speeches and public broadcasts which that entailed. Then his elder brother, King Edward VIII, abdicated a mere eleven months into his reign.

As George's coronation approached, the Archbishop of Canterbury vetoed the suggestion of a live television broadcast, fearing that it might expose the muscular spasms in the King's cheeks and jaw as he struggled to pronounce a particular word. There was, however, the unavoidable issue of the live radio broadcast he would have to make from Buckingham Palace after the ceremony. The Archbishop noticed that although George's speech had greatly improved since he began treatment with his Australian therapist Lionel Logue, it was still far from fluent. He wrote to Lord Dawson, the King's physician, suggesting that they replace Logue with a new therapist, but Dawson dug in, arguing that any change would be merely unsettling.

George was already in a state of immense anxiety, asking rather desperately if the coronation speech could be pre-recorded with his stutter edited out, and then presented as if live. John Reith, the Director-General of the BBC, crushed the idea, suggesting rather archly that the King should decide himself 'whether the deception mattered'. Reith did, however, instruct Robert Wood, the engineer in charge of outside broadcasts, to deploy whatever technological means were available to assist the cause of fluency. Wood practised with the King, showing him how the amplification of the microphone meant he could speak more softly, rolling into words rather than coming at them hard.

In the final days before the coronation, the King, with the help of Logue, Reith and Wood, practised repeatedly. The speech was recorded and played back, and any words that proved problematic were removed. By the day itself, George was well prepared, and the speech – judged on how he read it more than the content – was deemed a triumph, in official circles at least. The press, which at the time was more deferential to royalty than it is today, reinforced this view: the King had become a great public speaker with a warm and strong voice. This remained the official line throughout the following years as war broke out, Britain's towns were ravaged by the Blitz, and the King repeatedly addressed the nation on the need to stand firm. It's the narrative that survives today due, in part, to the Oscar-winning film *The King's Speech* which shows George, supported by Logue, overcoming his impediment to become the people's King. However, thanks to contemporary diarists and sociologists, we know that the general public experienced these speeches rather differently.

'The King broadcast a speech last night which was badly spoken enough, I should have thought, to finish the Royal Family in this country,' wrote the poet Stephen Spender in 1939. 'It was a great mistake. He should never be allowed to say more than twenty words. His voice sounds like a very spasmodic often interrupted tape machine. It produces an effect of colourless monotony.'[2] The diplomat Harold Nicolson wrote that 'it is agony to listen to him – like a typewriter that sticks at every third word'. A more kindly account claims that one speech 'wasn't so bad'[3] but was still 'marred' by his stutter.

A striking example of the anxiety the King's stutter could cause, not only to himself but seemingly the entire nation, is provided by an investigator for Mass-Observation, a social research organisation whose mission was to record the everyday habits, concerns and speech of the British public. Investigations were carried out by mostly anonymous volunteers. An account by one particular woman brings to life a London pub on the evening of VE Day in 1945. While the enduring image of the victory celebrations is that of conga lines snaking round Eros in Piccadilly Circus, the atmosphere was reportedly much more subdued the moment you stepped a street or two away from city centres. While many people had spent the day at thanksgiving services or street parties, the overall mood suggested 'a dumb numbness of relief'[4] rather than joy. After all, the proclamation of victory had long been anticipated, but there was no end in sight to the prosaic realities of rationing and austerity. Lives were irreparably wrecked and all were affected in some way by the abstinence and sacrifices of war.

By nightfall, people were heading home or hunkering down in pubs for the final event of VE Day: a speech from the King. The pub our investigator went to, notebook in hand, was in Chelsea. It was packed full of people, many of whom were drunk, or simply trying to forget their wartime experiences through forced smiles and laughter.[5] The beer kegs were dry and only gin was available. At 9 p.m., the radio was turned on and the room became 'as hushed as a church' with several women at the back leaping to their feet and 'assuming reverent attitudes'. 'There is a sense that people have been waiting all this time for something symbolic,' our investigator wrote, 'and now they have got it.'

'Today we give thanks to Almighty God,' King George began, his voice echoing out through hundreds of thousands of radio sets across the land, 'for a great ...' And stopped. A brief moment passed, although it seemed an eternity. A young man in the Chelsea pub giggled. 'Deliverance,' the King said finally and moved on to the next sentence. He was but ten seconds into a thirteen minute address. The pauses and repetitions came thick and fast. The young man, probably drunk, began to impersonate the King's stutter, and became 'the centre of looks of intense malevolence from all corners of the room'. The worst moment came towards the end of the speech. 'Let us turn our thoughts', the King said, 'to this day of just …' He stopped again, tripping repeatedly on a 'T' sound. The investigator noted that 'several women's foreheads pucker and they wear a lacerated look'. 'T – t – t,' went the young man, giggling loudly. The King started the phrase again and had another run at it. 'Of just …' – and it worked – 'triumph and proud sorrow, and then take up our work again, resolved as a people to do nothing unworthy of those who died for us.' He finished his last words, the opening strains of the national anthem were played and everyone, except for a few Marxists, stood up to sing 'God Save the King'. One imagines nobody was more relieved than the King himself. It was inconceivable, as turned out to be the case, that he would ever give a speech of such import again.

George VI's stutter is one of the most widely known and oft-depicted examples of this most common of speech disorders. It highlights many of the mysteries associated with the condition; not least the enduring mystery of what causes it. Biographers have focused on his dysfunctional upbringing and how his rough, unloving father would bellow 'Get it out!' when the young prince got caught on his words. But these stories only explain how his stutter might have been exacerbated, not the root cause. There is the mystery too of how to cure or at least alleviate a stutter. George's relationship with his speech therapist was celebrated at the time, but most of Lionel Logue's techniques for fluent speech now have little currency and

– as contemporary diaries and memoirs reveal – they simply made the King's speech sound strange and hard to follow. Today there is still no undisputed cause or cure for stuttering, although there are theories and techniques which are as popular as Logue's once were.

But the biggest mystery is the one we rarely talk about: why it mattered so much at the time, as it still does, that the King of England should be – or at least appear to be – fluent; that his words should trip effortlessly from his mouth. On quick reflection, the answer might seem obvious. The monarch needs to be a good communicator, able to lead and inspire, particularly during wartime; and that this requires an ability to speak with power and eloquence. These are not qualities we generally associate with stuttering, but by all accounts George was able to express himself with warmth and directness in person. The fact that he stuttered did not interfere with his ability to form relationships, conduct the business of state and hold politicians to account. His problems with communication were exacerbated not so much when he stuttered as when he tried not to.

Imagine for a moment if George VI had broadcast the speeches he wanted to give in his own voice, rather than the one taught him by speech therapists and radio engineers. They would survive today full of stuttering repetitions, but also, I suspect, with the humanity that his friends found in him. They might be easier to follow because, although particular sounds might briefly be blocked or repeated, the cadences would match the meaning of the words he said. Instead, the pressure to hide his stutter meant he spoke through a veil of unnatural modulation.

Lionel Logue taught George to speak in small phrases – what he called 'three-word breaks' – so that he could pause before rolling into the next one. BBC engineer Robert Wood taught George a flattening 'tone formation and lip formation' to help him get his words into the microphone. The text of speeches was scrutinised, with problematic words replaced by synonyms. By the time George opened his mouth, every effort was focused on verbal tricks, which is why he sounds more like a 'tape machine' or 'typewriter' than a human being. His speeches were exercises in simulating fluency rather than hearts-and-minds rhetoric. Even today, they make for uncomfortable listening. Not only because this was a task he could never truly succeed in, but because in striving for fluency his performance was stripped of vigour and meaning.

George's speeches are a reminder that, although fluency and good communication often go together, they are not the same thing. There are those who have no trouble getting their words out, but fail to say anything convincing with them. And there are those who struggle with speech but still connect with a listener. Few would suggest that the scientist Stephen Hawking was a bad communicator, yet he spoke with a synthesised voice. I believe the reason why it was deemed so essential by the British state, the general public, and George himself, that the King should not stutter – even at the expense of his ability to deliver engaging speeches – lies not so much in the act of stuttering, but in the symbolic importance we attach to it.

Stuttering is widely considered a sign of both physiological and psychological dysfunction. According to that view, not only are people who stutter verbally incompetent, but the problem is exacerbated by childhood neuroses and insecurities. When we encounter a person who stutters, we seem to hear inner turmoil translated into sound. If that person is a stranger, it can feel like an unwanted exposure to somebody's deepest weaknesses. Our response, therefore, is often a combination of pity and repulsion, something which has been proven through repeated studies.[6] Stuttering is both a speech disorder and a social stigma.

But the symbolic potency of stuttering extends way beyond the unfavourable light it casts upon an individual. When a person stutters, the usual flow of speech and conversation is ruptured. This is challenging for us because we think of speech as the oil in the machinery of human society. Words enable us to communicate ideas, to decree laws, to share the secrets of the heart. Although email and social media have further empowered the written word as communication – much as letter writing did in the past – we still prioritise the spoken word for the things that matter. Only when our governments have debated and amended proposals do they become preserved in written law; political briefings describe what a public figure will say in an hour or a day's time, but remain speculative in the eyes of the media until the words have emerged from that person's mouth. In our private lives, we consider speech the appropriate mechanism for both the most joyous and confrontational moments of our lives. 'I love you' should be spoken first, and God forbid the person who tries to end a relationship by text message. A speech impediment like stuttering is more than a verbal handicap then, but an unwelcome blockage in the flow of life.

These negative perceptions are often unconscious, but they determine how we encounter people who stutter on the rare occasions that they are thrust upon us. In the case of George VI, this was magnified into a national concern. As King of the United Kingdom, the Dominions of the British Commonwealth and Emperor of India, George VI was the embodiment of the state. For him to be flawed in person suggested the State itself might be flawed – metaphorically at least. The fluency, or rather disfluency, of the King's speech became as symbolic of the nation's fate as the ravens in the Tower of London. No wonder the anxious, 'lacerated looks' across the country that accompanied every pause in his speeches, and the surges of relief when he pushed through to the next word.

George VI is one, admittedly exceptional, example of a person who stutters, just as stuttering itself is just one of many conditions that affect the human voice. Today, there are many who have what are called speech 'disorders' and spend their lives in fear of their own voices because of the accompanying stigma. We know such disorders exist, but what is rarely appreciated is just how widespread they are.

Statistically, well over a million people in the UK are deemed pathologically non-fluent in verbal speech. The Royal College of Speech and Language Therapists puts the number of children who have some form of speech and language impairment as high as 9 per cent and claims that 20 per cent of the population has some form of communication difficulty at some point in their lives.[7] They may have a stutter; the linguistic impairment of aphasia following a stroke; the coprolalia (swearing) of Tourette's syndrome; the dysarthria of speech associated with cerebral palsy and Parkinson's disease or the distorted voices of dysphonia. All conditions that would have sent the Archbishop of Canterbury in George VI's day into a spin.

The sheer number means that all of us in some way live with a diagnosable disorder, either because we have a condition ourselves or because someone in our family and wider social network does. How we engage with those who have a disorder – whether as a parent, friend or colleague – can dramatically affect their quality of life. Yet these are conditions we often have little understanding of, even when they disturb our own speech. One reason for this is that fluency is considered not just normal, but a necessity. Speech disorders are to be hidden rather than understood. Unfortunately, this all too often leads to exclusion and discrimination because they are, for the most part, not conditions which go away.

This is something I have a personal stake in, both as a person who stutters but also as part of an extended family that does so. That there are several of us is not unusual, for there is strong evidence that stuttering is a hereditary condition. My mother passed it on to me, just as my wife inherited it from her father. In fact, my struggles with speech and language go beyond stuttering. I had developmental delay in my speech as a child, and in my teens was diagnosed with both cluttering and dyslexia. But stuttering is the condition that defined me most. I am unable to separate it from my identity because it was always there, submerged but palpable in the murky half-memories of my childhood, and still present in the hidden blocks and word substitutions of my apparently fluent speech today.

When I enquire of my mother when it started, she

tells me she knew something was awry not long after my second birthday. While most infants chatter adoringly at this stage, stringing together short sentences, I was stubbornly mute. Eventually, she took me to see the famous paediatrician Hugh Jolly, who bounced me around a little, looked inside my mouth, and concluded that I was merely lazy. When I did finally deign to speak, coming on for three years old, a whole sentence fell out and they kept coming. But the words began to get stuck too. I have early memories of being stunned as relatively simple words like 'where' or 'when' disintegrated into a string of bizarre wah-wah sounds; the looks of mild concern on the faces of adults; and, inevitably, the look of indulgent malevolence on my sister's face at the discovery that her imposter younger brother was so wonderfully malfunctioning.

My awareness of having a problem was at first far greater than any trouble it actually caused me. It was something I experienced through the reactions of other people more than the mild inconvenience of sometimes not being able to get words out. I spent fifteen years in and out of speech therapy: from one-on-one sessions with a speech-language pathologist to a two-week bootcamp for chronic sufferers at the Michael Palin Centre for Stammering Children. My mother was a features writer and so my progress was tracked through a string of articles for *Good Housekeeping* and the *Guardian*, generally accompanied by a picture of me with bowl haircut, toothy grin and NHS specs. 'How My Son Lost the Edge of My Wretched Tongue', ran one headline in February 1991 with the byline: 'Anne Woodham on her family's battle against a stuttering blight'.

My anxiety about stuttering grew until it became a defining feature of my life. I put a great deal of energy into avoiding words or situations which might expose me. I was so scared of being bullied I would sometimes pretend to forget my own name when called upon to say it aloud in class. On my first day at university, I slipped a letter under my professor's door begging to be excused any group reading or recital exercises that might be required while completing a degree in English Literature. I so desperately wanted university to be an end rather than an extension of the humiliations of school.

At the same time, only those I was closest to knew my secret for I had developed a rapid-fire way of speaking, pivoting around difficult words or phrases and substituting or paraphrasing with others in a manner which passed for quick-wittedness. After leaving university, I was drawn to broadcast, film and theatre, but carefully built a career for myself behind the scenes. The people I work with are often hyper-fluent: breathtakingly articulate, brilliant performers, able to speak off-the-cuff on myriad subjects. I wonder if, without even knowing it, I became a linguistic groupie, hovering around people who speak in a way I never dared believe I might be able to imitate.

Over the years, my stutter and I reached an uneasy truce: as long as I didn't cross agreed parameters, it would leave me more or less alone. But in my early thirties it inexplicably worsened again. A speech therapy course lasting several months at London's City Lit Adult Education College resulted in a level of fluency I had never known before. Having some emotional distance was a relief, but I also found myself floundering. After so much time digging at the roots of my speech, I didn't know what to focus on and so I tried to make sense of everything I had gone through.

Ever since the age of five or six, I had been locked in a cycle of mitigating tactics to try and conceal my stutter, while discreetly and with a few trusted elders exploring what might be causing it and how it might be cured. Most books on the subject are what I consider cause-and-cure self-help manuals that look at a condition not only in isolation from others, but from fluent speech in general. I saw stuttering, incorrectly, as my unique stigma and could count on one hand the number of times I had encountered it outside of speech therapy. But increasingly I was aware of how prevalent it is. Many people who stutter are closeted or 'interiorised', going to great lengths to hide their condition because they believe it will prove detrimental to their careers as well as their social and romantic lives. And I became aware of other people who in their own way, whether with diagnosable conditions or in an uncategorised void, were struggling with speech. Looking back, it astonishes me how my most worrisome preoccupation was also the one I was most ignorant about. In my desperation to cure or hide it, I never had the courage to bring it into the light and decide for myself what it means to stutter. Ten years ago, I set out to do just this.

This is a book about what happens when speech breaks down, and why we are so afraid of it. It is about the disfluencies that impact all of our lives and their relationship with the prized but elusive state of fluency we hold so dear. It is both a scientific and cultural study. It has to be. While it is now widely accepted that most speech disorders are neurological in origin, they are highly attuned to social and cultural context. In some cases, as with stuttering and the vocal tics of Tourette's syndrome, they intensify or alleviate depending on where the individual is and who else is in the room. Other conditions like aphasia and dysarthria are diagnosed not only according to the symptoms of the subject, but by how intelligible that person is deemed by society. For this reason, I have not attempted a definitive survey but focused instead on the psychological and cultural significance of speech disorders as a whole, focusing on those I am most familiar with, rather than anatomising them all.

The sheer prevalence of speech disorders makes them a concern for everyone, but so do the wider truths they reveal about how we all experience language. While many of us have a diagnosable condition at some point in our lives, there are plenty of others who feel some degree of inadequacy about their speech. Not only do we often struggle to find the right words, but – amid the umming and ahing – sometimes struggle to get them out too. The fear of public speaking is in part a fear of falling on the wrong side of some invisible divide separating ourselves from a charismatic and fluent elite; no wonder it is one of the most widespread of recurring nightmares. Those with diagnosable speech conditions sit on the front line of these anxieties. The intensity of their experiences can provide invaluable insights not only into how the rest of us feel, but into language itself: the hold it has over us, the way it perplexes and torments as much as it clarifies and connects.

I believe that rather than merely tolerating speech

disorders, we need to celebrate them because of the diversity and innovation they bring to human thought and language. Despite first appearances, those who struggle with speech tend, out of necessity, to be linguistic virtuosos. People who stutter develop vast vocabularies of synonyms to replace troublesome words. Those with articulation difficulties choose their words more carefully, for each one is a precious commodity requiring more deliberation than the rest of us put into entire sentences. In finding themselves lost for certain words, people with aphasia learn to contort new meanings and combinations out of those they can recall. For the individual with vocal tics, this linguistic virtuosity is often beyond control, but no less remarkable for it.

Living with these disorders requires summoning a level of linguistic creativity each day that most of us experience only occasionally, if ever. In the right hands, such creativity becomes art. A strikingly disproportionate number of our greatest artists were and are people who have pathologically struggled with speech. Writers like Lewis Carroll, Henry James, Elizabeth Bowen and Christy Brown; philosophers Ludwig Wittgenstein and Stephen Hawking; actors Samuel L. Jackson, Nicole Kidman and Marilyn Monroe; songwriters Edwyn Collins, Kendrick Lamar, Carly Simon and Bill Withers; and political orators and visionaries Aneurin Bevan and Greta Thunberg. All of them are people who have a remarkable ability with language which I believe must, on some level, be connected to their struggles with it.

Through charting the stories of such individuals, we learn not only to appreciate speech disorders but also to look differently at the unquestioning reverence we have for fluency in our culture. Although many effective speakers are blessed with a 'smooth tongue' or 'the gift of the gab', this is not essential for good communication and can even be antithetical to it. Fluency deconstructed is often little more than a string of interconnecting clichés and figures of speech with relatively little content, that may even conceal untruths and manipulative lies – much like the 'fake news' we hear so much about today. Sociological studies continually show that much, or even most, communication between humans is non-verbal: gestures, tone of voice and body language.[8] Our speech is often little more than a cover or pretext for the far more primal yet elaborate exchanges going on beneath. This doesn't mean that language isn't important to us – it is, particularly when trying to articulate abstract emotions or ideas – but the way we use it has far more to do with conforming to social expectations than translating our deepest and most complicated thoughts into words.

In the first half of this book, I provide an overview of some of the most common speech disorders: not only their physical symptoms, but also the psychological impact they have on an individual, and the stigma they carry. (This is not as simple as it sounds as definitions and diagnoses continue to vary.) The point is to show how much those with such conditions have in common, and the benefits that come from thinking about speech disorders as a group.

The following chapters describe the role of culture in determining our attitudes to both disfluency and fluency. I introduce the notion of 'hyper-fluency' to describe the expectations that twenty-first-century communications and labour markets – from social media to gig economics – place on us to appear fluent at all times. Through emphasising the cultural perception of speech disorders, I aim to show that there is nothing objectively 'bad' about them; we have just learned to see them as deficiencies. Nothing reveals this more than the strange and barbaric story of their diagnosis and treatment over the last 150 years, which I follow with a cautionary reminder about how little we still know today. From there, I abandon the search for a cause and cure of speech disorders as (mostly) futile and propose a different way of thinking about them.

Neurodiversity is a concept which emerged in the late 1990s and looks at a wide range of conditions not as diseases but simply as forms of human difference that have unrecognised positive qualities as well as the much documented negative ones. It is rarely applied to neurological disorders of speech, however; an oversight which the second half of the book tries to address. I argue that speech disorders embody a set of traits that often result in better rather than worse communication, greater rather than diminished productivity, and play an important role in challenging some of the prejudices and errors of language as experienced by a fluent mainstream. Neurodiversity is significant because it presents the best opportunity to date of improving the experience of the many millions alive today who struggle pathologically with speech.

Mindful that many with speech disorders struggle to be heard – both metaphorically and literally – I refer to written accounts or the dozens of interviews I have conducted wherever possible. While some of the arguments that follow diverge from the dominant views of speech-language therapy, I hope none of them detract from a profession and body of knowledge that has ultimately had more impact in diagnosing and alleviating the suffering of those with speech disorders than medical science has. It is rarely acknowledged that the practice of listening to patients – not only literally, in terms of monitoring their speech, but also responding to their emotional and psychological state of mind – owes more to speech-language therapy as a discipline than psychotherapy, although it is rarely credited for it.

Finally, a note on terms: while there are those who increasingly talk about speech 'differences', I continue to use 'disorder'. This is because it will be more familiar to most readers and because it may well be retained and rehabilitated by those with such conditions in the same way that the term 'disabled' has. While everybody experiences some 'disfluency' of speech, the term here mostly refers to those pathological conditions where such interruptions become compulsive, problematic and ultimately diagnosable for an individual. I distinguish therefore between 'a disfluency' and 'everyday disfluencies'. In keeping with current practice, I talk about 'people with' stutters, aphasia and tics rather than 'stutterers', 'aphasics' and 'tourettics' – it may be cumbersome, but it is a small price for acknowledging that a speech disorder is a trait rather than the essence of a human being.

I began writing this book partly to alleviate the shame and fear I had about stuttering, but also as a call-to-arms for those who have experienced speech disorders to speak out – in their own voices – about the creativity and productivity, as well as the lows and frustrations, of disfluency. Only this way can we address what most needs to change: not an individual's speech, but the way society thinks about it.

In all of what follows, I have one very simple argument to make: what are generally referred to as 'speech disorders' are simply forms of vocal and linguistic diversity. Despite appalling stigmatisation, they still manage to enrich our language, our ideas and art forms. They forge stronger and more meaningful forms of communication between human beings. Just think what might be possible if we stop resisting and embrace them.

1

Maladies of Speech

It is the late 1940s and Kenya is under British rule. In a family compound some twenty miles outside of Nairobi, A young boy who will become known to the world as Ngũgĩ wa Thiong'o grows up among his four mothers and many siblings. At home he speaks Gikuyu, a Bantu language spoken by barely a quarter of the Kenyan population. But when he passes through the school gates, he is required to speak the language of the colonial authorities. Children caught speaking Gikuyu are often compelled to wear a placard saying 'I am stupid' around their necks.

Already Ngũgĩ is aware that speech is far more than an enabler of communication; it is also subject to dangerous prejudices and manipulations. He knows that some ways of speaking are considered superior to others, and that the enforcement of the English language is central to the subjugation of the Gikuyu people. It is enlisted in what he will later describe as 'mental colonisation'. Alongside such weaponisation of speech, he knows something else too: that the human voice often goes awry in unpredictable ways beyond anyone's comprehension.

'I grew up with stuttering in the family,' Ngũgĩ tells me, out of the blue. We are sitting in a rented apartment overlooking the Grand Canal in Venice on a wet, winter's day; a far cry both in time and place from his childhood home. As Kenya's most famous living writer, his life is a semi-nomadic one of lecture tours and residencies. Finding the opportunity to meet him is a question of getting a ticket to whatever city he happens to be in. For someone like me who is fascinated by the way language is both used and abused the trip is worth it.

Ngũgĩ has thought about this subject, and borne the brunt of its realities, as much as anyone alive. In the late 1970s, he even spent a year in prison, illegally detained by the Kenyan government, because of his decision to write a play in his native tongue, something perceived as a threat to a regime that promoted English and Swahili as its proper languages. There is something in the way Ngũgĩ has repeatedly described the marginalisation of minority languages that resonates for me with the way speech disorders are treated in our society. We have talked for almost two hours, but this intimate recollection of stuttering in the family compound comes as a surprise.

'I had four mothers and one father,' he continues. 'The senior mother had two kids, older than me. My brother Gitogo had a defect of speech. He could utter one word occasionally, but he always struggled to get the word out so mostly he spoke through gestures.' As a consequence, Gitogo wasn't deemed much use for anything at all. But Ngũgĩ loved him and was devastated when Gitogo was shot in the back by British soldiers who assumed, incorrectly, that this strange young man was a militant in the Mau Mau independence movement. Ngũgĩ was still a boy and the murder of Gitogo shaped him indelibly. Although he himself did not have a speech disorder, there was something in Gitogo's struggle with a language that was, in any case, marginalised, that made Ngũgĩ fascinated in the way speech functions and dysfunctions in human society.

Such a fate – face down in the dust, his life bleeding out of him – could easily have come to Ngũgĩ, as it did to so many other young Kenyans, but he was saved by his talent. While Gitogo had struggled to speak at all, Ngũgĩ mastered not only his people's language but the tongue of his masters too. This was critical: proficiency in any academic subject came secondary to the imperative of language. You could be a genius at maths or science, but without fluent English higher education was out of reach. Ngũgĩ's linguistic dexterity earned him a place at Makerere University in Kampala. His first English-language novel, *Weep Not Child* (1964), published when he was only twenty-six, brought him fame and the opportunity to escape the bloodshed at home.

Ngũgĩ never forgot the endless humiliations of his childhood. Their shadow and the fate of his brother Gitogo hang over his writing, in which the experience of inarticulation and repression are always combined. For fifty years his novels charted the changing fortunes of Kenya under British rule, the early hopefulness of independence, and the oppressive dictatorships that followed, but his characters – always pawns at the hands of indomitable forces – struggle to get their words out.[1]

Wizard of the Crow (2006), his late career masterpiece, is set in a fictional version of modern Kenya, rife with corruption and personal insecurity. Slowly a disorder takes over the land in which people are unable to speak.

It begins when they try to articulate their deepest desire with the words 'if' and 'if only'. The wizard of the book's title, a sort of accidental witch-doctor, gives his prognosis: 'There is a strange illness in the land. It is a malady of words; thoughts get stuck inside a person. You have seen stutterers, haven't you? Their stammer is a result of a sudden surge of thoughts, or calculations, or worry.' This malady of words proves contagious, affecting many hundreds of thousands including the corrupt President himself, and only alleviates when society itself begins to change for the better.

Ngũgĩ's image of a malady of words seems fantastical at first, but is less so when one remembers the overwhelming number of people who have speech disorders in real life. It reminds us too that despite the different diagnoses and complicated terms we use, they all serve to exclude such individuals from whole areas of human discourse; not only the affairs of the state and public life, but those of the heart too. And it reminds us that such disorders will only be 'cured' not when the afflicted individual changes, but when our discriminating society is willing to accommodate them.

All these are important observations to keep in mind as we chart the ways speech disorders are experienced in our society today. As is the central theme of Ngũgĩ's life and work: speech, whether 'fluent' or 'disfluent', is never just about communication, but power and subjugation. It is a source of prejudice and inequality. What is at stake goes far beyond day-to-day humiliation; it determines the potential of an individual's life.

Although statistics tell us that hundreds of millions

across the world experience a diagnosable speech disorder at some point in their lives, it is not immediately clear how many such conditions there are, nor indeed what separates 'disordered' from 'normal' speech. Addressing these questions is a necessary first step in any enquiry into the ways in which speech breaks down. After all, most of us encounter some problems with our speech, whether the perennial challenges of turning abstract thought into spoken word, or the passing hesitations, stumbles, malapropisms and blockages that are present in even the most fluent speaker.

These are usually mere hiccups. We are hardly aware of them at all, or, when they do pass through our consciousness, it may be as a passing irritant rather than a recurring problem. But then there are those for whom the process of speaking the words they have in mind is a consistent battle. Since their intelligence is unimpaired, the consciousness of a recurrent breakdown between thought and speech is intensely frustrating. It can feel like taking a step forwards only to find your leg doesn't move. And it is in such consistently bumpy or obstructed linguistic territory that we may identify a disorder.

There are many different types of speech disorder, but all of them share a single quality: the consistent and obtrusive struggle in communicating the words you want to say. Whatever the cause, whatever the symptom, the emotional impact on a life can be devastating. Often speech disorders are experienced alongside, or in consequence of, other conditions like cerebral palsy, stroke or motor neurone disease. One of the 'purest' in this regard, while also the most widespread and enigmatic, is my own condition: stuttering.

It is said that five per cent of children stutter at some point, while one per cent of the adult population continues to do so.[2] If that sounds small, we need only consider that it amounts to nearly 700,000 people in the United Kingdom, over three million in the United States and seventy million globally. In most cases we do not know the cause, although it is increasingly considered a neurological condition, something to do with the wiring of the brain, that affects speech. While it seems simple enough to those who don't experience it – it's the jack-hammering speech of popular caricatures like Porky Pig or Ronnie Barker in *Open All Hours* – for those who do, it covers a vast range of vocal dysfunctions.

Although the parameters of the term have changed, with different types of non-fluency creeping in and out, one well-regarded definition is that of American speech therapist Marcel Wingate. Stuttering, he wrote, is a 'disruption in the fluency of verbal expression, which is characterised by involuntary, audible or silent, repetitions or prolongations in the utterance of short speech elements ... These disruptions usually occur frequently or are marked in character and not readily controllable.'[3] This is a specific, unified definition, but there are also those experts, like linguist David Crystal, who identify 'stuttering' as a catch-all word to cover several kinds of non-fluency, each of which can vary considerably from speaker to speaker.[4]

Although the dominant characteristic is a physical struggle to get words out, no two people experience this in quite the same way. The most widely recognised symptom is the unnatural repetition of sounds, which writers tend to homogenise into a c-c-c-cliché of written form. Then there's the abnormal prolongation of sounds that seem to get trapped in the speaker's mouth. And then the silent block, where no sound comes out at all. There is no universal pattern for sounds more likely to cause obstruction. For some, plosives (like *p*, *d*, *g* and *b*) are particularly problematic, others struggle with fricatives (like *f* and *th*) or elongate vowels. Many experience stuttering as a pot pourri of all three. I have met one person who fears 'Rs and Ls', another who dreads 'K' and 'T' sounds, and another for whom it is 'M', 'W' and 'L'.

While one speaker's experience of stuttering is different from another's, an individual's own symptoms are equally inconsistent. From moment to moment, day to day, behaviour can vary wildly. People who stutter are frequently taken by surprise and if they sometimes look startled in the act it is because they are. Even the most reliable of sounds can prove false friends. This variability is reflected in the range of terms we have for it. Although some people insist on a distinction, 'stuttering' is entirely interchangeable with the word 'stammering'. Americans tend to use the former; British the latter (I use 'stutter' simply out of choice, because its repeated 'Ts' seem more suggestive). There are other words too: 'psellism' and 'dysphemia' are both medical terms; and there are obsolete Shakespearean words like 'mammering' and the prim Victorian euphemism of 'hesitancy'.

These days a distinction is drawn between stuttering and 'cluttering'. Rather than involving excessive breaks in speech, cluttering results from disorganised speech planning. Individuals speak too fast or in spurts which collapse into incomprehension. When I was a child, the therapists at the Michael Palin Centre for Stammering Children measured both the speed and flow of my speech and concluded I cluttered as well as stuttered. My speech would race along then fold into itself leaving me babbling and gasping. I experienced both stuttering and cluttering as different sides of the same disorder and found it hard to distinguish between them except by the sounds they made.

Quite understandably, and at the risk of tautology, there is a tendency to think of people who stutter as people who stutter. But many adults like me had traumatic experiences at school and our disorder became covert or 'interiorised'. You will probably know some of us without being aware of it. We can speak in a slow, incredibly considered and therefore slightly infuriating way, because we are using a great deal of energy and mindfulness to avoid stuttering. Or we might create long pauses at the wrong moments in our speech; not after making some clever or amusing point but simply mid-sentence or even mid-word. We may appear rather inarticulate, choosing unusual phrases and long, circumlocutory sentences to make quite simple points. I consider these to be vocal symptoms of stuttering just as much as the stutter itself.

For some, a stutter is a disability, narrowing access to vast areas of human experience – whether jobs, relationships or vocational fulfilment. For many others, like me, it is a concern but a manageable one that can be mitigated and even entirely concealed through word substitution and voice modification techniques. Then there are those who rarely get through a sentence without getting stuck, but are fluent when speaking a foreign language. When Cardinal Villeneuve encountered George VI in Quebec, he was struck by the way the King stuttered when delivering his speech in English, but was fluent when he repeated it in French.[5] Sometimes a mere change in accent can be enough. When I spoke to the Irish novelist Colm Tóibín about his stutter, he recalled knowing 'a man in rural Ireland who spoke with a posh accent because when he spoke posh he didn't stammer'.

Many find they can speak without a hitch if on their own at home; the problem arises once another person is involved. And there are actors and singers who stutter off-stage but become fluency itself when performing: Rowan Atkinson, Bruce Willis and Emily Blunt are famous examples. It is said Marilyn Monroe developed her distinctive whispery voice not as a technique for seduction but just for getting the words out, and built a career out of it. One theory is that when performing we use different parts of the brain, particularly our memory faculties, compared to when we're engaged in spontaneous conversation. In other words, if stuttering really is something to do with the wiring in the brain, then performance may rewire it – if only for a short duration.

This waxing and waning is one of the most perplexing aspects of stuttering. After all, many disabilities aren't quite so context-dependent, disappearing or re-appearing according to the type of activity the speaker is participating in. Through the Michael Palin Centre for Stammering Children, whose courses I attended as a child, I met British actor Oliver Dimsdale, who has appeared in such popular shows as *Father Brown* and *Downton Abbey.* Oliver is one of those who stammers in person but never on stage or on screen. He tells me how debilitating his stammer was ('cripplingly bad') throughout childhood until, at the age of thirteen, he discovered acting.

In conversation, Oliver's stutter is discernible, but within seconds he can conceal it. 'I sit down,' he says, suddenly speaking slowly, evenly and with regular pauses. 'I get to the core of my breath. I'm looking around the room. I look people in the eyes. I'm taking my time. And when I have an impulse to say whatever it is I have to say next, I could probably talk for hours and hours and not stammer.'

This self-conscious manner of speaking is similar to the process of rehearsing and ultimately performing a part; a process in which Oliver's speech becomes more fluent as the role develops. 'When you know exactly the sentences, the breath and the moves you're going to make – and you're in it, going from moment to moment – you have the freedom to forget you are a person who stammers. You are you, imagining yourself inside the words, inside the head, of another person. I find the fluency inside me for whatever character I'm playing.' I ask him why he doesn't do this the whole time. 'Because it's a bit more exhausting, actually,' he says, his stammer suddenly reappearing. 'There's so many layers of stress that come with auditioning, presentations and teaching, so I'd much rather feel that I was being completely myself in my day-to-day life rather than trying to come across as someone who is fluent all the time, even to my wife and kids.'

Another strange characteristic of stuttering is its

gender bias. Characters in films and popular media who stutter are almost always male, and there's good enough reason for this: throughout the world, there are around four or five times as many men as women who stutter. Nobody knows why. Carolyn Cheasman runs the revered speech therapy department at City Lit in London and is one of the leading therapists in the UK. She is also a person who stutters. When I ask her to explain this gender imbalance, she insists there are no facts, only theories, but they are intriguing nonetheless.

One theory draws a link with the way infant boys tend to lag behind girls in speech development. So while girls are better able to express their thoughts with words, boys struggle to do so. Since stuttering tends to emerge between the ages of three and six, at precisely the moment when the developmental gap between boys and girls is at its greatest, there could be some connection between the two phenomena; as if stuttering is caused in part by a lag between a child's conception of relatively sophisticated thoughts and feelings, and their ability to express them.

But Cheasman has another theory, based on her own experience, which is that females might be better, or more determined, to hide a stutter. One of the courses she runs, which I attended in my early thirties, focuses on interiorised stammering for those individuals who construct their speech and lives around concealing their impediment. More women take this course than any of the others. Is it possible that because of certain societal pressures – the expectation to be a certain way – women may be going the extra distance to conceal their struggle with speech? Men, on the other hand, whether for physiological or cultural reasons, seem less willing or less able to conceal it.

People with interiorised stutters can often pass as fluent, although we sometimes spot the tell-tale characteristics of word substitution or speech modification in one another. Sarah is an arts administrator in Manchester who I met through work. One evening, protected by the roar and noise of an industry dinner, we began to swap notes. Like me, she is in her forties and still constructs her professional life around concealing her stutter; avoiding not only words, but certain types of meeting or presentation. I ask her in what ways her experience as a woman might be different from that of men. To my surprise, she has found that stuttering is linked to her menstrual cycle. She can pinpoint almost to the day when her speech is likely to be most fluent or disfluent. As a result, she has long been in the habit of consulting her cycle before scheduling public speaking engagements.

With so many variables and unknowns, stuttering remains a mystery. Uri Schneider, a prominent American speech therapist who runs a large practice treating different disorders in several cities around the world, describes it to me as 'the most enigmatic of speech conditions. If somebody has cerebral palsy and dyspraxia,' he says, 'they don't wake up one day with one type of speech and another day with a different kind of speech. It's a consistent issue. Same with learning disabilities. But stuttering has that erratic, unpredictable quality to it.'

Stuttering is an enigma then. Always has been and perhaps always will be. But I would argue that there is one condition, which, while not in itself a speech disorder, often results in disordered speech and is scarcely less enigmatic or unpredictable than stuttering. It takes its name from the French physician Gilles de la Tourette who first argued in the 1880s that in certain cases motor and vocal tics were not signs of some other condition, but amounted to one in its own right: *La maladie de tics de Gilles de La Tourette,* as it became known.

These tics include involuntary movement of different parts of the body as well as uncontrollable sounds and speech. One of the speech disorders we associate with Tourette's is coprolalia, or the involuntary and repetitive use of obscene language. Although it affects only about one in ten people who have Tourette's,[6] it has become a defining feature because of media and public fascination. Other Tourettic speech disorders include echolalia, which is the repetition of one's own or others' words or phrases; and palilalia, in which a person repeats their own words. Many others with Tourette's find their words are unaffected, but they are interspersed with barks, grunts, yelps and coughs. Once considered extremely rare, it is now thought that Tourette's syndrome – with or without its accompanying speech disorders – affects about one per cent of the population at some point in their lives.[7]

Jess Thom is a performing artist with Tourette's with whom I have collaborated on a couple of television programmes over the past few years. Like stuttering, Tourette's often begins in childhood and alleviates as people grow older, but it is more part of Jess's life in her thirties than ever. Because her motor tics affect her limbs, she uses a wheelchair and other aids to help her through the day. Since people who tic are often treated as exotic curiosities by the public, I asked what the experience is like for her. 'My tics have a physical sensation attached to them,' she says. 'It's often described by doctors as a "premonitory urge", but that doesn't really describe what that feeling is for me. I feel it like itching powder in my blood or the sudden experience of being tugged in a particular direction.'

Vocal tics are influenced by social context. While they can be random, they can also give voice to the unsayable – manifesting as personal insults as well as swear words – in a way that is deeply distressing for anyone implicated in what has been said, but also for the person with Tourette's who may not even share the sentiment coming out of their own mouth. Most tics are not personally insulting, but they can be disruptive in other ways: subversive, surreal, even amusing. 'People think saying "fuck" in the fruit aisle is funny,' Jess says, reflecting on one popular stereotype, 'but that's nothing on the reality of living with Tourette's. I am the one who's being an involuntary Sat Nav while my friends are playing Mario Kart [a racing simulator game] or who's explaining to airport security that there's not really a bomb – or a springer spaniel – in my bag.' Gradually, Jess has come to think of her tics as creative as well as distracting and incorporates them into her stage shows.

There are many intriguing similarities between Tourette's and stuttering, in which I have a personal interest. As well as stuttering, I have experienced motor tics in my face and body all my life – nose twitching, repetitive blinking and sniffing – which I endeavour to conceal throughout the day. While I have never sought diagnosis, the experience of a premonitory urge is deeply familiar to me, and it is not dissimilar to the sensation of an approaching vocal block. I'm struck by the fact that both conditions have elusive origins or causes. Only since the 1990s has there been a growing consensus that they are inherited neurological conditions, suggesting some sort of dysfunction in neural connections. MRI scans show differences in the make-up of the brains of people who stutter or tic: signs of disturbance or 'dodgy wiring', as one neurologist described it to me, which are not there in fluent speakers.

Both are conditions which emerge in childhood, they are around four times more prevalent in males, and in many cases wane after adolescence. And both are dramatically inconsistent and shift according to social context; symptoms come and go for no apparent reason and may disappear altogether. In the same way that a person who stutters can be fluent when performing or speaking a foreign language or on their own, those with Tourette's can often hold tics in reserve then 'release' them later. In one case study, the neurologist and writer Oliver Sacks described a Canadian surgeon who could suspend his tics for long periods of time while performing operations or flying his private airplane.[8]

Like stuttering, tics come and go, affecting people differently day-to-day and over the course of their lives. This dramatic variability in symptoms goes some way to explaining why stuttering and Tourette's have historically struggled to be recognised as neurological disabilities. Such inconsistencies have allowed observers to conclude an element of 'putting it on' as if variability implies voluntariness. Yet it is precisely this variability that renders them so distressing to the individual. Daily life is imbued with an unpredictability that can prove both physically and mentally exhausting, never quite knowing where the boundaries of one's capabilities lie, and always wondering if just a little more effort might enable one to pass as 'normal'.

The coprolalia, echolalia and palilalia of Tourette's syndrome refer to an excess of language. Aphasia, on the other hand, refers to a decline in linguistic ability, affecting speech as well as reading and writing. It is most commonly associated with stroke victims who struggle to speak or whose words are jumbled up. So while stuttering and Tourette's are inherent to an individual, quickly emerging as a child reaches speaking age, aphasia is something that – for the most part – happens to you. It is acquired rather than innate to an individual. It is generally a symptom or consequence of another condition and therefore accompanied by other symptoms: for instance, a stroke victim with aphasia will often have some degree of physical paralysis from the same primary cause. Determining the number of people who have aphasia is therefore a bit of a totting-up exercise, but it has been estimated to affect around a quarter of a million people in the UK.[9]

Like so many names in the world of speech disorders, aphasia is a bit of a catch-all term and there is continuing inconsistency in where the barriers are drawn. Some neurologists believe 'aphasia' should be reserved for linguistic impairments caused by damage to the left hemisphere of the brain; others that it should include damage to the right hemisphere; and others that it should include language impairments caused by dementia and other progressive conditions. When British neurologist Henry Head gathered his case studies of aphasia in soldiers returning from the trenches of the First World War, it was the lack of a general pattern that struck him most of all. 'No two examples of aphasia exactly resemble one another,' he wrote. 'Each represents the response of a particular individual to the abnormal conditions.'[10]

Even the term 'aphasia' covers a wide range of different symptoms, each with their own name.[11] There is *anomia*, which describes a difficulty in recalling the words for everyday objects. There is *paraphasia,* where words which have some logical connection or similarity are confused, like saying 'knife' for 'fork' or 'night' for 'light'. There is *jargonaphasia*, where paraphasia becomes unintelligible: a sentence may make perfect sense to the speaker but comes across as peculiar jargon to the listener. And there is *agrammatism*, where the syntax of speech becomes affected or scrambled, like saying 'I to the house go' rather than 'I go to the house', or is diminished, as in 'house go'.

Aphasia is often accompanied by *apraxia of speech* when a person may know what they want to say but the mouth is unable to perform the task as required. They may say a completely different word or make one up. The tongue and lips may 'grope' to say a word that would once have emerged automatically. While speech-language therapists stress the difference, they are often inseparable. A person with aphasia may both struggle to find the words, then having found them, struggle to get them out. In some cases, people with aphasia also experience stuttering. This sort of stuttering is often called 'neurogenic' or 'acquired' stuttering and, unlike most other forms of stuttering, normally has a clear cause in the underlying stroke, head injury or tumour that brought it on.

Although aphasia generally accompanies other symptoms, including localised paralysis in the arm or leg, people often describe it as far worse than physical immobility because it impedes their ability to communicate. By nature it is something more often described by physicians or family members than by the individuals themselves, something which a few books like *Jumbly Words, and Rights Where Wrongs Should Be: The Experience of Aphasia from the Inside* have tried to rectify. 'Thoughts are clear as bells,' says one individual, 'but come out so muffled and jangled.' 'New words form,' says another, 'lazy words marry each other and the gaps go on.'[12]

The range of severity in aphasia is even greater than with stuttering. 'The individual with mild aphasia may experience only minor problems such as hesitancy in word-finding, or difficulty following a group discussion,' writes speech therapist Gill Edelman. 'In severe cases, unable to understand what is said, to utter more than a few meaningless sounds, or to read or write, the individual may be locked into a private world where normal communication is impossible.'[13] Because it normally occurs later in a person's life it can also be the most debilitating of speech disorders. If you grow up with a stutter, both your personality and relationship with language is indelibly shaped by the experience. Idiosyncratic techniques for managing it are developed over a long time. Aphasia, however, comes out of the blue, ripping away abilities one has always taken for granted.

Fortunately, after the original shock, many with aphasia find the condition improves and they relearn some of their capacity for speech. In *The Word Escapes Me: Voices of Aphasia*,[14] an American woman called Yvonne describes how her aphasia appeared in advance of her stroke. After hopping onto a treadmill at her gym, she tried to make some friendly comment to the person beside her, but her voice came out slurred and garbled. Then she collapsed. As people from across the gym gathered around her, she opened her mouth to speak but no words came. Then she slipped into a coma. 'I was unable to communicate in words,' she recalled, 'I was rendered infant-like again – literally speechless, helpless.' During the long months of rehabilitation, she learned to walk again, although with a limp, and her speech began to return. But recovery was only partial. 'When I try to speak, I'm outed as having trouble talking. "Ss" become "Shs", "single" becomes "shingle", "spell" becomes "smell", and so forth.'

For many with aphasia, this rehabilitation is incredibly slow and arduous. Few ever recover the capacity for speech they previously enjoyed. Since language is central to how we think and express ourselves, this transformation can be experienced as a fundamental change in personality. This is often, but not always, described in negative terms. But while many talk about the overwhelming frustration and even anger, particularly in the early stages, others (admittedly, a minority) describe a necessary reassessing of priorities and values, a sense of enhanced empathy and eventual peace of mind.

The fourth, and last, of the most common speech disorders is dysarthria. However, it is not a word people use much. Even more than aphasia, it is often one symptom among many of an underlying condition. The term describes the distorted articulation, the slurred or slow speech, of those with cerebral palsy, muscular dystrophy, Parkinson's disease and any other condition which causes damage to the nerves or muscles involved in speaking. It can also include stuttering-like symptoms. Understanding someone with dysarthria can be difficult and, as a result, intelligibility is one of the key indicators in determining an assessment. Because of the wide range of causes, we do not know exactly how many people have dysarthria, although if one considers that Parkinson's is thought to affect 127,000 people in the UK,[15] while around 166,000 have cerebral palsy,[16] then its frequency may be as common as aphasia.

While few people see themselves as having dysarthria as such, its presence within a broader condition can often prove the most painful symptom. Jamie Beddard is a playwright, actor and director who was born with cerebral palsy. He can walk, but increasingly relies on his wheelchair now he is in his fifties. His speech, in his own words, is both 'guttural' and 'hard to understand', although it is easy enough to follow with a little concentration. We first became acquainted through our work in the arts, often finding ourselves at the same events. After a year or two of knowing one another by sight, I realised I was doing what so many do: avoiding direct conversation because I was afraid of not understanding and causing offence. So I invited him for coffee.

'I used to say the only thing that bothers me is my communication,' he tells me. 'My speech has been the biggest element of my disability.' To enable better communication, Jamie puts a lot of physical effort into articulating. As a result, the act of speech can be physically exhausting, requiring a certain economy over what he does and doesn't say. While dysarthria often lacks the dramatic variability of Tourette's or stuttering, it still changes from day to day. 'It's not consistent,' he says. 'If I'm relaxed, it's probably a little better. When I'm nervous, it's a little bit worse. When I've had two beers, it's a little bit better. When I've had four beers, it's a little bit worse. Basically, the more relaxed I am the better.'

While people with cerebral palsy are normally born with dysarthria, there are many others who acquire it later in life. Motor neurone disease (MND) refers to neurodegenerative disorders affecting the nerves in your brain and spinal cord, including the capacity for speech. It is rare, affecting around 5,000 people in the UK.[17] Fortunately, there is greater awareness than there used to be because of the distinctive image and voice of scientist Stephen Hawking who lived with it for over fifty years. But Hawking was the exception: life expectancy following diagnosis of MND averages between two and five years.

My cousin Gilly Truman was diagnosed in her early thirties. Seven years on, she now uses a wheelchair and her ability to communicate is in what she calls the 'transition' phase with an increasing dependence on her augmented and alternative communication (AAC) device. 'I have to fill in a form every quarter in my clinic about dysarthria,' Gilly tells me. 'The questions ask about how difficult I find talking. I say don't ask me about how difficult it is. It's more the effort. If I've had a massive weekend of socialising, I find I just can't talk any more. I can't make myself heard in restaurants anymore so I find it easier to socialise at home.'

Like Beddard, Gilly emphasises the variability and inconsistencies of life with dysarthria. 'If I don't know someone, I find it harder to speak. The effort is tenfold. Or when I'm emotional, like when I'm talking about MND, my mouth gets a bit breathy. Basically, I can't hide any emotion or anger in my voice.' But the greatest inconsistency stems from the unavoidable process of transitioning, week on week, year on year. 'It will only get worse,' Gilly says. Increasingly, she is using EyeGaze, a sophisticated technology that tracks the movement of her eyes on a computer screen to spell out and pronounce words. This is partly because it can be a welcome break from the effort of speech, but also because she knows EyeGaze, rather than her worsening dysarthria, will be the voice of her inner thoughts and feelings for the rest of her life.

Together, stuttering, vocal tics, aphasia and dysarthria encompass most cases of pathologically disordered speech. But there are also conditions which affect speech in other ways. The most common of which are voice disorders, or dysphonia, caused by abnormalities in the voice mechanism in the larynx. The causes are manifold: from certain types of cancer and multiple sclerosis through to exhaustion, smoking and the temporary symptoms of the common cold. People with such disorders may be perceived, by themselves as well as others, as having voices which are too low, high, quiet, loud, monotonous, rough or hoarse. These symptoms may be accompanied by a physical difficulty in speaking.

One high profile figure with dysphonia is broadcaster Nick Robinson who describes his voice troubles following an operation for lung cancer in his book *Election Notebook* (2015). Because there is a strong element of subjectivity in diagnosing a voice disorder (one person's too hoarse, is another's just right), studies on the prevalence of dysphonia in the UK vary widely, although one estimate suggests around 2.5 per cent of the population.[18] As with stuttering, I think it is an individual's own perception of struggle that should determine a diagnosis most of all.

There are other conditions, but they are far rarer. Spasmodic dysphonia, for instance, is a neurological disorder in which the muscles that generate a person's voice go into periods of spasm. This creates breaks or interruptions in the subject's voice as frequently as every other word, making speech very difficult to understand. Dysprosody, known as foreign accent syndrome, is an extremely rare neurological speech disorder, usually caused by brain damage from a stroke or tumour, in which the variations in pitch and timing control go askew: people know what they want to say but can't control the way the words come out of their mouths. Often this results in the subject speaking in a pseudo-foreign accent.

There are also conditions which fundamentally change the way an individual communicates but are not speech or voice disorders as such. Selective Mutism is a severe anxiety disorder that affects around 1 in 140 children.[19] They find themselves unable to speak in certain social situations and, left untreated, it can continue into adulthood. 'Having selective mutism can feel like you're living your life in a box,' writes Sabrina Branwood, a thirty-something woman from Rochdale, in an interview with the BBC. 'The box is see-through so you can see out and hear people, but you can't leave no matter how hard you try. You can shout inside the box as loud as you like but nobody can hear you. They can't hear you cry when you're hurt or scared.'[20] One famous person with Selective Mutism is enviromentalist Greta Thunberg who has described her anger at the climate crisis as an overwhelming force that makes her speak in spite of her condition.[21]

Finally, there are those deaf people who use speech but struggle to articulate their words in a way many can easily understand. Increasingly, such 'oralism', the term used to describe the practice of teaching deaf people to communicate using speech and lip-reading, is considered old-fashioned. It is rejected as something imposed by intolerant societies rather than chosen and the use of sign languages is on the rise. In the 2011 Census, for instance, 22,000 people in England and Wales reported using Sign as their main language.[22] However, the term 'speech disorder' is inappropriate for the communication methods of the deaf. The difference comes down to choice. While those with speech disorders experience a consistent and obtrusive struggle in speaking the words they want to say, deaf people may use verbal speech or sign language, or a combination of both, in a way that is 'fluent' and effortless.

So far, I have described some of the main speech disorders on their own terms, as unique conditions with occasional overlaps. Stuttering is an impairment in fluency; aphasia in use of language; dysarthria in articulation; and vocal tics in intent, with unwanted words interrupting speech. For good reason, these conditions are generally, and appropriately, considered in isolation, and the literature around them is specific to each. Yet there is another way of looking at it. Rather than stressing the differences between speech disorders, we can emphasise what they have in common and think of them as a family: a sprawling one with different personalities, but a family nonetheless.

This is not an arbitrary exercise, but one that is critical for any serious attempt to tackle widespread discrimination against those who have them. Considered individually, they can appear rarified or obscure conditions. As a result, the case for research funding has sometimes been hard to make, and campaigns to tackle social prejudice have rarely reached critical mass. But if we consider them as a family, we are forced to acknowledge that they impact all of our lives. We may not be one of the millions who have them, but somebody in our life almost certainly does. What is more, we may develop one in years to come; whether the aphasia of a stroke or the dysarthria of a late-life condition like Parkinson's disease. It is in our interest, and that of people we care about, to ensure that such conditions are better understood and cease to be discriminated against.

Perhaps the most significant breakthrough for this viewpoint is the increasing scientific consensus that most speech disorders are neurological in nature, resulting from disturbances to the brain and nervous system. This is an idea we are still getting used to. Up until the end of the twentieth century, both stuttering and vocal tics were widely considered psychological complaints, putting them in an entirely different medical category to aphasia and dysarthria. Going further back, stuttering was explained in physiological terms, as the result of a large tongue or lack of moisture in the body.

Brain scanning, however, suggests that while the causes of a speech disorder can range from cerebral palsy to stroke as well as the 'enigma' of stuttering, in each case there is some difference in the circuitry of the brain. This would explain why many people experience more than one speech disorder. For instance, neurogenic, or acquired, stuttering often co-occurs with aphasia and dysarthria.[23] It would explain too why variations in dopamine, a chemical neurotransmitter in the human brain that sends signals between nerve cells, impact so many speech disorders. Drugs that suppress dopamine have proved effective in treating Tourette's syndrome and stuttering, while those which enhance it have diminished the symptoms of dysarthria in conditions like Parkinson's disease.

The gradual streamlining of speech disorders into a neurological framework has been accompanied by a similar streamlining of treatment. In the past, depending on your condition, you might be treated by a surgeon, a psychoanalyst, or just written off as a hopeless case. Today, if you seek a diagnosis or treatment for symptoms of aphasia, dysarthria, cluttering or stuttering, you will almost certainly find yourself in the company of a speech-language therapist. This is entirely appropriate because the techniques a therapist uses often apply equally well to different disorders. Yet such mainstreaming of the profession was hard won.

Speech therapy developed as an outsider discipline, frequently dismissed by the medical establishment right into the twentieth century, but gradually gained currency because of its ability to mitigate the symptoms and negative experience of speech disorders more effectively than other practices. The techniques used can seem deceptively simple, whether teaching better articulation or breathing, but it often overlaps with psychotherapy, helping a demoralised or despairing client to self-confidence and better understanding. Today, the experience of speech therapy – often, but not always, a positive one – is something that people with many different types of speech disorder share.

But more than their shared neurological origins and similar methods of treatment, I believe what unites all speech disorders is their relationship as a minority 'other' to fluency or 'normal speech'. Anyone with a speech disorder experiences some form of disruption between what they want to say and their ability to say it. The person with aphasia or a stutter, or the coprolalia of Tourette's finds that words either won't come out or do so differently, or are interrupted by other words that seem to appear from nowhere. Such people have a fundamentally different relationship with language than fluent speakers do; it is something to be distrusted as much as enjoyed.

This is why I find Ngũgĩ wa Thiong'o's description of a 'malady of words' in his novel *Wizard of the Crow* so powerful. When I was a boy, and long into adulthood, I believed I was cursed by a rare affliction. I had little idea how many people pathologically struggle with their speech. For me, Ngũgĩ's vision of a nation where millions are afflicted by a 'malady of words' is more than a metaphor for political voicelessness, but a description of reality. The phrase cuts through the medicalisation, the terminology, the cordoning off of myriad conditions, and reminds us that collectively a significant proportion of our population struggles with speech and feels humiliated by it.

'Humiliation can leave scars for life,' Ngũgĩ told me on that winter's afternoon in Venice:

> You can cover it, but the humiliation can be internalised. You begin reacting against certain things, not because you are consciously thinking about rejecting this or that. It becomes almost like the way we avoid spaces of pain because we like to inhabit places of comfort. So if you've been humiliated in relation to language, even if just the register of your voice, without realising it you don't want to have anything to do with that register.

As he said this, I realised that the physical symptoms of speech disorders – the stuttered sounds, unexpected interjections, lost or mumbled words – are not the defining qualities of those conditions. Running beneath them, and far more overwhelming for the individual, are the negative emotions: the feelings of isolation and shame that shape a person's life. On the flight home from our meeting, I opened the copy of his prison memoir, *Wrestling with the Devil*, which I'd hurriedly asked him to sign as I left. Above his name, he'd written: 'In solidarity in the struggle for the right to one's language.' Not a commiseration then, but a call to arms.

2

The Mouth Trap

In the winter of 1878–79, the novelist Henry James famously dined out 140 times in and around London. As a young man off the boat from America, he was fascinated by the glamour and sophistication of the Old World. His notebooks and letters are full of observations about people's speech and conversation. He reflects on the 'high superiority of French talk', encounters 'one of the most charming and ingenious talkers I ever met', is relieved at a dull soirée to stumble upon 'a flowering oasis in conversation sands', disapproves of an acquaintance who is 'rendered more inarticulate than ever', and worries that his own standards of 'what makes an easy and natural style of intercourse' might be dropping.[1] This fascination with the art of human conversation fills the novels and stories he is best known for, including *A Portrait of a Lady, Daisy Miller* and *The Wings of the Dove*.

His linguistic snobbery could also make him a bore. Having spent much of his life avoiding lower-class establishments, he unwittingly found himself in an Upper East side café in New York (the city had changed a great deal since his previous visit) where he felt himself in 'the torture-rooms of the living idiom'.[2] The experience was so traumatic, he addressed it head on in a lecture on 'The Question of Our Speech'. Speech is sacred, he said, and warned that 'the human side of vocal sound' was being corrupted by slovenly speech and kept 'as little distinct as possible from the grunting, the squealing, the barking or the roaring of animals'.[3] When the young Winston Churchill met James he couldn't resist winding him up by using as much slang as possible.[4]

Such preoccupation with language, and its correct usage, is understandable in a novelist determined to write both exquisite prose and capture the speech patterns of the sophisticated Londoners and Americans he encountered. But something else motivated it too, a secret he shared with very few.

That there was something strange about James's own speech was impossible to ignore. And just as he wrote about the speech of others, many people wrote about his. James's manner of speaking was long-winded, full of pauses and circumlocutions, and it proved divisive. Some found it irritating: 'I don't think he talks remarkably well,' wrote William Hoppin, an American diplomat in London. Constance Fenimore Woolson, a fellow novelist, tactfully struggled to explain his 'unusual flow of language', while the poet Ezra Pound remembered him 'weaving an endless sentence'.[5] The young Virginia Woolf left a satirical sketch of their encounter:

> 'My dear Virginia, they tell me – they tell me – they tell me – that you – as indeed being your father's daughter nay your grandfather's grandchild – the descendant I may say of a century – of a century – of

> quill pens and ink – ink – ink pots, yes, yes, yes, they tell me – ahm m m that you, that you, that you write in short.'[6]

Like most men of his time, James was not good at talking about his deepest feelings. He was almost certainly gay, but seems to have chosen the (arguably) less complicated life of celibacy. In the same spirit, he never acknowledged his stutter. But stutter he did. Some of those who encountered him hint at it. His nephew noted his uncle's 'perpetual vocal search for words even when he wasn't saying anything'. Urbain Mengin, a French poet, noted that 'he speaks with a slight hesitation [a word often used in polite circles at the time as a euphemism for stuttering], repeating the first syllable of certain words.' Miss Weld, James's typist, also acknowledged the 'hesitation', but promptly adds that it 'was simply nervousness and vanished once he knew you well'.[7]

One of the few people James confided in was fellow writer Edith Wharton, who had a knack for drawing people out:

> His slow way of speech, sometimes mistaken for affectation – or, more quaintly, for an artless form of Anglomania! – was really the partial victory over a stammer which in his boyhood had been thought incurable. The elaborate politeness and the involved phraseology that made off-hand intercourse with him so difficult to casual acquaintances probably sprang from the same defect. To have too much time in which to weigh each word before uttering it could not but

> lead, in the case of the alertest and most sensitive of minds, to self-consciousness and self-criticism; and this fact explains the hesitating manner that often passed for a mannerism.'[8]

What is most striking about Wharton's claim is the extent to which it suggests Henry James's life was shaped by a speech impediment few ever actually heard. It determined not only his elaborate and long-winded way of speaking, but the way he thought about himself. Above and beyond Wharton's theory, I think it may have informed his obsession with the way language is used by others; and, as a writer who dictated many of his novels, it is present in many of the books he is most famous for (I will say more about this later). But in all this there is nothing unusual.

We define and diagnose speech impediments by their overt symptoms: the strangulated repetitions and blocks of stuttering, the outbursts of vocal tics, the distorted articulation of dysarthria, and the pauses and malapropisms of aphasia. Yet for anyone who has a speech disorder, it is not the sound of their condition that most impacts their lives, but everything that follows. Speech-language therapists sometimes use an iceberg metaphor to describe this.[9] The act or sound of a speech disorder is just the part others are aware of, if at all, but underneath it are complex behavioural and psychological responses. What is experienced by others as a disorder of speech or even just an unusual manner of speaking can shape an individual's entire personality.

As an overt, and then interiorised, person who stutters,

I developed techniques for managing my speech from a very early age; not only avoiding problematic sounds and words, but situations where I might be required to use them. The experience of being and feeling humiliated damaged my self-esteem, ultimately impacting the choices I made in life. I'm one of the many who, like Henry James, manage to pass as fluent, if sometimes unusual, speakers. We keep our disorder invisible but at great cost, restricting and narrowing our lives to do so. In this regard, I both do and don't have a speech disorder, for stuttering is the thing I have spent a lot of my life energetically not doing.

Of course, there are many others for whom concealment is not possible. The sense of shame they feel and are made to feel by others can result in low self-esteem, isolation, loneliness and, in extreme cases, dissociative disorders and suicidal feelings. One of the reasons why I believe we should talk about speech disorders collectively is because their impact on an individual is primarily psychological. There is a consistency of negative feelings and avoidance behaviour that applies to those across the spectrum, whether they stutter, tic, struggle to articulate or to recall words. By understanding the way these disorders impact on an individual's life, I hope we can respond and better support those affected.

For people with a speech disorder that manifest itself in early childhood, like stuttering, vocal tics or certain forms of dysarthria, it can be the reactions of others that inform their sense of something being wrong rather than any innate consciousness of something awry in their speech. 'Adverse listener reactions can play a part,' writes linguist David Crystal. 'A typical example is when parents prematurely correct their children for non-fluency, or become impatient when their child is non-fluent; this causes insecurity and anxiety, which in turn causes further growth in the non-fluency.'[10]

Shame, it seems, often starts at home not out of malice, but from love. Parents want their children to lead 'normal' lives after all. 'I know people whose families are uncomfortable with them ticcing,' artist Jess Thom tells me, 'and there's an unconscious pressure to suppress which can have a really negative knock-on effect on their mental well-being and their mental health.' If symptoms continue, parents may seek a diagnosis. This can result in a child being told they have a problem before they are even aware of having one.

Francesca Martinez is an actor and comedian with cerebral palsy. When she was a baby, doctors told her parents she was physically and mentally disabled and would never lead a normal life. 'I'm not quite sure what a normal life is,' she writes in her memoir *What the **** is Normal?!*. 'What I am sure of is my bemusement now at the ease with which these professionals make such weighty pronouncements. Words that take seconds to utter and decades to cast off. Unknown to me then, they disappeared into the ground around me and, over time, would emerge as the bars of a cage, hemming me in from the outside world.'[11] As she grew older, her parents encouraged her, lovingly but forcefully, to overcome her slurred speech, although it wasn't a problem she recognised. 'I couldn't see why I needed to do exercises at all,' she writes. 'What was the logic in practising certain words to improve my speech when I talked perfectly already? A fact clearly demonstrated by the clear voice I heard every time I spoke. Or in the suggestion that certain mouth exercises might help me not to dribble.'

While self-consciousness about speech and labelling can aggravate a problem, the pioneering American speech therapist Wendell Johnson went one step further. Stuttering, he claimed, begins not in the child's mouth, but in the parent's ear. The act itself is nothing more than 'the simple repetitiousness of preschool-age children.'[12] It becomes a clinical problem 'not before being diagnosed, but after being diagnosed ... The more anxious the parents become, the more they hound the child to "go slowly", to "stop and start over"... the more fearful and disheartened the child becomes and the more hesitantly, frantically and laboriously he speaks.'[13]

To some extent Johnson was right: 5 per cent of children stutter at some point, generally between the ages of three and six. And there is surely some significance in the fact that children who stutter have faster speech rates on average than children who do not. For many, it may be a verbal version of the stumbling they do when learning to walk and run, yet few if any parents fixate on a toddler's tripping over as a sign of congenital lameness. In fact, 80 per cent of children who stutter become fluent speakers and it is sometimes hard to tell whether speech therapy alleviated or exacerbated the problem.[14]

In the 1930s, Wendell Johnson put his theory to the test in the now infamous 'Monster Study'. Under his supervision, graduate student Mary Tudor selected six children between the ages of five and fifteen at an orphanage in Iowa for an experiment. The orphanage was important because she wanted children unencumbered by protective parents. 'You have a great deal of trouble with your speech,' Tudor told each child, all of whom were already vulnerable from a life in care. 'These interruptions indicate stuttering. Don't ever speak unless you can do it right. Whatever you do, speak fluently and avoid any interruptions whatsoever in your speech.'[15]

Tudor studied their behaviour in the following months and found that they spoke less, more slowly and with greater hesitations. Their behaviour changed too; they became shy and easily embarrassed children. Years later, Franklin Silverman, a revered speech therapist and one of Johnson's students, recalled that Tudor continued to visit the children in following years out of a sense of responsibility because some of them had actually developed stutters as a result of the 'experiment'. 'The implications of the findings seem clear,' Silverman wrote. 'Asking a child to monitor his speech fluency and attempt to be more fluent can lead to increased disfluency and possibly stuttering.'[16]

Knowing all this now, it is hard not to look back and wonder to what extent my own stutter was shaped by my family and nursery teachers. My earliest memories aren't of actually stuttering, but my family's reaction to it. Since stuttering runs in families (and there is even some evidence of a stuttering gene), parents who experienced it themselves may be particularly sensitive to any telltale signs in a child's speech. They may hear an echo of their own affliction in the perfectly normal repetitions of speech development and seek a diagnosis and treatment before it is necessary.

My mother stuttered from school age well into her

twenties, an experience she remains sensitive about to this day, so it is understandable she was highly attuned to any obstacles in my own speech. But I am only partially convinced by Wendell Johnson's theory. He was working at a time when the influence of psychoanalysis was at its peak, and there was a tendency to over-emphasise the role of neurosis in many pathological conditions. While I believe it possible in some extreme cases that a child can start to stutter purely through suggestion, the evidence of brain scanning suggests many more are born with a disposition that may be lessened or intensified, but not caused, by how it is treated by the adults around them.

Johnson wrote about stuttering, but a hereditary pattern has also been found in Tourette's syndrome, suggesting family influence could play a similar role. Johnson's insights are clearly less relevant to the speech disorders arising from conditions like cerebral palsy, where symptoms may be evident long before the speech development process begins. Even then, as Francesca Martinez describes, the process of diagnosing a condition is a sensitive one that can affect a child's confidence for the rest of their lives. In all cases, I think parents would do well to worry less about disordered speech in a child and consider it instead as a perfectly normal process in speech development, even if 'normal' is never going to be the same as for other children.

The loving concern and implicit pressures of anxious parents may generate a sense of shame, but it is only aggravated when that child is thrown into a larger and less sympathetic social environment. Joshua St Pierre, a Canadian philosopher and speech activist, vividly remembers the frequent humiliations of school. 'There'd always be shame and embarrassment,' he tells me on the phone. 'And after these awkward social situations, I'd mutter things like "stupid Josh, stupid Josh, stupid Josh" as a way of mitigating that awkwardness.' The Irish novelist Colm Tóibín tells me about 'a little fucker called Titch Hogan. He would follow me home going "duh-duh-duh-duh" the whole way. I put his mother into one of my books.' The American writer Darcey Steinke writes about the occasion some kids from her school tossed a book called *The Mystery of the Stuttering Parrot* onto her family lawn.[17]

'My absolute worst nightmare,' the poet Owen Sheers tells me, 'was the idea of reading round the class in English because you can see your turn coming: you can see the paragraph with the words – and blocks – you're going to have.' Oliver Dimsdale, long before he even dreamed of being an actor, remembers 'looking around at John or Fred who was next to me, nonchalantly reading line after line, and thinking you lucky, lucky bastards. How on earth are you able just to pick something up without thinking about it and read fluently? It would get round to me and I'd spit out two or three sentences. More often than not, I'd run out and find a place to have a cry.' My mother experienced this situation differently: for her it was about exclusion rather than humiliation. Even today she recalls bitterly the way her teacher in the 1950s wouldn't let her speak, simply saying, 'I think we'll skip Anne and pass on to the next.'

It was partly to counter the misconceptions of teachers and the taunts of children that a group of worried parents formed the Tourette Association of America in the early

1970s, supporting new medical research as well as awareness-raising campaigns. Fifty years on, the TAA continues to gather the experiences of parents and children impacted by a condition that remains widely misunderstood. One mother describes her horror at hearing her seven-year-old announce that he wanted to kill himself. 'Here was my son telling me in the clearest words possible that he felt he had no value,' she writes, 'that having Tourette's syndrome meant his future would never be equal to his peers. He was giving up … I thought of the mistakes I'd made before his diagnosis, remembered every time I'd begged, "please, just stop!" I thought about the times he'd been removed from class, punished, and sent home.' One man recalls his worst anxieties about Tourette's being around the age of eleven, 'when establishing your "cool" took a lot of hard work and one little snag – like tripping down the stairs, spilling soda on your pants or, God forbid, an episode of uncontrollable sounds and movements – could set you back years, if not eternally.'[18]

It is all too easy to blame children and teenagers for humiliating schoolmates who struggle with speech, but I believe our education system promotes such behaviour. Schools are built around relentless displays of public speaking: reading aloud in class, assembly presentations, plays, debates, oral examinations. In all of this, they do little to accommodate those, and there are many, who do not respond well to such tasks. Not only people with speech disorders, but introverted or easily embarrassed children.

Despite being diagnosed very young as a person who stutters, I was never exempted from such rituals. At the age of nine, I occasionally pretended to forget my own name in class roll-calls to avoid stuttering on the troublesome 'J'. Ten years later, I failed the oral in a French exam because I blocked so severely throughout the test. In between those two events is a long line of humiliations in which I recall my teachers in part as threats who could expose me at any moment through the tasks they set.

The argument that such tasks are a necessary preparation for life to come is half true at best. Few people embark on careers that require anything close to the amount of public speaking they were compelled to do at school, and there are many whose experiences were so bad that they choose careers precisely to avoid it. An education system developed with an awareness of the number of children who experience speech disorders would place less emphasis on performative speaking, ensure what tasks they do participate in are not humiliating for them, and place equal attention on other forms of communication that may play better to their strengths.

Although many speech disorders are developmental and dissipate over time – only 20 per cent of children who stutter or have vocal tics continue to do so in adulthood – the damage may be already done, with self-respect and social confidence forever diminished. For those who continue to struggle, a pattern of avoidance and low self-confidence is already set. Life choices, whether careers or relationships, may be determined by the desire to blend in.

Jim Smith, a leading UK scientist who happens to stutter, tells me that he only went into his field because of a misguided idea of the 'lone boffin'. He had no idea of the amount of lecturing, seminars, committee meetings and policy speeches he would have to do. In her early twenties, my mother was a junior reporter with the *Sydney Telegraph*. She would never ask a question at a press briefing because you had to say your name first, something which caused her to stutter. In the aggressive culture of journalism, she was reluctant to expose herself to public humiliation. She even adjusted her first name from 'Anne' to 'Annie' because the 'e' sound gave her a bounce into 'Woodham'. After a while, the hopelessness of being a news reporter who wouldn't open her mouth at junkets became too much and she went into research-oriented features writing instead. It still involved asking questions, but without a dozen other journalists listening in.

As a young man, I made similar choices. I considered, and dismissed, professions that revolved around performative speaking. The law, politics and journalism were intriguing but doors better left closed. Instead, I went into documentaries, an art form which generally tells stories using the voices of others. It turned out I had a limited idea of how they are made. My early jobs as a researcher involved endless cold-calling while sitting in an open plan office, which is a trigger for stuttering. I ran up vast bills with my late 90s brick-shaped mobile phone making calls in the stairwell or outside, for which I could never claim reimbursement as I had no plausible reason for not using the perfectly functional phone on my desk. Another accessory was a pack of beta blockers which I drew upon before important pitching meetings or interviews to help me relax and therefore speak a little more fluently.

Although there is certainly an element of self-censorship

in such career decisions, discrimination remains a real problem. Francesca Martinez writes that, as a comedian, she has been dropped from BBC radio shows because of her 'funny voice'. Walter Scott, a civil servant in the Ministry of Defence, tells me he was rejected for a scholarship with the Armed Forces as a young man because of his disfluent speech. 'I had subsequent experiences in job applications in my early twenties,' he says, 'where I was rejected because I stammered. Eventually, I entered the civil service by applying for a job nobody else had applied for. I have chosen my career path carefully, generally avoiding jobs where I thought there'd be other people applying. Why would you take the candidate who has a stammer?' And there are many with acute aphasia or dysarthria, or who communicate with Sign, who cannot get any work at all.

Discrimination in the workplace may not be as overt as that of the schoolyard, but it is no less damaging to the esteem and potential of an individual. Think of how often job adverts specify the need for 'fluent and effective' communications. And it is still widely assumed that there are certain jobs that are entirely incompatible with speech disorders: jobs which require giving quick orders (traffic control), or representing a company to the outside world (public relations), or talking to customers (sales), or cold-calling (research). Each employer will have their own set of positions for which a basic mastery of fluency seems essential. Case-by-case, there are always arguments and justifications which seem sound, but looked at collectively people with speech disorders unwittingly form a social caste better suited – in the eyes of society – to manual or lower-income desk jobs. The problem isn't so much one of wilful prejudice, but of ignorance. There are, in fact, very few jobs that people with speech disorders cannot do, particularly since technology has provided devices and apps that can compensate for the words an individual struggles with. Social attitudes are not going to change overnight but a powerful first step would be for companies to build an awareness of speech disorders, as they do with other types of diversity, into their employment policies to avoid discrimination. This is currently patchy at best and it is usually down to an individual whether they consider and are willing to describe their disorder as a form of disability; something which in theory protects them under the Disability Discrimination Act.

While most speech disorders develop in childhood, there are many which emerge later in life. In such cases, feelings of shame are no less pronounced. The person with aphasia following a stroke might feel half the person they were before, reduced by the loss of speech to a state of near-infancy. 'Just because I can't speak like them and I look a bit different,' writes a man called Jim who experienced a stroke at twenty-nine, 'they turn away, ignore me or speak to my wife or speak to somebody else.'[19]

Those who find their ability to articulate affected by Parkinson's disease or motor neurone disease are acutely aware of slipping, in the eyes and ears of those they encounter, from the status of the able-bodied to that of an invalid. My cousin Gilly tells me of the shock of becoming socially invisible, both because of her wheelchair and her dysarthria. 'When your voice goes, people assume your brain has gone too,' she says. 'A few months ago, I went into a clothes shop with a girlfriend. The shop assistant would only talk to her. Eventually, my friend looked at me and said, "What clothes do you want?", and I could see the shop assistant realise that I did have a brain.'

Faced with the prejudices of an intolerant society, and the sense of shame which that often creates, people with speech disorders develop a complex range of tactics for managing their speech. Those who can will try to conceal a condition for as long as possible. This is particularly true of stuttering which, unlike vocal tics, aphasia and dysarthria, is often self-contained rather than a symptom of a more multifaceted and widespread condition like Tourette's, stroke or cerebral palsy. As a person grows to understand the words or situations that affect them most, they also become more adept at avoiding them.

Like most people who stutter, I developed these techniques through my teenage years. I did so instinctively, grasping at anything that might get me through or away from a difficult word. Only as an adult, when I finally began talking to others and reading books on the subject, did I realise how universal these 'dodges' are, effectively amounting to a grammar of stuttering. There is *word substitution*, where you simply replace a difficult word with a synonym (and this might explain in part why there are so many words for stuttering, including the softer, less plosive 'stammering'). There is *deliberate hesitation*, where you wait until a word can be more effectively broached, much in the way George VI did in his radio broadcasts; and *pitch modulation*, where you adjust the speed and tone of your voice, generally by slowing and flattening it, so it is less bumpy. There is also *deliberate repetition*, where a speaker bounces into a difficult word, but without the involuntary grimaces of stuttering.

Used together, these techniques can result in a highly idiosyncratic way of speaking, like the descriptions of Henry James's speech. Looked at again, with an awareness of the full range of techniques used, and considering James's intention to avoid actually stuttering, his speech no longer seems strange but extremely logical and structured. The American journalist Elizabeth Jordan befriended James late in his life and wrote an article, published long after his death, describing the way he spoke. In it she recalls that he broke his sentences into 'little groups of two, three, or four words', just as speech therapist Lionel Logue taught George VI to speak in three-word breaks. In a transcript of one such sentence, she also captures all the blocks, elongated vowel sounds and varying rhythms we have identified as common tactics:

> Eliminating – ah – (very slow) eliminating – ah – eliminating nine-tenths – (faster) nine-tenths of-of-of (very fast) what he claims (slower) of what he claims – of what he claims (very slow) there is still – there is still – there is still (very much faster) enough – left – e-nough left (slower) to make – to – make – to – make – a remarkable record (slow) a remark-able record, (slower) a remarkable record (very slow).[20]

When I attended Carolyn Cheasman's course at City Lit for 'interiorised stammering' in my early thirties, I didn't even know such a phenomenon existed beyond my own secretive and shameful behaviour. I was astonished to find that nearly all the people in my group, about ten in all, were only 'out' to family and close friends. There was one man who had even managed to keep it a secret from his fiancée. 'It goes far beyond physical acts,' Patrick Campbell, an alumnus of City Lit and co-author of *Stammering Pride and Prejudice,* tells me. 'People who stammer talk about not being able to say what they want to say; changing their words; not speaking out when they want to speak; being the quiet one in the room; shaping their whole life around this thing. That is what stammering is, much more than the physical issue it causes in your mouth.'

Patrick's comments remind me that although I use words like 'tactics' and 'strategies' to describe the ways in which people who stutter conceal or mitigate their disorder, it implies more agency than they feel. Interiorised behaviour ceases to be a conscious choice but second nature. The words I speak today are vetted by an internal and unconscious mechanism I rarely pause to acknowledge. In the same way, I do not think Henry James's strange way of speaking arose from him consciously avoiding particular words, but from a long and deeply ingrained habit of which he was no longer aware.

Avoidance strategies are by no means restricted to stuttering. While many with aphasia, dysarthria or vocal tics have speech that is palpably disordered, affecting every word they utter, many find their condition is both moderate and variable: with great effort and numerous tricks they can also pass as something close to 'normal'. In my experience, the more an individual is able to appear fluent, the more they may attempt to do so. Ben Brown, an American with Tourette's syndrome and the founder of the Tourette's Podcast, writes how he 'kept a lid on my TS and crafted ways to mask my tics or blend them into normal routines, even as the subterfuge could be exhausting and often unsuccessful'.[21]

Similarly, those with degenerative conditions that affect speech will often try to conceal their condition for as long as possible. Writer and documentary filmmaker Jon Palfreman describes the patient support group he attended after being diagnosed with Parkinson's disease. There was a long conversation about 'coming out'. One-by-one, patients admitted they hadn't told anyone but their closest family about their condition. A woman in the group warned them that 'if you kept matters secret, people might interpret your behaviour – the slow movements and slurred speech – as something else. "They might think you'd been drinking … that you're an alcoholic."'[22]

The actor Michael J. Fox has talked about his desperate attempts to drug his Parkinson's into submission long after diagnosis. 'I can vividly remember all those nights when the studio audience, unknowingly, had to wait for my symptoms to subside,' he wrote, recalling his third season in the sitcom *Spin City*. 'I'd be backstage, lying on my dressing room rug, twisting and rolling around, trying to cajole my neuroreceptors into accepting and processing the L-dopa I had so graciously received.'[23]

Attempts to conceal a speech disorder, or the condition causing it, often largely succeed in their aim, but they come at a high cost. 'You can imagine the pressures of having to keep those levels of secrecy going," says Willie Botterill, one of the founders of the Michael Palin Centre for Stammering Children, and my speech therapist for many years:

> I had a woman who worked for the health service who had just got to the point where she was having to make speeches to quite big audiences about technical stuff. It is very difficult to find your way around a specific word which applies to something there is no other word for. She came to me because she was having terrible migraines as a result of the stress of trying to keep it all secret.

Betony Kelly is a civil servant who decided in her mid-thirties to stop hiding her stammer. She wrote a blog on the civil service website announcing her decision and why. 'Depending on whether it was a good or bad day,' she tells me when we meet in a cafe in Whitehall, 'between 10 and 30 per cent of my brain was taken up managing my fluency. When you start to speak and you have a stammer, the seamless connection between your thoughts and your mouth just isn't there.' As a result, a disfluent speaker is never quite in the moment. However present they appear, an inner process is at work: scanning ahead; determining when to engage and how; sifting words like sand to remove the clunky grit.

'In many ways you have to be able to see other paths, other ways of expressing yourself,' Kelly says. 'All those strange things we do, like pretend we've forgotten a word and get someone to spell it for us. Or speak in a different accent. All those little playful things just to get through a sentence.' When Kelly came out at work, she didn't feel ashamed but liberated from the 'huge emotional and physical drain of trying to produce fluent speech'. She accepted what so many deny: that fluency-performing techniques have the adverse effect of worsening rather than improving communication. The person who endlessly substitutes words to avoid stuttering confuses a listener far more than one who allows those same passing blockages to occur.

Of course, there are many whose speech disorder cannot be concealed. For them, a different set of tactics needs to be cultivated. These are about mitigation; rendering themselves and their speech more palatable to a fluent majority. Actor and director Jamie Beddard describes how his cerebral palsy requires him to disarm a listener just to enable a simple conversation. He has a sophisticated strategy and set of techniques for achieving this. 'If I can make people relax, they are able to understand me. But people who think, "Oh my God, I don't know what he's saying" are unlikely to focus to do so.' Humour is an essential tool. 'Often I say, "if you don't understand me – tough!" and they understand I am taking the piss.' Laying out the ground rules is important too. 'I tell them it's okay to say "what?" I don't mind repeating myself again and again. The moment I give permission to not understand, it makes it a lot easier. I prefer that to when people pretend to understand me when they clearly haven't.'

The imperative to conceal, to moderate, to explain and apologise joins with the shame an individual feels and exacerbates what is undoubtedly the dominant psychological symptom of a speech disorder: a sometimes overwhelming sense of isolation and loneliness. One

Victorian speech therapist described the 'habit of secrecy' of the person who stutters: 'of feeling himself cut off from his kindred; of brooding over his thoughts, of fancying himself under a mysterious curse'.[24] Francesca Martinez recalls the 'growing unhappiness and sense of isolation' of life with cerebral palsy, and those with aphasia talk – when they can – about being lost and lonely.

Isolation and loneliness are symptoms of the lived experience of many disabilities, but are peculiarly heightened by the very nature of a speech disorder. Given that speech is a tool for communication, then anything which hampers its efficacy separates an individual, even just a little, from the usual comforts of human discourse. My cousin Gilly finds herself being increasingly silenced in certain social situations. 'My projection is woeful and people talk over me all the time,' she says. There are certain types of interaction she struggles to participate in. 'If somebody is really aggressive or dogmatic, I can't take them on.'

While there are many different speech disorders, and immense variations within each, one thing above all unites them: the disfluent speaker has a fundamentally different relationship with language to fluent speakers. It is something that cannot quite be trusted. This is more than a matter of wrestling with an unreliable tool, like a cheap vacuum cleaner, because language is what ties human society together. No wonder, then, that feelings of alienation, of simultaneously observing and participating in any social situation, of never quite being in the moment of verbal communion, are so frequently described. This forced distrust of speech not only unites those who have a speech disorder but creates a gulf between them and everyone else.

The isolating qualities of a speech disorder are manifold. There is the isolation of humiliation, of having to forge one's own path through life, of feeling estranged from human communion. But there is something else too, although it is the hardest quality to describe: a feeling of detachment not only from others and from language, but from oneself. In psychology, the term *dissociation* describes the occasional but unsettling feeling of disconnectedness from yourself and the world around you. As a recurring condition, it is linked to childhood trauma and stress. When we consider the bullying that a child may experience because of a speech disorder, as well as the stress of continually needing to manage one's own speech with avoidance and substitution techniques, it is understandable why so many describe the symptoms of dissociation.

Darcey Steinke describes the out-of-body experience she had in speech therapy as a child:

> My mind unfocused and I floated up, watching the skinny, pathetic girl in the sundress and tyre-tread sandals trying so desperately to find a little grace. Flash forward twenty-five years. After a plethora of speech therapy, my stutter was less disruptive; I moved through the world trying to pass as a fluent person, one unmarred by disability. Whenever I stuttered, I disassociated: that struggling human was not me.

But I think there is a bigger cause of dissociation in

speech disorders than just stress and social alienation. We use speech to describe our thoughts and feelings. When this faculty is disordered we find ourselves at one remove from the thoughts in our mind. The mental process of word substitution, for instance, is one of adjusting what I want to say to what I can say. It means looking at my own thoughts as an outsider. This might explain why I began to experience intense and disturbing attacks of dissociation when I was still a child, roughly around the same period I began to stutter. These attacks have never gone away although, like my stutter, they are less frequent and more easily managed. The two are forever connected in my mind and I see dissociation as an extreme expression of the internal distancing and editing I do with the thoughts and words I want to express.

While stuttering, vocal tics and dysarthria often develop from infancy over many years, the sudden onset of aphasia later in life is also explained in terms of intense dissociation. Some of these are captured in *Jumbly Words, and Rights Where Wrongs Should Be: The Experience of Aphasia from the Inside*: 'I live outside myself'; 'There was somebody else in my skin'; 'My mind sits on the fence'; 'I felt I was neither here nor there, just flotsam and jetsam'.[25] Understandably, such people also experience overwhelming depression, loneliness and anger.[26] One approach in treatment involves looking at aphasia through a grief paradigm – equating its impact to the loss of a loved one, although the person lost is oneself – moving through stages of denial, anger, bargaining, depression and acceptance. This can be far more than an emotional transition: an individual's personality itself can fundamentally change, as if unanchored and searching for some other mooring to drop in.

Speech disorders, then, are far more than conditions affecting the ability to say the words you want to say. They create moments of immense humiliation, estranging you from families and peers, unbalancing – often permanently – your sense of worth. They determine the paths you choose through life: the careers you embark on, the circles you move in, the associations you forge. They inform your performance in a social context: what you say, as well as when and how you say it. And, because speech disorders redefine your relationship with language, your very personality may change.

Often the experience of all these things feels like a closing in of horizons. Speech therapists find themselves supporting an individual through emotional crises as much as imparting techniques for the voice. I saw the same speech therapist, Willie Botterill, on and off from my pre-teens well into my twenties. On certain occasions, we barely spoke about my speech at all, but the anxiety I felt about it. Sometimes these enhanced periods of stuttering coincided with difficult periods in my life, like the death of a grandparent or the break-up of a relationship, so the boundary between speech therapy and counselling became negligible.

Many others reach far greater depths of despair than I ever imagined. American speech therapist Charles Van Riper described his many thoughts of suicide driven by his stutter, a condition he compared to being 'naked in a world full of steel knives'.[27] In the UK, one of the few charities that supports research into stuttering is the

Dominic Barker Trust, named after the twenty-six-year-old who tragically took his own life in 1994. It is a great sadness that every support organisation that deals with speech disorders can testify to those who have experienced despair or committed suicide.

This is why it is so important that we strive to understand speech disorders better. Not only as neurological conditions impacting speech, but as disorders of the mind, impacting mental health and life choices. And there is a third element too, which has emerged over the previous pages. The scale of psychological suffering an individual experiences is determined not so much by their inner resilience, but by the discrimination of the society in which they live. That sense of ever-narrowing horizons may be more than metaphorical but real, because humiliation, bullying and workplace prejudice undoubtedly eliminate opportunities for personal fulfilment. Like any social behaviour, the scale of such discrimination is not fixed, but varies both within and across different societies. Speech disorders, or at least the experience of them, are therefore shaped by culture. In this regard, they should be considered social disorders as much as neurological and psychological ones. This is both a cause for hope and concern. Social prejudice can get worse, but it can also, in the right conditions, get much, much better.

3

Talking Culture

In the late 1970s, the American linguist Daniel Everett began a life-long study of the languages of hunter-gatherer communities in the Amazon; in particular, the Pirahã people who live by the Maici river. The tribe, and the people who speak Pirahã, number less than a thousand. Besides the odd Portuguese word, they are monolingual. Their language is a closed circuit with its own unique structure and grammar: a precious rarity in a globalised world, where cultures seamlessly blend into one another. While wary of viewing contemporary hunter-gatherer communities as a paradigm of the forgotten origins of the West, Everett found it impossible not to draw insights into some of the ways language may have developed in the obscured past of our own civilisation.

In comparison to technologically advanced societies, Pirahã vocabulary and grammar is relatively narrow. Everett soon discovered how limited the role of verbal speech is in communication. 'You can recount jokes or lie, talk about the hunt, ask about the family or tell tall tales – all by whistling,' he wrote. 'In addition to whistle speech, the Pirahãs have hum speech, another form of communication that only uses pitch, loudness, and length, yet none the less communicates all the richness of normal human speech.'[1] Because industrialised societies pride themselves on their vast vocabularies (The Oxford English Dictionary Online, for instance, boasts over 600,000 words), they struggle to take notions like whistle and hum speech seriously, yet for Everett those modes of communication reveal a nuance and sophistication no less remarkable than our linguistic dexterity. In revering speech above all else, we may be missing out on other forms of communication. While we can express the abstract nuances of political ideology or religious belief in words, we struggle to express anything more than the most basic emotions of jauntiness or exasperation when it comes to whistling or humming.

Gradually, Everett became convinced of a simple idea that would nevertheless prove immensely divisive in the world of linguistics. His theory is an old, but unfashionable one: that language is simply a cultural tool aimed at communication and social cohesion. It is something human societies create, like any other tool, to serve a purpose. This may sound like common sense but it runs counter to some modern theories of language. In particular, it brought him head-to-head with his former teacher, the legendary linguist and political theorist Noam Chomsky.

Since the late 1950s, Chomsky has tried to prove that certain basic grammatical structures are innate to the human brain. As human societies develop they simply unfold this inner formula, or 'universal grammar', into reality rather than building it from scratch. While vocabularies need to be created, some of the grammatical structures they sit within are hard-wired into us. This is very different to a tool like the wheel or the hammer, neither of which existed as concepts in the human brain before they were invented. Everett argued that, after actually studying hunter-gatherer communities rather than speculating about them, there was no evidence of a universal grammar at all, nor any apparent benefit to be had if one did exist. By flying in the face of a sixty-year-old theory that has been institutionalised within universities, Everett brought the wrath of academia upon his head; he has been called a charlatan and a fraud by both Chomsky himself and his followers. The sheer level of vitriol in these attacks against what is, after all, a commonsensical theory of language only suggests the extent to which he has rattled them.

As a cultural tool, the Pirahã language evolved to suit the lifestyle and needs of its speakers. While it has a comparatively limited vocabulary and grammar, it is more diverse in its different types of speech. Whistle speech, for instance, is useful when out hunting: it enables people to communicate at a distance without shouting and startling the prey. In industrial societies, on the other hand, the complexity of a language evolves alongside scientific innovation with an ever greater prioritisation on uniformity and exactness. Theories of gravity, of relativity and quantum physics expand the limits of a language, creating a bedrock for further theories in the process. They would be impossible without a large vocabulary of words that are both specific but also abstract. We can't see gravity, for instance, but we all agree what it is.

But if speech and language are culturally determined, it raises the question of the extent to which speech disorders are too. In contrast to the speech of a fluent majority, the sound of somebody who stutters, emits vocal tics or has trouble articulating strikes us immediately. It sounds wrong and can even be unsettling. But what seems obvious may not be objectively so. This is the question I asked Everett when we met up, not in the Amazon, but in Liverpool where he was on an academic residency. 'In every Western society, the reactions to disfluency are fairly similar,' he told me:

> There's a real pressure to conform. Whereas I've noticed in some of the smaller societies there is more variation at the individual level in pronunciation, all sorts of variation you wouldn't find here. So I have encountered disfluency in Pirahã speakers. But nobody even comments about it or appears to notice it. I have seen people who had severe difficulty articulating consonants like p, t and k and instead would use a glottal stop [an explosive consonantal sound produced by obstructing airflow in the vocal tract]. And I've asked questions about it because I'm a linguist and I need to know what's going on and they almost get offended by the question.

While we are highly attuned to even the most barely perceptible disfluencies of speech, in Pirahã they are just characteristics of an individual's way of speaking. Even when an outsider introduces a Western 'speech disorder' into their language, the reaction is the same. 'One of my co-workers when I was a missionary had the worst stutter I ever heard,' Everett says. 'The Pirahã may very well have noticed there was a difference, but they never showed the slightest interest or concern in it.' Gradually, Everett began to experience it the same way. 'When I first met her, it was very hard for me not to act like there wasn't anything abnormal happening. I knew what she wanted to say, everyone knew what she wanted to say, and she was taking a while to get it out. But after I got to know her, I didn't even think about it any more because we spoke to each other all the time.'

Everett's observations about the lack of interest or even awareness of speech disorders in Pirahã highlights the extent to which they may be culturally determined. Disfluencies like stuttering may simply be idiosyncratic ways of speaking that are pathologised as medical problems within a particular social and cultural context.

I have described both the behavioural and psychological dimension of speech disorders, but this third – the cultural dimension – is the hardest to grasp. It is easy to understand the physiological notion that some people struggle to release their words in the effortless way others do. The idea that a person's psychological response antagonises this makes it a little more complicated. That culture might minimise or exaggerate the effect of a disorder, or even determine its existence entirely, seems to contradict the behavioural evidence. Surely a stutter or a tic is a neurological fact: it occurs, involuntarily, and we all recognise it when it does. But Daniel Everett is by no means a lone voice in questioning these assumptions.

In their essay 'Diversity Considerations in Speech and Language', two speech-language pathologists called Brian Goldstein and Ramonda Horton-Ikard argue that 'Speech and language acquisition does not occur in a vacuum but is mediated by the culture from which the child comes.

This environment is defined broadly and includes, but is not limited to, parents, siblings, extended family members, peers, teachers, and so on.' Speech is only considered defective 'if it deviates from the norms, expectations and definitions of his or her indigenous culture.'[2] In a small community like Pirahã, that deviation is simply everything that is not Pirahã. Indeed, the term they use to describe other languages translates as 'crooked head'[3] – something askew. But any variation within, by virtue of being Pirahã, is accepted. 'The Pirahã is like one big family,' Everett says, 'so I think that has something to do with the toleration of much wider degrees of individual diversity. There would be no reason to comment on your stutter, for instance, because I've known you all my life and that's no shock to me.'

In industrialised societies, you can spend all your life in the same small market town, let alone a big metropolis, and still not know everyone you encounter. In this context, small variations in speech and dialect become incredibly important: a way of denoting us and them. Sometimes we describe these differences as dialect or accent; sometimes as defectiveness. Historically, children in the United States who spoke African-American Vernacular English (AAVE) were frequently diagnosed with a language disorder. This continued right up until the turn of the century when AAVE, also known as ebonics, began to be recognised as a systematic and rule-governed dialect in its own right. There is also evidence that the very nature of speech disorders varies across languages and cultures with physiological traits that are unique to each community.[4]

Within a society, attitudes towards speech disorders

may vary according to class. To take one example: Elizabeth Bowen, author of *The Death of the Heart* and *The Heat of the Day,* stuttered all her life. The circles in which she moved were distinctly upper class. Those she encountered socially found her stutter simply enhanced the eloquence of her speech. One friend described 'the stammering flow of her enthralling talk', another how her impediment gave 'an attractive touch of diffidence to her wide-ranging conversation'.[5] One British Council representative who booked her to give a talk in Zurich, described her speech impediment as 'endearing' in his official report. He concluded, 'She is a *most* successful lecturer with a *most* successful stammer.' These attitudes were typical of the British upper class at the time. Speech impediments suggested a certain unworldliness and rarified existence, like the stutter Evelyn Waugh gave to his 'aesthete par excellence' Anthony Blanche in *Brideshead Revisited,* in contrast to the smooth talk of the world of business.

And then there was the opinion of the wider population. In 1956, a BBC radio producer wrote an internal memo explaining why they had kept Elizabeth Bowen away from the airwaves, while embracing so many lesser-known writers. 'Elizabeth Bowen', it begins, 'is a stammerer. That is why we have never used her on such a big undertaking before we had tape.' Now, empowered by the innovation of pre-recording, their recommendation was to give her a try. 'We believe that she will be able to speak rather more fluently, however, if she is allowed to speak unscripted from notes and is allowed – if necessary – to rest during recording or to repeat difficult passages.'

Whatever permission that was required was soon granted and, from the insights of the BBC's Audience Research Department, we know how the general public reacted to Bowen's ensuing broadcasts. Despite the best efforts to re-record and edit out her trickier moments, listeners were irritated by Bowen's 'slow, jerky and hesitant delivery' and found her stutter 'painful to hear'.[6] It seems that what was endearing and scarcely disruptive for Bowen's upper-class associates was grating and distracting for the rest of the population.

The role of culture in defining and describing speech disorders is unsettling. The trouble a person has with stuttering, ticcing, using or articulating words seems innate, a physiological fact, even if symptoms are variable and exaggerated through the psychological experience of them. But by foregrounding the cultural dimension of speech disorders, we don't negate these other elements. We do, however, broaden and enrich our understanding of them.

This cultural dimension is in itself complex, although easily broken down into three main areas. The first is sociological: how a society, or elements within a society, react to any form of difference, turning what another society might consider negligible into an intractable problem. The second is linguistic: how a society's attitudes to language, and the labels it uses, enhance artificial constructs about good and bad speech. And the third (the subject of the next chapter) is culture in the more traditional sense: how the ideas and arts of a society work to include and exclude different ways of speaking.

Together, these three elements create an exaggerated

divide between those who are deemed fluent and those who are deemed disfluent or disordered in speech. The only way to debunk that binary perception is to expose the stereotypes and assumptions that support it. This is, in turn, the necessary first step to the rehabilitation and even appreciation of speech disorders within society.

Let's start with the sociological aspect. I have defined a 'speech disorder' as a consistent and obtrusive struggle in communicating the words you want to say. For the majority, that struggle is small and doesn't, in the case of the person with a slight stutter or early stage Parkinson's, prevent them from saying what they want to say. For others, as in severe aphasia or cerebral palsy, it is fundamental, becoming the defining or determining factor in how they communicate (sometimes an individual ceases to struggle, often because they choose to use alternative means of communication like Sign or Augmented and Alternative Communication devices, and when that happens we rarely think of them as having a speech disorder as such).

For some, the physical sensation of struggling with words may not be particularly negative. Any pain it causes, the additional labour in verbal performance it requires, or the impact on overall words spoken, may be small. The real difficulty emerges when that disorder is placed in a social context. This is almost always unavoidable because speech is, after all, a social tool. We can think of speech disorders, therefore, as mostly dormant conditions that are triggered when an individual comes into contact with others. It is only then that the worst symptoms – avoidance and concealment tactics, alienation and depression – are also activated. But unlike the physical symptoms, these psychological ones do not dissipate outside of social contact: they become all pervasive, haunting an individual's solitary hours. So while speech disorders are increasingly acknowledged and talked about as neurological in origin, their development and fruition is dependent on social factors. As we saw in the last chapter, the main determinant in a person's psychological response to the experience of a disorder is how family, schoolmates, teachers, co-workers and strangers react to it.

In his descriptions of the Pirahã, Daniel Everett offers the enticing vision of a society that simply ignores such disturbances in speech and communication. Unfortunately, this is far from the case with ours. From the schoolyard bullying of the kid with dysarthria to the infantilisation of the person with aphasia to the frequent discrimination in job interviews against the person with a stutter, the litany of acts of exclusion against those with speech disorders is endless. The trauma of these encounters encourages a secretive and self-censoring mentality in an individual who may retreat from society, or even attempt suicide to avoid further humiliation.

In some cases, social responses not only exacerbate a speech disorder, but transform its primary, or behavioural, symptoms. For people who stutter, problematic sounds and words shift and evolve according to the anxiety they cause. It is no coincidence, after all, that after years of stammering during school and even workplace roll-calls, the sounds of my own name became the hardest for me to utter. Similarly, when first describing the symptoms that would later become known as Tourette's syndrome in 1825, the physician Jean Itard concluded that the more his patient Madame de Dampierre was revolted by a word's 'grossness ... the more she is tormented by the fear that she will utter them, and this preoccupation is precisely what puts them at the tip of her tongue where she can no longer control it'.[7]

'Rude tics are about social context,' says Jess Thom. 'Those I'm most frightened of are the ones that I think would most damage other people because I don't want to damage anyone else's confidence or self-esteem or sense of self.' As a result, she tries to curate what language she is exposed to, avoiding situations, television programmes or music that might highlight racial stereotypes or derogatory names. 'It seems bizarre on the face of it,' writes medical historian Howard Kushner, 'that something as rooted in culture as the utterance of inappropriate phrases or obscene words could be attached to organic disease ... Even if neurobiology and biochemistry play an important role, a brain cannot "curse" without knowledge about what a culture views as a linguistic taboo.'[8]

The role of context is less vital in aphasia and dysarthria as they are generally linked to brain damage or neurodegenerative conditions, but many still report their speech varies according to how relaxed they are. Anxiety or humiliation are stressful emotions that temporarily worsen speech performance. My own stutter activates in certain social situations, such as public speaking, particularly if I am doing so off the cuff. But it also occurs, on the opposite end of the spectrum, in moments of great intimacy and emotional vulnerability. While I don't entirely share Wendell Johnson's view that a stutter is created by the ears of others rather than the mouth of a speaker, I think it is clear that the scale of a disorder is connected to the willingness, or lack of willingness, that a society has to accommodate it.

While speech disorders are considered neurological conditions in their medical context, in sociological terms they may be classified as a form of stigma. In his landmark 1963 book *Stigma: Notes on the Management of Spoiled Identity*, the sociologist Erving Goffman defined his subject as 'the situation of the individual who is disqualified from full social acceptance'. The word is Greek for a bodily sign like the branding of a slave, designed to show something unusual and bad about the bearer. 'We believe the person with a stigma is not quite human,' suggests Goffman. 'We tend to impute a wide range of imperfections on the basis of the original one.'[9] This is why we often suspect that those with speech disorders may have some sort of mental impairment or psychological trauma.

As Emperor of Rome in the first century AD, Tiberius Claudius Caesar was both man and deity. But not even his divine status could save him from the unpardonable offence of having a speech disorder. For centuries it has been assumed this was a stutter, but recent scholarship suggests that he had a form of cerebral palsy called Little's disease that may have prompted symptoms of stuttering as well as difficulty in articulating. Either way, he was considered the most ungodlike of living deities. According to Suetonius, his own mother considered him a 'monster of a man'.[10] Shortly after the Emperor's death, Seneca the Younger wrote a satire describing his apotheosis, or ascent to the heavens. In this work, Claudius's last words roughly translate as 'O no! I think I have shat all over myself.' He arrives at Olympus, but none of the gods can understand him because of his unintelligible speech.[11]

There is another side to the story though. Surviving documents suggest he could be effective at public speaking, even if his voice sounded a little odd.[12] Clearly there was a disjunction between the actual difficulty his speech disorder presented to communication and the way Roman society decided to interpret it. This, then, is the difference between a physiological condition and a stigma. The first is real; the latter a collective fiction which through critical mass takes on the appearance of reality.

While the neurological disturbances behind a speech disorder may be fundamentally the same across continents and epochs, a stigma is culturally dependent and therefore fluctuates. Not only across different societies, but also within them. Even in my lifetime attitudes to different types of speech in the United Kingdom have changed immensely. When I was born in 1975, minority dialects and accents were treated as stigma akin to disfluencies. In *The Presentation of Self in Everyday Life,* Goffman linked 'dialect and sub-standard speech' as negative character traits.[13] Geordie, Mancunian, stuttering and dysarthria all thrown in the same bucket. In the UK, the term 'Received Pronunciation' (RP) emerged in the 1920s to describe approved or 'normal' pronunciation. RP has been called at different times 'public school pronunciation', 'Oxford English', and more recently, 'Standard Southern British English'.[14] Because the BBC emerged at the same time as RP, a clipped, southern tone became the official lingua franca of the nation's broadcaster. Everything else was 'other' and implicitly inferior.

When my parents began their careers as journalists in the 1960s, they cultivated RP to get on in the world. For my father this was simply a question of exaggeration. His working-class father had already hacked away his cockney roots and catapulted his family to Home Counties splendour. When my sister and I found old recordings of dad doing interviews or reports we used to roll around laughing because he suddenly sounded like Prince Charles. Such reinvention in the United Kingdom was harder for my mother who was just off the boat from Australia, but her accent quickly found an inoffensive middle-ground somewhere between Sydney and London.

Forty years on, regional accents are celebrated in the media and in professional services (particularly call centres). In the BBC, where I work, RP has given way to a plethora of accents not only from across the UK, but the world (there is even a BBC News Pidgin service which, although considered a language rather than a dialect, is mostly comprehensible to the English speaker). There are many reasons for this change, but they all come down to the same thing: we no longer find it acceptable to openly discriminate on the basis of class or regionality.

For those with speech disorders, the dramatic and ongoing shift in attitude towards regional dialect is enviable but also a source of hope. But while there are signs of some change (I will describe some of these later), the stigma remains. Except as an occasional novelty, people do not stutter, tic or struggle to articulate on media outlets and certainly not call centres. It might be argued that this is because dialect is more intelligible than disordered speech to a fluent mainstream, but this is not the case. Most of us can recall situations when we've struggled to understand other dialects. On the other hand, speech disorders are unusual but generally intelligible, except when extremely advanced.

I have talked about two historical leaders, Claudius and George VI, whose difficulties with speech became a form of stigma. At the time of writing, Joe Biden has been selected as the President Elect of the United States of America. Biden has reminisced over the years about his childhood stutter. He has even implied his sense of political justice comes in part from the humiliation he experienced at school: his first act of protest was walking out of a classroom when a teacher mocked his struggle to say his surname. Now in his late-seventies, Biden's speech seems affected in different ways. During campaign speeches, he sometimes appeared to forget words or say the wrong things. He once referred to himself as a 'gaffe machine'.[15] This led to frequent claims, mostly by rivals, that 'Sleepy Joe' suffers from the memory lapses symptomatic of mental decline and is not fit for office.

Around the summer of 2019, John Hendrickson, political editor of *The Atlantic*, became convinced that Biden's childhood stutter and late-life gaffes were not separate issues. Hendrickson, also a person who stutters, noticed a pattern to Biden's gaffes. They tended to happen around words with similar sounds, for instance. Often it was obvious that Biden hadn't actually forgotten what he wanted to say, but was trying to find other words with which to say it. Hendrickson concluded that Biden had never 'overcome' his stutter, but was in fact stuttering the whole time: blocking on words and using circumlocution to avoid them.[16]

Hendrickson's theory is that Biden, confronted with a choice to stutter openly or feign forgetfulness, was choosing the latter. The cost of this is immense. 'At an August town hall', Hendrickson writes, 'Biden briefly blocked on Obama, before subbing in 'my boss'. The headlines afterwards? 'Biden forgets Obama's name.' Hendrickson suggests Biden's reluctance to admit to stuttering was partly because of the story he was trying to tell about himself: his stutter was one of those triumphs over adversity that presidential candidates like to talk about. But there is another reason too. Political campaigns are carefully choreographed events with candidates and their advisors shaping the message they want to present to the world. If Hendrickson's theory is true (and I find it compelling), then it is possible Biden felt more comfortable suffering regular accusations of mental decline than admitting to stuttering. Whether this decision occurred at a conscious or unconscious level is impossible to tell as concealing a stutter becomes second nature for those, like me, who can. Either way, Biden's story is another reminder that while Claudius and George VI are figures of bygone times, the issues they faced haven't gone away in the slightest.

So why has the stigma of speech disorders proved so intractable? Goffman suggested one theory. While support groups and activist movements have long existed for almost every type of social stigma (whether alcoholics, ex-convicts, the aged, the obese, the physically handicapped), he claimed, 'there are speech defectives whose peculiarity apparently discourages any group formation whatsoever.' Goffman found this perplexing considering how disabling such conditions could be. Since isolation and secretiveness are key psychological symptoms of speech disorders, this is understandable. But I believe it also emerges from a tendency to look at speech disorders in medicalised silos ('Tourette's syndrome', 'aphasia', 'dysarthria') rather than as different expressions of the same discriminating social framework.

For most of my life, I embodied the 'peculiarity' that Goffman writes about. I refused to talk about my speech except in safe institutionalised spaces like the Michael Palin Centre for Stammering Children. I maintained this silence even when I encountered other people who stuttered. On one occasion, in a restaurant in Newcastle, I stared blankly at a clearly distressed waiter who stuttered throughout our exchanges when I'm sure one kind word of solidarity would have alleviated his suffering. And I still recoil in self-disgust at my inexplicable laughter in the face of a stuttering German student in a youth hostel in Rome some twenty years ago. I can only explain it as a moment of irrational hysteria, as if coming upon a doppelgänger of myself, as I had encountered so few people who overtly stuttered at that stage in my life.

With so little empathy even for other people who stutter, the idea that I had anything in common with other speech disorders never even occurred to me. Sometime in the late 1980s there was an attempt to set up a National

Speech Day to raise awareness of speech disorders. My mother and I joined a press event in Hyde Park where I was photographed alongside children with other conditions and speech disorders. I remember looking down the line and thinking, 'what am I doing here?' In keeping with Goffman's theory, National Speech Day soon disappeared. The only evidence I have of it is an old newspaper photograph of a minor celebrity advocate, a row of children and my strained smile. It is only in the last five years that I have started talking to people with the whole spectrum of speech disorders and realised how much we have in common.

There is one other reason, but perhaps the biggest, why the stigma of speech disorders remains so entrenched. It is not to do with such disorders themselves but of what they are defined against: the notion of fluency. Although an ongoing process, dismantling the stigma of dialect has been immensely enabled by a growing awareness that RP is a sacred cow worth killing. For while 'public-school pronunciation', 'Oxford English' and 'Standard Southern British English' may dominate our culture still, they are also associated with privilege, elitism and inequality. But how does one go about denigrating a notion so apparently virtuous as 'fluency'? It may not be possible to do so, yet without it speech disorders will always be considered a sub-standard expression of language.

How a society thinks about its languages and the labels it gives to its different usages enhance ideas of good and bad speech. The very term 'speech disorder', after all, determines from the outset how we are to think about stuttering, aphasia, dysarthria and vocal tics. As a child, just knowing I had a 'stutter' made me extremely conscious of the blockages and repetitions in my speech. Similarly, many of the social prejudices about speech disorders are determined the moment they are labelled as conditions, and those prejudices, like the label itself, inform and exacerbate both the psychological and behavioural traits of those conditions.

Our ability to even think about this issue is hampered from the outset: *disfluency, disorder, abnormal* and *impediment*. These terms are radically different, even oppositional, to another set: *fluency, order, normal, unimpeded*. Linguistically, a thick line implicitly separates normal speakers from those with speech disorders, often through the use of binary, negating prefixes like *dis-* or *ab-*. The moment we start talking about disfluency or disorder, we are already assuming a degree of defectiveness; an influence that is difficult to evade. This is a trick of linguistics rather than a reflection of reality, for once we label something in a negative way it determines how we view it. (For instance, if somebody tells me that a particular person is 'immoral', it will colour my perception of them until I am convinced otherwise.) So if we strip away these binary positive and negative terms, how much difference is there really between 'fluent' and 'disfluent' speech?

When we encounter a person with a speech disorder, our brains try to make sense of a difference that may be extremely pronounced or even quite subtle. Labelling is key to this process. If I meet someone whose eyes are different colours (a condition called heterochromia iridum), it may take me a moment to realise what is unsettling me, but once I identify the difference I feel more relaxed.

Likewise, if somebody's speech is scattered with disfluencies, it will perplex me until the point that I determine that they have a stutter; or if interspersed with vocal tics, I may start to suspect Tourette's syndrome. Such labelling doesn't require knowledge of medical terms. After all, many people who have dysarthria aren't even aware of this term. But it requires knowledge or experience of a type of vocal dysfunction. Sometimes labelling may just be a suspicion that one stranger who speaks slowly and uncertainly might have had a stroke, while another who is unsteady and has unusual articulation may be in the early stage of Parkinson's disease or motor neurone disease.

Whether named or not, this process of labelling is important for us, as all those individual disruptions in the way a person talks suddenly become expressions of a single cause or characteristic. It is often accompanied by a sense of relief. We don't like uncertainty, particularly when dealing with strangers. 'People are so used to whatever their concept of normal human interaction is that when someone different comes along they are thrown,' says Lee Ridley, a stand-up comic with cerebral palsy. 'They're not used to a bloke who can't communicate in the usual way. They're not getting the well-versed social signs through body language and facial expression, so they're not sure how they're doing. Am I saying the right things? Am I keeping eye contact in the right way?'[17]

The problem is that once we label a person in this way, we burden them with all the preconceptions and prejudices we may have about a condition. Labels, like all forms of categorisation, are useful illusions that help us make sense of the world, but they also lead us to attribute general qualities that may not be relevant to particular individuals. Our assumption is that a *dis*order of speech is a breakdown of function. This leads to discrimination in the workplace and other social environments.

Take, for instance, the common perception that word flow – and, therefore, productivity itself – is slower or reduced in a person with a speech disorder. While this is true in some cases, it is by no means a universal trait. People who stutter often compensate by speaking quickly between stuttering events. The rhythm of their speech may swing between extremes but they don't necessarily get less words out. While for people with Tourette's syndrome, vocal tics often fill up the natural pauses that arise in speech rather than creating them. Even if speech is rendered slower, it may not be less effective. For Jamie Beddard, dysarthria makes him more economic in his choice and use of words, but not in his overall ability to communicate. Rather than letting our labels and prejudices determine the capability and limits of a person's speech, we would do far better to simply familiarise ourselves with their unique speech patterns just as we unconsciously do with all the 'fluent' speakers we encounter.

If certain people have speech disorders, impediments or disfluencies, then those who don't – a sizeable majority – are implicitly 'fluent'. Studies of speech disorders rarely attempt to define what we mean by this, dragging the reader into an oppressive and sometimes airless space in which the notion of a 'disorder', and the gulf separating it from normal speech, is assumed from the outset. Yet it is impossible to truly make sense of such conditions unless we are clear about what it is they are apparently failing to perform. Just as we need to define disfluency, we also need to define fluency.

'To be a fluent speaker of a language means to be able to enter any conversation in ways that are seen as appropriate and not disruptive,' writes linguist Alessandro Duranti.[18] According to David Crystal, fluency is the 'ability to communicate easily, rapidly, and continuously'.[19] The word itself derives from the Latin 'fluere': to flow. The fluent tongue is like a river, gathering momentum and speed as it moves from a mountain spring into a great estuary opening out to sea. But despite images of flowing rivers and unimpeded tongues, 'fluency' is far more complicated than at first appears. It's a quality that applies to a lot of people and yet there is a huge amount of variation between them. A great orator like Barack Obama as well as the mumbling teenager in the upstairs bedroom; the clipped tone of the Queen of England as well as the broadest dialects of our remotest regions: all these may be considered fluent.

While there are those who have a quiet, or not so quiet, confidence in their speaking ability, just as many of us feel tongue-tied, lacking the ease and naturalness of speech that fluency implies. Rather than setting up fluency and disfluency as binary opposites, it would be more accurate to think of fluency as a spectrum in which people move back and forth over the course of their lives. Even this is of only limited value for it might capture the sound of somebody's speech but not how they feel about it. There are fluent speakers who experience as much anxiety about their voices as those with diagnosed speech disorders. According to a YouGov poll from 2014, fear of public speaking, or *glossophobia,* is the third biggest phobia in the UK after heights and snakes,[20] fuelling an industry of voice coaches, workshops and self-help books.

The etymology and ideal of 'fluency' suggests an ease and rapidity of verbal performance, but what does it sound like in reality? In recent years, projects like CANCODE (Cambridge and Nottingham Corpus of Discourse in English) have recorded millions of words of everyday conversation. In transcribing conversation, researchers develop a grammar of symbols to denote the breakages in speech that don't occur in the written word. In the case of CANCODE, '+' marks the point where one speaker's utterance is interrupted by another. A common sign is '=', which shows when a speaker has either changed their course in mid-sentence or in the middle of an individual word, as in the following exchange:

Speaker 2: Yeah. I wonder now about people who go into the army these days like m= I had a friend erm who went who was a good friend of mine when I was at school you know+

Speaker 1: Mm.

Speaker 2: +up till sixteen. After that we lost touch a bit but he only lives round the corner from me now. But he went erm on a army course recently and he did really well and he got to the last thing at Sandhurst where you would go+

Speaker 1: Yeah. [laughs]

Speaker 2: +in as an officer+

Speaker 1: Yeah.

Speaker 2: +and he did the thing there and he fa= he fell at the last hurdle. And

Speaker 1: What he he, you're talking metaphorically here?

Speaker 2: and and er fitness trainings and did really well and now he's gotta go in as a, as a yu= you know as a regular.[21]

Struggling to keep up? What such exchanges repeatedly demonstrate is how disfluent 'fluent' speech really is, with persistently awful grammar, verbal stumbles, torturous and rather inarticulate attempts to express the ideas in our minds. 'The voice is supposed to be suffused with spirit,' writes linguist Steven Connor. 'But the voice is not always quite itself … it is full of poltergeists, noisy, paltering parasites and hangers-on, mouth-friends, vapours and minute jacks.'[22] Those qualities we associate with everyday fluency, an uninterrupted ease and rapidity of delivery, are extremely rare. We are, in fact, all disfluent, but in such a large variety of ways that each individual slip is scarcely noticeable. It is only when one type of disfluency eclipses all others, like a vocal tic or the block of a stutter, that we describe someone as having a speech disorder.

All this is well known to speech-language therapists. In defining the traits of stuttering, for instance, the important distinction is not between disfluency and fluency but between abnormal and everyday disfluency. According to *The Handbook of Language and Speech Disorders,* disfluencies like *interjections* ('he went-um-home'), *word repetitions* ('he-he-he went home'), *phrase repetitions* ('he went-he went home'), *revisions* ('he went-he ran home'), *incomplete phrases* (he went …'), and *broken words* (he we-[pause]-nt home) are all part of fluent speech.[23] None of these should be considered symptomatic of stuttering, which is identifiable by part-word repetitions, some forms of word repetition, prolonged sounds and tense pauses. Add it up, and there are actually more types of disfluency in everyday fluency than in stuttering. Fluency, like disfluency, is an illusion. Once you accept this, it is difficult to hear human speech in quite the same way, but the repercussions are only positive. There is no need for anyone to feel overwhelming anxiety about their speech because there is no perfect standard to aspire to, while any discrimination against those with speech disorders is hypocritical.

The discovery that 'normal' speech can be just as disfluent as many speech disorders comes as a shock. One reason for this lies in the processing of the brain. In order to make sense of the conversations we participate in, it is necessary at an unconscious level to strip away all the non-essential information – the 'poltergeists, noisy, paltering parasites and hangers-on' – scattered throughout our speech. We only notice such disruptions if they have a pathological regularity that repeatedly draws our attention. The human brain looks for patterns in the material world and a speech disorder is just one such pattern. What is in reality a sliding scale is given a binary separation in our minds: normal, and therefore unnoticeable, disfluency; or abnormal, and therefore disruptive, disorders.

While ignoring the ums and ahs, the blockages and repetitions, we also over-emphasise the role of speech in communication. While we fixate on (and often regret) the things we say, sociological studies repeatedly show that much, even the majority, of human communication is nonverbal, based on body language and tone of voice as well as words.[24] Yet it is the words themselves we hang onto, perhaps because they seem more tangible and less ambiguous. There are, after all, many dictionaries that tell us exactly what they mean, while interpreting atmosphere and gesture is more often a question of instinct. But we also know that if somebody is hurt by our behaviour, it is more likely to be because we didn't look at them or turned our bodies away rather than any specific comment. And this is why we, in turn, are sometimes relieved or triumphant when somebody we have long suspected doesn't like us says something that actually confirms it.

If words aren't so important this should mean that speech disorders scarcely present a problem to the ease and rapidity of communication, but the opposite is true. In the 1970s, the psychologist Albert Mehrabian famously devised a rule which argued that our emotional response (liking, disliking or indifference) to a person is determined mostly by their body language (55 per cent), then their tone of voice (38 per cent), with comparatively little depending on the words they say (7 per cent).[25] Unconsciously, it seems, we are far less trusting in the power of language than we profess: and wisely too, bearing in mind what we know through speech corpuses like CANCODE. But it also explains why the immediate reaction to somebody with a speech disorder can be so negative. Since such conditions affect not only the tone of voice, but are often accompanied by further physical contortions in the face or body, listeners are more likely to notice them. They react far more to the behavioural signs of the disorder, allowing it to influence and even determine their emotional response to that individual, than anything they might have to say – and that, in turn, interferes with the process of communication.

The illusion of fluency and disfluency is partly down to human nature. It is created by our brains which prejudice in favour of what is tangible (words rather than gestures) and by our memory which simplifies the mess of conversation. Not only do we edit conversations as and after they occur, ignoring recurring and unobtrusive slippages of the tongue, but we overemphasise the role of speech in all interpersonal exchanges. It is hardly surprising then that many societies treat speech disorders as grand human failings that compromise the preciousness of communication.

But this illusion is also cultural: the reverence for fluency varies across human societies. In the post-industrial societies of the twenty-first century, it is considered far more than an enabler of communication, but the key to all success; the glue that ties society together; the essence of being human. This false conception has evolved through our 'culture', in the traditional sense of the term, shaped by philosophy, politics and aesthetics. As we are about to discover, our society defines disorders not only against fluency but an extreme version of it: a *hyper-fluency* that sits on the other end of a spectrum to disfluency, and is as far from everyday fluency as that is from disfluency.

4

The Tyranny of Fluency

In February 2002, a forty-five-year-old British entrepreneur stepped onto the stage of a lecture theatre in California and made an announcement that would change the course of his life. The event was an annual conference devoted to speakers from the worlds of technology, entertainment and design. It had been running for eighteen years but was on its last legs: its peak seemed past, its founder was retiring, attendance was down to only seventy. In theory, it had little power to make or break anyone's career except this man had made the dubious decision to buy it. TED was his gamble and he needed all the people in the room to back him.

Chris Anderson's vision was to take the content of TED – which, after all, had a track record of attracting some superb speakers – and put it on the internet. Making videos is straightforward enough, doing it in a way that people want to watch them remotely is far harder. In selling TED as a brand, Anderson had to sell an aspirational idea of what a lecture can be. His breakthrough was to recast the public speaker as hero.

This emerged through the aesthetics of what was soon recognisable as the TED style. There is the speaker's platform: empty, uncluttered, spotlit in the centre and fading away into darkness. There is the audience itself, revealed in dimly lit, wide shots that communicate their admiration but prevent any distraction from the solitary character on stage. There is the posture of the speaker, liberated of lectern and microphone through the means of a headset to stand alone, vulnerable and defiant before the crowd. But most of all, there are the speaker's words. These are talks that are full of humility, revelation and human stories. They are rehearsed over and over again, timed to the second, resulting in sometimes breathtaking performances of charismatic verbal fluency.

While some TED talks are more successful than others, there is a set of principles that runs through them all. Anyone can learn these simply by watching the content or reading the publications, official and unofficial, that reveal TED's 'secrets'. All emphasise the same things: the importance of authenticity and vulnerability, of telling stories rather than giving facts, of delivering jaw-dropping revelations, as well as what to wear and how much to rehearse. Most of all, the importance of eighteen minutes, which Anderson described as 'long enough to be serious and short enough to hold people's attention'.[1]

'Great speakers find a way of making an early connection with their audience,' Anderson writes in his book *TED Talks*. He takes as an example a talk by a successful health psychologist:

> Take a look at the first few moments of Kelly McGonigal's TED Talk on the upside of stress. 'I have a confession to make.' [she pauses, turns, drops hands,

gives a little smile] 'But first, I want YOU to make a little confession to me.' [walks forward] 'In the past year' [looks around intently from face to face] 'I want you to just raise your hand if you've experienced relatively little stress. Anyone?' [an enigmatic smile, which a few moments later turns into a million-dollar smile]. There is instant audience connection there.

For me, the most striking thing about this transcription isn't necessarily how effective Kelly McGonigal's talk is, but how mannered and choreographed it is compared to everyday speech and communication. The term Anderson uses to describe this is 'presentation literacy': the art of 'unlocking empathy, stirring excitement, sharing knowledge and insights, and promoting a shared dream'. Anyone who worries about their ability in this regard is right to do so. 'Presentation literacy isn't an optional extra for the few,' he writes. 'It's a core skill for the twenty-first century.' The success of TED suggests that he is right.

Within a few years, Anderson had turned TED around from a small conference of waning influence to a global phenomenon. The high contrast, visual simplicity of the content – a lone individual against a dark backdrop, often with hands thrusting out before them like a twenty-first-century prophet – worked well for the early years of internet streaming. Even pixellated, its power carried. Thinkers, academics, entrepreneurs and activists, who had struggled for mainstream recognition, became celebrated overnight with immediate impact on book sales and businesses. Ken Robinson, Amy Cuddy and Simon Sinek: brilliant but formerly low-profile intellectuals whose talks have now been seen by over forty million people around the world. This in turn attracted major celebrities like Bill Clinton, Bono and Bill Gates. Seats at the conference itself became hot tickets and now cost thousands of dollars – just to see people talking. Before long, TED franchised the brand. According to their website, there are TEDx conferences in over 130 countries a year, with an average of eight events taking place every day: from Iran to India as well as America and the UK.

The global triumph of TED is symptomatic of a transformational moment in our relationship with a particular linguistic register. Neither Anderson's term 'presentation literacy' nor the more old fashioned 'public speaking' seem to quite describe it. While there are those individuals who become a different personality on stage, there are also those whose heightened fluency transcends both private and public discourse. They speak with extraordinary eloquence and expressiveness, both personable and memorable, seemingly without the everyday disfluencies of fluent speech. In this regard, their speech is as removed from everyday fluency as disfluency is supposed to be – and it explains in part why so many perfectly 'fluent' people feel such a sense of inadequacy. Not so much fluency, therefore, as hyper-fluency: speech without the ums and ahs.

The pressure to be hyper-fluent is something many of us know, fear, and are unable to avoid: not only job interviews and PowerPoint presentations, but also (less regularly) stage-of-life addresses, like those at weddings and funerals. It pursues us into seemingly innocuous social scenarios. The party piece and pub anecdote are second nature to some, but sources of anxiety and feelings of inadequacy for the many who struggle with them. We work hard at improving our performance in these arenas. The success of organisations like TED, as well as a large industry of voice coaches, public speaking gurus and self-help books, testifies to this. But how desirable is hyper-fluency really?

In *Quiet: The Power of Introverts in a World That Can't Stop Talking*, Susan Cain argues that our culture is dominated by what she calls an 'Extrovert Ideal'. Cain is convinced that the power of the introvert is lost in our culture and the Extrovert Ideal dominates everything we do: not just our professional lives, but our social and even domestic selves as well.

> Talkative people, for example, are rated as smarter, better-looking, more interesting and more desirable as friends. Velocity of speech counts as well as volume: we rank fast talkers as more competent and likeable than slow ones. The same dynamics apply in groups, where research shows that the voluble are considered smarter than the reticent – even though there's zero correlation between the gift of the gab and good ideas.[2]

While volubility, the quality of talking fluently, is identified as a common characteristic of the extrovert, the absence of it doesn't always imply introversion. Many with speech disorders struggle to get their words out irrespective of where they sit on the introvert–extrovert spectrum. But I do think we can apply the same scepticism about the supposed superiority of extroversion to hyper-fluency because of the considerable overlap between both qualities.

Undoubtedly, hyper-fluency can be a powerful and influential means of communication, as the finest TED talks show. But it has inherent risks and dangers too. Even when used with the best intentions, there is a gravitational pull to glibness and simplification, 'style over content' as the saying goes, that seems astonishing in the moment, but considered afterwards often seems nothing more than the obvious said well. While there is a popular misconception that the best ideas are simple (a statement which lends itself conveniently to a culture increasingly built around the power of short-form content), there is nothing simple about the Theory of Relativity: even Einstein struggled to make sense of it. Often in rendering complex ideas palatable, we strip them of their potency precisely by making them simple.

Hyper-fluent speakers can also be charlatans, con-artists and corruptors, exercising their skill for personal gain or just drunk on their own power. During the 1930s, the German linguist Victor Klemperer charted the way the Nazis secured their ascent through the manipulation of language.[3] The political success of Adolf Hitler and Joseph Goebbels lay in their oratory skills first and foremost, honed through years of public meetings and rallies. They consciously developed a technique that controlled a crowd through the repeated use of buzzwords, euphemisms and outright lies, but all under a veneer of supposed common sense and heartfelt passion. Klemperer provides many examples revealing just how elaborate this was.

The words *artfremd* (alien to the species), *ewig* (eternal, as in 'the eternal Reich'), and *volk* (people) were repeated endlessly. The word for 'murder' was replaced by 'special treatment', 'mass-murder' by 'final solution', while the war was always 'imposed' on a peace-loving Führer.

Less harmful, but worrying in a different way, is the way hyper-fluency can conceal an absence of content: verbal performances that are dazzling in the moment, but leave nothing behind. Our politics is polluted by a fluency prejudice which means leaders are often chosen by their resemblance to after dinner speakers rather than on the length and quality of their experience in public service. Meanwhile, social media is the making of multi-millionaire teenage YouTubers, who have a knack for talking compellingly about make-up or gaming with often little more than a bedroom wall behind them.

One of the most successful is Logan Paul, who began posting videos from his family home in Ohio when he was only ten years old. In his world, and that of thousands like him, hyper-fluency is not reserved for rare public speaking occasions, but is continuous: addressing an audience while in bed, on the way to school, out with friends. By the time he was twenty, Paul's videos had over 300 million views, and he was loved by kids for his banter and shameless boasting about his new-found wealth. The banter briefly ran out after he filmed and posted a video of a dead body in Mount Fuji's 'suicide forest'. Growing up on YouTube meant he was unable to separate the tragedy of somebody's dead son from clickbait. Over the real footage of the body he even pasted sentimental piano music to enhance its emotional power. Paul's response was no less bizarre. Rather than empathising with the victim or the victim's family, he said, 'this is a first for me,' as if the significance of the suicide lay in his experience of it.

Another problem with hyper-fluency is the way it both raises and narrows public perception of what qualifies as good communication. We come to think that there is only one acceptable style of speaking in public, which most of us aren't particularly proficient in. What gets lost in the mix is a diversity of public speaking styles: rambling talks which don't have an obvious message; uncharismatic talks by people too shy to look at the audience; talks which are just weird stories that don't obviously connect; talks which don't tell any stories at all but just give you facts; talks which haven't been learned by heart but sound like good prose when read from the page; talks which are very short or very long; talks by people who speak differently to others. All of which have a place in our culture, but of which our shortened attention spans are increasingly intolerant.

Marina Abramović is a world famous performance artist who has extolled the power of nonverbal communication through her work. She is perhaps best known for a show called *The Artist is Present* which ran for three months in 2011 at the Museum of Modern Art in New York. The concept was simple: Abramović sat in the same chair eight hours a day for three months. Visitors to the museum were able to sit opposite her and commune through silence and eye contact. It's not an immediately promising idea, but the response was extraordinary. Something happened in those silent exchanges. People claimed it changed their lives; many wept. Before it closed, people queued round the block overnight to seize the last opportunity for a silent encounter with Abramović.

Because of the success of the show, TED approached her to give a talk. The result is an odd marriage: an artist famous for advocating nonverbal communication restrained within an inflexible speech format. She looks uncomfortable. 'TED was really frustrating,' Abramović tells me when we speak on the phone. 'They time you. They wanted me to repeat and to verbalise things which I hated so much. I went crazy. I can't repeat things twice. It's just against me.' The difference between Abramović as a public speaker and as a nonverbal communicator is palpable in the videos of her TED talk and *The Artist is Present*. The latter have by far the greatest power. Hyper-fluency is a form of communication but by no means the only one, nor the best.

There is one final reason why I think we need to resist simply accepting hyper-fluency as an imperative for twenty-first-century life. As well as narrowing the diversity of communication styles, inclining to glibness and, in the wrong hands, deception, it is also exclusive. We are told that, with a bit of practice, anyone can speak well. But as much as we're told the potential is within us all, many of us have communication styles of one sort or another – whether speech impediments or introverted personality traits – that make the pithy, charismatic talk as out of reach as the four-minute mile.

The truth is that some people are better predisposed to hyper-fluency and 'presentation literacy' than others. So when we're told it is a core skill for life, we are right to worry, just as we would if told that a 'high IQ' or 'toned body' isn't an optional extra for the few. It is just one linguistic register in a spectrum that includes endless manifestations of everyday fluency as well as diagnosable disfluencies. By elevating it to an imperative we risk what has in fact happened: widespread social and economic discrimination against those who speak differently.

I believe that it is only when we challenge the supremacy of hyper-fluency in our society that we also challenge the discrimination against other ways of speaking, including speech disorders. Doing so will not be easy, yet we can learn from the discrepancies between cultures. 'Westerners are typically uncomfortable with silence, which they find embarrassing and awkward,' write Adler, Rodman and du Pré in *Understanding Human Communication*. 'On the other hand, Asian cultures tend to perceive talk quite differently ... Japanese and Chinese people more often believe that remaining quiet is the proper state when there is nothing to be said. To Asians, a talkative person is often considered a show-off or a fake.'[4]

In *Far From the Tree*, Andrew Solomon describes visiting a small village in northern Bali where a congenital form of deafness affects around 2 per cent of the population. Everyone there can use the unique sign language, called Kata Kolok, that they have developed. But what eventually struck Solomon wasn't the remarkable phenomenon of a community that was bilingual in spoken and sign language, but how secondary both were to community cohesion:

> For educated Westerners, intimacy requires the mutual knowledge achieved as language unlocks the

> secrets of two minds. But for some people the self is expressed largely in the preparation of food and the ministrations of erotic passion and shared labour, and for such people the meaning embedded in words is a garnish to love rather than its conduit. I had come into a society in which, for the hearing and the deaf, language was not the primary medium through which to negotiate the world.'[5]

Even within the West, there are unique traditions that revere non-verbal communication. In many Native American communities, silence is considered the appropriate way to express deep emotions like grief and anger:[6] hence the stereotype of the silent Apache in many Western films. And in Europe, social order was maintained throughout the Dark Ages largely due to the network of Christian monasteries that reached across the continent, generally founded on strict rules that regulated speech to a minimum. When the writer Patrick Leigh Fermor began staying at monasteries in the 1950s, he found that 'the desire for talk, movement and nervous expression that I had transported from Paris found, in this silent place, no response or foil, evoke no single echo'. Instead, he needed less sleep and found himself with 'nineteen hours a day of absolute and god-like freedom'.[7] The difference is that these Western traditions of silence have now been enclosed within reservations or small compounds, forgotten amid the noise of a culture addicted to chatter.

These examples don't negate the fact that hyperfluency can be useful in 'unlocking empathy, stirring excitement, sharing knowledge and insights,' as Chris

Anderson describes it, but they do remind us that there are other approaches. While we consider hyper-fluent speech a virtue, whether in the formal context of a presentation or the storytelling of the pub wag, we do well to remember that our perception is culturally determined and therefore relative, just like our attitude to speech disorders, rather than a reflection of something objectively good.

If hyper-fluency is cultural rather than innate to human nature, the question is how it developed and what purpose it serves. In *TED Talks*, Anderson offers an answer. While recognising 'presentation literacy' as a particularly twenty-first-century imperative, he suggests it is a modern embodiment of rhetoric, or the art of persuasion, drawing an evolutionary line between the assemblies and market places of the classical world and the TED URL. There is some truth in this. While first described in Mesopotamian and Egyptian texts, rhetoric emerged as a major discipline in Greece around 500 BC, inseparable from the political notion of democracy that it both informed and was shaped by.

Democracy is a politics of consensus and debate (often frustratingly prolonged) rather than the individual prerogative of a tyrant, in which a command can be brief and irrational, but effective. The uses of rhetoric, therefore, extended beyond lawgivers and a priest class to all those who participate in some way in the city life, or *polis*, of Athens. By the time Aristotle came to write *The Art of Rhetoric* in the fourth century BC, it had evolved into a highly codified and ritualistic practice: a sort of martial art, or Tongue Fu, of the voice.

In Rome, which saw itself as both conqueror and inheritor of Greek civilisation, rhetoric became even more revered. Roman Law, which contains the origins of our legal system, is based on spoken testimony and rhetorical advocacy rather than the rough justice of many non-democratic communities. Both Cicero and Quintilian, the great theorists of Roman rhetoric, began their careers as lawyers, and developed theories that position rhetoric more holistically as the external expression of a virtuous and enquiring individual rather than a self-contained discipline. In this regard, rhetoric gradually became a social signifier, evidence of a distinguished background and good education, as much as a pragmatic tool for persuasion.

'In the world of the Roman aristocracy,' writes classicist Christian Laes, 'achievement in oratory was as glorious as success on the battlefield.'[8] This is the beginning of a subtle difference between rhetoric and hyper-fluency, for where rhetoric has a purpose, hyper-fluency is a quality that an individual may reveal during even the most banal and purposeless of exchanges. A hyper-fluent individual, rather than a merely fluent one, is somebody clearly well-bred and intelligent; somebody you can trust and do business with, while hoping to gain access to the rarified social circles they have access to.

Rhetoric is not the only legacy from the classical world informing the fluency-prejudice of the twenty-first century. Just as important is that of another group of wordsmiths who had a difficult, sometimes outright hostile, relationship with those who practised the art of rhetoric. While we tend to think of philosophy today as a solitary and silent practice (thanks in part to iconic images like Rodin's *Thinker* who is locked in an intense and mute reverie with mouth literally stoppered by his own fist), for most of our history it has been an intensely social and conversational practice. In Ancient Greece, philosophy was dominated by 'schools': groups of pupils and peers who gathered around revered thinkers. The term signified 'love of wisdom'. Its focus extended beyond the (often obscure) riddles of existence we tend to associate it with today, and included natural science, physics, astronomy, mathematics. In short, everything one might consider as wisdom – until the drive to specialisation of relatively recent times.

Philosophy depended, then as now, on the use of words. The movement of the heavens, the atomic structures of invisible matter, the moral quandaries of daily life: all this could be explained, if only we tried hard enough, through speech alone. One early philosopher, Heraclitus, even elevated the term for word or speech, *logos,* to mean knowledge and cosmic order itself, as if human language contained all of natural law within its structures.

Socrates, perhaps the most famous of all philosophers, preferred dialogue and collective reasoning, the so-called Socratic Method, over abstract thought or demonstration as the means to all knowledge. He never wrote anything down and we depend on the writings of his pupils, particularly Plato, to know his teachings. Plato's works are all dramatic dialogues, in which he presents his master Socrates and his friends uncovering the secrets of the universe by simply talking to one another. Their speech is effortlessly fluent and idealised, unhampered by any sort of disfluency, whether the hesitations or repetitions of everyday speech or the stumbles, tics and distortions of speech disorders.

Greek philosophy is often described by scholars as logocentric, fixed on the word. While logocentrism has undoubtedly helped us to understand our lives better, it can also result in mere wordplay or, in certain cases, dangerous untruths. In Plato's *The Republic*, a series of genial, urbane conversations between Socrates and his friends seem to follow an irrefutable logic to an Orwellian nightmare of individual repression and banishment of art – slavery in everything but name. Yet these works set the tone and template for many of the great works of political philosophy to this day.

Together, the classical traditions of rhetoric and philosophy form the origins of modern hyper-fluency. They remind us that it is a way of speaking that has as much to do with class and verbal gymnastics as well as communication. As a result, the Greeks and Romans came to see fluency as synonymous with civilisation itself. Those who weren't civilised were barbarians. The Greek word 'barbaros' is related to the Sanskrit word 'barbara', which referred to the speech-defective and fool as much as the uncivilised outsider. This in turn informed the Latin word for a speech defect: *balbus*.

Throughout the classical world, there is a deliberate association of citizens who had speech disorders with the barbarians beyond the frontier. This is reflected in the broader attitude to speech disorders which is marked by lack of interest and occasional contempt. Christian Laes has found that in all the documents of the classical world there are only fourteen instances where it is suggested a particular individual has a speech disorder. In each case it is often hard to tell what type of disorder they had because their terms were so vague, in itself a sign of indifference. *Balbus* was a catch-all word for the person who stutters, lisps or is even just a bit clumsy. Increasingly, it is acknowledged that the two most famous examples of people who stutter in the classical world are false. Demosthenes, the famous Greek orator, who overcame his stutter by putting pebbles in his mouth, probably had little more than a slightly weak voice and a lisp. Claudius, as we have seen, probably had Little's disease.

What is significant is that in each of these instances the individual in question is somebody attempting to participate in public life. Since this revolved around the traditions of rhetoric and logos, anything that impeded their flow, like a speech disorder, could – and did – prove a barrier to success. There was no question of educated society tolerating such a defect: not even Claudius, as Emperor, was free from relentless disgust and mockery about the disorder in his speech. The general view was that he was unfit for such service, but must be tolerated because of who he was. Only those who completely overcame a speech disorder, like Demosthenes, would be truly accepted. The vagueness of Greek and Latin terms is symptomatic of these attitudes: there was little point in closely analysing the speech of somebody unfit for public life because they were, after all, little more than barbarians.

Bizarrely, it seems that for the rest of the population, the vast majority who were not of aristocratic birth and unable to participate meaningfully in public life, a speech disorder was scarcely a problem at all. While it must be assumed that as many people had speech disorders as they do today, it is impossible to tell for certain because, as Laes says, 'difficulty in speech was not often used as an identifying characteristic'. In other words, it was ignored. This suggests it is only in the context of an elite culture which has come to revere fluency of speech that disorders first become problematic.

Over the following millennia, those societies across the world that have viewed themselves as inheritors of classical civilisation, have automatically assumed a fluency-prejudice that is culturally determined rather than innate to human behaviour. In the eighteenth century, this prejudice became even more enhanced in Europe and North America with the perceived gulf between fluency and defective speech widening ever further. At the heart of this shift was a changing attitude to speech itself. 'Nothing deserves the name of man except what is able to speak,' wrote the scholar Friedrich Max Müller.[9] The German philosopher Johann Gottfried von Herder argued that speech was the single differentiating quality that set humankind apart from other animals.[10] Similar statements appear repeatedly in texts of the time.

The emphasis on speech alone as the distinguishing mark of humanity is a peculiar narrowing of Aristotle's famous and enduring statement that 'man is by nature a social animal': for while speech is a social tool, it is one among many and human societies can, if they choose, communicate without it. There are many reasons for this change. The intellectual 'Enlightenment' of the eighteenth century foregrounded the role of language and reason in defining human knowledge. But the most important shift arguably wasn't scholastic, but economic. For thousands of years, European society had been predominantly feudal in nature with individuals born and dying in the same status. Social mobility, as we understand it, was extremely difficult. But from the 1500s, the merchant class we associate with Tudor England or the Florence of the Medicis had grown both larger and more powerful, and by the early eighteenth century, our economies depended on the fluid movement of capital as much as fixed ownership of property.

In the world of capitalism, historic class and feudal structures were starting to break apart: a person born into service might, with ambition and some luck, rise to the top and watch their former masters passing on their way down. The centres of this new economic order were the cities and the colonies. The increasingly large class of people born neither into land ownership or servitude traversed this landscape searching for opportunity.

The novelist Daniel Defoe's fictional heroine Moll Flanders charts this transformation: one that Defoe had witnessed over the course of his own life.[11] Born into penury, Moll becomes a prostitute in London, then a businesswoman and finally plantation owner in America: her status and wealth continually shift. At all times, within this fluid social order, she depends upon the gift of the gab as much as her sexual prowess. Fluent and charismatic speech, Defoe suggests, is what enables one to lie, impress, cut deals and survive.

For the emerging 'middling classes', who considered themselves above the hustle of the streets, but were also painfully aware of their inferiority to the aristocracy, mastering a certain register of speech was an important way of showing their worth. Books like Thomas Sheridan's *Lectures on Elocution* (1762) and John Walker's *Elements of Elocution* (1781) proved immensely successful. Elocution lessons were invaluable for businessmen of humble origin trying to navigate rarified circles, but also for women needing to pass in polite society or marry above their status. Unlike the schools of rhetoric of the classical world, which had included elocution as just one element in a more holistic approach to persuasion and political consciousness, these schools were simply about speaking well. While somebody with a speech disorder like stuttering can still prove competent at rhetoric, they cannot but fail at elocution unless they eradicate their disorder.

In 1750, Lord Chesterfield wrote to his eighteen-year-old son expressing immense concern at the 'hitch or hobble in your enunciation' which made him almost unintelligible. 'No man can make a fortune or a figure in this country without speaking, and speaking well, in public,' he writes. 'Your trade is to speak well, both in public and in private ... Be your productions ever so good, they will be of no use, if you stifle and strangle them in their birth.'[12] With the stakes so high, it is no coincidence that the first speech therapists, or 'artists', emerged around the same time.

In a recent study, Cambridge historian Elizabeth Foyster dated the earliest practitioner to 1703, several decades earlier than previously thought. An advertisement states that James Ford, 'who removes stammering, and other impediments in speech', can be found every

Tuesday and Thursday at Mr Merriden's, the sword cutler, during the day and at Rainbow Coffee House at six in the evening.[13] 'Speaking well was crucial to being accepted in polite society and to succeeding in a profession,' Foyster says. 'Speech impediments posed a major obstacle and the stress this caused often made a sufferer's speech even worse.'

Social and economic change explains the increasing emphasis on fluency in the modern era. And it is this aspirational speech, instrumental for social mobility, that joins with the deeper traditions of rhetoric and philosophy in creating what we recognise as hyper-fluency: the need to speak well at all times. Dale Carnegie, the American pioneer of self-improvement, saw this change clearly. 'In the days when pianos and bathrooms were luxuries,' he wrote in 1913, 'men regarded the ability in speaking as a peculiar gift, needed only by the lawyer, clergyman, or statesmen. Today we have come to realise that it is the indispensable weapon of those who would forge ahead in the keen world of business.'[14]

The new economic order, and the implications it had for speech, changed everything. Not only was fluency deemed a necessary trait for business, but the term became synonymous with the effective workings of capitalism itself. 'Flow', which shares the same etymological source as 'fluency' and is a common metaphor for admired speech, was requisitioned by economists trying to describe how capital works. We talk of 'cash flow', the 'flow of wealth', and 'stock and flow'. There are even asset management companies called Fluent Investments and Fluent Financial, while Deloitte Fluent Capital Adequacy is a piece of software that helps banks navigate financial regulations. In this way, what were once neutral, descriptive terms become virtues and we forget that all things that flow, like the course of a river, also require control and moderation. Gradually, these changing terms and values infiltrated our understanding of the world in which we lived.

In the 1950s, Erving Goffman captivated the English-speaking world with a radical interpretation of human behaviour as a form of performance. In *The Presentation of Self in Everyday Life,* he likens social interaction to an informal, intimate version of theatre and human beings to performers. As a sociologist rather than an anthropologist, his examples were predominantly taken from industrialised societies and, indeed, those societies are where his theories were most applicable. It is Goffman who applied the word 'front' to how we project ourselves in social situations. This is the version of ourselves we want the world to see. It is different to the 'backstage language' we use at home or among closest intimates which includes swearing and open sexual remarks as well as 'dialect or sub-standard speech'.[15]

Maintaining a front is hard enough in itself, but the stakes are heightened because individuals are continually participating in 'team performances'. These are not rare, formal events like football matches but happening continuously. They occur every time two or more individuals who have established a certain dynamic find themselves engaging with other individuals: work colleagues pitching to a client; a couple of friends trying to pick up at a party; immediate family spending time with in-laws. This means not only being aware of our own front, but those of our partners. 'The whole machinery of self-production is cumbersome,' Goffman writes. 'But, well oiled, impressions will flow from it fast enough to put us in the grip of one of our types of reality – the performance will come off and the firm self accorded each performed character will appear to emanate intrinsically from its performer.'

The problem is we're continually rupturing this flow, undermining our efforts, with 'unmeant gestures'. This is when backstage behaviour leaks into our performance. Unmeant gestures include things like stumbling, belching, flatulence – and speech disorders. For Goffman, encountering somebody with an involuntary speech impediment is painful because we are forced to watch somebody failing to maintain a front. It's rather like seeing an actor who keeps slipping out of character or momentarily forgetting their lines. The worst thing is that an unmeant gesture not only undermines an individual's front, but that of the entire team they are operating within at any given moment. People with pronounced stutters, Tourette's syndrome, aphasia and dysarthria are implicitly unsuited for mainstream team behaviour, which in Goffman's view means social intercourse itself. Goffman does not endorse this discrimination: it is an observation, borne out by everything we have seen, about how our society stigmatises speech disorders.

In the 1970s, another influential psychologist, the American-Hungarian Mihaly Csikszentmihalyi, incorporated values of fluency into his theory of human happiness. 'We have all experienced times,' he writes, 'when, instead of being buffeted by anonymous forces, we do feel in control of our actions, masters of our own fate.

On the rare occasion that it happens, we feel a sense of exhilaration, a deep sense of enjoyment that is long cherished and that becomes a landmark in memory for what life should be like.'[16] The name he gave to this state of mind is Flow. The terms we choose put a particular prism on our concepts and even Csikszentmihalyi is seduced into confusing verbal fluency for flow and therefore for happiness itself. 'When words are well chosen, well arranged,' he writes, 'they generate gratifying experiences for the listener. It is not for utilitarian reasons alone that breadth of vocabulary and verbal fluency are among the most important qualifications for success as a business executive.' Csikszentmihalyi's assumption is that there is something objectively pleasing about fluency rather than it being culturally determined.

By conflating ideas of flow and verbal fluency, Goffman and Csikszentmihalyi – two of the most influential thinkers of the last seventy years – contributed to the fluency prejudice that puts the disfluent speaker forever at a disadvantage. Disfluency, like any impeder of flow, is not only antithetical to an individual's professional and personal fulfilment, but of little use in an increasingly fluid and globalised economy. Dale Carnegie may have identified the shift in hyper-fluency from a 'peculiar gift' to an 'indispensable weapon' as early as 1913, but, over a hundred years on, this change has only intensified. The collapse of the jobs-for-life ethos in the last fifty years, matched by the rise of the gig economy, means there is no exemption for anyone. With few of us able to know what we'll be doing a couple of years hence, we have to be prepared to impress at any given moment in interviews, meetings and presentations – and that means being able to talk well.

Joshua St Pierre, a Canadian speech activist and philosopher with a long personal experience of stuttering, describes to me the way twenty-first-century capitalism 'incites our tongue to speech the whole time'. It has transformed 'our capacities of speech into a form of human capital'. In so doing, it has compromised the effectiveness of speech as a tool of protest or change. While 'speaking up' was once daring to say the unsayable, whatever the consequences, now it is just part of capitalism itself: the very thing such protest is often directed at. Social media – the benign, collective term we give to vast global corporations like Google, Amazon and Facebook – depend upon us 'speaking up at all times and as much as possible' in order to fuel their data economies.

A hundred years ago, Dale Carnegie considered charismatic speech indispensable for the 'businessman'. The conceptual leap from there to Chris Anderson's 'core skill' for everyone is immense, but accurate. How else do we explain the global success of TED, or indeed the relentless eloquence of social media, in which teenagers can become multi-millionaires delivering low-fi make-up or gaming tutorials from their bedrooms? What makes our twenty-first-century society exceptional isn't the existence of hyper-fluency, therefore, but its universal imperative: a core-skill not for a small priest class, but for us all. And because this society is increasingly globalised, it is ever harder to sit it out. In doing so, we have lost a great deal.

'Non-verbal communication is the highest form of

communication,' Marina Abramović tells me, speaking English with her pronounced Serbian accent:

> The Buddhist teachers say that the most ordinary communication between master and a student is the former talking to the latter. Verbal communication. Then the second communication, which is much higher, is gesture. But the highest communication of all is sitting in silence with no words ever exchanged. So when I'm looking a total stranger in the eyes and not having any conversation with them, I will know more about that stranger than I will ever know through any conversation at length. There is something about non-verbal communication that opens doors no other communication can open.

How do we get back what we have lost? How do we start to challenge our cultural reverence for a singular way of speaking; one which comes at the expense of tolerance for other ways of communicating and is, in any case, prone to misuse and error? Doing so involves sharing an awareness of the limitations of hyper-fluency, but also celebrating the virtues of different types of speech, even though hyper-fluency encourages us to be intolerant of them.

Abramović describes one attempt. Shortly after her unpleasant TED experience, she decided to try something different:

> Giving up is the beginning of everything ... Lately I gave a talk in front of two thousand people. I was

> terrified: I sit in the bathroom before. Finally, I go to the stage. Before I didn't trust this feeling but because it's happening constantly now I trust it. I don't prepare. I stand in front of the audience and the first thing I do is just try to empty my head of any kind of conception, of anything I want to tell, so that liquid knowledge comes to me. It's something that comes organically: realisations about life, about perception, about humanity, about who we are. Anything that comes out of my mouth comes from a state of non-thinking and that state of non-thinking is the best Marina lecture you could possibly have.

Later, I will describe the role speech disorders can have in challenging the cultural dominancy of hyper-fluency, but there is another story to tell first that explains the stigma that still surrounds them. It is the story of how, from the mid-nineteenth century, when the emphasis on fluent speech as the key to human happiness and success became most entrenched, disorders of speech in contrast became diagnosed, medicalised, and even treated with contempt.

5

A Muted History

Everything we think we know about speech disorders dates back a mere 150 years. Up until the mid-nineteenth century such conditions were either ignored, misdiagnosed or misunderstood. This doesn't mean they didn't exist: there are Ancient Egyptian texts from as early as 3000 BC connecting speech and communication problems to head injury,[1] and their existence in the classical world and beyond is (thinly) documented. While catch-all terms like the latin *balbus* gradually gave way to specific terms for stuttering or lisping, other disorders like dysarthria, aphasia and the vocal tics of Tourette's remained unnamed and were seen simply as symptoms of other problems: stroke or infirmity or some obscure palsy. But in the mid-nineteenth century, the increasing specialisation of medicine and advancements in our understanding of the human brain brought them into view. Of particular importance were the emerging fields of neurology and psychology which studied the brain from different angles: the first looking at the nervous system, the second at human thought and behaviour. Practitioners were asking questions that had never been asked before about how speech is produced and how it breaks down, and gathering evidence to answer them.

These investigations ran throughout the century, but in 1861 two important events occurred that proved hugely influential on our understanding of speech disorders today. They occurred in the cities of Paris and London: two great centres of science and innovation. One was a discovery made with a scalpel knife; the other a set of illuminating ideas contained in a book. These revelations, and those they inspired, were game changers, but they were frequently contested.

The first took place in Paris. Aged only thirty-six, Paul Broca was already a leading light of French medical science in 1861. Although a surgeon by trade, he had become the world's leading authority on aneurysms; made outstanding contributions to our understanding of cancer and the nervous system; and founded the Anthropological Society of Paris to extend the work of Charles Darwin in understanding human evolution. Along with his anatomist friends, Broca had become interested in human language and how it is produced. Was it something with an almost mystical origin that simply emanated from our consciousness, or could it be localised to a part of our anatomy? Those of a religious persuasion favoured (or hoped for) the former: the fact that no one knew where the faculty of language lay, left a space open to argue for the existence of the human soul. Those of more godless, Darwinian leanings hoped to dash their faith – if only they could uncover a bit of human flesh that seemed to be doing the job.

The search for the origin of human language, therefore, was more than an anatomical enquiry but an agitator on the fault-line between science and religion. As an ambitious and curious scientist, Broca hoped to claim this particular discovery for himself, sitting perfectly as it did across his skills as both an anatomist and anthropologist. The problem was how best to go about it. It wasn't acceptable to open the skull and dig around the brains of perfectly healthy individuals with a scalpel, hoping in the process to deactivate, and therefore locate, a language switch. Nor was it much use if those experimented on were already dead, as even if one did hit upon the right place there was no way of knowing since they were no longer able to speak.

Early in 1861, Broca was alerted to the case of a patient at Bicêtre Hospital in Paris who had an unusual condition. The man was a fifty-one-year-old farmer who had slowly lost control over his ability to speak, as well as experiencing paralysis through the right side of his body. His name was Louis Victor Leborgne, but he was known as 'Tan', because for many years it was the only sound he could make. Ask him his name, how he was doing, what he wanted to eat, and the answer was always the same: 'tan', 'tan' and 'tan'. In every other regard, his intelligence was unimpaired. For Broca, this strangely afflicted farmer presented a unique opportunity. Because Leborgne had already lost the use of his speech, it opened the tantalising prospect that if a fault could be found somewhere in his body, some damage causing the speechlessness, then the source of language itself would be located.

Broca had Leborgne, now bedridden and speechless, transferred to his care. He subjected him to tests to try and locate the source of his infirmity, but none was obvious. His nervous system was clearly working, even on the right side of his body, because of the 'flinching and screaming' that he made when Broca tested his scalpel on him. 'The tongue was perfectly free,' wrote Broca. 'The muscles of the larynx did not seem impaired at all, the timbre of the voice was natural, and the sounds the patient made in pronouncing his monosyllable were perfectly pure.'[2] Broca was at a loss. Then, shortly after these early examinations, Leborgne died. Within hours, Broca conducted an autopsy to try to understand once and for all where the root of his condition lay.

As Broca worked his way through the cadaver, he found Leborgne was in every way a perfectly functioning individual. Then he discovered deep lesions in the frontal lobe of the left hemisphere of his brain. This, Broca concluded, was the source. 'All evidence,' he said, in an address to the Anatomical Society of Paris later that year, 'leads us to believe in this case that the lesion to the frontal lobe was the cause of the loss of speech.' The implication appeared obvious: if a lesion to the frontal lobe could deprive an individual of speech, the same area must also be the origin of it.

In the following months and years, autopsies on patients with similar conditions seemed to confirm his proposal. This part of the brain soon became known, as it is called to this day, the Broca's Area. Speech deficiencies arising from damage to this area were called 'aphasia'. Broca had claimed both language and its disorders for neurology. And if aphasia could be diagnosed and explained, it was possible other disorders of speech might be too.

Across the Channel a different breakthrough, but of equal import, was under way. This was not a surgical innovation, but a way of seeing, a paradigm shift. The instrument was a book rather than a scalpel and it concerned stuttering rather than aphasia. The author was James Hunt, an extraordinarily precocious, prim-looking twenty-eight-year-old who had become the leading expert in stuttering. He was not a surgeon or neurologist; scarcely a scientist at all, although he had managed to scrape through a doctorate abroad to claim a qualification. He was one of the speech 'artists' who had emerged in London over the previous century.

While the origins of this profession undoubtedly had an element of hucksterism, with unqualified quacks reaping the benefits of the placebo effect from their supposed cures, it had gradually developed a degree of peer review among its members, becoming highly sophisticated in the process. Speech artistry continued to sit outside, often at odds, with the medical profession, yet by the mid-nineteenth century it was clear these practitioners were consistently having better results in the development of partial cures. Although we now talk of speech therapists, there was as yet no universal term for this sort of practice and little in the way of literature presenting a consistent method. Hunt was on occasion referred to as a 'psellismolligist', although this ungainly term did not last long (probably for no better reason than the fact it is almost unpronounceable, particularly to those who might have recourse to use it).

James Hunt's *Stammering and Stuttering, Their Nature and Treatment* (1861)[3] not only summarised the collective achievements of this unofficial, almost underground profession, providing a blueprint for later speech therapy, but convincingly challenged the dominant conceptions of what stuttering is. Hunt was the first to chart the history of stuttering and the different ways it had been treated. In doing so, he showed how, as with other speech conditions, it had been repeatedly misunderstood. The first part of his book is a powerful chronology of human folly.

The earliest descriptions of stuttering, Hunt reveals, go back to the Old Testament, where Moses claims he is not fit to lead the Israelites because he is 'slow of speech and tongue', which has often been interpreted as a sign of stuttering. In the fourth century BC, the Greek physician and 'father of medicine' Hippocrates speculated that it is a consequence of disease and is accompanied by enduring diarrhoea. Hippocrates concluded that stutterers who are tall and baldheaded are good people; those with large heads and small eyes are passionate; and anyone with a little head will not stutter or go bald unless they have blue eyes. Celsus, another Greek philosopher, suggested the stutterer should exercise himself to retain his breath, wash the head with cold water, eat horse-radish, and then vomit. His contemporary Galen stated that stuttering is caused by either excessive moistness or dryness of the tongue.

The thread goes slack with the Dark Ages, but Hunt picks it up several centuries later, showing how little the understanding of stuttering had changed in that time. Guy de Chauliac, a medieval French physician, proposed blistering and bleeding as a cure. The Italian Girolamo Mercuriale agreed with the blistering, but also insisted that people who stutter should never wash their hair because it just adds to the excessive moisture in the tongue that is at the root of the problem. In the eighteenth century, Gottfreid Hahn identified the hyoid bone in the neck as the culprit; Anthony de Haen favoured a cavity in the lung; while Santorio Santorio blames the width of the incisive canal connecting the nose and mouth. Depending on who is writing, cures involve speaking with a bullet, a role of linen, a silver fork, a bride-langue (a sort of human bridle) or a whalebone in the mouth.

Again and again, Hunt identifies the misdiagnoses and inappropriate treatment of the medical profession. And for anyone convinced these are the errors of the distant past, he points to the recent atrocities of the surgical profession. Only twenty years before, Johann Friedrich Dieffenbach recounted the apparent success of his surgical cure on a group of teenage boys:

> The tongue being drawn as much forward as possible, I pushed a curved bistoury [scalpel] through it, as near its root as I could, and cut through its whole muscular thickness, leaving the mucous membrane inviolate ... The substance of the organ was so completely cut through that a slight additional pull with the forceps would probably have torn it off. The blood streamed from the apertures made by the knife as vehemently as from a large artery.[4]

The results of these operations were, in Dieffenbach's words, 'beautiful'. He claimed his patients had not stuttered since. This apparent success encouraged other scalpel-happy surgeons across the continent until it became clear that any temporary alleviation of stuttering was simply a combination of placebo effect and shock that soon wore off.

The fundamental error, Hunt concludes, from Hippocrates to Dieffenbach, is a conviction that stuttering is physiological in origin, with the poor tongue more often than not getting the blame. 'There is perhaps no affliction to which the human frame is liable,' he writes, 'which has been attempted to be cured in so many different ways. The famous pebbles of Demosthenes; a bullet in the mouth; a roll of linen under the tongue; the fork of Itard; the bride-langue of Colombat; the whalebone of Malebouche; the stick behind the back; intoning; speaking through the nose; talking with the teeth closed.' Yet no physician had got any closer to solving the enigma.

Hunt's message, delivered within the first chapters of the book is clear: traditional medicine, having had ample time to find a cure for stuttering, had failed. It failed because it assumed there must be a single physical cause of the problem, usually the tongue, and because it took so little account of a patient's own experience and insights. But over the previous hundred years, according to Hunt, a different approach had slowly emerged alongside. It was developed by a combination of people who stuttered themselves, and fluent speakers who were willing to listen carefully to those who did. It was a way of thinking that would ultimately evolve into the practice we today call speech therapy.

The 'speech artists' of the eighteenth century tended to focus on an individual's habits of speech rather than their tongue, encouraging them to improve articulation and pronunciation[5]: simple techniques which help far more than whalebones, silver forks and surgery. And, increasingly, there were other individuals who believed the cause of stuttering had little to do with the speaking apparatus at all. The German philosopher Moses Mendelssohn suggested as early as 1783 that the main cause might not be physiological, but rooted in the experience and attitude of an individual. The English philosopher Erasmus Darwin (grandfather of Charles) concluded much the same. 'Impediment of speech,' he wrote, 'is owing to the association of the motions of the organs of speech being interrupted or dissevered by ill-employed sensations or sensitive motions, as by awe, bashfulness, ambition of shining, or fear of not succeeding.'[6] The cure involved practising 'for weeks or months upon every word, which the stammerer hesitates in pronouncing. To this should be added much commerce with mankind, in order to acquire a carelessness about the opinions of others.'

Significantly, both Mendelssohn and Darwin were also people who stuttered (as was Darwin's more famous grandson, Charles). Their theories came from personal insight rather than wild speculation. Because they foregrounded psychology over physiology, James Hunt considered them forerunners of his own way of thinking.

In the second part of *Stammering and Stuttering*, Hunt presents his own theory of stuttering. In his view, there is no single cause. It is not an organic disease at all, but a habit – and a bad one – of articulation, reinforced by the negative associations attached to it. In this regard, stuttering is primarily psychological, although the term Hunt uses is 'psychical'. He takes great pains to describe the mental condition of the stutterer: 'the habit of secrecy, of feeling himself cut off from his kindred; of brooding over his thoughts, of fancying himself under a mysterious curse'. All of which was reinforced by a medical profession that was not only completely confused in its diagnosis, wilfully spreading misinformation, but also infantilised people who stuttered by prescribing ill-conceived cures rather than listening to them.

Just as he rejects a single cause of stuttering, Hunt also rejects the idea of a single cure. His method consists of listening and studying the patient to understand how the habit had become acquired and what methods might be necessary to help them control it. His aim is to help an individual to self-awareness, clearing away the clutter of ignorance and misconception that surrounded the condition, building their confidence and helping them 'to speak consciously as other men speak unconsciously'. By learning about themselves and the mechanics of their speech, Hunt's 'pupils' (he preferred this word to 'patient') can steer their own path to fluency.

Putting theory to practice, James Hunt opened a country house residency near Hastings where pupils would come and study for weeks at a time. Each day, they would undertake certain activities together: reading aloud, debating and delivering speeches. In this safe environment, they could address the often insurmountable fear of public speaking, or even just everyday conversation, and build confidence and self-reliance as talkers. We all have a mental image, based on personal experience or movies, of what group therapy looks like – and it doesn't include men and women in Victorian dress.

Stammering and Stuttering did a number of things. It put to bed once and for all the idea that stuttering was a physiological problem that could be treated through surgery or any other tricks of the physician's bag. And it also comprehensively made the case for a multifactorial understanding of stuttering, recognising that the symptoms are psychological as much as behavioural. By focusing on literary as well as medical history (and the book is full of references to Shakespeare and the philosopher John Locke as well as the likes of Hippocrates), Hunt opened up the third dimension of stuttering, recognising the condition is shaped by the social and cultural attitudes of the time.

Finally, it was immensely influential in legitimising the emerging field of speech therapy. Hunt's pupils included some of the most prestigious writers and scientists of the day who contributed to the future integration of speech therapy into medical practice. Lewis Carroll and Charles Kingsley, author of *Alice in Wonderland* and *The Water-Babies* respectively, studied under him and were passionate believers in his methods. W.H.R. Rivers, one of the pioneers of British psychology, was Hunt's nephew and grew up in and around the practice. Without Hunt the legitimisation of speech therapy might have taken far longer than it did.

Hunt's thinking was not without its flaws. In ensuing years, he concentrated increasingly on the emerging field of anthropology. In 1863, he set up the Anthropological Society of London, where he delivered a disgraceful paper *On the Negro's Place in Nature* in which he defended slavery in the Confederate States of America. But in the field of speech therapy, which was his expertise, his impact and influence was almost wholly positive. *Stammering and Stuttering* remains a book of immense wisdom: the oldest practical guide to alleviating the symptoms of stuttering that continues to have merit.

In the same year, Broca and Hunt had made the case for both the neurological and the psychological roots of aphasia and stuttering respectively. These approaches are not mutually exclusive but complementary; today, it is widely thought that speech disorders are neurological in origin but subject to psychological factors. The three decades following 1861 proved a golden age with more achieved than in all human history up to that point.

An important successor in this endeavour is the towering figure of Jean-Martin Charcot. In the 1880s, he opened the first neurology clinic at Salpêtrière Hospital in Paris, gathering a group of brilliant physicians around him. Like Hunt, Charcot has a chequered legacy: his ill-conceived theories on female 'hysteria' created a toxic stereotype that lingers to this day despite being refuted within his own lifetime.[7] Charcot's real achievements lie in his work around neurological disorders. He was the first to define multiple sclerosis and Parkinson's disease, recognising dysarthria as an important symptom of both conditions. Under his guidance, students and colleagues made further breakthroughs. It was Charcot who named a newly identified 'malady of tics' after the groundbreaking work of his pupil Gilles de la Tourette.

As with multiple sclerosis and aphasia, there was no previous recognition that ticcing could constitute a disease or disorder in its own right. Jean Marc Itard had first described the symptoms in 1825, but the most widespread theory was that such conditions were exclusively an after-effect of rheumatic fever. This was not as ridiculous as it sounds: the tics of Sydenham's Chorea, known colloquially as St Vitus's Dance, were caused by fever. But at Salpêtrière, the young Gilles de la Tourette began collecting case studies of individuals who had similar types of tic but no experience of rheumatic fever. He became convinced of three things: that there was clear evidence for a malady of tics in its own right, that it was hereditary, and that it couldn't be cured.[8]

De la Tourette's theory struggled to catch on. Among his critics were the traditionalists who continued to insist such tics were an after-effect of rheumatic fever. Then there were those who said that 'la maladie de tics' was neither a syndrome nor an after-effect of Sydenham's chorea, but simply an elaborate manifestation of hysteria. Such florid hysteria was in itself a sign of advanced genetic 'degeneracy': a greatly discredited theory that argued negative mental and moral traits could be passed down from generation to generation, particularly among the poorer populations, leading to a weakening of the human species.

Gilles de la Tourette struggled to defend himself. He was severely debilitated after a mentally unstable patient shot him in the head, and suffered increasingly from mental confusion owing to syphilis. In 1899, he managed to publish an article salvaging what was left of his theory by conceding that the syndrome 'almost always exposed a condition of mental instability characterised by numerous phobias ... and all the stigmata which today are referred to as mental degeneration', although he preferred the term 'unbalanced'. What he would not endorse, though, was the notion that it was just an extreme form of hysteria. It was, always had been and always would be, a syndrome in its own right.

But the most damaging opposition to his theory ultimately came neither from the traditionalists nor the proponents of degeneracy, but from a new and emerging field that was to entirely change the way we understand the human condition. By the 1890s, some physicians and neurologists at Salpêtrière were fascinated by, and actively contributing to, the emerging discipline of psychoanalysis. They were close to Sigmund Freud who had briefly studied with them under Charcot in 1885. Freud, a neurologist by trade, was in turn influenced by the work they were doing into speech and other neurological disorders. It was while studying children with aphasia that he became convinced there were neurological and psychiatric conditions without any organic cause, driven instead by unconscious mental processes: a conviction that would become the bedrock of psychoanalysis.

One by one, the neurological breakthroughs in speech disorders that suggested they were linked to organic dysfunction in the brain were overcome by psychoanalytical theories. In 1891, Freud published his first book, *On Aphasia,* in which he dismissed Broca's claims of a localised disorder linked to brain damage as 'overrated' (he was right, but not for the reasons he supposed), leaving the field open for other theories, particularly his own. Over the course of the decade, he became increasingly emboldened. In *The Psychopathology of Everyday Life* (1904), he delivered a psychogenic reading of all forms of speech disturbance, or 'speech-blunders', where words are confused or inappropriately used. All such blunders, he suggests, are motivated by an unconscious drive such as repression. The famous 'Freudian Slip', as it became known, where one word is substituted for another, reveals 'self-criticism, an internal contradiction against one's own utterance'. Freud claims these principles apply also 'to those speech disturbances which ... affect the rhythm and execution of the entire speech, as, for example, the stammering and stuttering of embarrassment. But here, as in the former cases, it is the inner conflict that is betrayed to us through the disturbance in speech.'[9]

By linking major speech disorders with everyday slips of the tongue, Freud marginalised the role of neurology, foregrounding instead the role of a repressed and conflicted unconscious. People with 'speech disturbances' should not just be considered physical and verbal oddities, but psychological ones too.[10] None of this would have mattered if Freud's work had been forgotten, as so many of his contemporaries' treatises were, but *The Psychopathology of Everyday Life* proved one of the most influential books of the coming century.

For a long time, Freud and his contemporaries were viewed warily by the medical profession, but then thrust into the mainstream when a new ailment of the mind swept through Europe on an epidemic scale. In the First World War, hundreds of thousands of soldiers on the front line developed what we now call post-traumatic stress disorder (PTSD). The official term at the time was 'shell shock' and reactionary physicians believed it was literally caused by the impact of artillery explosions on the nervous system. For the still emerging field of psychoanalysis, shell shock was all too clearly a form of hysteria caused by the unbearable conditions of trench warfare. Because speech disorders were one of the most common symptoms, Freud and his followers had what amounted to a smoking gun connecting shell shock to psychogenic rather than neurological origins.

In *Psycho-Analysis and the War Neuroses* (1921), Sigmund Freud introduced the work of two of his disciples, including the Hungarian psychoanalyst Sándor Ferenczi. In his article, Ferenczi talks of shell shock as 'a museum of glaring hysterical symptoms' including 'all the varieties of tic … stuttering and stammering, aphonia [mutism] and rhythmical screaming'. With a certain triumphalist glee, he insists, 'There could be no question of a mechanical influence, and the neurologists have likewise been forced to recognise that something was missing in their calculations, and this something was again – the psyche.'[11]

Over the course of the war, some army hospitals had reluctantly integrated elements of psychoanalysis into their practice, for the simple reason that it seemed effective in helping soldiers return to the front line. This comparative success, in contrast to the conspicuous failings of the medical profession, seemed a public vindication of a new discipline that had been widely considered an oddity. Emboldened, Freud and Ferenczi grew ever more cavalier in their speculations. Their great error was to mistake the benefits of therapy, where a professional and the patient talk through negative feelings, as vindication of their elaborate mythology of the role of repressed sexual and erotic functions on the behaviour of individuals. In one letter, Freud suggests to his colleague that stuttering is a displacement upwards of a psychological conflict over excremental functions.[12] Ferenczi, evidently not one to worry about a word like 'might', ran with the idea. In *Thalassa: A Theory of Genitality* (1924), he observed that stuttering on consonantal sounds suggested 'sphincter action, with anal inhibition'.[13]

Others followed in quick succession. 'Psychoanalysis of stutterers reveals the anal-sadistic universe of wishes as the basis of the symptom,' wrote Otto Fenichel. 'The expulsion and retention of words means the expulsion and retention of faeces, and actually the retention of words, just as previously the retention of faeces, may be either a reassurance against possible loss of a pleasurable autoerotic activity. One may speak, in stuttering, of a displacement upward of the function of the anal sphincters.'[14] Another psychoanalyst, Isador Coriat, saw stuttering as an extension of the suckling that an infant does on its mother's nipple. It is a form of mother fixation that explains 'the unconscious or latent homosexuality so frequently encountered in stammerers'.[15] The anxiety that people who stutter feel about their speech isn't a fear of embarrassment, 'but is a protective mechanism to prevent complete betrayal of the primitive oral and anal-sadistic tendencies through speech'.

If stuttering supposedly evidenced an erotic retentiveness, the phenomenon of ticcing suggested the opposite. Needless to say, psychoanalysis did not recognise ticcing as a neurological condition but simply as another symptom of a fretful unconscious. In 1921, Ferenczi published his 'Psycho-analytical Observation on Tic', in which he announced tics were 'stereotyped equivalents of Onanism [masturbation]'.[16] Coprolalia was 'nothing else than the uttered expression of the same erotic emotion'. Ferenczi drew great significance from a theory 'that tics often increase in power at the time of early puberty, pregnancy and childbirth, at the time therefore of increased stimulation of the genital regions'. The presence of coprolalia simply confirms 'the impression that the significant "displacement from below upwards" so strongly emphasised in neurotics as well as in normal sex development plays no inessential part in the formation of tic'. Astonishingly, in reaching these conclusions, Ferenczi confessed he had never examined a patient with profound tics but drew instead on the reports of others.

Yet, as a form of treatment, psychoanalysis seemed to have little effect on ticcing. The more it failed, the more outlandish its claims were. In the 1940s, Margaret Mahler, an exile from Nazi Europe living in New York, published a series of psychoanalytical studies of children with 'tic syndrome'.[17] While she acknowledged a hereditary predisposition in particular individuals, it remained latent, she claimed, unless brought out by unique psychosomatic conditions. According to Mahler, all people with the syndrome were emotionally immature with a 'preoedipal mother fixation' and 'homosexual claims directed towards the father'. She described the ticcing of the various patients she encountered as deriving from a 'masturbatory conflict', or a 'psychosexual conflict on an anal-sadistic and masochistic level'. And yet, having done extensive first-hand research (unlike Ferenczi), Mahler was forced to conclude that there was 'no direct correlation between recovery from the tic syndrome and length or method of psycho-therapy'.[18]

In an astonishing twist of logic, Mahler claimed this was of no detriment to her profession: tics were a way of releasing sexual and unconscious tension. If the symptoms of the syndrome disappeared, then that same tension usually resolved into a 'severe personality maladjustment'. The role of psychoanalysis, therefore, was not to eliminate tics, because they might be the last bastion preventing a complete disintegration of an individual's personality, but to tackle the underlying masturbatory and psychosexual conflict that Mahler believed was causing them. In her case studies, she repeatedly engages young, often prepubescent, children in prolonged and explicit interrogations about sex in a manner which, from a twenty-first-century perspective, borders on abuse.

Retrospectively, it is easy to see that while none of these individuals intended harm, they were locked in a culture of groupthink – of conferences, periodicals and personal correspondence – that led them from one insupportable assumption to another. The astonishing thing isn't that they wrote such nonsense, but that these theories gained mainstream credibility. For most of the twentieth century, the Freudian or psychoanalytical understanding of stuttering and Tourette's syndrome was the dominant one in both the medical and the popular imagination. Even the treatment of aphasia, a condition so clearly linked to brain damage, was impacted. For a while after Freud, there was a tendency not only to address the impairments of speech in a patient but what one psychotherapist called their 'total personality',[19] as if aphasia offered the opportunity to perform some general housecleaning of the soul.

Under the influence of psychoanalysis, the popular perception of a person who stutters was, and remains, that of an individual with an excess of neurotic tendencies. There's the stuttering Billy in Ken Kesey's novel *One Flew Over the Cuckoo's Nest* and Miloš Forman's iconic film adaptation, whose speech impediment is a sign of his repressed Oedipus complex and harbinger of his eventual suicide. Nicholas Mosley, son of the British fascist leader Sir Oswald Mosley, spent many years in psychoanalysis trying to understand his speech impediment. 'A stammer is the indeed often ludicrous outward sign of an inward contradiction,' he wrote in his autobiography.[20] He also believed 'it is a protection against the stammerer's own potential aggressiveness towards others.' No wonder that sociologist Erving Goffman, writing at the height of psychoanalytical influence in the 1950s, listed stuttering as one of those 'unmeant gestures' like stumbling, belching and flatulence, that embarrassingly expose one's private self in a public arena: when you stutter, you're advertising your most intimate neuroses to the world.

Whatever the successes of psychoanalysis in treating other conditions, it remained the case that it just didn't work for speech disorders. Worse, it actually hindered our understanding of them, pushing to one side some of the advancements made by neurologists and speech therapists in the late nineteenth century. By the 1950s, an increasing disillusionment sent professionals scavenging for other cures. While James Hunt reserved his worst scorn for the surgeons of his own generation, one wonders what he would have made of some of the atrocities to come. Not only the excesses of psychoanalysis, but passing fads like the carbon dioxide therapy of Hungarian psychiatrist Ladislas Joseph von Meduna,[21] or a brief experiment in lobotomising children with Tourette's syndrome (in a later study, it was found that of sixteen such children, only five were deemed to have improved: the remaining eleven appeared worse than before the operation).[22]

Unsurprisingly, by the 1960s there was a growing resistance to psychoanalytical theories of speech disorders. This was partly due to the failure of empirical evidence to support them, reinforced by the fact that psychoanalysis itself offered little in the way of effective treatment. A new generation of neurologists and psychiatrists began to look elsewhere for solutions. Broca's theory about localisation, that both the faculty of speech and the cause of aphasia lay in the front lobe of the brain, had lost influence in the first half of the century, but was now reappraised. This was largely due to American neurologist Norman Geschwind who found that, despite its simplicities and flaws, there was more evidence in favour of what he called 'the classical neurologists' (Broca and Carl Wernicke) than the 'holistically oriented neurologists' of the twentieth century who integrated elements of psychology and psychoanalysis into their practice.[23] While nobody would argue that speech sat exclusively in Broca or Wernicke's areas, they were clearly important in speech production and damage to them, as well as other parts of the brain, provided a better focus for neurologists than the mysterious workings of the unconscious.

Stuttering was also slowly being reclaimed from psychoanalysis. The independent speech artists of the nineteenth century had always sat to one side of the medical profession, if not in outright hostility. After the First World War, speech-language therapy, as it was now called, was increasingly integrated into hospitals and universities. Not least because the number of returning soldiers with significant speech disorders, whether caused by shell shock or brain damage, required it.

Wendell Johnson and Charles Van Riper met in the 1930s in the newly-formed speech pathology department at the University of Iowa. Both men had stutters themselves and so were instinctively wary of some of the excesses of psychoanalytical theory. Instead, their ideas show the influence of Behaviourism, a psychological method which focuses on an individual's environment and past experience. The important thing wasn't to waste hours dredging the unconscious for a cause of stuttering, but to create a more constructive environment and support network for the stutterer, and to give them techniques for improving fluency. They developed a range of practical techniques to support this. These included voluntary stuttering which desensitises the experience of stuttering and builds confidence by making an individual stutter on purpose, but in a controlled way. Another was stuttering modification therapy which enables a person to tackle difficult words through a softening and slowing of sounds. These techniques were simple but effective and had a far greater impact than psychoanalysis ever achieved.

But the greatest setback for psychoanalysis followed the discoveries made about dopamine in the 1960s.

Dopamine is a natural chemical that works as a neurotransmitter, sending signals throughout the brain and the body. Nobody knew a great deal about it, but it was found that drugs which reduced or enhanced dopamine impacted a wide range of neurological conditions. In his book, *Awakenings*, Oliver Sacks described the experiments he was involved in at Beth Abrahams Hospital in the Bronx. Sacks and his colleagues gave the dopamine precursor, L-DOPA to patients who had been immobile with *Encephalitis lethargica*, or 'sleeping sickness', for decades. Astonishingly, they emerged from their catatonic state, but soon developed violent side effects, including ticcing. The connection between neurotransmitters and tics caused pause for thought: had Gilles de la Tourette been right after all? Was it possible that 'la maladie de tics' wasn't psychosomatic, but a neurological condition?

Around the same time, two married doctors, Elaine and Arthur Shapiro, began prescribing haloperidol, a drug that reduces dopamine transmission in the brain, with startlingly successful results. In 1968, they published their findings, directly challenging the psychoanalytical community, arguing that the success of haloperidol suggested ticcing was not psychogenic in origin.[24] Gilles de la Tourette, they concluded, had been on the right track in the 1890s before psychoanalysis undermined his findings. By giving the illness a name – Tourette's syndrome – and insisting it was a neurological condition that could be pharmaceutically treated, parents of children with tics found themselves overwhelmed with relief. One father wrote of his joy 'to finally meet with an unusually competent psychiatrist who stated with assurance that the tic symptoms did not indicate that our son was psychotic, neurotic, or emotionally disturbed because of his family environment and parental inadequacy'.[25] The Shapiros joined with a handful of such parents to form the Tourette Syndrome Association which over the 1970s led a sustained media campaign, placing adverts and articles that proclaimed these findings and building a vast support network across the United States.

The importance of dopamine quickly emerged in other disorders affecting speech. Haloperidol has been effective in the treatment of stuttering, although it is rarely prescribed because of the side effects. The Austrian biochemist Oleh Hornykiewicz became convinced of the link between Parkinson's disease and dopamine deficiency as early as 1961. When he first experimented with L-Dopa on his patients, he was astonished to see them stand up and walk. 'Speech became better,' he recalled, 'they started laughing and actually crying with joy.'[26] It remains one of the few effective treatments available today, although the side effects, ranging from involuntary writhing to impulse-control disorder, can prove as unpleasant as the disease itself.

Whether prescribed or not, the effectiveness of dopamine enhancers or inhibitors was vital in diminishing the psychoanalytical hold over speech disorders and reclaiming them as neurological conditions. In effect, the 1970s saw a resumption of the work that had begun in the golden age of neurology, lasting thirty years from Broca's and Hunt's breakthroughs of 1861 to the emergence of psychoanalysis in the 1890s. This meant that, apart from the overdue recognition and integration of speech-language pathology as a practical discipline, decades of progress had been compromised.

Even today, the Freudian paradigm doggedly refuses to quite lie down. Every time we talk about someone having 'a nervous tic', we are reinforcing a notion that tics are caused by anxiety. 'They are,' says Jess Thom, 'but they're also more pronounced if I'm excited or happy. *Any* heightened emotion has an impact.' Before I was married, I remember going on a date with a woman who, after hearing me stutter repeatedly, squinted her eyes and asked, 'Are you a very angry person?', as if my impediment was nothing more than a sign of some repressed and unconscious fury.

Many people who stutter unwittingly contribute to trauma-based theory, not realising that in doing so they encourage people to think of stuttering as evidence of some emotional or neurotic crisis. Most people I speak to have their theory: poet and rapper Scroobius Pip tells me his speech disorder arose after nearly drowning as a boy; author Colm Tóibín says that his appeared when his father almost died; artist Brian Catling believes it may be the result of a teacher forcing him to be right-handed; and the writer Margaret Drabble was told by her mother that her stutter came on after she fell in a river. But while therapist Uri Schneider has encountered a couple of people who have undeniably trauma-induced stutters, he tells me it tends to be 'trauma with a capital T' like battle fatigue. Otherwise he's not so sure. 'Sometimes the story is that there was a dog that barked and mummy wasn't holding Johnny's hand,' he says. 'We want to make sense of things.

There's a human desire to understand and come up with a story that seems plausible because the worst thing is to sit with something as an unanswered question. People are looking for answers.'

We still are. The history of speech disorders is a long and painful narrative of misguided diagnosis and treatments that have tended to do more harm than good, failing to significantly alleviate the physiological symptoms while contributing to a stigmatisation which is, after all, the biggest problem for most sufferers. For me, the insights of neurology and psychology first developed in the late nineteenth century, then largely ignored, and finally integrated over the last three decades, are the most significant periods of advancement in our knowledge of speech disorders.

There are clear lessons to be drawn from this obscure history. The first is that we should never doubt the role of cultural determinism in the labelling of speech disorders. The fact that most didn't even have a name until relatively recently, or that their very existence was contested, confirms it. The second is that many of the greatest insights and breakthroughs come from personal experience. These may be from people with conditions themselves, such as Moses Mendelssohn, Erasmus Darwin, Wendell Johnson and Charles Van Riper. Or they may be through the close partnerships between experts and those with conditions, as in the examples of James Hunt and his 'pupils', or the Shapiros and the parents of children with Tourette's.

A third lesson is that we should never under-estimate the accumulative effect of centuries of misdiagnosis. It casts a long shadow over the way we hear and respond to speech disorders. Changing public perception will require tackling the legacy of psychoanalysis and proving that speech disorders have nothing to do with repressed emotions and disintegrating personalities. Most of all, we should be extremely wary about accepting any contemporary orthodoxies about the causes and cures of speech disorders. The surgeons of the nineteenth century and the psychoanalysts of the following were just as certain about their scalpels and anal fixations, yet have been rightly discredited. What appears convincing today may be equally discredited in a hundred years time.

6

Unfinished Stories

The history of speech disorders may be a catalogue of misdiagnosis and ill-conceived treatment, and obviously so when considered with the benefit of hindsight, but that does not automatically make the present an age of enlightenment. Our understanding of these conditions continues to change by the year. There remain more unanswered questions than answers. And broader awareness in our society, which is the key to acceptance and rehabilitation, is next to non-existent. Even in my lifetime, theories and treatments have come and gone like seasonal fashions, making it hard even for people with speech disorders to make sense of their experiences. When I look back, I see myself drifting between different approaches, sometimes achieving a brief improvement in my fluency and confidence, then adrift once more.

Although I have memories of stuttering from a younger age, it only became a significant problem for me around the age of ten. The mid-1980s was, however, not a great time to be diagnosed with a speech disorder. Psychoanalytical assumptions about stuttering lingered on and it was still seen as a sign of inner conflict and weakness that could benefit from a firm hand. Implicitly, there was a sense that many people who stutter chose to do so, if only at an unconscious level, and that if they toughened up or sorted out their hang-ups it would no longer prove such a problem. I think this is why laughing at stuttering was actively encouraged within society. This was the time, after all, when the UK's favourite sitcom (*Open All Hours*), its Oscar-winning film (*A Fish Called Wanda*[1]) and one of its hit singles (*The Stutter Rap*) all hinged around characters with supposedly hilarious stutters performed by people without them.

'Interviewers turn away, who wants to be covered in spray?' – rapped Morris Minor and the Majors in *The Stutter Rap*. 'Talkin' to me for more than an hour is equivalent to an April shower.' The song reached number four in the UK singles chart. It was an unfortunate backdrop to my early experiences of stuttering. When I blocked on a word at school, the class would roar with laughter and impersonate me. I learned *The Stutter Rap* in self-defence. If somebody quoted a line, I could pick it up and finish the verse, then change the subject.

The story of my treatment is preserved in my mother's newspaper cuttings folder. 'By 10, he had become almost incomprehensible,' she stated, rather bluntly, in an article for the *Guardian*.[2] I was taken to see a local speech therapist, but have few memories except a sense of hopelessness. I remember hearing about Demosthenes and his wretched pebbles, a few tips on how to slow down, followed by silent drives home. 'Months of treatment seemed fruitless,' my mother wrote, and I was deemed problematic enough to be referred to an intensive two-week course at the Farringdon Health Centre.

What I didn't know when my parents and I arrived at a rather shabby pre-fab building in central London was that we were guinea-pigs in a radical new treatment that was being watched with fascination by speech-language therapists across the world. I was one of eight children with pronounced stutters, all accompanied by both parents.

The course at Farringdon was led by three women – Lena Rustin, Willie Botterill and Frances Cook – who brought different skills and experiences to bear. They had discovered what all therapists know: it's easy to make someone fluent in the consulting room, but almost impossible to make it stick outside. It's the everyday environment (family, school, the work place) that reinforces stuttering behaviour. The very format of therapy, the lone subject with the lone specialist, was therefore both a help and a hindrance. What they needed was a form of therapy that would not only change a stutterer's speech, but the day-to-day environment in which they moved. But that's not something that can be done by sitting down for an hour once a week.

'Lena made the case,' Willie Botterill tells me, when we meet up thirty years later. 'She was the pioneer. She managed the whole National Health Service in Camden and Islington. So she had a big organisation and could decide how the money was spent. And because stammering was her particular thing, she prioritised it.' The course they founded did three things. First, it brought children together in group therapy so they could develop a peer-to-peer support network in the following months. I was twelve years old and remember feeling immensely safe in those over-lit, barely furnished institutional rooms, but also part of something edgy and experimental. Second, it applied Fluency Shaping therapy, taught to us as Smooth Speech, through which we learned to speak from scratch. I recall Willie recording my speech, working out that I spoke well over 200 words a minute, and feeling very special when she told me that only John F. Kennedy spoke as fast.

Finally, and most significantly, it kept all the parents in another side of the building for the entire two weeks, where they were both scrutinised and taught to recognise and change negative environmental factors. 'Impatient with Jonathan's fumbling fast-forward narratives,' my mother wrote (this time for *Good Housekeeping*), 'I'd done what so many people do with stammerers, and looked away when he spoke; and he, in response, kept his eyes on the floor when talking. To help our children become fluent we had to examine ourselves and the way in which we communicated as a family. This meant becoming aware of basic social skills, listening, turn-taking, praising, problem-solving.'[3]

This was the spring of 1987. It was the first time a group of therapists had attempted both behavioural and environmental changes on such a scale in the UK. And the results were spectacular. None of us were 'cured', but we became more fluent. Most importantly, we found ourselves more resilient and with savvy, supportive families who were able to connect with how we were feeling, how we were being treated at school, and intervene appropriately. A few years later, an evaluation of one cohort showed that around 45 per cent of children became, to all extents and purposes, 'normal' speakers with fewer than three stammered words a minute.[4] The work of the Farringdon Health Centre (now the Michael Palin Centre for Stammering Children) was widely celebrated and replicated in different ways around the world.

I assumed I'd experienced the last word in speech therapy. As a young adult, I would practice 'smooth speech' whenever my stutter got particularly unruly. But in my early thirties, I felt overwhelmed once more and feared it was negatively impacting my work. I got in touch with Willie Botterill, having not seen her for over a decade. It was strange returning to the same building and rooms I had spent so much time in as a child. Willie recommended I sign up for the adult speech therapy group at the City Lit Education College. After an assessment with Carolyn Cheasman, I was placed in the 'interiorised stammering' class.

In those first sessions at City Lit, a couple of things took me by surprise. The first is that stuttering was no longer talked about as a predominantly psychological disorder, but a neurological one: something different in the wiring of our brains. We, a group of around ten adults, were bluntly told that there was no cure and, in any case, that wasn't the point of therapy. The important thing was to change our thinking so we didn't feel so negatively about it. In place of Fluency Shaping therapy, the 'smooth speech' of my childhood, was seemingly the reverse: voluntary stuttering. We began by having conversations in pairs, during which we had to fake a stutter while maintaining eye contact. This latter part was essential: over the decades, we had learned to always look away when stuttering as if caught in the performance of some terrible, shameful act. Eventually, we were sent outside in pairs, where we had to accost strangers, asking for the time or directions, and deliberately stutter. In doing so, we couldn't break eye contact or apologise for our speech. I found this horrifying at first, but it soon became easy and, as a result of worrying less, I eventually stuttered less.

What stuck with me most was how much the emphasis of speech therapy seemed to have changed since my childhood. The shift from smooth speech to voluntary stuttering, for instance, felt a complete turnaround. I didn't know whether this was simply a reflection of the difference between treating children and adults, or whether something more fundamental had changed within the discipline. When I ask Willie about this, she suggests it was a bit of both:

> When we started out, it was simple, our job was to get you fluent. Now it's different. How much you stammer is not particularly important. There are people for whom the physical act of being fluent needs so much management that it compromises other things and they end up not communicating in the way they'd like to. If you can get to the point where the amount of fluency is not the issue and communication becomes the important bit, then that substantially alters both the way the individual and the world around them manages and thinks about it.

This change, from a practice focused on curing to one of individual empowerment, is perhaps the biggest in the history of speech therapy. It is not an absolute reinvention

– Fluency Shaping therapy still remains popular, while voluntary stuttering dates back to the 1930s – but it is a shift in balance that is only increasing. One can speculate as to the different reasons for it, not least a general shift in many societies towards greater tolerance for difference or diversity. But I believe the most important factor is the growing acceptance that most speech disorders are neurological conditions antagonised by secondary, psychological considerations. This change is significant because it means that stuttering and ticcing are no longer signs of a disturbed unconscious, or embarrassing 'slips' in an individual's front (to recall the formula of Erving Goffman), but just something different in the structure and workings of the brain.

If most speech disorders are neurological conditions, then the whole notion of trying to conceal them through mitigating techniques becomes morally dubious. There may be people within society who still believe that those who are disabled or different should be invisible, but they, rather than those they despise, are what needs most to change. It explains too why the emphasis of speech therapy has moved to empowerment, changing the way a person thinks and feels about their disorder, rather than trying to suppress its existence. This shift is still recent history. Howard Kushner, author of *A Cursing Brain?*, recalls being convinced, as so many others were, that Tourette's syndrome was psychoanalytic in nature as late as the 1980s. The tipping point for both stuttering and Tourette's occurred through the following decade.

The change in emphasis has helped to reduce the stigma of some conditions, but there is a risk that, unless clearly defined, the word 'neurological' becomes as jargonistic as all those terms – from 'psychogenic' to 'narcissistically-fixated' – that psychoanalysis thrived upon. To take one definition, this one from the World Health Organisation: 'Neurological disorders are diseases of the central and peripheral nervous system. In other words, the brain, spinal cord, cranial nerves, peripheral nerves, nerve roots, autonomic nervous system, neuromuscular junction, and muscles.' Neurological conditions are compounded by psychological considerations. After all, anxiety, pessimism and despair can exacerbate the symptoms of almost any ailment through obsessively thinking about them. Yet such conditions are not in themselves caused by negative emotional states, but by fundamental differences in the brain and wider nervous system.

Since aphasia and dysarthria are usually secondary consequences of brain injury or progressive disorders like Parkinson's, their neurological rather than psychiatric origin seems beyond dispute – and, to an extent, has been since the late nineteenth century. Stuttering and ticcing, however, have no obvious cause. Studies since the 1960s have shown how changes to the levels of dopamine in the brain can both exaggerate and diminish ticcing and stuttering, just as it affected the dysarthria of neurological conditions like Parkinson's. Then, from the 1980s onwards, advances in neuroimaging technology made it possible to peer inside people's brains. Again and again, scans show that there are significant differences in brain structure and activity between 'fluent' speakers and those who stutter and have Tourette's syndrome.[5] Yet compared to other fields of medicine, such technology is still in its infancy and the role of neurology remains theoretical. 'There are still many inconsistencies across studies,' concludes one recent report, 'and a comprehensive understanding of the specific mechanisms underlying Tourette's syndrome remains incomplete.'[6]

At the Oxford Centre for Human Brain Activity, Dr Kate Watkins is leading a cutting-edge programme called INSTEP (a near acronym of Investigating Noninvasive Stimulation to Enhance Fluency in People who Stutter) looking at the brains of people who stutter. I went to spend an afternoon shadowing her team at work. In one room, a volunteer from Bristol called Ahir waved cheerfully at me before rolling back into a vast state-of-the-art scanner. In the observation room next door, I watched his brain light up as he performed a series of verbal exercises. 'What we're finding,' Watkins tells me, 'is that people who stutter have a difference in the organisation of the white matter: the fibres and fatty insulation connecting the different brain areas that are needed to communicate. So it could be that the fibres are less well connected in stutterers or not as well insulated. What's significant is where we're finding this difference: close, almost in, the Broca's area.' Although Broca's theory of a single location of language has given way to one which emphasises the role of modules throughout the brain, the Broca's area is still considered of vital importance to speech production.

Researching this neurological difference is notoriously problematic. While many scans have been made of the brains of people who stutter when at rest, it is extremely difficult to conduct them during the act itself. The scanner is noisy, rhythmic and isolating: stimuli that generally make people stutter less. From what data Watkins has managed to produce, there is a great deal of activity in both sides of the brain at the moment of stuttering, but what is prompting this firework display – whether it is the cause of the stutter or the brain's reaction to the experience – is uncertain. And the evidence of neuroimaging doesn't quite explain the extreme variability of the condition; why a person who stutters might be unable to speak one moment and entirely fluent the next.

Watkins suggests one way to think about it is as a tendency, like a weak knee: 'When you're tired or anxious, it gets worse and reinforces itself. If one day you struggle and can't say your name, the next time you have to say your name, you are going to get more anxious. It becomes a vicious circle. Anxiety is not the cause of stuttering, but the result of having stuttered.'

Even the mystery of how people who stutter can become fluent when speaking in a foreign language, or singing or acting, can ultimately fit within a neurological framework. 'When you are speaking in a different language or as someone else, like an actor,' Watkins says, 'you're switching from your habitual manner of speaking into another one. This engages another part of the brain in speaking: a part of the brain which might work quite fluently. And when you revert to your habitual part of your brain, you start stuttering again.'

Brain scanning of people with Tourette's syndrome has produced some similar results. According to Tourettes Action UK, 'some structures in the basal ganglia part of the brain and in the fronto-temporal brain areas' are different in individuals with TS. But while neuroimaging can show difference in the structures or connections of the brain, it can't explain why. In the case of people who stutter or have Tourette's, it seems that people are simply born with it. This is reinforced by genetic research that suggests both a stuttering and a ticcing gene, and by the anecdotal evidence that both run in families. 'Around half of our cases report a relative who also stutters,' Kate Watkins says. 'And there have been mutations identified in the GNPTAB gene which seem to correlate to stuttering.'

While these breakthroughs are all significant, there are those who caution against assuming too much. 'I think we're moving the ball forward but it's still highly enigmatic,' says American speech-language therapist Uri Schneider. After all, it isn't beyond doubt that the differences in brain structure and connections are the cause of a speech disorder rather than a consequence of them. The brain is highly adaptable and can change to match human behaviour as well as being a cause of it. The genetic work is, likewise, promising but limited. 'There are many stutterers who do not seem to have any genetic history,' says Schneider. 'And while many do, you can have genes for all kinds of things but that doesn't mean they're activated. Ten, fifteen, twenty years, we may be there in terms of understanding the true nature of stuttering, but we're nowhere near yet.' And, of course, none of the scans help explain one of the biggest mysteries of all: why there are up to four times as many men with stuttering or Tourette's as women.

Unsurprisingly, caveats and uncertainties continue to run through the literature about speech disorders. Many bold claims are saddled with conditionals: the devil is still in the small print. 'Tourette Syndrome (TS) is an inherited, neurological condition,' begins *What Makes Us Tic*, an explanatory leaflet provided by Tourettes Action. This is an important statement because it helps shift societal prejudice away from notions that sufferers are psychologically disturbed or deliberately provocative individuals. But this firm claim is soon moderated: 'Although the cause has not been established, it appears to involve an imbalance in the function of neurotransmitters (chemical messengers in the brain), dopamine and serotonin. It is also likely to involve abnormalities in other neurotransmitter systems of the brain.' As for the hereditary roots, it concludes that 'the genetic cause of TS is complex as not one single gene has been identified to be the cause of the condition.'

Official statements about stuttering tend to remain even more cautious. According to the NHS website: 'It isn't possible to say for sure why a particular child starts stammering, but it isn't caused by anything the parents have done. Developmental and inherited factors may play a part, along with small differences in how efficiently the speech areas of the brain are working.' *The Handbook of Language and Speech Disorders* acknowledges there is probably 'an underlying neurological cause', but emphasises that most theories today are 'multifactorial': stuttering is a perfect storm of genetics, brain structure, environmental factors and the unique psychological response of each individual.

To the physicians of antiquity through to the nineteenth century, multifactorial theories would have seemed wishy-washy: they wanted a single, smoking gun (or, in this case, tongue). While posterity may disfavour this current tendency, just as it has those of the past, the advantage of multifactorialism is that it is non-exclusive, permitting and accommodating new theories. To take one example, Naheem Bashir, an experimental psychologist at the University of London, is researching the extreme variations in stuttering behaviour within an individual's own experience. When I saw him speak at the Wellcome Collection in London, he described it, as it generally is, as 'neurological, with a genetic and developmental base', but his use of neuroimaging has uncovered an intriguing characteristic.

While brain activity in fluent speakers is similar in most speaking scenarios, Bashir claims it varies significantly for people who stutter depending on whether they are speaking alone or speaking in company. When speaking alone, their brain activity is the same as those who are fluent, but it transforms when they're speaking in company. It isn't the act of speech, therefore, that prompts unusual activity in the brain but the act of interaction. To explain this, Bashir suggests stuttering could be linked to what is called 'social information processing', or how our brains interpret and react to social situations. Whatever the neurological and genetic basis really is, stuttering appears to be activated by certain social scenarios. It may not have an on-off switch, but it seems to have a dial that goes from low to high. The same is true to an extent with Tourette's syndrome in which both the frequency and very nature of tics are influenced by social context.

Greg Snyder, a Professor of Communication Sciences and Disorders at the University of Mississippi, goes one step further. He highlights a small number of studies over the decades suggesting that speech disorders occur in sign as well as spoken languages. While it is easy enough to conceive how the articulation difficulties of dysarthria (linked as they are to wider motor disabilities), the cerebral disconnect of aphasia and the tics of Tourette's all translate into Sign, there is evidence that the involuntary repetitions, prolongations and blockages of stuttering do so as well, enacted by the hands and body rather than the mouth. Yet it is impossible to account for why this is the case, unless we are willing to acknowledge that stuttering is more than a speech disorder but a condition that affects communication skills more generally.

The enigma causes Snyder to argue that 'the traditional views and definitions of stuttering as a speech disorder fail to account for the stuttering phenomenon', for while they account for stuttering as it occurs in the mouth, they fail to accommodate or even acknowledge similar behaviour in the gestures of a Sign user.[7] His recommendation is that researchers and clinical scientists should consider 'abandoning much of the prevailing paradigmatic thought on stuttering ... a new paradigm will need to emerge to account for this new perceived reality.'

As theories about the cause of speech disorders have changed, so too have the recommended treatments. Looked at over time, speech therapy can appear remarkably faddist in nature. The methods of Lionel Logue in the 1940s seem odd but harmless, while those of psychoanalysis misguided and often cruel. Of far greater and enduring credibility are the methods that emerged in the American midwest from the 1930s. Stuttering modification therapy is associated with Charles Van Riper, but early variations of it were practised by nineteenth-century speech artists like James Hunt. The course I attended at what would eventually become the Michael Palin Centre for Stammering Children owes a debt to the theories of Wendell Johnson, the architect of the controversial Monster Study, who emphasised the importance of changing the environment and mindset of a person who stutters, rather than their speech alone.

The Lidcombe Programme in Australia, which started around the same time, boasts immense success in promoting fluency by teaching parents to congratulate and therefore reinforce fluent behaviour. And since the 1990s, the McGuire Programme in the UK has become extremely popular, combining breathing techniques and sports therapy with exposure therapy. Participants are given a series of increasingly daunting public speaking challenges, from cold-calling on the telephone to addressing a crowd of strangers in public spaces like Trafalgar Square or in whatever urban centre the course is being run. It instigates a highly emotional and dramatic journey of personal transformation, although critics suggest it doesn't address the core problem, and improvements in fluency are often temporary.

There are technological tools too. The SpeechEasy is an audio device that has helped many: rather than increasing volume like a hearing aid, it loops and adjusts the sound of your own voice creating a 'choral effect' as you speak. In another of the strange variables of stuttering, this is enough to render some speakers mostly fluent. Kate Watkins is achieving some promising results with transcranial direct-current stimulation, which involves running a very low electrical current through the brain. Pharmaceutical treatment is rarely endorsed because of the side effects, but there is evidence that dopamine reducers[8] and SSRIs (selective serotonin reuptake inhibitors) like paroxetine[9] are effective. But both technological and pharmaceutical treatments are increasingly out of favour, partly because they are cumbersome interventions but also because they fail to address the core of the problem, which is not the individual's speech but how their attitude and their environment exacerbate it.

While certain practitioners and programmes will talk, as they have always done, about providing a cure for stuttering – even presenting the testimonies of individuals to support this – the reality is that there isn't, and never has been, such a thing. If current theories about the cause tend to be multifactorial, the most effective treatment tends to be as well, rooted in pragmatism rather than ideology. 'There's no one size fits all in therapy,' Uri Schneider tells me. 'We're not surgeons, we're there more like a midwife to help someone through a challenging process with a lot of guidance, support and tips. But ultimately it's their journey and we're there to be along for the ride.' Schneider's method involves taking all the tried-and-tested techniques of speech-language therapy over the decades, without any ideological prioritisation depending on which school of thought they support, and offering them as an armoury to choose from.

Any hope of a miracle cure for the vocal tics of Tourette's syndrome is slowly being abandoned as well. While the impact of dopamine-reducing haloperidol played an essential role in making the case for a neurological rather than psychoanalytic basis for the condition, the side effects were soon apparent too. By the late 1970s, many parents were complaining it wasn't a miracle drug after all, but had a deadening effect on their children. One mother described the dilemma: 'squelching a child's tics completely, to make it possible for us to deny he had a problem, or for him to stay in public school or be on a team or in a club, is as ghastly as child-beating – it's only more subtle and more sophisticated.'[10] While drugs continue to be prescribed, the emphasis (as with stuttering) is increasingly on behavioural therapies. Habit reversal therapy, much like stuttering modification therapy, teaches an individual to identify their tics in detail, increase their awareness of when one is about to happen, and then to find a competing response that sidesteps the tic. Exposure and response prevention exacerbates the force of a premonitory urge so that an individual learns to ride it without actually ticcing.

In the case of aphasia and dysarthria, the presence of significant brain damage or a progressive neurological disorder means treatment is almost never about cure. Although these conditions have been less vulnerable than stuttering or ticcing to misdiagnosis, this greater certainty brings pitfalls of its own. In the late nineteenth century, the conviction that damage to the Broca's area was both the cause of aphasia and also irreversible led to what one psychiatrist called 'nihilism': a sense that nothing could be done or was worth doing. Another doctor wrote that 'the actual therapeutic side of the question is relatively little discussed and comparatively scant attention is paid to the interest of the patient.'[11] This hasn't entirely gone away: patients sometimes complain, when they have recovered enough speech to do so, of being infantilised or ignored by the doctors who are supposed to understand them best.

Just because full recovery may be impossible, it doesn't mean immense leaps still can't be made that immeasurably improve a patient's quality of life. As with other symptoms of stroke, therapy focuses on recovering lost capability and evidence shows that through sustained practice progress can be made.[12] The ability to do this has been enhanced through cognitive neuropsychology, a data-based approach that has enabled therapists to understand the ways in which language-production is transformed by aphasia. As well as helping an individual to recover lost language skills, therapists also focus on acceptance and adjustment. In most cases, the aim isn't to recover all of the ability one once had but to find other ways of achieving good communication. Conversation training teaches family and friends to speak slowly and clearly, avoiding abrupt changes in topic and keeping background noise to a minimum. Non-verbal techniques are often introduced: pointing at a visual analogue mood scale (not dissimilar to emojis), drawing, or enhancing the use of facial expression.

As with aphasia, treatment of dysarthria is generally about mitigation rather than cure. Mostly this involves behavioural techniques, like the Lee Silverman Voice Treatment, which focus on increasing the strength and clarity of a person's voice. In more extreme cases, instrumental aids, medication (like L-Dopa) and surgical procedures may be employed. For those who have spoken fluently for most of their life, these treatments may be precious: a way of achieving continuity with their past selves. But for those born with cerebral palsy it can be a bemusing process too, with an excessive emphasis on rendering them socially acceptable rather than helping them to communicate. For Jamie Beddard, years of therapy had little impact and are lost among the other memories of childhood. 'I can't remember, to be honest,' he tells me. 'There was a lot of focus on pronunciation. I used to dribble a lot more than I do now.'

Sometimes dysarthria is linked to a neurodegenerative disorder like Parkinson's or motor neurone disease. In such cases, practising articulation techniques can feel like a losing battle. When I ask my cousin Gilly what techniques she practices in her weekly speech therapy sessions to help alleviate the dysarthria that stems from MND, she is under no illusions about the future. 'Nothing,' she says. 'It will only get worse. Energy conservation is key.' Although she can still make herself understood through speech, she is transitioning into a life that will be less dependent upon it. Gilly's speech therapy isn't really about speech at all. She works with a therapist to develop and master alternative forms of communication. Some of these are incredibly rudimentary. For instance, she shows me a set of communication cards in her bag that are coloured to signify different scenarios: yellow for travel, green for social, red for managing daily life around the town. One of the red ones reads, 'Hi, can you put the groceries in my backpack in my wheelchair after I've paid.'

Gilly's main hope lies in her AAC (augmentative and alternative communication) device. These come in many shapes and sizes and, because of advancements in digital technology, the last twenty years have been something of a golden age. Gilly uses EyeGaze, which by tracking the movement of her eyes across a screen, speaks the words that she spells. Historically, those using speech synthesisers have to choose from a limited cast of voices, like the distinctive, American-accented 'Perfect Paul' we associate with British scientist Stephen Hawking. But a new wave of voice banking technology has appeared in the last couple of years enabling those with progressive conditions to record thousands of words and phrases before their voice deteriorates, which personalises the sound of the AAC devices they increasingly depend upon. Gilly banked her voice a few years ago, but I am struck by the fact that she doesn't use it, preferring a generic Australian female voice that comes with the technology. When I ask about this, she says that her old voice isn't who she is any more. She doesn't want to hide from the present or her future. EyeGaze is part of her voice now, factory settings and all.

Although AAC devices tend to be used by those who have lost the capacity for easily comprehensible speech, it is not inconceivable – as they become more personalised and easier to use – that those with borderline disorders of speech may use them too.

In the last chapter, I showed how throughout history theories of what causes and might cure speech disorders have been ill-conceived, often damaging. Didactic treatment, the belief that there is a single and universal cure like surgery or psychoanalysis, tends to end badly. What worked best then is still what works best today: pragmatic approaches that are flexible and based on trial-and-error with an individual. Most of all, the principle of partnership between therapist and patient, listening and guiding rather than declaiming and prescribing, has proved enduringly effective, building both self-awareness and reliance in tackling the continuing difficulties a disorder may present.

While treatments that are both pragmatic and productive have taken many different shapes over the centuries, they share one ingredient: a desire, and a record of success, in building self-confidence in an individual. This isn't the general or generic confidence of the Dale Carnegie salesman, but specific: the confidence to communicate, express oneself and follow the paths one wants, even if verbal flow continues to be significantly disturbed or entirely eliminated. The primary aim of treatment shouldn't be to cure or render a person more palatable to an intolerant society, but to build or rebuild an individual's self-confidence that has often been left in tatters by years of stigmatisation and humiliation. 'You want someone you can cry with,' broadcaster Nick Robinson has said about his experience with dysphonia, 'you want someone who can listen to your fears, who believes in you, who convinces you if you work hard enough you'll get better. A huge part of a therapist's role is not just the technical and the mechanical and the medical, it's the emotional support.'[13]

In her memoir, band manager Grace Maxwell describes the extraordinary dedication of her husband's two speech therapists following a near fatal stroke:

> They learn from Edwyn and their other patients, and are continuously adding to the sum of their professional knowledge. But there is more to this dynamic

> duo than any of these words can convey. They are creative geniuses, fascinated and humbled by the unknowable nature of the brain and the spirit of its possessors. This really is the key thing. It's impossible to predict the path recovery will take. There are as many routes as there are human faces.[14]

The personality of the therapist and their relationship with an individual is therefore of equal, if not greater, importance than any of the techniques they wield, which are prone to faddism. As with any form of therapy, the right practitioner can transform a person's life as much as a bad one can hamper it, by coaxing an air of optimism or despair in their client. Many 'cures' or treatments of the past, which have been revealed as bogus or empty, were immensely fruitful at the time simply because the practice of them created a sense of optimism.

Earlier, we saw how Lionel Logue helped King George VI to greater fluency, but his actual techniques, like 'three word breaks', are an ungainly form of speech modification therapy and pale in effectiveness compared to his willingness to stand beside King George VI and smile encouragingly during every broadcast. Yet this is an unsatisfactory kind of therapy, creating a sense of confidence not in the self, but in a guru figure who can guide one through difficult situations. Nicholas Mosley was also treated by Logue. 'He taught me to speak in cadences so that I could declaim like a politician in front of an audience,' Mosley recalled. 'I could do this quite well: then, when I was not with him, I would stammer as before.'[15] It seems the further one was from Logue himself the more one's speech diminished. A good therapist is somebody who guides an individual to both confidence and self-reliance and, in the process, renders themselves unnecessary: the opposite, in other words, of those celebrity therapists whose fame depends upon their enduring indispensability to their clients.

In many cases, greater fluency is a by-product of increased confidence, but not always. Either way, fluency comes to matter less to an individual. 'I had a lot of speech therapy,' says Patrick Campbell, co-author of *Stammering Pride and Prejudice*, 'but what I've found most empowering lately is just seeing stuttering as my voice and part of who I am rather than something to be fixed.' Jess Thom describes a similar change in her attitude to Tourettes. 'It was developing the language and confidence to start explaining my experiences to other people,' she says. 'That's what's been transformative – more so than any other intervention.' Comedian Lee Ridley uses similar language: 'I'm a lot more at ease with using my talker. In the past, it used to stress me out when I had to speak to new people because I knew they wouldn't know what to expect … But now I feel differently. I don't care if I take a bit longer to reply … I just feel more confident in myself as a whole.'[16] For me, the surge in confidence that I acquired from the Michael Palin Centre for Stammering Children in 1987 and the City Lit course for Interiorised Stammering in 2009 contributed to ensuing periods of greater fluency. But it's a particular sort of confidence: that which comes from self-knowledge, understanding what makes me tick, rather than just feeling good about myself.

The cultivation of acceptance and self-confidence is now recognised as more important than the imperative to fluency, but knowing this doesn't make it easy and the number of people who genuinely reach a place of acceptance about a speech disorder are still few. The problem is that the odds are stacked against those with speech disorders by the sheer scale of social prejudice. Even if they have the potential to overcome their own psychological barriers, they still face the daily discrimination – sometimes overt and bullying; sometimes polite and unspoken but equally debilitating – of peers, employers and families. And then there is the cultural ideal of fluency permeating all our values about language and speech which such individuals have to (imperfectly) navigate their way through each day. 'People are very judgemental,' my cousin Gilly says when I ask what she would most like to change about her experience of dysarthria. 'So the minute you are in a wheelchair or you open your mouth and you don't sound right, you're done. And your intellect is judged. And that will only get worse as my voice gets worse. I want society to be more accepting, more open and not so ready to label everyone.'

It follows that if we can prevent society from stigmatising speech disorders, then half the struggle is solved. But how does one go about changing the world? It may feel like an impossible task, but of all the options it may be the best we have. After all, over two thousand years of medical enquiry have created as many dead ends and even dangerous miscalculations (like the surgery of Dieffenbach) as they have effective mitigating tactics. While such enquiry needs to continue, and deserves support, it is not enough simply to wait for a magic cure bearing in mind how little we still know about the workings of these disorders and how resilient they have all proved against the best efforts to eliminate them. The priority is to empower individuals to experience them more positively and develop alternative forms of communication. Nobody can do this on their own: they need a receptive environment to achieve it.

It may not be easy, but we need to cultivate a new way of thinking about speech disorders within our society and culture. Not as something whose origin must be uncovered; a cure found. But something to be understood, accepted – even celebrated. The greatest hope for this lies not so much in speech therapy, which can only tackle the inner life and behaviour of an individual, but in neurodiversity: a conceptual and social movement which has rapidly gathered momentum over the last two decades.

7

Extraordinary Minds

In the late 1960s, a young British neurologist called Oliver Sacks began a long residency at Beth Abraham Hospital's chronic-care facility in the Bronx. New York was the perfect place for a doctor with an interest in the human brain: a vast metropolis with a seemingly endless supply of strange and fascinating characters. At Beth Abraham, he encountered patients with extreme symptoms of 'sleeping sickness', aphasia, amnesia and Parkinson's disease, as well as rare conditions with names like agnosia, hemispatial neglect and somatoparaphrenia.[1] Many of these individuals experienced great suffering, others were barely aware of their difference from others, all of them were unique.

Sacks quickly realised how inadequate the prognoses and treatments of the past had proven by the simple fact that such an extraordinary range of human beings were lumped together, as they were in many countries, in hospital wards cut off from the outside world. Often they were considered lost causes and received only the most perfunctory attention from the staff. Because of the overpowering influence of psychoanalysis, understanding of many neurological conditions had scarcely progressed since the 1890s. But seventy years after Charcot and de la Tourette, Sacks and others of his generation were starting to look afresh at conditions which psychoanalysis had ultimately failed to make sense of.

More often than not, these conditions affected speech. For instance, Sacks observed how patients with extreme symptoms of autism were deemed incapable of communication. Passing doctors would try and get through using the same verbal language they used with children and then give up. The more Sacks studied these patients, the more he realised they were communicating the whole time: not with words, but gestures and nonverbal expressions.[2] Crossing New York to and from work each day, he began to notice people with Tourette's syndrome not just in the hospital wards, but on the streets of the city. He realised not only how prevalent it is but the extent to which many of them managed to maintain normal lives. Following the lead of Arthur and Elaine Shapiro, Sacks tried one of his patients on haloperidol. Both doctor and patient were delighted at how effective it seemed. But, to Sacks's surprise, 'Witty Ticcy Ray', as he called him, felt increasingly conflicted about this 'cure': he complained his speech was less quick-witted, less funny, even his dreams were 'straight wish-fulfilment with none of the elaborations, the extravaganzas, of Tourette's'.[3] In the end, he settled on a compromise, spending the working week on haloperidol, but letting his Tourette's fly at weekends.

On another occasion, Sacks found a group of patients with aphasia in the ward roaring with laughter while watching the slick, hyper-fluent patter of a politician on television. At first he struggled to understand what they found so amusing: after all, this was a level of fluency they could only dream about. Then he realised it was the emptiness of the politician's rhetoric that was making them laugh. 'In this, then, lies their power of understanding,' Sacks wrote. 'Understanding, without words, what is authentic or inauthentic. Thus it was the grimaces, the histrionisms, the false gestures and, above all, the false tones and cadences of the voice, which rang false for these wordless but immensely sensitive patients. It was to these (for them) most glaring, even grotesque, incongruities and improprieties that my aphasiac patients responded, undeceived and undeceivable by words.'[4]

For the young Sacks this was a surprising revelation, but I believe people with speech disorders have always been well placed to expose the tendency to glibness, occasional deceitfulness and intolerance of other modes of communication that is inherent to hyper-fluency. They do so because they have a fundamentally different relationship to language than those who consider themselves fluent. It is still a tool for communication, but one that is inherently unreliable and requires constant vigilance to avoid tripping them up. By looking at their own speech in this way, they become aware of the way others use and misuse language.

The more time Sacks spent with his patients, the more he became convinced they were misunderstood. Historically, their conditions were always described in negative terms, as displaying a 'deficit' of ability. But what, Sacks wondered, if this was only part of the story? What if their conditions were also 'ebullient' or 'productive' in character? This question instigated a fundamental change in how we understand neurological disorders. He asked it again and again in his books, for instance in *The Man Who Mistook His Wife For a Hat* (1985) in which the life stories of his patients are offered up as demonstrations of the richness of human experience. 'Defects, disorders, diseases can play a paradoxical role,' he wrote, 'by bringing out latent powers, developments, evolutions, forms of life, that might never be seen, or even be imaginable, in their absence.'[5]

Over the ensuing decades, an increasing number of doctors and patients joined Sacks in a new celebration of neurological difference. Such conditions could be limiting, frustrating or painful, but these deficits were often partially compensated by insights and capabilities denied to others. Gradually, but with increasing momentum, the narrative around certain conditions began to shift, and it is here that I find the best hope of alleviating the suffering that accompanies speech disorders in our society. These changes occurred quickest and most demonstrably around autism and dyslexia. While not speech disorders, they impact language and provide an example and precedent by which we might think about speech in new ways.

Autism, a condition in which people experience the world and communicate differently to others, is said to affect around one in a hundred people. It was first 'discovered' (that is: identified and named) as recently as the 1940s.[6] This was at the height of psychoanalysis and for a long time it was widely believed to be caused by 'refrigerator mothers' who neglected their babies' emotional needs, turning a child in on itself.[7] As a result, the parents of autistic children experienced appalling guilt, while those with autism were seen as stunted and half-formed individuals. But in the 1970s, evidence increasingly compelled a neurological rather than psychoanalytic interpretation of autism. Neuroimaging seems to confirm this, suggesting something fundamentally different in the make-up of the brain.[8] This, coupled with an awareness of just how many people have some form of autism, has resulted in a shift in treatment. Rather than trying to force individuals into a 'normal' life, we increasingly try to understand the way they engage with the world and provide them with the tools to navigate society more easily.

'I think in pictures,' writes Temple Grandin, a world famous professor of animal science who has also provided invaluable insights into her experience with autism. 'Words are like a second language to me ... When somebody speaks to me, his words are instantly translated into pictures. Language-based thinkers often find this phenomenon difficult to understand.'[9] In 2009, American blogger Amanda Baggs posted 'In My Language', a short film using images, text and voice over, which attempts to show how she experiences the world. Rather than being trapped within herself, as people assume, she simply interacts with her surroundings more through her senses than speech. 'The thinking of people like me is only taken seriously if we learn your language,' she says. 'It is only when I type something in your language that you refer to me as having communication.' Parents of autistic children often describe breakthrough moments where they suddenly discover a new way of communicating. A famous example is that of Owen Suskind who as a child seemed unable to speak but had an obsessive interest in Disney movies.

He and his family began to communicate using dialogue from those films in the roles of animated characters.[10]

Over the decades, ever greater recognition has been given to the unique talents that people with autism display. Occasionally, we hear stories of those who perform seemingly super-human feats of memory and cognitive processing: playing an entire Tchaikovsky concerto after one hearing or learning to speak Icelandic fluently in a week. These are inspiring if extreme examples. More prosaically, evidence shows that everyday jobs built around systems rather than human interaction lend themselves well to autistic thinking. The popular stereotype of 'on the spectrum' computer programmers is not as lazy as might seem: there is a greater percentage of people with autism spectrum disorders living around Silicon Valley than anywhere else in the United States.[11] Their contribution to emerging technologies has benefited us all and is testament to a growing conviction that we need to enable those with autism to find their niche. We hear a lot about the importance of presentation and communication skills in the twenty-first century, but the world turns just as much, if not more, on the strength of those who understand systems, algorithms and patterns better than the erratic behaviour of human beings.

Autism primarily impacts social interaction and communication. Dyslexia, on the other hand, impacts reading and writing ability. It affects more people than almost any other neurological condition (according to the British Dyslexia Association around 10 per cent of the population is dyslexic; 4 per cent severely so). It was once, and still is, confused for stupidity, but it is increasingly recognised as a difference in information processing rather than intelligence. Since the 1970s, it has been carefully repositioned in public discourse.

'Children with any form of dyslexia are not "dumb" or "stubborn,"' writes Dr Maryanne Wolf, Director of the Centre of Reading and Language Research at Tufts University, Massachusetts.[12] 'Their brain is differently organised for written language. Brain imaging research suggests that some people with dyslexia appear to have a very strong right hemisphere that appears atypically activated when they read.' Since reading depends on left hemisphere activity, this explains why it takes them longer to read. However, it also explains the tendency for creative and original thinking, which is associated with right hemisphere activity. Wolf describes how, 'Inventors and artists like Thomas Edison, Leonardo da Vinci, and Pablo Picasso; modern day entrepreneurs like Charles Schwab, Rt. Hon. Michael Heseltine and Richard Branson; actors and writers like Johnny Depp, Keira Knightley, and the late Agatha Christie; all had histories of dyslexia.'

Debris Stevenson is a contemporary artist from London who works across different art forms. She is a poet, playwright, actor and dancer: skills she occasionally brings together as in her play, *Poet in da Corner,* which she both wrote and starred in. She is also profoundly dyslexic. I'm interested in how dyslexia has shaped her use of language and whether there are any lessons to be drawn for how we rethink speech disorders. When we meet, she describes the difficulties it has given her: not just around reading and writing, but also how she speaks and listens. 'If things don't have really strong context I don't understand them,' she says, speaking with rapid-fire speed and pronunciation. 'So often I'll be in a position where I have no idea what someone is talking about, but if they go back to basics and really build the foundation of what they're talking about then I'm fine.'

At the same time, Debris believes there is something intrinsically creative about her condition, beginning with a unique mental spatiality: 'Thinking three-dimensionally is a big part of it and that can be really overwhelming. I keep A3 notebooks and write in eight different colours in eight different directions and that's quite a good visual idea of what my brain is like. Something that helped me is touch-typing. It's enabled me to get as much out as possible. I can touch-type while having a conversation with you about something else.' Debris thinks the multi-dimensionality of her dyslexia is why she works across so many art-forms, but also why she works the way she does within each art form. 'In a good poem, every word has the utmost meaning,' she says. 'The rhythm of the sentence is saying something. The verbs I've chosen in context say something. The way that I say it out loud says something. Me moving says something. If you've seen me doing a poem that's the easiest way to see how I think because a poem is 3D, it's not a sentence.'

While a positive shift in perception of dyslexia is far from universal, there is far greater awareness in the public mind of both its unique qualities and the fact that it does not signify a lesser intelligence. In turn, there is less stigma attached to it than there once was. Schools are more effective at spotting it in children and supporting their needs, although there is still a long way to go. There is even a certain glamour attached to the notion of being dyslexic, fuelled by the growing list of extraordinarily creative and entrepreneurial people associated with it. When Apple ran its famous 'think different' campaign at the turn of the century, a disproportionate number of the exceptional individuals it celebrated (and implicitly linked to its own brand) are or were believed to be dyslexic: Pablo Picasso, Albert Einstein, Richard Branson and John Lennon. And it has been repeatedly claimed that Steve Jobs, the man behind the campaign, was dyslexic himself.

It may be early days still, but those changes to the way we think about autism and dyslexia since the 1970s have been seismic and continue to gather momentum, impacting how other neurological conditions are perceived. In 1998, this paradigm shift was given a name: neurodiversity. The term was coined by an Australian sociologist called Judy Singer,[13] although Oliver Sacks is rightly seen as 'the godfather' of the movement.[14] Neurodiversity describes a way of looking at neurological conditions like any other form of human difference, acknowledging the difficulties it may present to an individual but also the unique insights and abilities it gives them.

According to theorists of neurodiversity, this way of seeing is neither an abstract, academic concern nor woolly political correctness. It is urgent. We live in a diagnosis culture: the number of listed psychiatric conditions trebled in the second half of the twentieth century. Today, the NHS claims that one in four adults and one in ten children experience mental illness.[15] These statistics throw down a gauntlet: either we consider a vast and ever-growing percentage of the population as ill, or we accept that many neurological conditions may not be diseases or disorders at all. This means trying to understand as much as medicating them, celebrating their productive qualities as well as their negative ones. Most importantly, it is a 'neurotypical' majority that needs to change to accommodate a neurodiverse population rather than the other way round.

The beauty of neurodiversity is that simply subscribing to the concept is the trigger for change. An individual who begins to view their condition or disability as a unique and essential variation on societal norms becomes empowered to demand the opportunities previously denied them. Often this rejection of discrimination is enough to convince neurotypical individuals and organisations, whose prejudice may have been rooted in ignorance rather than malice, that change is necessary. Like a virtuous circle, this in turn further empowers neurodiverse communities, which leads to greater social awareness.

Although over twenty years old, neurodiversity is still a new way of thinking, and the range of conditions it encompasses has varied and expanded. Judy Singer introduced the term specifically around autism, based on her experience as the mother of an autistic child. But over the ensuing years, neurodiverse accounts of dyslexia, ADHD (Attention deficit hyperactivity disorder), mood and anxiety disorders and schizophrenia have followed in quick succession. A core argument is that such terms are all culturally determined, much as we have seen speech disorders to be. 'Whether you are regarded as disabled or gifted depends largely on when and where you were born,' writes Thomas Armstrong, author of *The Power of Neurodiversity*. 'Instead of regarding traditionally pathologised populations as disabled or disordered, the emphasis in neurodiversity is placed on *differences*.'[16]

Neurodiversity has much in common with another challenge to mainstream perception, which emerged at the same time but has focused on physical disability. In 1975, a small activist group in the UK called the Union of the Physically Impaired Against Segregation released a statement that tried to upturn several thousand years of discrimination. 'In our view it is society which disables physically impaired people,' it announced. 'Disability is something imposed on top of our impairments by the way we are unnecessarily isolated and excluded from full participation in society.'[17] The disabled academic Michael Oliver coined the phrase 'the social model of disability' to describe this conceptual shift.[18] It is a fundamental inversion of the way many people see disability and, as a result, those encountering it for the first time can struggle to get their heads around it.

One example often used to explain the social model of disability is that of a wheelchair user. Despite popular perception, a wheelchair user may be incredibly mobile, able to turn and move faster than many 'able-bodied' people. The problem arises when you put an obstacle in their way, like a flight of stairs or a bus without a ramp or a curb that is too high. All these are things produced by a society that is prejudiced towards a single, dominant type of mobility. They are creations which, in enabling an able-bodied person to do something, exclude a wheelchair user. The social model of disability argues that it should not be beholden to the disabled individual to adapt themselves to an intolerant society, but for society to adapt itself to the millions of people within its entirety who it renders disabled. It was, and is, an important stepping stone in the development of 'neurodiversity', which proposes an equally radical reframing of neurological difference.

The internet, particularly social media, has both fuelled and created a tipping point for neurodiverse and social model activism. This is partly because it allows individuals who are often isolated in their immediate environment to form micro-communities with other individuals across the world. But it is also because the form itself has opened up new opportunities for people who struggle, as so many neurodiverse and people with disabilities do, with neurotypical forms of communication. For many autistic people, language itself is not a problem, but the way human beings use it: they understand what words mean perfectly, but struggle to 'read' the facial expressions, body language and emotional subtext that provide a counterpoint in their usage. Sarcasm, for instance, is a technique of tone and manner that undermines, even contradicts, the words it accompanies. Not only does the internet put a greater focus on written language, it also empowers other forms of communication like memes, emojis, Instagram photos and short-form video that neurodiverse or disabled people may be more comfortable using.

In fact, the internet can be rightly called the first truly neurodiverse form of communication in human history, which is hardly surprising considering the role that neurodiverse people have played in designing and expanding digital technology. In a world where everybody is communicating through their computers and phones, the use of AAC devices by those who have disordered speech or are non-verbal no longer stands out as it once did. In my childhood, Stephen Hawking and his synthesised voice felt like a figure from the science-fiction programmes that I watched on television. Today, a comic act like Lost Voice Guy, who delivers his routine through his AAC, is just somebody doing what we all do: communicating first-and-foremost through the aid of a device. He just happens not to use it in tandem with vocal speech.

While far from complete, the success of these social movements is evident in the culture around us. The size of the audience watching the last Paralympics on television would have been unthinkable fifty years ago, while popular series like *Homeland* or *Grey's Anatomy* have central characters who are bipolar and dyslexic respectively. Hollywood has played an under-appreciated role too. Whatever the accuracy of iconic films like *Rain Man* (1988), *My Left Foot* (1989) or *A Beautiful Mind* (2001) in representing the conditions or characters they claim to display, their success in the box office has softened attitudes to autism, cerebral palsy and schizophrenia. This increased awareness has impacted our legal system and company policies – in particular, the Disability Discrimination Act of 1995 – making it far easier to call out and rectify discrimination when it occurs.

As theories, both neurodiversity and the social model of disability have their critics. One common complaint levelled at both is that they ignore the genuine pain many people with disabilities and neurological conditions experience. Instead, they are looked at through the brightly-lit, warm-coloured filters of the films they inspired. As a result, the medical model of disability, which sees them as problems to be treated, remains dominant. They are not, however, mutually exclusive. Both medicine and society have a role to play in alleviating the suffering of the disabled individual.

There are also huge gaps still in the achievements of disability activism. One of them is speech disorders. Discourse and debate around neurodiversity rarely acknowledges speech disorders as a category unless they are symptoms of a broader condition like cerebral palsy. Popular understanding and prejudice against stuttering and aphasia has scarcely changed since Oliver Sacks's day. This is surprising considering the central role that language and its disorders played in his writing. It may be because the movement is still developing. At the end of *The Power of Neurodiversity* (2011), author Thomas Armstrong speculates on the future of the term. 'We should probably make our definition of it as inclusive as possible,' he writes. The next wave, he predicts, will be around 'dyspraxia, Tourette's syndrome, nonverbal learning disabilities, and speech and language disorders.' Clearly, rehabilitating these conditions within society has felt less urgent and they are picked out almost as an afterthought. While this may simply reflect the vast number of people who have conditions like autism and dyslexia and the scale of discrimination against them, there are other reasons to consider too.

Earlier, I described a 'peculiarity' (to use Erving Goffman's description) about speech disorders that makes those who have them less likely to organise themselves compared to people with other forms of disability. It may have something to do with the way many speech disorders, unlike other disabilities, can be partially or even completely concealed – even if it involves reshaping every aspect of a life (career, relationships and hobbies). This ability to pass as neurotypical means that most with speech disorders don't even think of themselves as being disabled and it rarely occurs to them that the curtailing of experience is in itself a form of disability. And it also results in the 'habit of secrecy, of feeling himself cut off from his kindred; of brooding over his thoughts, of fancying himself under a mysterious curse' that James Hunt described one hundred and fifty years ago.

Such secretive, loner behaviour is hardly compatible with activism, which depends upon collaboration and outspokenness: an outspokenness that many with speech disorders feel physically incapable of performing or have learned to avoid. Finally, there is the modern tendency to compartmentalise speech disorders into distinct and self-contained silos, a differentiation that is not made in other societies at other times and discourages collaboration. By even talking about people who pathologically stutter, tic, struggle to articulate or translate thoughts into speech as sharing a problematic relationship with language, we run against contemporary practice that resists drawing comparisons across these speech disorders.

Yet this 'peculiarity' must be overcome. Since the causes of many speech disorders remain murky or poorly understood, and the long-held hopes for a 'cure' as elusive as ever, the achievements of neurodiversity and social model activism present the most promising, if not the only, opportunity for achieving lasting improvement in the well-being of those with such conditions. This is not a modest or pessimistic pursuit: remove the stigma against speech disorders and half the trouble goes. Those with borderline conditions will find their speech scarcely bothers them at all, while those with more problematic ones, like extreme aphasia, will achieve greater communication with a society more willing to engage patiently with them on their own terms.

One speech disorder already benefitting from neurodiverse thinking is the vocal ticcing of echolalia and coprolalia that we associate with Tourette's syndrome. This may be because Tourette's is not a speech disorder in itself, but a broader condition that can affect the entire body; in some cases, bringing mobility aids like wheelchairs into play. Early attempts at raising awareness of the condition tended to focus on the more spectacular and disruptive symptoms of coprolalia. Documentaries like the BBC's *John's Not Mad* (1989) had the double-edged outcome of convincing a mass audience that people with TS weren't insane, but that it was also predominantly a 'cursing' disease. The writings of Oliver Sacks were (again) instrumental in shifting attention away from the cursing of Tourette's to its creativity: not just his iconic 1981 essay 'Witty Ticcy Ray', but in ensuing books like *An Anthropologist on Mars* and *Musicophilia*. It is because Tourette's has an involuntary but nevertheless productive quality that it is more easily rehabilitated within a neurodiverse perspective, in contrast to other conditions affecting speech which seem defined, like stuttering or aphasia, simply by an inability to get words out.

Jess Thom readily attributes her sense of personal liberation to neurodiversity and the social model of disability. 'I feel very clear that the moment where my life really changed was the moment that I started talking about Tourette's and giving myself space to think about it rather than push it away and hide it,' she tells me. Soon she realised the extent to which her experience of Tourette's had been determined by the perception of others.

> The Social Model of Disability has been really important to me. We live in a society where the messages we get from a very early age are that there's one way of doing things; there's one body, there's one mind. We can't really cope with fluctuations and don't even want to describe them as grey areas. If you deviate from the norm then you are wrong or broken. But that is such a lie. And it's a lie about our bodies, it's a lie about Disability.

Gradually, Thom came to realise that these social and cultural conventions, more than her own body, are what need to change. This isn't just ideology, but pragmatism too. 'At the moment there is not loads that can be done to change the experience of Tourette's from a physical point of view,' she says, 'but there is something that we can all do about the social impact immediately which is about increased understanding.'

While there have long been organisations that raise awareness and help people who stutter, the focus has traditionally been on support for the individual rather than a radical repositioning of how stuttering is perceived. But in the last couple of years a more defiant and radical spirit has emerged: a movement which calls itself, depending on which side of the Atlantic you are on, Stuttering Pride or Stammering Pride. Central to this new spirit was a blog called *Did I Stutter?*, started by a couple of academics in North America, which became a virtual gathering space for stuttering activists across the world. One of the founders is Joshua St Pierre, a lecturer in philosophy at the University of Alberta, Canada.

'I've stuttered my whole life,' St Pierre tells me, when we talk on the phone. 'For the majority of that time I had incredible shame about my speech. And I would always assume that if communication would "break down" it was my fault because I was the disabled, negative subject.' The turning point came in the summer of 2012.

> I was working a summer job, and I'd been struggling hard to get out a sentence with this guy I was working with. I was stuttering and it came out really slowly but still clearly. In response he said, 'huh?'. So I said it again. And he said 'huh?'. Suddenly I realised that it wasn't my fault in this case. He was the one being the poor interlocutor. And I felt anger in a way I'd never felt before.

St Pierre became convinced that although he stuttered, the breakdowns in communication he experienced were more a consequence of people unwilling to listen or take the extra time to pay attention to stuttered speech. This is when he became interested in the social model of disability. 'I realised the first wave of disability activism was based on physical disabilities and those who could claim cognitive parity,' he says. 'People who could say we're just like you and therefore we deserve the same rights you do. But there wasn't any activism yet for speech disorders.' St Pierre teamed up with a colleague called Zahari Richter, who also stuttered. 'The idea of having a blank slate enabled us in some ways to decide what we wanted this to be. We took a fairly radical stance as far as disability studies go in that we didn't just want inclusion, but we wanted to call out the imperative to be fluent across society and how that affects a wide range of speakers.' They were soon joined by an American poet called Erin Schick, whose performance of an activist piece called *Honest Speech* had recently gone viral on YouTube.

In 2014, the three launched *Did I Stutter?* which became a spearhead for the newly emerging Stuttering Pride movement. From the start, the traditional aims of therapy and treatment were deemed inadequate. 'Inclusion or acceptance is a big buzzword in speech-language pathology,' St Pierre says. 'But I think that's just a watery, weak goal, because we're being asked to accept ourselves on the terms of the medical, ableist world. I think we can do better than acceptance. I think there's room for a disfluent pride. There are huge variations in how people communicate and speak and this is just one of those variations.' Through the blog and social media, St Pierre, Richter and Schick came into contact with thousands who felt the same way: people who didn't want to be accepted by society, but to change it. When I first encountered their work, it was intensely exciting to hear convictions I had felt but never shared with anyone expressed in the public realm.

Bizarrely, the first line of resistance came not from the prejudiced and discriminating masses, but from speech therapists who worried their views were too extreme and uncompromising. 'It became an issue of challenging the authority of who gets to speak the truth about the stuttering body,' St Pierre says. 'Speech-language pathologists and geneticists are the ones who have the authority to speak the truth about what stuttering actually is and therefore how we should go about dealing with it.' You can hear this in action on two editions of *Stuttertalk*, a podcast presented by speech-language pathologist Peter Reitzes, from 2014. Over the last ten years, *Stuttertalk* has been important in raising awareness about the nuances and issues around stuttering and building an online community. But confronted by *Did I Stutter?*, Reitzes gets audibly queasy. The whole social model of disability is one he admits he's never considered before, but he is open-minded. Then the controversial issue of 'informed consent' comes up.

According to St Pierre and Richter, children should not be submitted to speech therapy because they are too young to comprehend what they are really getting into. Needless to say, this is something Reitzes, as a therapist who works with children, cannot abide. Therapy, he insists, has progressed: it no longer reinforces stigma, but gently helps children to both understand their stutter and develop some management tactics if they choose to do so. But St Pierre disputes whether this is possible: once a child is in therapy they are trapped in a perception that their speech is a problem that must be dealt with. What's more, this is happening at such an early age it is likely to determine how they view themselves for the rest of their lives, a phenomenon that Wendell Johnson had identified decades before. St Pierre argues that until an individual can make a decision to enter therapy for themselves it should not be thrust upon them. The issue of 'informed consent' becomes a line that neither side can compromise on.

'Our position has always been that it's every person's right to go to speech therapy,' St Pierre says.

> We don't have anything against speech therapy in itself because we understand that we live in a shitty, ableist world that makes it hard for people. Our problem with speech therapy is that we don't think there's actual, genuine choice. Speech therapy is seen as a necessity because fluency is seen as a necessity and we don't make space for other ways of communicating. In lots of ways it becomes compulsory even if it isn't actually ever said. It's an imperative if you want to be happy. If you want to have a good life you have to go to speech therapy and fix your speech. And I did that for years and years. I had been trapped in this world of self-hate for my whole life and then I was liberated by disability activism. It isn't just this heavy thing I do: it's changed me, I'm a different person. We want other people to have the option to experience this too.

The issue of consent is a difficult issue to resolve, and ultimately a personal one. I benefitted immensely from speech therapy as a child, because I was lucky enough to be among the first intake of what would become the revered Michael Palin Centre for Stammering Children. I can also see how the wrong therapist, or at least a bad dynamic with one, might have exacerbated my stutter. I think a lot about how I will respond if my own children begin to stutter. If they do, my approach will be to wait until I am absolutely sure it has become a problem for them personally before seeking help. Even in this outcome, the important thing is to resist unquestioning faith in the authority of a therapist but monitor closely the dynamic they create with my child; prepared, if need be, to change therapist or desist entirely.

The impact of *Did I Stutter?* has been in the discussion around stuttering, largely online. It's no coincidence that the growth of Stuttering Pride, as with so many identity movements, has developed alongside the emergence of social media. 'Before *Did I Stutter?*,' Joshua says, 'there wasn't much critical dialogue that was happening, but I've been in contact with tons of people, little activist communities are popping up everywhere.' And here's the double bind: social media, which has done so much to promote hyper-fluency, fake news and trolling, has also enabled the group formation and speech activism that Erving Goffman once considered impossible. It's a reminder that technology in itself is rarely to blame, but the uses it is put to. The imperative to organise becomes greater than ever in order to outweigh the spirit of intolerance that governs so much social media usage.

In the last couple of years, Stammering Pride has emerged in the United Kingdom. One particularly dynamic cohort includes therapists and alumni of the City Lit adult speech therapy department in London, who are applying a neurodiverse and social model of disability theories to stuttering. Patrick Campbell, co-editor of *Stammering Pride and Prejudice: Difference not Defect*,[19] is central to this movement. 'I no longer believe in all these speech techniques to try and improve fluency,' he tells me when we meet in a Manchester café.

> I think that almost hinders people who stammer because it just encourages the thought that they shouldn't be stammering. It all links back to the stigma which came to stammering over the years: the idea that people who stammer are less competent, less able than other people. And this seems ingrained in our whole culture. People who stutter on TV or film are always the bad guy or stupid. As a child who stammers in that environment you take on those views of yourself, you become self-stigmatised to think those things of yourself. You think you're less able, less competent because that's what society has been telling you throughout your life.

Changing that wider perception of stuttering is an arduous process of day-in day-out activism. Even as we talk, Campbell confronts me on the adjectives I use to describe stuttering. 'You used the term "flared up" when you said you had a bad stammering period which is like saying it's got worse,' he says. 'But why did you use that term? Why did you not say "stammer more"? "It's got worse" implies there's a subjective value judgement against a person.' Having grown up using the binary terminology of fluency and disfluency, of normal and disordered speech, I struggle to think of my speech outside of a positive to negative spectrum. Following this encounter, I resolved never to use negative adjectives to describe anybody's speech disorder unless used by the individual in question.

The emergence of an activist movement around stuttering is immensely significant, a rebuttal of the peculiar inability to organise that Erving Goffman identified, but it is early days still and mainstream attitudes to stuttering remain fundamentally unchanged. And then there are those disorders of speech which threaten to be left behind entirely. Perception of dysarthria is tied to that of those conditions it accompanies, so while experiences of cerebral palsy have been central to the evolution of the social model of disability, one can hardly say the same about Parkinson's disease or brain damage. In each case, irrespective of how often people with such conditions say it is their speech which troubles them most, dysarthria is always seen as a by-product or symptom of a broader condition rather than one which warrants a neurodiverse analysis in its own right. Many people who have dysarthria don't even know the name for it, which makes it even harder to educate a fluent mainstream how best to respond and behave when they encounter somebody who struggles with articulation.

In some ways, this situation of semi-acknowledgment is preferable to the unremittingly bleak perception of aphasia. Many exceptional individuals have had aphasia, but their exceptionality is deemed to have preceded it. In fact, aphasia is often understood as the very thing that has deprived them of such exceptionality, tearing away abilities they took for granted and seeming to offer nothing as consolation. If it appears in the biography of a great personage, it tends to be in the final chapter when a series of strokes carries a person speechless to their grave. The testimonies of those who experience aphasia, and live a long life after, are often filled with frustration and despair. And since activism depends upon a degree of verbal eloquence and fire in the belly, the experience of aphasia, which is confusing, frustrating and diminishes self-confidence, is hardly conducive to changing mainstream perception. After all, how do you 'speak up' when you are lost for words?

The strength of neurodiverse theory is that it argues for a productive value within neurological conditions as a counterpoint to traditional notions of deficit. Yet this is also its weakness, for it creates an implicit hierarchy between conditions based on which are the most 'productive'. Neurodiversity has prioritised autism, dyslexia and, more recently, Tourette's syndrome, where such an argument can be fairly easily made with the aid of celebrity advocates and the retro-diagnosis of historical figures. But it has floundered with conditions where arguments for unappreciated productivity are hard to identify or when the suffering of individuals resists any positive spin. How can one make the case for the blocked, distorted and lost words of stuttering, dysarthria and aphasia when they seem to offer no productive qualities whatsoever?

This then is the immense challenge we face: the greatest hope for alleviating the suffering and stigma of speech disorders currently lies not with medical science, which acknowledges there is no 'cure' for such conditions, but with the dynamic movements of neurodiversity and the social model of disability. They, at least, attempt to diminish many of the worst aspects of such conditions by tackling the prejudices held by both society at large and even by individuals themselves. Yet speech disorders are rarely included in such discourse, partly because they are considered disorders rather than disabilities, partly because those who have them have been (mostly) reluctant to organise. But most of all because the argument for their productive or ebullient nature has, with the exception of vocal ticcing, been hard to make.

In the following chapters, I present the case for the productive qualities concealed within speech disorders. Despite the suffering they cause, they can also enrich an individual's experience of life and day-to-day communication. They inspire a creative energy that is not only productive but unique, with consistent and recurring qualities. And they play an important part in challenging some of the more dangerous and intolerant tendencies in our society.

In doing so, I aim to tie speech disorders closer to the benefits of neurodiversity, to achieve not only acceptance but appreciation too. This is not a plea for tolerance: all individuals, and all neurological disorders, deserve to be treated with dignity and respect without having to justify themselves. Yet the methods of neurodiversity are undeniably effective in speeding up the process of assimilation, alleviating stigma and, in this case, liberating us all to think about our speech in different ways. This is something everyone can benefit from. Since the rampant fluency prejudice, or hyper-fluency, in our culture has the unexpected effect of narrowing as much as expanding human experience, then learning to appreciate disfluency may enable us to speak and think in different ways. 'Diversity is always hard for us,' linguist Daniel Everett tells me. 'But new information comes from innovation or difference. If everyone talks the same, we don't think about the nature of our speech. Just a simple case of one child stuttering can cause us to learn about what speech is and what tolerance is.'

8

Virtuous Disfluency

As a child, the future George VI was ragged mercilessly by his siblings for his speech while his father, the King, watched on. Although he didn't know it, this humiliation connected him to thousands of other children growing up around the country. One was Aneurin 'Nye' Bevan: two years younger, born in the Welsh mining valleys, with a stutter to rival that of the prince. While George's was to be a life of unrivalled privilege, Bevan had little more to look forward to than one of ill health and physical suffering in the local colliery where his father worked. The idea that he would one day found the National Health Service would have seemed to him deluded fantasy. Yet when the two men became acquainted later in life, their shared experience of stuttering meant they enjoyed talking together.[1]

Like most of his classmates, Bevan left school at thirteen and went to work. The conditions were intolerable and he became increasingly aware of the injustices of society: the vast gaps between rich and poor, the strong and the weak, the healthy and the sick. 'A young miner in a South Wales colliery,' he later wrote, 'my concern was with the one practical question: Where does power lie in this particular state of Great Britain, and how can it be attained by the workers?'[2] Bevan concluded the best hope for addressing this question lay with the trade unions so he joined the local chapter of the South Wales Miners' Federation, known simply as The Fed, and became one of its most tireless and dedicated activists.

Even as a teenager, Bevan was recognised as an asset, but there was a problem: union activity turned upon speech, whether chapter meetings, conferences, rallies, or one-to-one advocacy. The ability to talk well and persuasively was the pre-eminent quality necessary for an effective trade unionist. William Abraham, one of the founders of The Fed, was an orator first and foremost, renowned for his deep booming voice and ability to switch effortlessly between English and Welsh. Bevan, on the other hand, stuttered. It broke his flow, muddled the meaning of his words, created opportunities to be interrupted or dismissed. It seemed that the fire within, the potential to change the world, would remain unharnessed.

Bevan did what few others would: he simply kept at it. He spoke up falteringly but regularly in meetings. He volunteered himself for every public speaking opportunity imaginable. He addressed groups of tired and angry miners on the importance of personal sacrifice, on the need to do more for the union, on how new rights and greater power would be claimed. In his recreational hours, he studied the dictionary and thesaurus in the library, building up a vast vocabulary so he could replace difficult words with synonyms at any given moment. He stalked the hills above the town reciting poetry against the wind to develop his voice, before returning down to address another meeting.[3] Decades later, when asked how he overcame his stutter, he replied, somewhat grimly, 'By torturing my audience.'[4]

Bevan was still a young man when he won a seat as a Labour MP in the 1929 general election. His years of activism and incendiary speaking saw him quickly emerge as one of the most formidable forces in parliament: a large, fleshy-faced man in a trademark pinstripe suit. He soon rose to the senior ranks of the Labour Party, not least because he was one of the few who could take on the great orator of the other side of the house: Winston Churchill.

Churchill, of course, had his own speech impediment. While there is continuing uncertainty about what exactly it was, experts believe it was probably a severe lisp rather than a stutter.[5] As a young man, he consulted a speech therapist and it is thought that the strange and distinctive pronunciation he became famous for ('Narzees' rather than 'Nazis') was in part a way of broaching difficult sounds. In an early essay on rhetoric, he argued that a speech impediment, rather than being a handicap, could prove 'of some assistance in securing the attention of the audience'.[6] Bevan, likewise, learned to put his stutter to good use. Once, in a particularly vicious exchange with Churchill, who tended to dismiss Bevan as 'a squalid nuisance', he leapt to his feet in the House of Commons, exclaiming, 'I welcome this opportunity of pricking this bloated bladder of lies with the …' For a moment he stuttered on the letter 'p', while the room looked on expectantly, then released: '… poniard of truth.'[7] The MPs listened carefully to what he then had to say.

Bevan's hour came immediately after the war. When Churchill was ousted in a Labour landslide, Bevan was appointed Minister of Health in Clement Attlee's government. With a large majority behind him, this was his moment to address some of the structural inequality in society that had so hampered the mining community from which he came. Bevan pushed through the National Health Service Act in 1946, pledging free healthcare for all, and launching the NHS that is so close to British hearts today. Bevan's achievements were great and, we might conclude, happened in spite of a debilitating speech disorder. But then again, maybe it wasn't debilitating at all. Maybe he achieved what he did not in spite but because of it.

Bevan's story is one of many concerning extraordinary individuals who both have a speech disorder and also scale the heights of their chosen profession. It is inspiring because the odds seemed so against him, yet the prize – the founding of the NHS – was so great. It raises these questions: can a speech disorder be of benefit to an individual, and are there circumstances where the loss of control and struggle to speak result in better speech and more effective communication? Drawing up a list of these benefits is often used in speech therapy: rather than dwelling exclusively on the negatives, those in treatment are encouraged to identify some of the positives too. This may be difficult at first because the experience of humiliation and frustration tends to eclipse all else, but gradually some are teased out.

Such 'benefits' range from the trivial (extra time in oral examinations) to the pragmatic (a legitimate reason not to participate in public speaking exercises that fluent speakers may dread just as much) to the holistic (an enhanced sense of compassion because of one's own suffering). From the testimonies I read in books and articles, as well as the interviews I conduct, there are certain benefits that emerge repeatedly as themes. Considered together, I think they provide the basic material for a neurodiverse account of speech disorders; one which seeks to celebrate their difference rather than simply, and grudgingly, tolerating it.

One group of such benefits concerns the personality of an individual. The psychological impact of a speech disorder is vast, resulting in another set of symptoms often more debilitating than the physical ones. A personality can be shaped by a disorder, as it generally is through stuttering and tics, or it can be reshaped, as it is by aphasia and acquired dysarthria. The experience of these conditions is mostly negative: humiliation and shame lead to secretive, internalised behaviour. People with speech disorders can lack confidence and avoid careers and relationships. But these psychological traits are by no means always detrimental to an individual's well-being: there are always those who strive to compensate or to achieve despite, or rather because of, those negative feelings. As artist Brian Catling tells me, 'There's a restlessness and a sort of bloody mindedness' to his character, derived from a lifetime of struggling to get his words out.

The French revolutionary Camille Desmoulins, Aneurin Bevan and – to take a contemporary example – Joe Biden are all renowned orators who stuttered. All of them grew up believing their speech disorder would likely render them unfit for public life. No less remarkable is the way that young people who struggle with speech seem to be preternaturally drawn to acting. Rowan Atkinson, Samuel L. Jackson, Nicole Kidman, Marilyn Monroe and Bruce Willis – to take a handful from a long list – all had, or have, stutters.

'My parents took me to speech coaches and relaxation coaches,' says English actor Emily Blunt. 'It didn't work. Then one of my teachers at school had a brilliant idea and said, "Why don't you speak in an accent in our school play?" I distanced myself from me through this character, and it was so freeing that my stuttering stopped when I was onstage. It was really a miracle.'[8] Blunt is one of many who stutter in everyday speech but are inexplicably completely fluent when performing a role. The best theory I have heard for this is the one suggested to me by Dr Kate Watkins at the Oxford Centre for Human Brain Activity, which posits that recital and performance use slightly different parts of the brain, circumventing those which prompt a stutter.

The link between stuttering and acting extends to other speech disorders too. The comic actor Dan Aykroyd experienced vocal tics in his early teens. 'I had a slight touch of Tourette's,' he has said, 'which means you talk to yourself and bark and cry out at night.'[9] Dash Mihok is an American actor best known in the UK for playing Benvolio in Baz Luhrmann's *Romeo + Juliet*. Through his life, he has experienced the full range of symptoms of Tourette's including coprolalia. As a teenager, acting became a way of concealing his tics, but also what made him interested in embodying other roles. Whenever he noticed other people with tics or quirks on the subway, he would mimic them, trying to feel what tics were like for others.[10] Jamie Beddard, who has dysarthria (as a result of cerebral palsy), struggles to explain his own experiences on stage and screen. 'It was completely bizarre becoming an actor,' he says, 'because as a kid a lot of people stared at me and I tried to normalise myself, and then you suddenly become an actor where you want people to stare at you.' All these examples tell us that although most people with speech disorders avoid professions that require constant public speaking or verbal performance, there is a smaller but high-achieving set who embrace them, determined to succeed in precisely the area in which others most expect to fail.

Drive and ambition (often in precisely the one area that is meant to be out of bounds) are frequently cited as compensatory qualities that emerge alongside fear and stigma. Another is that of empathy. The person with a speech disorder may be able to lead the life of the neurotypical: riding the same train, going to the same office, socialising in the same places. Yet their disorder, often encountered most forcibly in their youth, gives them an experience of and insight into the perspective of other marginalised or disabled people. This ability to not just perceive but feel the vulnerability of others can seem like a special power.

'I do believe in a strange way that stammering is a gift,' writes a young woman called Felicity in *Stammering: Advice for All Ages* (2008). 'To the outside world I appear fluent, happy and confident; inside I am constantly carrying around the burden of ensuring that as few people as possible find out about the stammer I've been hiding for as long as I can remember … I am so much more aware of other people and their feelings because of my heightened awareness of myself.'[11] According to Joe Biden, stuttering is 'the best thing that ever happened' to him. Like Bevan, he strove for greater fluency as a young man by reciting poetry (although he did so in front of his bedroom mirror with a torch before his face rather than tramping the hillsides), becoming a better orator in the process. And it gave him the empathy that a great politician needs. 'Stuttering gave me an insight I don't think I ever would have had into other people's pain', he has said.[12] In my case, I am sure the experience of stuttering has made me a more empathetic person because I know how much lies beneath the surface of the words we say. I'm forever listening for the emotional subtext in even the most mundane exchanges. While this is not a quality unique to people who stutter, what capacity I have for it comes from my troubles with speech.

A wonderful quality about empathy is that it is contagious. When I ask my cousin Gilly, rather tentatively, whether there are upsides to dysarthria and motor neurone disease, she is quick to reply: 'I'm a better listener. I'm a better communicator. I don't interrupt people any more because I can't.' This has transformed her relationship with her two young children. 'I'm a better mother,' she says. 'I can't yell at the kids. I can't lose my shit. I'd love to run around like a whirlwind, but I can't. Everything is so much more planned and orchestrated. And I think they become better people for it. They have to listen to the words I can say. And then they listen at school. And they understand they can't talk over people.'

Of course, there are those speech disorders that effectively remove someone from the mainstream; a world they may have long been part of. The testimonies of people with aphasia tend to focus unremittingly, if understandably, on the frustration and moments of despair. Yet, over time, as some speech returns, certain individuals describe a particular wisdom and sense of peace caused by their experience. In *The Word Escapes Me: Voices of Aphasia,* one woman describes how her 'faith became even stronger', another describes how she 'felt inexplicable, loving empathic feelings for everyone' around her.[13] 'I came to understand that aphasia is not something the clients resent (at least not all of the time),' writes one therapist. 'On the contrary, many of them experience gratitude, not in spite of, but because of their aphasia, explaining how it has rendered them wiser, stronger, and more humane than was possible before. One client mentioned a higher level of consciousness and a sense of interconnectedness with others and with the world at large that was achieved as a result of aphasia's impediment on his ability to work.'[14]

Drive, compassion, wisdom: all these are qualities that may arise in an individual because rather than in spite of their disorder. At the same time, this does not amount to a universal rule. There are just as many individuals whose ambition is thwarted by a greater loss in confidence, who are quite understandably too consumed in their own suffering to feel much compassion for others, and who never translate the frustration of disordered speech into wisdom. They will all be different for it, though, and any workplace or social network that values diversity of experience will value the insights that a person with a speech disorder might bring to a group.

A speech disorder affects the personality of an individual in both positive and negative ways. Likewise, the impact on their use of language can be constructive as well as an impediment. People with dysarthria and aphasia may find that their speech falls short of achieving its primary goal of communication. They may increasingly depend upon augmentative and alternative communication tools like pictures, mime and gesturing as well as speech synthesisers. Because the utterance of simple words and phrases requires a great deal more energy, language becomes a precious commodity. As a result, each word has more value and potency because of the deliberation that has gone into the choosing and delivery of it: a joke can be funnier, an observation more astute. There is a precision of language not generally present in the loquacious patter we associate with hyper-fluency.

Jamie Beddard describes how cerebral palsy makes him a more efficient communicator: 'I need to be more economical in my language,' he says. 'I think about what I say more because it's more effort and I don't want to spend effort talking shit.' He continuously substitutes words that are simpler and easier to understand beneath his 'guttural' voice. 'All the time I'm looking for short cuts,' he says. 'For instance, I swear a lot more than I might do because swearing is a short cut to sentiment. Everyone understands a swear word, but I never swear when I'm writing and whenever other people swear I have a go at them.' This imperative for verbal precision makes him acutely aware of how much others might benefit from it. 'I've always wanted to test this idea that you only get a few thousand words in a day and once you've used them you have to shut up,' he says. 'I think that would make us a better a society.'

My cousin Gilly agrees. 'I used to be a lot more wordy,' she says, 'but I can't be. I have no stamina so I've had to adapt. You think about what you're going to say before you say it, because you don't want to say it twice.' This change is evident in her speech patterns. She speaks in short sentences and has mostly disposed of conjunctive adverbs (like 'accordingly', 'however' and 'indeed') that connect clauses or sentences. This necessary economy of speech has given her abilities she previously didn't have. She describes her astonishment at hearing herself suddenly speak up in a book group and succinctly summarise a chapter that was causing confusion for others. 'That is not my skill,' she says. And yet, now it is.

Everyone with a speech disorder has to learn, as James Hunt claimed, 'to speak consciously as others speak unconsciously'. This should not be confused, as it so often is, with inferior linguistic competence. Rather, the reverse is true. Through struggling with speech, those with disorders become more aware of the ways in which it is used and develop compensatory tactics for managing their own. For the person who stutters, speech is far more than the utterance or performance of words you have in your head. There is a feedback loop between brain and mouth in which both send out warning signals about words or sounds which are proving or likely to prove problematic. This, in turn, allows the brain to draw upon a range of tactics and techniques to mitigate or entirely avoid the stuttering event.

Like dyslexics, many people who stutter talk about their three-dimensional or lateral way of thinking. The best metaphor I can think of is that of a slot machine: I both see and feel the sound of possible words, like the symbols on the reels, that are kept in play until the right combination locks into a place and a phrase I can utter without stuttering comes out. Everyone finds their own way of describing this. 'If I see an L or an R coming over the horizon,' says Brian Catling, 'or if I stick on one I don't even know is going to come, I will then step aside, open the door to the next room. It's a bit like a memory theatre. I find another word, an alternative word, sometimes a word I've never used before. And then I step back in the room with that word and bring it into the conversation. And when you look back you say I've never said that before, that was quite an interesting room, there's nothing in it except that word.'

Dr Clare Butler, a senior lecturer at Newcastle University, has researched stuttering in the workplace. In an interview on BBC radio, she talked about how people who stutter 'draw on a different sense of space. They use their own space in their heads to have two or three conversations on-going at the same time. They will use different words dependent on which word they can say.'[15] Dr Kate Watkins describes the difference in white matter in the brains of people who stutter, as well as the heightened activity at the moment of stuttering, suggesting a demonstrable rather than purely speculative difference in neurological activity. These differences aren't just a reflection of the compensatory energy needed to achieve what others do effortlessly, for the whole experience of language is different. To consider this simply in terms of 'impediment' or deficit is to misunderstand a relationship with language that is generally more, rather than less, productive.

'If stuttering is an impediment,' writes linguist Steven Connor, 'it is also oddly generative. Stutterers tend to become skilful synonymisers, trick-recyclists, unbelievers in the church of the mot juste.'[16] David Mitchell, the author of *Cloud Atlas*, has said that 'your stammer informs your relationship with language and *enriches* it, if only because you need more structures and vocabulary at your command'.[17] It is more than likely that the stuttering kid in the classroom who can't get their words out, who is laughed at and called an idiot, has – paradoxically – a superior linguistic versatility than any of those laughing at them. As a kid, I fell in love with rap music even as it was still developing as an art form because of the way it plays with words. At a time when reactionary critics were dismissing the entire genre out of hand, it seemed to me endlessly inventive and the only lyrical form that came close to the way words rushed and danced through my head.

The cultural historian Marc Shell aptly uses the term 'bilingualism' to describe the way a person who stutters always translates the words they want to say into those they can say.[18] American author David Shields gives an amusing, if exaggerated example of this in his novel *Dead Languages*, when his hero wants to say in class that the American Revolution was caused by an unfair distribution of wealth. He dodges so many danger words, he ends up saying, 'The Whigs had a multiplicity of fomentations, ultimate or at least penultimate of which would have to be their prediction to be utterly discrete from colonial intervention, especially on numismatical pabulae.'[19]

Like the synonyms used by people who stutter, the vocal tics of Tourette's are an intervention in verbal flow: the difference is that they are neither chosen nor deployed but happen against an individual's will. As with stuttering, there is now evidence suggesting enhanced rather than reduced neurological activity between those who do and don't have Tourette's. 'Research examining children with disorders such as Tourette's syndrome usually explore difficulties or weaknesses,' wrote the authors of a recent study.[20] 'We wanted to examine potential areas of strength, as a way to broaden understanding of this disorder.' What they found was that children with Tourette's seem to process language faster than other children. They are quicker at assembling both the words of speech (morphology) and its sounds (phonology). Rather than representing a deficit in linguistic function, the presence of tics signals an enhancement. Jess Thom describes her own discovery of this as a Damascene revelation:

> One day my friend Matthew said to me that 'Tourette's is a crazy, language-generating machine', and told me not doing something creative with it would be wasteful. That sentence transformed how I thought about it. I have no idea why that resonated in that way. I think it was partly because I liked the idea of a machine and the idea that maybe the tics are an amazing product, they're a sort of overflow. And also because I'd been brought up believing being wasteful was very very bad.

From that moment, she saw her condition as a rare and beautiful quality as well as a disability:

> The thing I most value about Tourette's is that my tics will often draw attention to the details in the world around us that I would never otherwise recognise. For instance, I've got a really surreal and strange relationship with the lamppost that I can see from my bedroom window. Every night when I go to sleep, I brush my teeth, I put on my pyjamas as I get into bed and then I shout at the lamppost until I fall asleep. And there's no rhyme or reason for that other than my tics draw attention to these things in the world that I wouldn't normally notice. For whatever reason or however randomly, I feel really lucky to have that relationship with the world.

While we associate vocal tics almost exclusively with Tourette's, they can develop alongside other speech disorders. In her diaries, the eighteenth-century writer Fanny Burney shows how George III used to cry 'what? what?' at the end of sentences. 'In the King, it is a mere habit,' she wrote, 'got from a disposition to stammer, which it seems something to relieve.'[21] 'If the King laughs, all laugh' – as an old saying goes – and 'what!' became a trademark exclamation of the upper classes throughout the 19th and early 20th centuries. It even became a common greeting in the term 'what-ho!'. Although they didn't know it, it is possible all who used it were unconsciously participating in a form of stuttering modification. While the sound of a stuttered word may not in itself be creative, the tricks we develop – whether consciously or unconsciously – to get around it are.

Vocal tics are also common in forms of aphasia where words are not necessarily lost but scrambled. In *Jargonaphasia*, edited by Jason W. Brown, a number of transcripts are presented, including that of a professor whose speech takes the form of an involuntary dialogue with a somewhat undermining alter ego:

> My trade? Well, I have a trade that is nearly identical to that of others to that. However, he is a professor. He is a professor. Well! It is. It is hard. It is hard for me. It is difficult because hm I am. I am in charge of – wait! – I am a professor. I am. I am a professor. How can I put it? I do nothing at all. I am in charge of seeing to it that baked clay is being conditioned for most people ...[22]

Because such interventions in linguistic flow are either involuntary (as with tics) or compensatory (as with synonyms), we tend to ignore any productive value they might have. But I think this is simply because they don't fit any of our pre-existing notions of creativity. One dominant definition, for instance, revolves around intent: deciding and striving to turn some idea in the mind into material form or action. It is because it is involuntary and without an obvious organising principle that I think jargonaphasia is named so pejoratively. In direct contrast, another popular notion of creativity is that of the genius, plucking fully formed compositions out of thin air. To some extent, this is involuntary, although the work itself is deemed god-given and inspired. Tics, on the other hand, are seen to be the refuse of a disordered brain. Yet despite not fitting into existing theories of creativity, it seems to me that they, along with the involuntary synonyms and jargon that also accompany speech disorders, are extraordinarily so.

The writer David Crystal defines linguistic productivity as 'the capacity to express and understand a potentially infinite number of utterances, made by combining sentence elements in new ways and introducing fresh combinations of words'.[23] Children are naturally very creative in this regard because they are experiencing language for the first time (twenty years ago, a popular television show called *Kids Say the Funniest Things* capitalised on this for entertainment). But, as we get older, we increasingly speak in set phrases that are part of our culture. When we say 'in a manner of speaking' we do not say the word 'in', wonder what to say next, add 'a', then decide to say 'manner' and so on; we simply pluck the phrase from a mental stockpile for deployment before launching into the next one. This is why transcribed speech often seems a string of clichés, and it is why we value speakers who can produce an original turn of phrase so highly.

Arguably, the potential for linguistic invention depends not on enabling, but on resisting flow. 'If a speaker is interrupted at a random point in a sentence,' Steven Pinker writes in *The Language Instinct*, 'there are on average about ten different words that could be inserted at that point to continue the sentence in a grammatical and meaningful way.'[24] The problem is that without such interruption the opportunity to use any but the most obvious words rarely arises. While we admire the conscientious speaker who internalises such interruption, scouring ahead even as they speak for the most effective rather than predictable words to use next, the very act of interruption – whether voluntary or involuntary – has a creative potential. It opens up the possibility of using one of the (on average) nine other words that are more rarely employed, but which might make for a more striking and original sentence. Fluency, on the other hand, is not an enabler but a blocker of such creativity.

Speech disorders are ostensibly conditions that impede the smooth, clear delivery of language. The perception of them, reinforced by the language used to describe them, is always of deficit: words are 'blocked', 'distorted', 'lost' or 'unwanted'. Yet the anecdotal evidence, increasingly supported by neuroscience, suggests this is precisely what makes them so productive and even (to use Oliver Sacks's term) ebullient.

The language of stuttering is defined by its ornate and sophisticated synonyms as much as its blockages; that of Tourette's is as playful and witty as it is primal or obscene; that of dysarthria is as economic and precise as it is obscured and hard to understand; while that of aphasia is as precious as anything that is hard-won, through its very absence forcing greater emphasis on other forms of communication that we may have long neglected. After all, if we were as skilful at hum speech as the Pirahã people of the Amazon reportedly are, then a problem with words would be of far less import than it currently is, for our dependency on them would be smaller. All these disorders create regular interruptions in the flow of language, opening up a space of creative potential to say or do something unexpected.

It isn't only a subject's speech that is both impeded and enriched by a disorder. Conversation requires two or more people, and so it is communication itself that is impacted. Generally, this is viewed in negative terms – as disruptive, time-consuming and a source of awkwardness. The more advanced a speech disorder is, the more other interlocutors are obliged to adapt. For anyone not used to disfluent speech this can be disconcerting, even nerve-racking at first, but it is also productive. 'Stuttering breaks down normal modes of communication,' activist Patrick Campbell tells me. 'It can make conversations which are normally superficial suddenly very deep. If you stammer when you're saying "how are you?" it shows you value who they are as you have to put more effort into what you're saying. It's not just a superficial question to you, it's something you have to push through. Stuttering adds value to almost every word you say.' The American writer Darcey Steinke describes it powerfully: 'Stuttering is a violent incantation that can break open normal conversation. What happens in that breach is up to the stutterer and her listener.'[25]

Recent history shows that the case for difference rather than deficiency tends to stem from activists within a neurodiverse community. In the case of speech disorders, fluent speakers will continue to be disconcerted and deride stuttering, tics, aphasia and dysarthria unless a counter case is presented to them. Much of this will depend upon showing, through example and argument, not only that there are productive qualities as well as deficits to such conditions, but that the prejudices of a hyper-fluent society, which recognises only one way of communicating, are flawed. This isn't just about raising awareness of disorders, but showing how much is lost when we ignore them.

Popular perception imagines a sliding scale in which the closer one is to exemplary fluency, the better and more fulfilling one's attempts at communication are likely to be. Yet sometimes the reverse is the case. Jonathan Bryan is a teenager who has cerebral palsy and can only communicate with his eyes. In his memoir, written with the aid of a spelling board, he describes the near-transcendental experiences he shared with another boy who is also 'non-verbal'. 'Friends have always been important to me, but my relationship with Will is unique... Bonded by our similar disabilities, we have never needed words; instead we look deeply into each other's eyes and together we disappear into our fantasies.'[26] On one occasion, such a moment of transport is torn back to earth by the clumsy interruption of a carer. 'Looking into his [Will's] piercing blue eyes we connected at a level beyond words,' he writes. 'Together we travelled the landscapes of our imaginations; outwardly vacant, inwardly amusing ourselves, until our journey was abruptly interrupted. "Hello, Jonathan," sang a voice dripping with enthusiasm. "How are you today? Hello, Jonathan, are you here today?"' One of the reasons Bryan wanted to master the spelling board was so he could complain about the endless disruptive and infantilising interventions from well-meaning but unconsciously prejudiced social workers.

The case against hyper-fluency (for that is what the

case for speech disorders depends upon) may not be so hard to make. Increasingly, there is something in ourselves that acknowledges its limitations. I think this explains why the response to Marina Abramović's non-verbal performance art has been so ecstatic. Not only *The Artist is Present* in New York's Museum of Modern Art, but *512 Hours* at the Serpentine Gallery in London. In the latter work, Abramović was simply present in the gallery space for 512 hours, occasionally directing individuals in meditation, or leading them through the rooms, but largely in complete silence. Over 130,000 people visited the show – a large number for a small gallery.

The experiences of Jonathan Bryan and Marina Abramovic are a world apart, but they reveal in different ways how little our ability to communicate is dependent upon speech, and how enriching it can be to allow space for other types of communication. In contrast, the symptoms of speech disorders may seem quite mild: a slight stutter that repeatedly trips up a speaker and forces a listener to wait or interrupt less; the vocal tics of Tourette's syndrome that require a disentangling of involuntary from intended sounds; the distorted sounds of dysarthria that compel harder, better listening; and the lost or garbled words of aphasia that require us to use gestures or draw pictures, opening up entire communication experiences we otherwise might never have. Viewed one way: these are small prices to pay for the linguistic inventiveness, deeper connection and unique insights that speech disorders also bring.

These, then, are some of the productive qualities of speech disorders. Although it is rarely acknowledged, they have a positive, as well as negative, impact on an individual's personality: the desire to achieve, a tendency towards compassion, a unique wisdom. They change the way that language is used, in a way that is creative and imaginative as well as limiting. And they disrupt the otherwise predictable flow of language and communication, allowing for new experiences to emerge.

Aneurin Bevan was one of many millions who experienced these productive and ebullient qualities. Rather than saying he achieved in spite of a speech disorder, we can see how it was because of it. His stutter gave him ambition, ensuring that he was a famous orator before he was even twenty, as well as informing the compassion that saw him relentlessly fight for and create the National Health Service. It caused him to studiously cultivate a wide vocabulary and range of synonyms, making him one of the most articulate, even poetic of parliamentary adversaries. And the act or moment of stuttering could disrupt the usual formalities and patterns of debate, allowing him to wield what he called the 'poniard of truth'.

These three tendencies – of personality, language and communication – are the bedrock for a neurodiverse appreciation of speech disorders. Those with such conditions have the potential to contribute to a more empathetic, linguistically innovative and communicative society, yet rarely get the chance because they are so discriminated against. There is a beauty and even a logic to these conditions that is smothered beneath the word 'disorder'.

I believe that as they become more accepted and integrated within society, we will all find ourselves learning to communicate in new and subtly different ways, for to engage with a person who stutters, tics, has aphasia or dysarthria on their own terms requires better listening, less interrupting and looking beyond the words people say to the other ways in which they may be communicating. It means everyone reaping the benefits I have gained from the hundreds of interactions over the past few years that have only enriched my understanding of human nature and language.

This is just the foundation. Around it develop other productive traits that might otherwise seem merely speculative, but follow as a consequence. If the combination of these qualities in an individual can stimulate enhanced and unique creativity in verbal communication, in the right hands speech disorders also inspire great art.

9

The Art of Disorder

As long as he could remember, Charles Dodgson struggled with speech. He might be halfway through a sentence and suddenly a word would stick in his throat and he'd be left mouthing silently like a fish out of water. At home, it didn't matter: most of his siblings were the same. They were a big household, tucked away in the country. A micro-community of their own. Charles was the family joker and wrote a poem gently mocking their strong-willed father, describing the 'Rules and Regulations' of the household. 'Learn well your grammar, and never stammer' it begins, followed by a list of petty instructions: 'love early rising', 'go walk of six miles', 'shut a door with a handle', then 'once more, don't stutter.'[1]

At school it was bad. The other boys were noisy and sporty and quick to spot weakness in others. Charles was a bookworm with a speech impediment. All the hardship and lack of friendship was summed up in the school-book where, underneath his name, someone wrote '…is a muff'.[2] That's all he was to them: a fool, a weakling, a stutterer. He got through his time, but left knowing that nothing on earth would make him go through such experiences again.

The day he arrived at Christ Church to study mathematics, he knew he never wanted to leave. Other people loved Oxford for the society, but for Charles it was the reverse. It was quiet and solitary. People left him alone. He was happy. Fellow students struggled to remember him: he seldom spoke and his impediment was not, as one contemporary recalled, 'conducive to conversation'.[3] After graduating, he simply joined the faculty, spending his days researching obscure mathematical problems. In his spare time, he developed a few hobbies: drawing, poetry, photography, writing letters back home. Things that took place away from human society. He became part of the furniture of the university; another eccentric loner. Over the years, though, he managed to make a few friends. 'Those stammering bouts were rather terrifying', remembered May Barber:

> It wasn't exactly a stammer, because there was no noise, he just opened his mouth. But there was a wait, a very nervous wait from everybody's point of view: it was very curious. He didn't always have it, but sometimes he did. When he was in the middle of telling a story... he'd suddenly stop and you wondered if you'd done anything wrong. Then you looked at him and you knew that you hadn't, it was alright. You got used to it after a bit.[4]

He drew a picture in a letter to another friend: 'a little thing to give you an idea of what I look like when I'm lecturing. The merest sketch, you will allow – yet still I think there's something grand in the expression of the brow and the action of the hand.'[5] There is nothing grand in the accompanying picture, though: it shows a man with a hand clamped over his mouth, eyes bulging in alarm, mute and ridiculous.

Occasionally, Charles dreamed of becoming a man of the world – a public figure, a great speaker. But he knew his stammer would let him down. He gradually accepted that a quiet life as a respected but uninspiring professor might be the best he could hope for. Then he heard reports of the speech therapist who was, by all accounts, a miracle worker. James Hunt had established a country retreat called Ore House where pupils could come and study together for weeks at a time. Charles Dodgson enlisted and spent the summer of 1859 participating in Hunt's pioneering experiment in group therapy.[6] Each day, clients were required to do certain activities together: mostly reading aloud, debating and delivering speeches. Often Hunt would leave them to it while he worked on the manuscript of *Stammering and Stuttering* in his study. In this safe environment, his pupils could address the often insurmountable fear of public speaking, or even just everyday conversation, and build confidence and self-reliance as talkers.

James Hunt's literary and philosophical approach to speech therapy would have appealed to Dodgson. Hunt was fond of quoting the philosopher John Locke's claim in *An Essay Concerning Human Understanding* (1690) that it is hard to determine whether 'language, as it has been employed, has contributed more to the improvement or hindrance of knowledge among mankind'. On the one hand, Hunt may have been emphasising the importance of his pupils mastering a better usage of words. On the other, he may have been encouraging them to be less tough on themselves. Rather than seeing language as perfect and their use of it imperfect, they should take courage from the fact that language itself is full of flaws.

It is the latter interpretation that seems to have influenced his pupils. For around Hunt gathered three writers, all with stutters, who were to prove pioneers of a new genre of literature: the modern fairy story, or what would become fantasy fiction. There was Charles Kingsley, who after being treated by Hunt wrote a public endorsement of *Stammering and Stuttering* and went on to write *The Water-Babies*. There was George MacDonald, future author of *The Princess and the Goblin*. These iconic books share a playful use of language, creating worlds where you can meet Mrs Doasyouwouldbedoneby or Prince Harelip, and visit strange places like Gwyntystorm. And, of course, there is the work of Charles Dodgson himself, that he would publish under the pseudonym Lewis Carroll.

Charles continued to visit James Hunt at Ore House in the years after 1859. During this time, he began experimenting with language in different ways. He wrote strange notes to friends that he called Puzzle Letters. Words were mixed with drawings and squiggles like a form of hieroglyphs; or they were reassembled into forms that require some decoding. There were mirror letters, back-to-front letters, circular pinwheel letters, fairy letters in tiny writing and letters with riddles and acrostics.

He also took ever greater delight in the company of his colleagues' children. He would invite them with their mothers or nannies to his rooms at Oxford, where he would take photographs of them in fancy dress. To entertain them, he would tell strange stories invented on the spot. Their questions and suggestions would send the narrative in unexpected directions. And all the time he would be preoccupied with taking his photographs. 'In this way,' remembered Alice Liddell, the little girl whose name became the title for one of the most famous books in the English language, 'the stories, slowly enunciated in his quiet voice with its curious stutter, were perfected.'[7]

One summer's afternoon in 1862, *Alice's Adventures in Wonderland* stuttered into existence. Dodgson composed it on the spot, verbally side-stepping, darting off in new digressions, much like the adaptive techniques he used to get through a conversation. He and a friend had taken Alice Liddell and her two sisters for a jaunt in the country. It was overwhelmingly hot and they took refuge in the shade of a hayrick in a meadow. As they rested, one of the sisters begged Charles to tell one of his whimsical stories. He began and couldn't stop. The children were entranced. His friend couldn't help interrupting, asking if it was improvised. 'Yes,' Charles said, laughing, 'I'm making it up as we go along.'[8] Later, when this moment had become legendary, Charles recalled how 'in a desperate attempt to strike out some new line of fairy-lore, I had sent my heroine straight down a rabbit-hole, to begin with, without the least idea what was to happen afterwards'.[9]

I believe *Alice's Adventures in Wonderland* and its sequel, *Through the Looking-Glass* (both published under his pen-name Lewis Carroll), are books that could only have been written by a person with a speech disorder.

Most writers use language to try and capture ideas, to convert abstract thought into argument and story. They value linguistic precision. Dodgson does the reverse. He loves language that is unruly and can't quite be controlled, as if he wants to continually remind us how unreliable it is, how little it can be trusted.

For instance, when Alice first arrives in Wonderland she cries so much at being lost in this strange place that she almost drowns herself and a gathering of animals in her own tears. Having pulled themselves onto land, the question arises of how to get dry, which prompts a 'very dry lecture' by a Mouse on William the Conqueror. This same Mouse then announces it will tell 'a long and sad tale' which transpires to be a concrete poem in the shape of its own tail. This is less a plot than a series of bad puns that rest on the potential of words to mean different things in different contexts. At other times, the story grinds to a halt entirely as when Alice's attempt at a logical discussion with the Red and White Queens in Looking-Glass land is rendered impossible because of their incessant word play. You can almost hear the voice of James Hunt behind it all: quoting John Locke, describing how unreliable and tricky language is, telling his pupils to be less uptight and more forgiving of themselves.

In his essay 'The Stuttering of Lewis Carroll', linguist Jacques de Keyser identifies Dodgson's use of portmanteau words as a consequence of his unusual speech.[10] Portmanteau words are created when two words are crushed into one, as in 'motor' and 'hotel' becoming 'motel'. They are accidentally created by children when stuttering or cluttering. Charles Dodgson's portmanteau creations include one-offs like 'borogove' and 'uffish', as well as a few which have joined the English language, like 'chortle' (chuckle/snort) and 'galumphing' (gallop/triumphant).

One of the first things Alice does after stepping through the looking-glass is to pick up a book lying on a table and read 'Jabberwocky'. In gloriously arcane and invented language, the poem recounts a young hero's successful attempt to slay the dreaded Jabberwock: a mythical beast of Dodgson's own invention. 'The Anglo-Saxon word 'wocer' or 'wocor' signifies 'offspring' or 'fruit', Dodgson explained later: 'Taking "jabber" in its ordinary acceptation of "excited and voluble discussion", this would give the meaning of "the result of much excited and voluble discussion."'[11] The Jabberwock is, literally, the fruit of jabbering: also known as nonsense. But jabbering is symptomatic too of certain forms of stuttering and also cluttering, where speech becomes so fast and animated that it collapses into babble and repetitive sounds. Astonishingly, Dodgson turned such speech into one of the best-loved poems in the English language. De Keyser concludes: 'most probably Carroll used the phenomenon of stuttering, with which he was confronted daily, as a literary device, as a kind of positive contribution to the language in reaction to the negative influence of stuttering on his personality.'

Despite continuing to study with James Hunt, Charles Dodgson never overcame his stutter. In his last book, *Sylvie and Bruno*, published when he was sixty, he even appears as a stuttering narrator. And it was still foremost in his mind at the time of his death in 1898. In a letter composed just nine days before he died he wrote, 'the hesitation, from which I have suffered all my life, is always worse in reading (when I can see difficult words before they come) than in speaking. It is now many years since I ventured on reading in public – except now and then reading a lesson in College Chapel. Even that I find such a strain on the nerves that I seldom attempt it.'[12]

In the century since his death, people have searched for other appearances of Dodgson in his work. It has been suggested that the Dodo in *Alice's Adventures in Wonderland* represents a stuttered abbreviation of his own surname. More convincing is the notion that he appears as the White Knight at the end of *Through the Looking-Glass*. In this guise, he takes his leave of Alice Liddell, who was, by the time of publication, already grown into a young woman. The White Knight escorts Alice before her last move across the chessboard landscape of Looking-Glass land to become a queen, but he cannot make the move with her. Everything about this clumsy, eccentric knight represents a form of stuttering: he can't even stay on his horse, but falls off with a crash every time he gets back on. And when he sings his song, which has a range of different titles like 'Ways and Means' or 'Haddock's Eyes', he sings of an old man he used to know, whose look was mild, whose speech was slow, and muttered mumblingly and low, as if his mouth were full of dough: a fairly accurate description of Dodgson's 'hesitancy'. When at last he can accompany her no further, Alice races on ahead, pausing briefly to look back upon this kindly if somewhat ridiculous man – but only briefly, being far more preoccupied with the exciting future before her.

Lewis Carroll's speech disorder not only inspired him

to make art, but shaped the form and plots of the stories he wrote. To his name can be added a long list of artists with a speech disorder. I have already referred to writers, actors, scientists and philosophers like Elizabeth Bowen, Marilyn Monroe, Charles Darwin and Stephen Hawking, and there are many songwriters too, like Marc Almond, Edwyn Collins, Noel Gallagher, Kendrick Lamar, Carly Simon and Bill Withers. They are all artists who deal with words. On the page, on the stage, in song: words are easier to manipulate in these formal environments, away from the haphazard chatter, the give and take, of social interaction. 'The central irony of my life remains that my stutter, which at times caused so much suffering, is also responsible for my obsession with language,' writes American author Darcey Steinke. 'Without it I would not have been driven to write, to create rhythmic sentences easier to speak and to read. A fascination with words thrust me into a vocation that has kept me aflame with a desire to communicate.'[13]

In certain cases, art may be more than creative liberation but the only way of communicating beyond carers and institutions. Memoir writing by people with dysarthria or non-verbal conditions has become a literary genre in its own right, from Jean-Dominique Bauby's *The Diving Bell and the Butterfly* to Joey Deacon's *Tongue Tied* and Jonathan Bryan's *Eye Can Write*. 'I couldn't speak with my lips,' writes Christy Brown, author of *My Left Foot* and *Down All the Days*, describing the moment he discovered he could write with his toes. 'But now I would speak through something more lasting than spoken words – written words. That one letter, scrawled on the floor with a broken bit of yellow chalk gripped between my toes, was my road to a new world, my key to mental freedom. It was to provide a source of relaxation to the tense, taut thing that was I, which panted for expression behind a twisted mouth.'[14] These books are powerful works of art written by people for whom every word is chosen more carefully than those of even the greatest poets: they are compelling, sometimes strange reports from a world the rest of us cannot begin to imagine.

Alongside this long list of the famous are the many millions who have turned to art, not to make their name, but simply to facilitate the communication that is denied them by speech. I have always been most fulfilled when writing, making music or films. Most of all, I am drawn to people who do these things well, which is why I have always worked close to artists. I love seeing the connection between performers, creators, writers and their audience: forms of communication that go far beyond what is possible in daily conversation. Art fills me with the hope I never quite found in speech. Amy Samelson, a clinical social worker, captures this optimism when describing her work with people with aphasia: 'Creativity is in play, and this is where it gets interesting. Two people with good will and intention, wishing to reach one another, work to find ways to reach out. Sometimes single, words, drawings pictograms, written words (when possible) … and pantomime are part of the new language.'[15]

On 18 February 2005, the Scottish songwriter Edwyn Collins was interviewed by BBC Radio 6 Music about his new album. He had composed one of the indie anthems of the 1980s in 'Rip It Up' and had a worldwide hit with

'Girl Like You' in the 90s. There was some curiosity about his next release but, at forty-five, most fans supposed his best years were behind him. Famously outspoken, Collins was uncharacteristically lacklustre in the interview and explained he was feeling unwell: a nausea and vertigo he attributed to food poisoning. Back home, the symptoms worsened and he was soon hospitalised. In quick succession, Collins suffered two cerebral haemorrhages that put him into a coma for a week and saw him bedridden for the next six months. Complete recovery was impossible. The stroke had left him severely paralysed on the right side of his body and with acute aphasia, but he had youth on his side.

Over the following years, much of his speech returned, although he faltered and stuttered continuously. Aphasia continued to create a fog in his brain. Yet he found there were unexpected compensations: his creativity was not only unimpaired but enhanced. Although conversation was difficult, he experienced no problem with words when he sang and so songwriting became a vital way of communicating the innermost hopes and fears he struggled to express in speech. He had lost the use of his right hand, but he found a way of playing the guitar using his left alone. And he rediscovered a love of drawing. 'My brain relaxes when I draw, and can see the pages unfolding,' he told a journalist later. 'Before my stroke. My drawing. Was taking me ages to do it. For example a wigeon [a type of duck], but … one week to do! But after my stroke, I became free. As a bird! I came terribly relaxed, and I'm working on things, a quick sketch, and it's much better than the "artiste" stuff I did before the stroke – I became much freer.'[16]

In 2010, Collins surprised his fans and the music press with the release of a new album. *Losing Sleep* charted his emotional journey to acceptance and partial recovery. The lyrics, by his own description, had the 'simple language' of aphasia: 'Losing sleep, I'm losing sleep, I'm losing dignity, everything I know is right in front of me, and it's getting me down.' 'My new style? It's simple and direct,' Collins has said. 'But I like it. I used to be an intellectual; my words were complicated. Now, I'm straightforward. I have to be.'[17] The cover was a collage of his drawings of British birds.

Collins had depended upon the contributions of friends to the songwriting, but his next two albums were all his own.[18] The clever wordplay of his early songs had returned. These were not just recovery albums, but among the best work of his entire career. Collins has never entirely regained his previous capacity with language – he finds it hard to read or speak in fluent sentences – but as an artist his work has evolved and is revered by fans and critics. He has released records, toured the world, collaborated on a film about his experience and published a book of his illustrations. There have been a rare longevity and inventiveness to his career that arguably might not have been sustained if he had never experienced stroke and aphasia.

If speech disorders are a spur to art-making, they can also shape the form and style of output. After all, Edwyn Collins's work over the last decade is not what it would have been if he had never had aphasia. The word Aristotle used to describe the study of art (in his case, drama) was 'poetics'. Since then, the term has been used to describe a wide range of creative forms with their own internal rules and tendencies: from poetry to Caribbean patois, classical music to cinema. Is it possible, then, to talk about a poetics of disfluency, identifying qualities that run as enduring concerns through the art of people with speech disorders?

The story of Charles Dodgson/Lewis Carroll is important in this regard because he is the earliest artist of any discipline whose biography offers enough detail to draw specific links between his work and his speech disorder. He is also the first to have consciously done so, acutely aware of the strangeness of both his spoken and written use of language. But it is compelling too because the *Alice* books are among the most influential and loved in the entire literary canon. They are, therefore, a plausible and precious keystone in a neurodiverse account of speech disorders. This, the earliest work of art we can claim with some certainty to be influenced by a speech disorder, also contains the enduring, productive qualities that artists who stutter or have other speech disorders have shared since.

I will describe each in turn, but they include the unique insight (having 'something to say') that is key to making art and comes in part from the experience of disfluency: the way Dodgson often kept to himself or hid behind his camera in social situations, but let his words fly in bizarre and compelling directions when with children. It includes the linguistic dexterity and playfulness that those with speech disorders develop as a way of concealing or mitigating their condition but can have startling results when used in art-making. And it includes a tendency to experiment in form; to break the rules of language that hamper a disfluent speaker's ability to participate in conventional forms of communication.

As we have seen, there are many personality traits common to people with speech disorders. Many are negative: a sense of isolation and secretiveness, of carrying a stigma, sometimes of despair. But there are positive ones too: a drive to succeed against adversity, an acquired empathy and a unique wisdom about human experience. These are all qualities that are frequently associated with those of the artist. Since art depends on the originality and authenticity of 'voice' (in its broadest sense), and since in any case no maker can remove their personality from their output, these qualities may be ones that consistently translate into the creations of those with speech disorders.

In his book *Stutter*, cultural historian Marc Shell wonders if there could ever be a 'Stutter Culture'. If so, it 'would be informed by awareness of isolation as an inescapable condition'.[19] This is certainly true of Charles Dodgson, who was immensely shy in person and heard James Hunt's theories about the 'habits of secrecy' that emerge from stuttering directly from the man himself. Charles Dickens was a fluent speaker, but he nevertheless observed astutely that 'stammering rises as a barrier by which the sufferer feels that the world without is separated from the world within'.[20]

One person who managed to turn this psychological predicament into art was Somerset Maugham. Through a long and productive career, he emerged as one of the most famous writers of the twentieth century, best known for novels like *Of Human Bondage*, *The Moon and Sixpence* and *The Razor's Edge*. 'The first thing you should know,' he once said, 'is that my life and my production have been greatly influenced by my stammer.'[21] While he discusses his impediment in some autobiographical sketches, it isn't immediately clear how his 'production' has been shaped by it. After all, in his vast oeuvre of plays, novels and stories, there isn't a single character who stammers. The closest is the impediment he gave to his alter ego Philip Carey in the semi-autobiographical novel, *Of Human Bondage*: not a speech disorder though, but a club foot.

The influence of stuttering seems instead to lie in the mood or atmosphere of his work. Maugham was a loner: he hated talking to strangers because he stuttered so much when he did and depended on garrulous lovers to manage social intercourse on his behalf. In later life, he created a loner's paradise for himself in the secluded Villa La Mauresque on a promontory of land jutting from the French Riviera into the Mediterranean Sea. The parties there were famous but Maugham, like Gatsby, would drift in and out according to his fancy. The narrators of Maugham's stories are generally loners like himself, whether it's the 'British Agent' Ashenden (Maugham himself worked as a spy for the British government at various times in his career), or the voluntary exiles eking out their existence in the furthest posts of the British Empire in works like 'Rain' and *The Painted Veil*. In *The Moon and Sixpence*, the narrator states:

> Each one of us is alone in the world. He is shut in a tower of brass, and can communicate with his fellows only by signs, and the signs have no common value, so

> that their sense is vague and uncertain. We seek pitifully to convey to others the treasures of our heart, but they have not the power to accept them, and so we go lonely, side by side but not together, unable to know our fellows and unknown by them.[22]

The loneliness that pervades Maugham's work is frequently attributed to his homosexuality, despite the fact that Maugham was, comparatively speaking, one of the most openly gay public figures of his day. It is a theory that ignores what Maugham himself claimed: his stutter, not his sexuality, was the 'first thing' one should know about his writing.

Many other writers with stutters describe how a sense of isolation and stigma cultivated at a young age finds expression in their work. The Irish novelist Colm Tóibín, author of *Brooklyn*, tells me his stutter arose after a traumatic episode when he was eight. His father had a brain haemorrhage and he was sent away.

> I was staying with an aunt, and I didn't know where everyone else was. I had been told I was safe and everything was okay, but it wasn't and I didn't know where I was or when I was going home. I always knew that some damage had been done to me. That experience of what happened in those months never left me. And if I'm writing I find it very easy to evoke that period. I have written about it a good number of times. It's a hurt. And the stammer was a symptom of that.

Brian Catling, sculptor and writer, tells me his stutter

means he is 'fascinated by all abnormalities of behaviour. I have to be careful: I can find myself following odd people round supermarkets because I feel a kinship.' All of his output, including the recent *Vorrh* trilogy, focuses on human abnormality: characters who are deformed, unhinged and lonely.

Because of this sense of isolation, of being an outsider, stuttering has a special relationship with the musical genre most associated with those same qualities: the blues. Two of the greatest bluesmen of all made this connection explicitly. 'As a child, I stuttered,' B.B. King wrote in his autobiography. 'What was inside couldn't get out. I'm still not real fluent. If I were wrongfully accused of a crime, I'd have a tough time explaining my innocence. I'd stammer and stumble and choke up until the judge would throw me in jail. Words aren't my friends. Music is. Sounds, notes, rhythms. I talk through music.'[23]

John Lee Hooker had a similar experience and impersonates himself in 'Stuttering Blues', where the singer's attempts to seduce a woman are undermined by his speech. 'Excuse me, baby, I can't get my words out just like I want,' he sings, stuttering as he does so. Then, with perfect fluency, 'but I can get my loving like I want it'.[24] According to biographer Charles Shaar Murray, Hooker's first producer 'claims to this day that his primary reason for deciding to record the young bluesman in the first place was that he was intrigued by the notion of a man who stuttered when he spoke, but not when he sang'.[25]

A certain romantic view of stuttering echoes in the popular rock music that the blues inspired. This speech disorder, so stigmatised in real life, in the mouths of rock and roll singers is charismatic and sexy. In 'My Generation', Roger Daltrey of The Who pretends to stutter in every line without an obvious reason why (although he puts it to great effect when he sings 'why don't you all …' and then blocks on an 'f', raising an appalling possibility for radio broadcasters in the 1960s, before following through with 'fade away').

In the early 1970s, when performing his song 'Cyprus Avenue', Van Morrison, a disciple of John Lee Hooker, would stutter for a long time on the word 'tongue-tied', a moment that always drew catcalls and cheers.[26] 'Morrison's work has always in part been about words failing,' critic Laura Barton recently wrote in the *Guardian*, 'about inarticulacy and the gulf between the emotion and the tongue. Many of his songs seem to sit at the precise point where language falls apart.'[27] On a live recording of 'Whole Lotta Love' from 1972, Led Zeppelin's Robert Plant fakes a long stutter on the final 'b' in the phrase 'You've got to let that boy boogie' before saying, 'I think John Lee Hooker said that.'[28]

There are several musicians who have claimed that singing and songwriting were a refuge from stuttering. 'As a kid, I used to stutter,' Kendrick Lamar has said. 'I think that's why I put my energy into making music. That's how I get my thoughts out.'[29] Ed Sheeran claims learning every word of Eminem's *The Marshall Mathers LP* when he was ten made him fluent: 'he raps very fast and very melodically, and very percussively, and it helped me get rid of the stutter.'[30] Carly Simon creates a charming image, straight out of *The Sound of Music*, of her family literally singing her to fluency. 'Because everyone in the family knew that it was very hard for me to speak but very easy to sing,' she has said, 'we began to sing around the house all the time, telling each other to go to bed, or get up, or come to dinner.'[31] But while all these artists were drawn to music because of their speech, only the blues and its derivatives have made music about stuttering, turning it into an overt act of rebellion and seduction.

The unique insights and emotions that emerge from the experience of a speech disorder inevitably influence not only an artist's vision, but also their use of language. Again and again, writers who struggle with speech have described their elation at the way words flow on the page. Colm Tóibín tells me his stutter is reflected not in 'the style so much as the wanting to do it, as much as the finding comfort in it ... One never really knew how problematic the speech was because you buried it. You put it aside. But when you had a pen in your hand you didn't have that problem at all. So there was almost pleasure but there was certainly release.' Poet and novelist Owen Sheers, who also stutters, describes to me the 'release and satisfaction in being able to be fluent on the page and to be very precise about words and their order'.

Unsurprisingly, the stuttering writer has often been prone to graphomania: a compulsive need to get words down because so many get caught in the mouth. Somerset Maugham wrote over thirty books of fiction, over thirty plays, and countless stories and volumes of essays and memoirs. Henry James wrote over twenty novels and over a hundred stories. Although Lewis Carroll published relatively little, he funnelled his creativity into his imaginative letters: over 100,000 in the course of his lifetime.

John Updike was scarcely less prolific and wrote about the satisfaction he took in having 'managed to manoeuvre several millions of words' around the 'guilty blockage in the throat'.[32]

Although the term Tourette's syndrome didn't exist in his lifetime, the eighteenth-century writer Samuel Johnson has been retrospectively diagnosed, based on the close observations of his friends Fanny Burney and James Boswell. He wrote many essays and biographies as well as a novel and a play, but his fame in his lifetime rested on his *A Dictionary of the English Language* (1755). At the time, and to this day, the task seems superhuman. There was no comprehensive English dictionary at the time; certainly nothing to compare with the French dictionary produced by the Académie française a half-century before. As Johnson himself famously observed, if it took forty scholars forty years to complete the French dictionary, he would do his in three. 'Let me see,' he joked, 'forty times forty is sixteen hundred. As three to sixteen hundred, so is the proportion of an Englishman to a Frenchman.'[33] In the preface to his dictionary, Johnson repeatedly talks about wanting to 'fix' the English language: not to correct it so much as pin it down so that words 'might be less apt to decay and that signs might be permanent, like the things which they denote'.[34] He sees language itself as unreliable, like the tics, gesticulations and involuntary ejaculations others observed in him.

More than the sheer volume of output, people with speech disorders often develop a unique style of writing that reflects some of the patterns of their speech. 'The way I write is very different to the way I talk,' says actor and director Jamie Beddard, reflecting on his experience of cerebral palsy. 'The language I use in speech is very functional because I know what works and what you're not going to understand. But on the page, I'm very pompous because I can't be pompous in real life.'

Earlier, we saw how Henry James's strange, circumlocutious way of speaking was the result of an interiorised stutter. In the autumn of 1896, a wrist condition prevented him from writing by hand and he was forced to employ a stenographer. Overnight, he went from writing novels to dictating them. As biographer Leon Edel observed, 'Henry James writing, and Henry James dictating, were different persons. Some of his friends claimed they could put their finger on the exact chapter in *Maisie* [*What Maisie Knew*] where manual effort ceased and dictation began. After several years of consistent dictating, the "later manner" of Henry James emerged.'[35]

The novels in the 'later manner' include *The Turn of the Screw*, *The Wings of the Dove*, *The Ambassadors* and *The Golden Bowl*. In them, he abandons the crystal clarity of his early work for a style that is obscure to say the least: long, very long sentences and sophisticated grammatical structures, or what has been called the 'complex' and 'indirect' style of these books. Characters no longer say what they mean; in fact, they tend to do the exact opposite. In *The Golden Bowl*, we are witness to a series of scenes charting an adulterous affair in which everything occurs beneath the surface of dialogue which is either so shrouded in secret hints and signals it is almost impossible to make sense of it, or completely off target altogether concealing some deeper form of communication. James's point is that human behaviour is too complex, too conflicted, too profound to reduce to definitive statements and articulate dialogue.

Most artists innovate in the early stage of their career, but James did so at the end, leaving behind the epic, moralising sweep of Victorian masters like George Eliot and Charles Dickens for something simultaneously vaguer but celebratory of human nature as it really is. This small group of books is recognised as a high point in the history of the novel, both because of their quality but also for the widespread influence they had on other novelists, fundamentally changing the art form for good. While there are many things that informed James's late, great period, the shift from writing to dictating is widely acknowledged as an important one. What we see is the carefully considered, circumlocutory, vast vocabulary and grammatical dexterity of the stutterer transformed with Midas-like alchemy into art.

Aphasia is known for depriving people of language and yet it also has its own poetic turn. After his stroke, Edwyn Collins could only say four things. Three of them were functional: 'yes', 'no' and 'Grace Maxwell' (his wife's name). But the fourth was seemingly random: 'The possibilities are endless.' Today, Collins has no idea where this phrase came from or what was really meant by it, except possibly being an enigmatic reflection on his own potential as a recovering stroke victim or a statement about life itself. As his recovery progressed, other strange phrases emerged from his mouth. His wife kept a record of them, noting that he wasn't 'really able to control these surprising announcements'. They included:

'Subtle differences' – 'The situation is evolving' – 'Life is an aphrodisiac' – 'Suffering is ordinary. Suffering is the place he is understanding. Means towards an end' – 'Different voices come. It rocks my world' – 'I think to myself, is it any wonder he's gone mad?'[36]

One writer who became fascinated by the seemingly random, yet poetic language of aphasia was Irish playwright Samuel Beckett. As a young man, he found himself questioning the 'official English' he heard and read all about him. It was 'like a veil that must be torn apart in order to get at the things (or the Nothingness) behind it,' he wrote to a friend. 'Grammar and style. To me they have become as irrelevant as a Victorian bathing suit or the imperturbability of a true gentleman. A mask. Let us hope the time will come, thank God that in certain circles it has already come, when language is most efficiently used where it is being most efficiently misused.'[37] For Beckett, speech disorders were often exemplary examples of efficient misuse. In the 1930s, he visited the French poet Valéry Larbaud who, following a stroke, could only speak a single sentence: 'Bonsoir, les choses d'ici-bas' (sometimes translated as 'Farewell material things of the earth').[38] Literary scholars have repeatedly pointed to the similarities between Beckett's theatrical masterpieces, such as *Not I*, and the transcribed speech of certain forms of aphasia. At the end of his life, Beckett experienced aphasia himself and his last poem describes the experience of trying and failing to articulate himself with the constant refrain: 'what is the word?'[39]

While a speech disorder can make an individual revere conventional artistic form, to excel on the page or on stage where they cannot in day-to-day speech, it can also push them the other way, to experiment. In some cases it is a natural consequence of that non-linear, spontaneous, almost three-dimensional way of thinking that accompanies a disorder. This is evident in the work of Charles Dodgson, who claimed he had no idea what he was up to when he composed the *Alice* books, and Henry James, whose late style effectively redefined the rules of the novel.

The American writer David Shields is mid-way through a career intent on taking this tendency to a logical conclusion. When he was in his twenties, he achieved literary success with his novel *Dead Languages*, a semi-autobiographical story about a boy growing up with a stutter, as Shields had done. *Dead Languages* is a conventional coming-of-age novel in many ways, and the perfect expression of his youthful desire to turn the nightmare of 'stuttering into lyric language'. 'Writing *Dead Languages* freed me up on some unconscious level to take stuttering no longer as subject matter nor as default mode of lyrical writing,' he tells me, 'and pivot into making stuttering the very methodology of my new found art form, namely literary collage, or montage or fragmentation.'

Shields began, tentatively at first but with ever greater ferocity, writing books which were neither fiction nor non-fiction but merged different genres, that were non-linear and often fragmented without connecting thoughts between sections, and that were built around the principle of collage, often putting in extracts from other writers' work. He has described this form as the 'lyric essay'. His influential 2010 manifesto *Reality Hunger* argues that conventional narrative form, or the novel, is no longer adequate for capturing the experience of modern life. Only work which merges different forms, shuttles between fact and fiction, leaves out long-winded set-ups and bridging thoughts, and in which the authorship of any single passage is unclear (all of which, incidentally, are qualities we associate with the internet) can do this. 'I am terribly distrustful of fluency of all kinds,' Shields tells me. '*Reality Hunger* is a sort of stutter-fest in a way. Stuttering understood as a metaphor for discordant literary form.'

In his article 'Tourette's Syndrome and Creativity' (1992), Oliver Sacks describes a writer who separates his practice: short, formal essays when he is repressing his Tourette's and 'huge, meandering, fantastical (and often coprolalic) novels, in which he gives his Tourettic fancies full reign'.[40] This description applies well to the theatre work of Jess Thom. Her show *Backstage in Biscuit Land* offered a unique insight into the surreal comedy as well as the difficulties of living with her condition. Rather than trying to write her tics out of the script, Thom embraced them. This included those that emerged during the production process. When she was asked what props she wanted for the show, she let her tics fly and, as one reviewer described it, on the stage were 'four ducks dressed as pterodactyls; a dinosaur balloon; an enormous loaf of bread named Steve; an anvil with the word "dinner" on it; a life-size statue of Mother Teresa; and "the smell of an ice cream parlour and bakery from a different age".'[41] The last one sprayed on the front row of the audience.

The British performance artist Brian Catling grew up with a stutter, dyslexia and tics, or what he has called 'the full set'. Although he suffered at school, it has been a long time since someone has dared mock him because, even in his seventies, he is an imposing presence: a highbrow bruiser like Dr Johnson. He began his artistic career as a sculptor, but as much as he loved making things with his hands it wasn't enough. He started writing poetry. Even then, there was something missing. Finally, for an event at the Whitechapel Gallery, he embarked, fairly spontaneously, on a work of performance art. He sat in the room tearing apart books and putting them together in new combinations.

Catling has created many performances since, but they tend to revolve around creatures played by himself, often for days at a time, with a heightened abnormality. This includes a cyclops (using a prosthetic mask) or a man with rape alarms attached to his head. 'All of the performance personalities are not heroes – the cyclops being the most obvious – all of them have an impairment that makes them more human,' Catling tells me when we meet at the Royal Academy in London. 'They're not there to demonstrate control of the world. They're not there to demonstrate a heroic posture or a posture of control. They're stumbling in it and so they become inventive.' Catling roots all of this back to his stutter: that feeling of struggling through the world with a handicap. 'I've consciously looked at verbal disability. I've made performance pieces about not being able to speak.'

Late in his career, Catling sat down one morning and began writing a piece of fiction that I think Lewis Carroll would have approved of. Not only was it a work of fantasy, but, like *Alice*, it began with a single image with no idea what would come next. He thought it would be completed in a day or two, but finished several years later. The *Vorrh* trilogy (*The Vorrh*, 2012; *The Erstwhile*, 2017; and *The Cloven*, 2018) became an immediate cult classic, celebrated as one of the great visionary works of the twenty-first century by Phillip Pullman, Terry Gilliam, Tom Waits and many others. Restlessly, Catling moves on to the next project: a sculpture show, a collection of short stories, a play and a film.

In the last chapter, we saw how a neurodiverse approach to speech disorders would recognise the immense difficulties people may experience with speech, but also acknowledge some of the productive qualities that may develop as well: the impact on an individual's personality, on their use of language, but also on the forms of social interaction they participate in. The unique forms of creativity that emerge alongside or because of a speech disorder mirror these areas shaping the personality or attitude of an artist, their use of language and imagery, and the tendency to experiment as they search for better ways of representing these insights. In other words, a speech disorder can impact on what an artist has to say and how they say it.

No wonder that Charles Dodgson had such a conflicted relationship with his own stutter. On one hand, he participated in intensive therapy for decades to try and alleviate it. But here is the strange thing: when he chose a pen-name for himself, a name he could choose out of any in the world, he settled on one that began with his most feared sound – a hard 'C'. This sound was so troublesome that Dodgson had to sometimes spell out what he wanted to say and even referred to it as 'my vanquisher in single-hand combat'.[42] Every time he said 'Lewis Carroll' he was reminded of his disfluency and the possibility it might trip him up at that moment. Since it is hardly likely this was a surprise to him, the likelihood is that he did it deliberately: a constant reminder of both his greatest shame and the oddity that made him unique.

10

Speech Acts of Resistance

Around 1916, a new front opened up in the Great War. It wasn't a territorial front, like the trenches surrounding Ypres or Gallipoli, for it was both invisible and pervasive, transcending borders, social divides and military loyalties. It was a conflict that had been simmering for many years but seemed suddenly to be bursting forth in the most unlikely of places. The target was immaterial: as light as air, as lethal as the biggest guns. Many of those participating in the assault were often unaware of their part in the conflict, but others had no doubt at all about their aim. This was a war against language.

Over the previous hundred and fifty years, since the emergence of what was called the Enlightenment in Europe, language had been increasingly claimed as the essence of human achievement: the vehicle of reason, of human co-operation and order. Countless politicians, philosophers, doctors, lawyers and clerics had repeatedly, and with ever greater force, expressed the view that our ability to speak and write was what separated us from other animals. Yet somehow this same civilising spirit, in the mouths and pens of those considered most adept at using it, had cajoled all of Europe into murder. The assassination of Archduke Franz Ferdinand in Sarajevo was incidental. After all, what did the murder of the heir to the Austro-Hungarian Empire by his own dissidents have to do with Britain? But for years, the words of priests, politicians, generals and polemicists had inveigled the paradoxical notion that war could prove a civilising force in the hearts of those they served. Within weeks of Franz Ferdinand's death, most of Europe was mobilising without most citizens quite knowing why, but nevertheless believing the voices of authority that insisted it was both necessary and noble.

The astonishing thing isn't that Europe went to war, but that so few resisted it. Doing so involved overturning every authority and certainty one knew. One of those coming to terms with this was the poet and soldier Siegfried Sassoon. Like millions, he had enthusiastically enlisted in the first months of the war. He was doing not only what the British Establishment wanted him to do, but what his friends, family, school masters and neighbours expected of him.

As an officer in the Welsh Fusiliers, he was revered for his bravery. Solo dashes into no man's land, even into enemy trenches, earned him a Military Cross and the affectionate nickname 'Mad Jack' from his men. To all appearances he was a fierce patriot, but the poems he wrote in private told a different story. While he had once written sentimental accounts of the honesty and loyalty of common soldiers, he increasingly satirised with terrible bitterness the authority figures who had betrayed them: a bishop who witters on about 'just cause' and 'the ways of God' when confronted by those whose lives have been wrecked,[1] and a general who is full of pleasantries with his men even as he devises the strategies that will kill them.[2] Sassoon later wrote that he wanted his poems to reveal what he called 'war's demented language'.[3] His friend Robert Graves described how British civilians were taken over by a 'war-madness' that appeared as 'a foreign language; and it was newspaper language'.[4] Both men still struggled to articulate it, but they sensed that the greatest enemy wasn't other humans but something rotten in the language we use.

In Zurich, Switzerland, this conviction was more flamboyantly expressed by a group of refugee artists and political activists, mostly from Germany, Romania and France, who were determined to sit out the slaughter in one of the few countries that had remained neutral. They declared themselves not only against reason and art, but against language too – or, at least, all existing forms of it – for it was words and argument that had created the war. They chose the nonsense word *dada* to describe their movement. On 14 July 1916, two weeks after the outbreak of the Battle of the Somme, the German poet and deserter Hugo Ball read out the first Dada manifesto in a public lecture. He described how language had become 'accursed' and covered in 'filth'. 'How can one get rid of everything that smacks of journalism, worms, everything nice and right, blinkered, moralistic, europeanised, enervated? By saying dada.'[5] He then illustrated his point with a shift into (semi) nonsense. 'Dada is the world soul, dada is the pawnshop. Dada is the world's best lily-milk soap. Dada Mr Rubiner, dada Mr Korrodi. Dada Mr Anastasius Lilienstein.' The poems he wrote 'meant to dispense with conventional language and to have done with it.' Like the name of the movement, they were nonsensical, full of made-up words and sounds.

The spirit of Dada wasn't isolated to a group of oddball deserters holed up in a mountain town. In Russia, a crew of poets was experimenting with an art form they called Zaum. One of them, Aleksei Kruchenykh, argued that language binds us to dominant hierarchies and ideologies. His manifestos call for a 'language that does not have any definite meaning (not frozen), a transrational language'.[6] In France, the poet Guillaume Apollinaire experimented in the trenches with what he called 'calligrammes': poems where words are laid out pictorially on a page without any sentence structure. Versions of the same iconoclastic turn against language took place among the soldier-poets of Vorticism in England and Futurism in Italy, although these artists tended to celebrate war as the force that would set language free once and for all.

All too often, avant-garde art movements sit in isolation, even against the broader trends of society, but for once the artists and armies were in alignment. The authorities weren't concerned about a few dissidents, but they were by the thousands returning from the front incapacitated by shell shock. Doctors, generals and politicians were at first reluctant to admit the cause might be psychological. The symptoms, they argued, were physiological. It was a form of concussion caused by internal damage to the nervous system brought on by the noise and shudder of shell explosions: hence its name. As the war progressed, the number of cases of shell shock developed into an epidemic. In Britain alone, it is estimated that somewhere between 80,000 and 200,000 soldiers were ultimately discharged from active service for it.[7]

Although shell shock had a wide range of symptoms, including paralysis, trembling, anxiety and nightmares, it was the disorders of speech in particular that captured the public's imagination. These ranged from mild stuttering to complete mutism. One of the best-loved songs of the war was 'K-K-K-Katy' – 'The Sensational Stammering Song Success Sung by the Soldiers and Sailors'.[8] In his poem 'Survivors', Siegfried Sassoon identifies shell shock victims by their 'stammering, disconnected talk'.[9] His friend Wilfred Owen, while convalescing, wondered in verse if he should 'mutter and stutter and wangle my ticket' out of the front line.[10] He was conscious that his speech impediment, involuntary as it was, might also save his life; what in peacetime was stigma, in war was a ticket to survival. In Virginia Woolf's *Mrs Dalloway*, the stutter of its hero, Septimus Smith, betrays the lingering shell shock that will ultimately lead to his suicide.

I don't believe that the speech disorders associated with shell shock were a conscious reaction against the authoritative and supposedly rational language that had both brought about and was perpetuating the war. At the same time, the notion that some unconscious and collective resistance was at work cannot be easily dismissed. Today, shell shock is considered a misnomer for what we now call post-traumatic stress disorder (PTSD). However, it is important not to conflate the two terms. All forms of PTSD, argues historian Peter Leese, are 'culturally shaped' at any given time. Shell shock, therefore, was the unique expression of PTSD in the context and culture of early twentieth-century Europe. It was, Leese writes, a 'malleable, subjective state' that 'absorbs too the sympathy of comrade and relative, the outrage of editor and MP, the censure of officer and pension doctor'.[11] Somehow, in this context, stuttering, tics and mutism emerged as dominant symptoms, the only occasion in history when speech disorders have reached epidemic proportions.

In a recent study of over 300,000 veterans of the Iraq and Afghanistan wars, it was found that only 235 (0.08 per cent) had 'acquired stutters'.[12] Even allowing for the higher number of Britons who fought in the First World War, this still suggests only a few thousand with acquired stutters, if the symptoms of modern PTSD and shell shock were the same. While there are no such studies from the First World War, the regularity of speech disorders in doctors' case notes – 'complete loss of speech'; 'mutism'; 'no stammer previous to shock'; 'speaks in a halting fashion'; 'a hesitation in his speech'; 'a tremulous tongue' – suggests it was, as the cultural stereotypes imply, far more prevalent. Something about the context of the First World War made disordered speech a fitting response to the horrors that soldiers experienced. Peter Leese concludes that shell shock was, in part, 'a bodily collapse of reason and language', like that described by the Dadaist artists, but one that 'demonstrated more eloquently than any artistic statement the modern era's failure of words'. That language was somehow to blame seems to have infiltrated the experience of shell shock in a way never quite matched in wars since.

Attempts to treat shell shock were mostly dire, the aim being simply to get people back to the front as soon as possible and avoid it becoming a shield for cowardice. Attempts ranged from massage to electric shock therapy to, most brutally, what was called 'firing squad therapy', threatening capital punishment for cowardice and in some cases following through. For a while, the army actually pursued a stiff-upper-lip policy of mixing shell-shocked soldiers with 'cheery chaps' who had minor physical wounds (this prompted an organised response from one group of shell-shocked patients that they would rather risk another air raid than be submitted to the enthusiasm of another 'cheery chap'). During the Battle of the Somme, by autumn 1916, the army was reporting over 15,000 cases of shell shock a month.

It was against this backdrop, the complete failure of traditional medicine to explain or treat shell shock, that the previously fringe theories of Sigmund Freud, Sándor Ferenczi and other psychoanalysts began to gain credence in the medical establishment. One exponent was W.H.R. Rivers, who set up a pioneering practice at Craiglockhart Military Hospital in 1916. He drew in part from psychoanalysis, but differed in one important regard. While the workings of an unconscious mind clearly seemed at work in shell shock, with symptoms an expression of the anxiety soldiers struggled to articulate in words, Rivers thought it had nothing to do with the childhood sexuality that was a cornerstone of Freud's theories.[13]

Rivers refused to stigmatise shell shock and its accompanying disorders of speech, perhaps for no better reason than he had stuttered all his life. By strange coincidence, he was a nephew of James Hunt and had grown up around his uncle's practice, meeting devoted pupils like Charles

Dodgson. Rivers's shell shock treatment owed just as much to James Hunt's methods as it did to psychoanalysis. He accepted patients for who they were, without passing judgement. Although it's hard to know exactly what Rivers spoke to his patients about, for that took place in confidence between them, Siegfried Sassoon gives one revealing insight about his own sessions with him. 'We talked a lot about European politicians,' he recalled, 'and what they were saying.' In other words, they talked about language.

The Great War was a turning point; the moment when many, rather than a few, began to challenge the infallibility of language. As a consequence, it was also a moment when the perceived inferiority of speech disorders was briefly brought into question. Stuttering became so common as to hardly merit comment. When Sassoon mentions in passing that he sat for dinner at Craiglockhart between 'two bad stammerers',[14] one feels he could be talking about brunettes or bald men. The song 'K-K-K-Katy' is unlike almost any other cultural depiction of stuttering because it is sincere and romantic. Its hero, Jimmy, may stutter, but he is 'brave and bold' and loved by a beautiful woman. Rivers shrugged off any concern about stuttering, claiming it was nothing more than 'a defect of the brain, which gives contradictory orders simultaneously when disturbed in a certain way', and that the best thing was to 'forget it'.[15] A hundred years later, his theory increasingly seems correct.

In the same spirit, people with aphasia were no longer perceived as 'intelligent dogs', as one pre-war doctor described a patient,[16] but as ordinary human beings struggling with a disconnect between thought and words. The neurologist Henry Head, a close friend of Rivers, tended soldiers recovering from head injuries. His influential 'Aphasia and Kindred Disorders of Speech' (1920) not only advanced understanding of the condition, but finally recognised that most sufferers were no less intelligent than they had been before and described them with great dignity.[17] Unfortunately, it was a moment that was soon betrayed by the theoretical indulgences of psychoanalysis.

I've shown how speech disorders can exert productive, as well as negative, influences on an individual's personality, their use of language and their creativity, but this account of the First World War shows how they can have a broader social purpose too. In the right context, speech disorders can prove a necessary disruptor: challenging groupthink and literally blocking the flow of a society that has run amok with platitudes and empty rhetoric. In the 1970s, the French philosophers Gilles Deleuze and Felix Guattari articulated this in explicit terms. Their collaboration as writers and political activists followed the violent and, ultimately, failed uprising of May 1968, when French students and workers briefly took control of the streets.

In their sprawling masterpiece *Capitalism and Schizophrenia* (1972–80), Deleuze and Guattari set out to show how every aspect of Western society is focused on controlling and cajoling us into people we don't want to be.[18] This is achieved not so much through guns or tanks, although they play a part, but through language. Words are used to fix and limit things with names and labels: male/female, black/white, straight/gay. Language is always in cahoots with the inherently repressive 'megamachine' of the state to keep us in our place. It is what determines class and gender, what controls our thinking, what holds back our development as individuals.

Language, Deleuze and Guattari write, is made primarily 'to be obeyed and to compel obedience', it is 'generalised slavery'. Mess with language, their argument goes, and you start to mess with the very foundations of human oppression. They even suggest some of the ways in which this might be done, including 'indirect discourse', 'atypical expression' and enforced 'breaks and ruptures' in our speech. All these are qualities we associate either with disordered speech or the compensating tactics used to conceal it.

The term they use to describe this strategy is 'creative stuttering'; creative because it is voluntary and planned rather than compulsive. 'Creative stuttering', they say, is 'an affective and intensive language' or 'a poetic operation' that can make us pause and become more aware of the way our tropes and phrases limit rather than expand thought. 'Creative stuttering is what makes language grow from the middle, like grass,' they write, 'what puts language in perpetual disequilibrium.' Unsurprisingly, Deleuze and Guattari revered Lewis Carroll, who had both a 'creative' and an actual stutter, and in whose hands language becomes gloriously irrational and unreliable.

When I first encountered the work of Deleuze and Guattari, I found this phrase pleasantly shocking. I had never seen the word 'creative' placed before stuttering and it made me think about it in a new way. I had always seen my stutter as an embarrassment that shouldn't be allowed to disrupt conversations. Now I began to wonder if there wasn't a certain power to it. Later, when I began to practise voluntary stuttering through City Lit, I put this to the test: deliberately blocking on words in professional meetings while maintaining eye contact, seeing the momentary unease it gave people and using that to then drive home a particular point I wanted to make. But could stuttering or any speech disorder ever be revolutionary, as Deleuze and Guattari suggested? I began to search for precedents and eventually found one in the Zimbabwean writer Dambudzo Marechera.

Growing up under British rule in the 1960s, in what was then called Rhodesia, Marechera saw the role that language played in enforcing colonialism in his country. At home and on the streets, Marechera spoke his native Shona, but at school – like Ngũgĩ wa Thiong'o in Kenya – he had to speak English. In his mind, like thousands of others, he associated his own tongue with the chaos of the ghetto and that of his colonial masters with order and wealth. 'Shona was part of the ghetto daemon I was trying to escape,' he recalled.

> Shona had been placed within the context of a degraded, mind-wrenching experience from which apparently the only escape was into the English language and education. The English language was automatically connected with the plush and seeming splendour of the white side of town. As far as expressing the creative turmoil within my head was concerned, I took to the English language as a duck takes to water. I was therefore a keen accomplice and student in my own mental colonisation.[19]

Whether it was as a consequence of that inner turmoil, or of the complexity of having to think and speak in two languages, or just coincidence, Marechera's speech failed him. 'I began to stammer horribly,' he said.

> It was terrible. Even speech, language, was deserting me. I stammered hideously for three years. Agony. You know in class the teacher asks something, my hand shoots up, I stand, everyone is looking, I just stammer away, stuttering, nobody understands, the answer is locked inside me. Finally the teacher in pity asks me to please sit down. I was learning to distrust language, a distrust necessary for a writer, especially one writing in a foreign language.[20]

Marechera got a place at the University of Rhodesia, but was expelled for his involvement in anti-colonial activism. His academic performance remained astonishing and he was accepted into New College, Oxford, but was soon expelled once more: this time for trying to set the college on fire. For the next few years, he was mostly homeless, sofa-surfing around the UK. And he started writing. If he couldn't burn down the buildings of the Establishment, maybe he could burn its language down. Could he write a book that would take all the confidence, that surety, of English and mangle it into something as uncertain and vulnerable as his native Shona had been rendered? A big ambition, but how to go about it? He found himself thinking back to that moment when he had begun stuttering:

> There was the unease, the shock of being suddenly struck by stuttering, of being deserted by the very medium I was to use in all my art. This perhaps is in the undergrowth of my experimental use of English, standing it on its head, brutalising it into a more malleable shape for my own purposes. This may mean discarding grammar, throwing syntax out, subverting images from within, beating the drum and cymbals of rhythm, developing torture chambers of irony and sarcasm, gas ovens of limitless black resonance. For me this is the impossible, the exciting, the voluptuous blackening image that commits me totally to writing.[21]

In 1978, Marechera's *The House of Hunger* was published in the Heinemann African Writers series. The book describes his experiences growing up in a township in Rhodesia and the student protests he was involved in, but it is no ordinary memoir. The language is violent, often surreal. He writes about losing his speech, beginning to 'ramble, incoherently, in a disconnected manner' as he tries to reconcile two languages in his brain. 'When I talked it was in the form of an interminable argument, one side of which was always expressed in English and the other side always in Shona. At the same time I would be aware of myself as something indistinct but separate from both cultures.' In one passage, he dreams he is the boy we briefly encountered earlier, operated upon by the over-zealous Prussian surgeon Johann Friedrich Dieffenbach, 'snipping off chunks from the tips and sides' of his tongue. He is woken by his mother telling him his father has been run over and killed.

The plot of *The House of Hunger* is non-linear: a series of passages inspired by the fragmented speech of his stutter, often ending abruptly mid-sentence and jumping backwards and forwards in time. In this way, the whole book is an attempt to turn his speech disfluency into both creative writing and political activism. Running through *The House of Hunger* is an overwhelming anger at colonialism, a self-loathing for writing in English (the language which, whether he liked it or not, he had been taught to understand best) and a desire to mangle it. The book caused an immediate stir. Doris Lessing said it was 'like overhearing a scream'.[22] It won the *Guardian* Fiction Prize. At the awards ceremony, Marechera threw plates at the other guests. Tragically, he never managed to reconcile the two voices in his head but increasingly suffered from poor mental health (either a form of schizophrenia or manic depression). He returned to Zimbabwe when it became independent in 1982, but lived a homeless existence before dying of AIDS-related illness at the age of thirty-one.

Marechera used his stutter as a form of resistance to colonialism. Today, nearly forty years later, a young Swedish woman is using her difficulties with speech and communication to fight a different battle: against human extinction. Greta Thunberg emerged to global consciousness in the summer of 2018 for her part in launching Fridays for Future, a school strike movement demanding environmental policies from government to match the scale of the climate crisis. Images of her standing with painted slogans outside the Swedish parliament went viral. Within a year, in what has been called 'the Greta

Effect', she became the face and voice of environmental activism. Publishers directly credit her influence on a surge in children's books looking at the climate crisis.[23]

Undoubtedly, there is a power in the image of a vulnerable fifteen-year-old girl standing like David before the Goliaths of the world. But it is far more than that. When Thunberg speaks, she does so with an extraordinary bluntness and simplicity, repeating the same messages again and again. Most famously, she berated the leaders of the world at the 2019 United Nations Climate Action Summit in September of that year, accusing them of depriving her generation of a future through wilful inaction. 'How dare you!' she said again and again. In a talk earlier in the year, she tried to explain this aspect of her personality. 'I was diagnosed with Asperger's syndrome, OCD and selective mutism,' she said. 'That basically means I only speak when I think it's necessary. Now is one of those moments.'[24]

Far more than the Instagram images, I think Thunberg's power lies in her use of speech. She does not use any of the normal tricks and techniques of hyper-fluency because she can't. There is no humour, no attempt to rein in her emotions and charm or seduce her audience. She speaks directly, honestly and with unrestrained anger. The value of her words is only enhanced by the fact she has had to overcome the constraint of selective mutism to say them. When she says that she only speaks when it is necessary, it is obvious she's telling the truth. And because of that inner struggle, because of the unique way the words do come out, they have a currency greater than those of even the most revered orator. They are perhaps the best hope we have of forcing our governments to change course.

Speech disorders, whether intentionally or not, can become agents of resistance or conscientious objection to oppressive regimes or in times of war. Just as importantly, although a little less dramatically, they can also undermine the patterns of thinking that support such regimes and conflicts. When I was researching neurodiversity and speech activism, I spoke to Joshua St Pierre, a Canadian speech activist and founder of *Did I Stutter?*. But as an academic at the University of Alberta, his work also looks at fluency and disfluency in the context of philosophy. 'A goal for a lot of political philosophy is mutual understanding or consensus,' he tells me. 'But I'm critical of consensus as a goal because I fear that smooths over differences in the appeal to some kind of common space or common ground.' This reminds me again of the works of Plato which depict Socrates and his friends uncovering the tenets of a perfect society through a process of consensus building: asking questions, disagreeing, adapting statements, moving forwards. 'It always assumes a certain kind of speaker,' says St Pierre. 'A political actor who's able to articulate themselves and able to do so without any help.'

Studying such works, St Pierre was acutely aware that, in most people's eyes, his stuttered speech hampers him from fully participating in such debate. This is not self-censorship or paranoia. When classicist Christian Laes surveyed all existing references to speech disorders in the ancient world, he was struck by the fact they all referred to the barrier they were perceived to present to public discourse.[25] Since our democratic traditions have their roots in that time, disordered speech remains problematic for political and philosophical practice today. This is something politician Ed Balls discovered when he was accused of lack of confidence and poor debating style in the House of Commons simply because he stutters.[26] 'Sometimes my stammer gets the better of me in the first minute or two when I speak,' he has said, 'especially when I've got the prime minister, the chancellor and 300 Conservative MPs yelling at me at the tops of their voices.'[27]

For St Pierre, this inability to accommodate different styles or registers of speech suggests something flawed in the practice of political philosophy. 'I worry about things that are far too smooth and things that desire to be smooth,' he says. Eloquence and flow are at the heart of consensus building, all of which tends to obscure the flaws in a particular way of thinking. Speech disorders, on the other hand, disrupt that process. If one of Socrates's friends had a speech disorder, for instance, the dialogues of Plato would read very differently. Rather than jumping from statement to statement, arguments might digress or even just pause, allowing time for doubt about a particular, and even erroneous, train of thought to settle. And what does the widespread presence of speech disorders throughout the population say about a mode of hyper-fluent reasoning that is supposed to be enlightened, but is nevertheless also discriminatory? 'To bring stuttering into the discussion,' St Pierre says, 'is to ask certain normative questions like why do we have to speak in certain ways to be taken up as rational, essential and political? Why does our world communicate in this highly technocratic and frantic way?'

Ludwig Wittgenstein, one of the greatest thinkers of the twentieth century, is somebody who did bring stuttering into philosophy.[28] As a young man, he came to believe the whole canon of western philosophy was built upon speculative and misleading wordplay. Language is more than flawed: it is a hindrance, preventing us from understanding the mysteries of existence. It leads us down mental culs-de-sac, wasting time on pointless exercises such as looking for the substance behind abstract concepts (for example, the question 'What is time?' assumes there is such a thing as 'time' to be defined). Any philosophy, Wittgenstein said, which is constructed around linguistic statements is nothing more than 'tidying up a room':[29] the mess being language itself; the room the narrow space in which it operates in the wider universe.

After publishing the only book of philosophy that appeared in his lifetime, Wittgenstein spent the last decades of his life inventing what he called 'language-games', playful scenarios that expose the limitations and falsehoods of language. 'What we are destroying,' he said, 'is nothing but houses of cards and we are clearing up the ground of language on which they stand.'[30]

According to some biographers, Wittgenstein stuttered as a child.[31] I believe he continued to do so at times throughout his life, but there is something unusual in the way in which he did. When you read descriptions of a person who stuttered by those who knew them, a pattern tends to emerge, giving a consistent sense of what they sounded like. But in Wittgenstein's case it is a struggle to find any continuity at all. There are accounts and transcriptions of his speeches and debates in which he seems unable to get the words out. The poet Julian Bell wrote a satirical verse about Wittgenstein saying, 'In every company he shouts us down/And stops our sentence stuttering his own.'[32] Another contemporary recalls his public performances being 'tense and often incoherent'.[33] Yet another: 'He had extreme difficulty in expressing himself and his words were unintelligible to me.'[34] Wittgenstein himself occasionally acknowledges these blocks. In one letter, he complains that his jokes 'get jammed and can't come out'.[35] But on other occasions, Wittgenstein seemed able to speak with great fluency. While stuttering is known for its inconsistencies, this variability is more pronounced in Wittgenstein than most others, raising the possibility that he deployed it as a tactic to draw attention to the limits and failure of language itself. In other words, it was another type of language-game.

'When he started to formulate his view on some specific philosophical problem,' writes one colleague, 'we often felt the internal struggle that occurred in him at that very moment, a struggle by which he tried to penetrate from darkness to light under an intense and painful strain, which was even visible on his most expressive face.'[36] In purely descriptive terms this philosophical struggle is indistinguishable from the appearance of a person wrestling with a block. 'My whole tendency was to run against the boundaries of language,' Wittgenstein wrote. 'This running against the walls of our cage is perfectly, absolutely hopeless.'[37] It is impossible to know for sure to what extent he used his impediment as a way of disrupting philosophical flow, but he did on occasion conflate his attempts at philosophy with the experience of a speech disorder. 'I never more than half succeed in expressing what I want to express,' he once said, 'often my writing is nothing but a form of stuttering.'[38]

I believe that stuttering, whether voluntary or involuntary, became for Wittgenstein a way of doing what he felt many other philosophers tended to neglect. It was a method for interrupting the momentum of linguistic flow and the errors of thought it leads us into, of continually pausing to take stock, reassessing his own ideas and language, then starting again on surer ground.

All speech disorders are disruptive. They break the flow of speech, drawing undue attention to the words we use and the way we say them. More often than not this causes a deep, almost inexplicable, discomfort for both speaker and listener. Normally, this phenomenon is described only in negative terms: it hampers efficient communication, limits public discourse, is a source of embarrassment for all involved. But a neurodiverse account of speech disorders turns this on its head. All those things may be true, but since hyper-fluency is a double-edged sword – able to conceal errors of thinking and prejudice behind pleasant words, as well as enable communication and new ideas – anything that slows it down and subjects it to closer scrutiny has value. In this regard, speech disorders have a social purpose above and beyond the affliction caused in an individual: as a disruptor, a creative spur, a memento of the limits of language or even an agent of resistance against oppression. Until the attitudinal changes that occurred around the time of the First World War, such an idea was implausible, but it has increasingly gained momentum to the point today where Greta Thunberg openly talks about her difficulties with speech as a 'superpower'.[39]

'The stutterer is faithful to human tension every time he talks,' writes American writer David Shields, echoing Wittgenstein, 'only in broken speech is the form of disfluency consonant with the chaos of the world's content. Stutterers are truth-tellers; everyone else is lying. I know it's insane but I believe that.'[40] Joshua St Pierre sees this in more practical terms. 'I genuinely feel that embracing disfluency within our midst changes how we can relate to each other, perhaps in important ways,' he says. 'Disfluency can call a kind of responsiveness from each other that is lacking. It can cultivate new ways of being in the world. At a different level, it's also a pretty strong critique of a lot of these capitalist forces that incite our tongue to speech the whole time.'

I would argue that the societal benefit of speech disorders lies in the same disruptive qualities that those who have them are often most ashamed of. Whether intentionally or not (and mostly the latter), they provide a healthy check on the dangerous errors of thought and action that fluent and hyper-fluent speech can sometimes cause. Along with those productive qualities I have already described – the unacknowledged positive impacts they can have on an individual's personality and creativity – the foundation for a neurodiverse appreciation of speech disorders is evident. Yet it remains far from widely accepted. The challenge lies not so much in describing these phenomena, but in convincing a fluent and prejudiced majority to recognise them. The stakes are high. Bearing in mind the failure of medical science to provide cures (and in some cases even effective diagnoses) of many conditions, neurodiversity presents the best opportunity to reduce the stigma and therefore many of the attendant psychological symptoms for those who have speech disorders. The challenge is to deliver it.

11

Communication Diversity

How do you change the way a society thinks? Shifting mainstream perception is notoriously difficult, particularly when it comes to something as fraught with ideology, custom and prejudice as language. All our instincts lean towards greater regulation rather than relaxation of linguistic performance. There are, after all, hundreds of books on how to speak with greater fluency, always with the threat that without this skill our careers and even our private lives may flounder.

If, as we have seen, there is a general belief that our civilisation is built and depends upon the efficient flow of speech and language, then the unreliability of words is problematic. 'English (or any other language people speak) is hopelessly unsuited to serve as our internal medium of computation,' writes Steven Pinker.[1] He points to its ambiguities, quoting newspaper headlines ('Drunk Gets Nine Months in Violin Case'), and also the fact that the linearity and comparative slowness of speech are almost at cross-purposes with the speed and lateral connectivity of thought.

Speech is particularly prone to sloppiness, partly because it is (mostly) spontaneous and partly because in addition to the ambiguity of individual words there are the additional ambiguities of dialect and intonation. When you put involuntary disfluencies into the mix, like a stutter, aphasia, dysarthria and vocal tics, it appears all the more unreliable. 'There is good reason why so-called laziness in pronunciation is in fact tightly regulated by phonological rules,' Pinker writes, 'and why, as a consequence, no dialect allows its speakers to cut corners at will. Every act of sloppiness on the part of a speaker demands a compensating measure of mental effort on the part of the conversational partner. A society of lazy talkers would be a society of hard-working listeners.'[2] It is assumed that such a society is unwelcome.

We are, it seems, hard-wired to resist variations in speech because we have put so much stock in an instrument that is dangerously unreliable. Yet despite the tendency to police our language, there are occasions when attitudes to linguistic difference or variation have relaxed, and in relatively short time too. By focusing on a couple of these, it is possible to uncover ways in which changing attitudes to speech disorders might be encouraged and achieved.

Martinique is a small island in the Antilles archipelago in the Caribbean. It was settled by the French in the seventeenth century and, aside from some back-and-forth with the British during the Napoleonic Wars, has remained French to this day. Most of the population are descended from the African slaves who were once imported on a mass scale to work the sugar plantations. Those slaves acquired the language of their masters, but in speaking to one another created a hybrid tongue called Creole using French, Carib and African languages, mixed with elements of English, Spanish and Portuguese, as well as inventing entirely new words. A couple of decades ago Martinican Creole was considered by the French, but also many Martinican natives, as it had always been: simply an inferior, mongrel dialect of the mother tongue; a childish babble incapable of carrying abstract thought or communicating knowledge.[3] This way of thinking dominated through to the 1980s, but then, in just a couple of years, Creole suddenly became respected and acknowledged as a linguistic register in its own right.

The seeds of this change date back to 1936 when a young Martinican student called Aimé Césaire returned from several years' study in Paris. He had imbibed the culture of his colonial masters, the excitement of Surrealism and jazz in the cafés and clubs, but also the racism and arrogance he encountered on the streets. He felt dislocated, yearning for the best of both places, but not feeling quite at home in either. He put his thoughts to paper in a prose-poem called *Notebook of a Return to My Native Land*, which captures both the beauty of the island and the subjugation of its people.

Césaire wrote in French, but he also recognised – as Ngũgĩ wa Thiong'o and Dambudzo Marechera would do in coming decades – that the imposition of a master's language is the most effective means of mental colonisation. For Césaire, French was an elegant means of expression but also an implement of domination, even torture. 'Who twists my voice?' he writes in the *Notebook*, describing this predicament. 'Who scratches my voice? Stuffing my throat with a thousand bamboo fangs. A thousand sea-urchin stakes.'[4] In response, Césaire decided, in his own words, to 'bend French': mangling existing words and inventing entirely new ones to say the things about Martinique that dictionary French, a language rooted in Europe, could not capture. It was said by one contemporary that Césaire even had a stutter at this time that began to alleviate with his political and linguistic awakening.[5]

After finishing the *Notebook*, Césaire continued to write but he also sought to liberate Martinique and its people from the worst elements of colonisation. As well as becoming mayor of the capital, he became a schoolteacher, educating the island's children to think for themselves. One of these pupils was a boy called Frantz Fanon. Under Césaire, Fanon learned to distrust the language of France as well as its uniformed authorities, but this also made him more curious about the Creole he and his friends spoke in the streets. Why were Martinicans so free with it in private yet so ashamed of it in public? What psychological impact did the use of two languages, one a subversive play on the other, have on a people?

During the Second World War, Fanon fought with the Free French Forces against Hitler and the Vichy government, but even while risking his life for the liberation of France he encountered appalling racism from those he served. Radicalised by these experiences, he devoted his life to fighting colonialism. He worked for revolutionary movements in both Africa and the Caribbean and provided a philosophical framework for post-colonialism in *Black Skin, White Masks* (1952) and *The Wretched of the Earth* (1961). In the former, Fanon addresses the subjugation of Creole in Martinique. 'The middle class in the Antilles never speak Creole except to their servants.

In school the children of Martinique are now taught to scorn the dialect. One avoids Creolisms. Some families completely forbid the use of Creole, and mothers ridicule their children for speaking it.'[6] Fanon doesn't make a claim for Creole as a creative language in its own right, but he does show that its repression is unsustainable, creating a sense of 'dislocation, a separation' in the hearts of Martinicans. Fanon had taken up the intellectual baton where Césaire left off and he handed it on, in turn, to a younger schoolmate who took this exploration of Creole to a surprising conclusion.

Beginning in the 1970s, Edouard Glissant, a philosopher and poet, argued that Creole was not a mongrel dialect, an inferior subset of French created by people too sloppy to obey the rules. It was a secretive means of communication within plantation life: a *lingua franca* for slaves, using elements of languages familiar to them, that their masters could not understand. When spoken quickly it appeared an 'accelerated nonsense created by scrambled sounds', but was perfectly comprehensible to those using it. As a form of linguistic subterfuge, it was arguably more rather than less sophisticated than the French it toyed with.

Glissant was friends with the French philosophers Deleuze and Guattari and seems to have been influenced by their notion of 'creative stuttering' as a means of resisting the conscription of language to oppressive causes. In *Caribbean Discourse*, published in 1981, Glissant turns on those who try to dismiss Creole. 'You wish to reduce me to a childish babble,' he wrote. 'I will make this babble systematic, we shall see if you can make sense of it.'

Glissant called his study of Creole a 'poetics': the term used for describing linguistic techniques in poetry and literature, but which he defines as 'the implicit or explicit manipulation of self-expression'. By doing so, he elevated its status from street patois to a conscious, organised and authentic language.

In identifying the qualities that synthesise Creole, Glissant articulates a set of techniques for making a dominant, imperial language stutter. He places the objective of 'diversion' as the driving force in its evolution: the need to conceal real meaning from the French administrators, while appearing to dutifully speak a clumsy version of their language. Diversion, in turn, leads to new possibilities: the use of 'ornate expressions and circumlocutions', 'antiphrasis' (using words in a way opposite to their real meaning), 'sudden changes in tone', 'continuous breaks in the narrative', 'asides' and 'the art of repetition'. All of these techniques are familiar to anyone who daily tries to conceal a stutter. According to Glissant, what was considered baby-talk was in fact a form of guerrilla linguistics.

Even as he was writing, a generation of young Martinican novelists used the techniques Glissant prescribed to create a new movement creolising the language of French literature. They called it, simply, Créolité. They put down their thoughts in an essay 'In Praise of Creoleness', which celebrates their language, in opposition to French, as 'an annihilation of false universality, of monolinguism, and of purity'.[7] They both revered Césaire as an intellectual antecedent who discovered the role of the French language in colonialism, as well as the 'bending' of it as a form of resistance, but also criticised him for not going far enough in recognising the beauty and complexity of Creole. In 1992, Patrick Chamoiseau, one of the founders of Créolité, published *Texaco*. It is a powerful and sprawling epic, written in a mixture of French and Creole, that tells the brutal story of the island from the early nineteenth century to his own time. It was quickly recognised as a masterpiece and awarded France's most prestigious literary prize, the Prix Goncourt.

In just a few decades, through organisation, hard work and creative inspiration, a handful of individuals had managed to change the perception of French (or at least the version of it dictated by the Académie française in Paris) from the language of poetry to that of authoritarianism and even oppression, and the language of Creole from degenerate street patois to high art. This, in turn, has contributed to an increasing respect for Creole and recognition of it as a language in its own right. Today, it is studied in books and taught in universities. The concerns about it are no longer a regret that it exists at all, but a fear that in a globalised twenty-first century where Creole is admired rather than ridiculed, it simply becomes assimilated into the dominant languages it once, by necessity, sought to distinguish itself from. Inspired by the lesson of Creole, I wonder if such a similar reversal in perception is possible for speech disorders. Could our reverence for hyper-fluency as the ultimate form of communication diminish, elevating in the process our appreciation of speech disorders, as well as all other forms of verbal and non-verbal communication?

This change has already begun with sign languages. These are forms of expression that use gestures (hand movements, facial expressions and body language) to communicate. They are developed and mostly used by those who are deaf or unable to speak, but they are also learned by those who are part of their lives: family, friends and interpreters. Like spoken language, there are many different forms of Sign across the world and throughout history. Their presence in smaller communities and in historical documents suggest they have always existed.

In the late nineteenth century, the 'oralist' movement sought to eliminate the use of Sign. In the United States, the Scottish inventor Alexander Graham Bell founded the American Association to Promote the Teaching of Speech to the Deaf. Like thousands of others, he believed sign language, something he referred to disparagingly as 'pantomime',[8] should be discouraged, that deaf people shouldn't mix with other deaf people at school or marry them. Whether his views were tempered or exaggerated by the fact that both his mother and his wife were deaf is hard to tell. His greatest invention, the telephone, was a form of oralist communication that many deaf people were (up until recently) unable to use. The success of the oralist movement was profound. By the time of the First World War, around 80 per cent of deaf children were being educated without any access to sign language.[9] Instead, their communication was limited to a poor and reluctant replica of the speech other children performed so naturally.

Gradually, a fightback occurred. In the same way that thinkers like Edouard Glissant revealed the complexity of Creole, a concurrent movement was making a similar case for sign language. In *Sign Language Structure*, published in 1960, the linguist William Stokoe convincingly demonstrated its complexity.[10] Over the ensuing years, he argued that it was not only a sophisticated alternative to spoken language but also a different way of thinking. Many who use Sign describe its physical, three-dimensional and non-linear qualities, in contrast to the linear sentence structures of spoken languages. 'Deafness is a culture and a life,' writes Andrew Solomon, 'a language and an aesthetic, a physicality and an intimacy different from all others.'[11]

In the 1970s, this movement, sometimes called Deaf Pride, gathered momentum and ultimately overturned the supremacy of oralism. One outcome was the formation of Bi-Bi schools (bilingual-bicultural education) where students are taught in Sign with English as a second language. Another, if unexpected, outcome has been the surge in popularity of American Sign Language (ASL) outside of the Deaf community by those exposed to it through personal experience or through seeing signed programmes on television. ASL is now the fifth most taught language in college, practised by as many as two million Americans. As Solomon writes: 'a broad population has been bewitched by the perceived poetry of a physical communication system.'[12]

Deaf culture is not a frictionless utopia. There are those who think Sign should not be assimilated into the mainstream because it is not just a language but the soul and identity of a marginalised community. Meanwhile, the emergence of hearing-enabling cochlear implants, readily available since the 1980s, has been immensely divisive in part because of the extent to which they enable deaf children to 'pass' in mainstream schools and then through professional life at a perceived cost to Deaf culture. But the very fact aid should be so controversial, with many opting out of using it, shows how successful Deaf activism has been.

Mainstream culture has gradually embraced Creole and sign language, yet it is a change that has occurred within my lifetime, even if the origins go back further. It is hardly inconceivable, therefore, that we may in a decade or two think in a similar way about speech disorders. We may recognise the 'ornate expressions and circumlocutions', 'sudden changes in tone', 'continuous breaks in the narrative' and 'the art of repetition' (borrowing the terms Glissant used to describe Creole) within stuttered speech. Likewise, we may celebrate the unpredictability of Tourette's, the economy of dysarthria and alternative communication strategies of aphasia. This is not to whitewash the psychological and physical suffering that can accompany those conditions, in the same way that recognising Creole as a poetic language does not alleviate the pain of colonial subjugation, but it does affirm that there are productive as well as negative ways of thinking about them.

While Creole and Sign are very different forms of communication, there are some similarities in the way the prejudice against them has been reduced, if not entirely overcome. They provide valuable hints for a strategy to shift mainstream perception of speech disorders from stigma to simply different forms of communication. In each case, three things are at play: the behaviour and actions of those within a particular linguistic register;

those, like parents and peers, who encounter them day-in-day-out; and those who do so only occasionally. In the case of Sign, for instance, there were the empowerment and organisation of deaf people; the support of their parents, as well as hearing friends and carers; and then an outside world that, responding to such activism, became more open-minded and ultimately appreciative.

A change in the perception of a minority interest by the mainstream depends, first and foremost, on the activism of that minority. It is the same activism that drove changes in attitude to Creole and Sign. It requires a shift from being a demographic category or percentage (like the million plus in the UK who have a speech disorder) to a collaborative community. Within the UK, the British Deaf Association was formed in 1890, the parents of children with autism formed the National Autistic Society in 1962 (just a couple of decades after it was first diagnosed) and the British Dyslexia Association formed in 1972. These organisations have raised awareness, lobbied the media and government, and enabled the formation of activist groups within their communities. Along with others, they have managed to change the way those conditions are perceived.

Similar associations for those with speech disorders emerged later. The British Stammering Association was founded in 1978, Tourettes Action in 1980 and the Tavistock Trust for Aphasia in 1992 (resulting in the Aphasia Alliance in 2004). Dysarthria is represented separately through organisations like Stroke Association, MND Association, Parkinson's UK and Scope. The closest thing to a single organisation that looks at speech disorders in their entirety is the Royal College of Speech and Language Therapists, although it ultimately represents the professionals who practise speech therapy rather than the individuals who have speech disorders. As Erving Goffman observed back in the 1960s, the 'peculiarity' of speech disorders 'apparently discourages any group formation whatsoever'. Although this has changed, and continues to do so, progress is slow and the handful of organisations in the UK were founded relatively recently and often struggle with funding.

Of course, institutions are just one measure rather than the sum of community activism. There is also what individuals can achieve on their own or with a few allies. Any change in mainstream perception of speech disorders needs to begin with the behaviour of those who have them. The Stuttering Pride movement emphasises the importance of self-empowerment. This means not apologising for stuttering by continually saying 'I'm sorry' or through those symbolic gestures, like the avoidance of eye contact, that imply it. It means eliminating internalised behaviour – word substitution, avoidance of particular situations – in favour of overt stuttering. It means changing the descriptive words used to describe the experience of stuttering: not a speech 'impediment' or even 'disorder' but a 'difference'; not a 'bad' or 'appalling' stutter, but an 'overt' or 'pronounced' one. And it means communicating the benefits and positive insights that come from a speech disorder as well as acknowledging the frustrations it causes. The same principles apply to vocal tics, aphasia and dysarthria. If the many people with speech disorders put as much energy into such overt behaviour as they currently do into avoidance and mitigating tactics, society would be compelled to think about them differently.

Whether as individuals or part of a group or institution, the important thing is to change the public perception of speech disorders. This means challenging wherever possible the popular but pejorative image of the isolated individual with an obscure condition who just can't get their words out. Together, people with speech disorders comprise a vast demographic segment that is full of variation, but also contains more shared characteristics (neurological, psychological and cultural) than has previously been acknowledged. They experience language differently, which means they think differently, and scans show important variations in brain structure. They have a long and overlapping history of misdiagnosis and maltreatment with some shared heroes, like Oliver Sacks, and also villains, like the anally fixated psychoanalyst Sándor Ferenczi. And there is a rich and ongoing tradition of cultural and artistic creation that is either made by or tries to capture the experiences of those with speech disorders: from Lewis Carroll and Samuel Beckett to Edwyn Collins and Jess Thom today. Most of all, they have an acute awareness of the traps and limitations inherent in language that we can all benefit from sharing.

The more people with speech disorders speak out – about their own experiences, about the prejudices surrounding language and the daily reality of discrimination – the more public perception will change. But they cannot be expected to complete this shift on their own. In some cases, they will struggle to change their own perception of themselves let alone that of strangers, for it requires unpicking a lifetime of habit and negative association such as I acquired. A person's behaviour is generally established early in their experience of a speech disorder, determined by how those around them react to it. For those conditions that emerge in childhood, like stuttering or tics, the response of parents and teachers is critical. While for those who develop one later in life, it is the immediate reaction of their family and friends as well as the professionals they are treated by that matters.

Unfortunately, advice for parents of children is conflicted. There are those who recommend acting as quickly as possible if symptoms of disordered speech begin to emerge in their child, intervening in such behaviour before it becomes entrenched. Then there are those who recommend ignoring it for as long as possible unless, or until, it becomes demonstrably upsetting for the child. Finally, there are those – a minority – who consider most intervention nothing more than neurotypical discrimination.[13] This is an ideological issue and each parent must choose their own path, but the priority should be the long-term mental well-being of the child rather than second-guessing the perceived demands of an intolerant society. Increasingly, as schools get better at teaching the benefits of diversity, there are children whose experience of a speech disorder is not quite so bad as it was in my day.

For those conditions which generally emerge later in life, like aphasia or progressive dysarthria, family and peers can help by enabling better communication, starting with themselves. That involves listening better and with greater patience, encouraging non-verbal communication strategies if appropriate, and being mindful of the language they use to describe these changes both with the individual and with their wider social network. Treating it as a sickness raises the possibility of cure but while the symptoms of aphasia can improve, and those of dysarthria may reach a plateau, they are unlikely to be alleviated altogether. It is far better to see it as a great change, fraught with complication and frustration, but one that can also lead to more imaginative and even better communication.

Whether the person in question is a child or adult, the priority should be to provide support and space for them to determine their own response to a disorder rather than unwanted or hasty interference. As parents, partners, friends or carers, we can help by being as matter-of-fact as possible, avoiding both emotive language and labelling before a solid diagnosis is given. It means listening and taking our cue from their signals about whether they want help and what sort of help might be appropriate. Since a bad therapist can worsen a condition, while a good one can alleviate it, and since no cure has ever been found for any speech disorder, it is worth every parent or peer being aware that the personality of the therapist, and the relationship they forge with a client, are probably going to matter more than any treatment or ideology they espouse.

Finally, there are those who neither have a speech disorder nor are intimate with anyone who does. How are they to behave to enable greater acceptance of speech disorders, and why should they bother? I have made the case for the advantages that those with speech disorders bring to our society and culture, but it is also a matter of empathy, whether one believes it is better to be kind than cruel, inclusive rather than divisive. The advice is simple and rooted in common sense:

- Do not avoid communication with somebody who struggles with their speech. Whether it is a person with a mild condition or who communicates through an augmented and alternative communication device, nobody wants to be isolated or avoided because of who they are.
- If they are helped by family or a carer, do not speak to that person as a substitute unless encouraged to do so. It is not up to you whether or when somebody speaks on their behalf.
- Do not be afraid to ask them to repeat themselves. If you find it hard to understand what they are saying, ask again or acknowledge you don't understand. They will be used to it and it is better to establish the terms of engagement than to be ignored.
- Do not speak for them. The temptation is to finish a person's words or sentences. This is literally robbing somebody of their voice and you will probably get it wrong.
- Do not judge or pity. Their experience of language and human society is not inferior to yours but likely to be more nuanced, full of insight that would never have occurred to you because their participation in both is so hard-won.
- Do not discriminate. There are very few experiences or jobs that people with speech disorders are really disadvantaged from

participating in or performing, although it might at times feel easier to dismiss them from the outset.
- Be generous and be brave, lean in rather than lean out. Life is about new experiences and ideas: speech disorders promise both.

The good news is that mainstream perception change is already occurring. Children and young adults with speech disorders seem not to report the same level of bullying and humiliation that older generations describe. The emphasis in speech therapy has shifted from cure at all costs to helping an individual find the level of fluency that is right for them. Workplaces and companies, compelled by anti-discriminatory legislation, are beginning to have policies in place that favour individuals for the work they do rather than the way they speak.[14]

This shift is increasingly reflected and stimulated in the culture around us. Comedy has always been an art form that uses laughter to broach taboo and challenge prejudice. Daniel Kitson and Drew Lynch are both stand-up comics who overtly stutter in their performances, rather than trying to conceal it. There are theatre companies like Jess Thom's Touretteshero and Graeae that showcase work rooted in neurological and physical difference. Lee Ridley (aka Lost Voice Guy), Francesca Martinez and Rosie Jones are all successful comedians who have cerebral palsy and dysarthria of speech. And, at the time of writing, four comedies are on television that feature characters with cerebral palsy, including *Special* and *Speechless* in America and *Don't Forget the Driver* and

Jerk in the UK. There are also those whose work does not revolve around a speech disorder but who have become more open about acknowledging their experience of one. The politician Ed Balls recently opened up about his lifelong stutter in his autobiography, and it is questionable whether talented celebrities like actor Emily Blunt or rapper Kendrick Lamar would have been quite so candid about their speech difficulties in a previous age.

I believe that positive mainstream exposure does and will lead to greater acceptance. 'Real exposure to difference is the only way to combat the fear and prejudice that arise out of ignorance and lack of experience,' says Martinez.[15] While Ridley describes how 'for the first time people seem comfortable talking to me, as a disabled person, right from the off'.[16] But there is still a way to go. Broadcast and streaming media are for the most part dominated by hyper-fluent communicators. Our newsreaders, DJs and talk show hosts are expected to have immaculate delivery. After his first day on Radio 4's *Today* programme following his operation for lung cancer, Nick Robinson's voice was ever-so-slightly croaky: something which drew a great deal of attention, even complaints, and for which he felt a need to apologise.

I am convinced that any progress is a trickle-down effect from the success of both neurodiversity and the social model of disability as movements. There is a growing acknowledgement that it is unacceptable to discriminate against difference and that it is the responsibility of society to accommodate rather than vice versa. But it also stems from an increasing appetite for alternative forms of communication to the relentless hyper-fluency that seems to dominate life in the twenty-first century. The current fashion for mindfulness meditation, which is rooted in the non-verbal communication practices of Eastern religions, is partly a craving to silence, if only briefly, the chatter in our minds, mouths and ears. And with many of us increasingly wary of sales patter, political bombast and corporate jargon, language that doesn't flow seems more intriguing than ever before. The so-called Greta Thunberg Effect is simply one example of an ever-increasing appreciation of neurodiversity and alternative forms of communication.

Undoubtedly, these changes are also fuelled by the emergence of social media that has given a voice to disenfranchised communities and individuals like those with autism and dyslexia. It is also inherent in the technology itself. Viewed on one level, platforms like Facebook and Instagram simply mainstream techniques that have been used in augmentative and alternative communication practice for decades. What we once thought was the last resort of the disabled is shown to be a preference for the millions who are happier communing on their devices than in verbal conversation.

In a report from 2015, it was shown that over 72 per cent of eighteen- to twenty-five-year-olds find it easier to put their feelings across in emoji than with words.[17] Something seen by an older generation as a light-hearted punctuation at the end of a text message has emerged as a linguistic system in its own right for the young. Emoji is not an alternative to the word, but a symbolic system that co-exists with it, enabling the easy communication of complex emotions that words alone struggle to capture.

An emoji can reinforce the emotional subtext of a message or deliver irony, humour or poignancy by contradicting it, while a combination of emojis can allow everyone to communicate difficult emotions that were once limited to a handful of poets adept at the sonnet form. 'Emoji is the fastest growing form of language in history based on its incredible adoption rate and speed of evolution,' claims Professor Vyv Evans from Bangor University.[18] Only recently, the Oxford Dictionaries announced their word of the year was U+1F602 (or 'face with tears of joy'). Like any emerging technology, we can only guess what this new language will ultimately mean for communication, but it certainly reduces the importance of the spoken word.

What are we to call this new movement that affects our understanding of speech and communication, that draws on not only the rise of neurodiversity, but also the advance of technology and a broader acceptance of alternative forms of communication? I spent months searching for the right term, then stumbled upon it while listening to a recent podcast encounter between two highly creative individuals with speech disorders. The first is a poet and rapper from Essex called Scroobius Pip. His career began in the early years of the new millennium, when a recording of a poem about his stutter drew the attention of radio producers and the music industry.

In 2013, the radio station XFM signed Scroobius Pip to host a weekly hip hop and spoken word programme. Some thought this was brave as Pip's stutter, which had made his name, hadn't gone away. Because the show was pre-recorded there was the option to edit his speech and Pip found himself with a golden opportunity that many with speech disorders strive for: he could present himself to the world as fluent. Yet Pip's stutter was part of who he was and it had inspired the work that first brought him attention. So, as he tells me when we meet in an east London café, he made a momentous decision. 'Look, if I really get stuck on something,' he said to the producer, 'I might start again. But other than that, I don't want you editing out my stutter. I don't want us doing retakes and retakes and retakes. As long as we can get everything into the hour show, as long as we're not missing any songs because of my stutter, it's all good with me.' Pip's show was the only programme I'm aware of anywhere in the mainstream media presented by a person who conspicuously stutters.

Then Pip went independent. He started his own label, which he called Speech Development Records, because he wanted something he could rhyme with 'speech impediment'. And he launched a weekly podcast called *Distraction Pieces*, in which he interviews artists and celebrities like Russell Brand and Killer Mike. It has built up a steady following: thirty million downloads in all. What is immediately noticeable about the podcast is that the host stutters a lot. 'A small radio slot I can probably get through without stuttering,' he tells me, 'but a ninety-minute podcast – there's going to be stuttering and I'm not going to edit it out.' He doesn't see himself as an activist though. He's not proud of his stutter, but simply recognises it as part of who he is. 'I think of it like an accent,' he says. 'I do have people hit me up and say it's so bold or so inspirational, but the fact is I've never considered it. I've just thought: I want to do a show. I haven't thought how empowering this is.'

Over time, Pip has come to think more about the values he stands by. 'I was coming up to my 200th episode,' he says. 'I had the option of Russell Brand coming back on. I had the option of a few huge names. And I realised that a huge name will get a lot of listeners at any time. The importance of the 200th episode is showing what the *Distraction Pieces* podcast is.' So he invited Jess Thom onto the show. The podcast is long (over eighty minutes) not because their speech slows them down but because they have so much to say. 'I realised that we've got the opposites,' Pip tells me. 'She can't stop things coming out and I can't make things come out. In that moment we realised that there's not been many conversations listened to by tens of thousands between people who don't speak in the traditional manner, who have some kind of restriction over what they say.'

In the podcast, there's a moment talking on this exact theme when Thom suddenly shouts out, 'communication diversity, motherfuckers!' The swear word makes it sound like a tic, yet the phrase 'communication diversity' perfectly sums up what is going on in episode 200 of *Distraction Pieces*: a programme, impossible only ten years ago, that gives space to two individuals with speech differences to communicate with a large audience, not only without concealing but actively celebrating those differences. It's not a phrase in common usage so when I ask Thom where it came from, she says that she doesn't know and it doesn't really matter. Whether or not the phrase 'communication diversity, motherfuckers!' was a tic or not doesn't detract from its potency but adds to it. The term itself might be the product of the sort of speech differences it seeks to accommodate.

Communication diversity recognises that, despite the tendency for fluency-prejudice throughout society, there are many modes of speaking and communicating. We should champion them all: not only because it makes life more rewarding for the many millions who do communicate in different ways, but because it is how we hold in check the normative tyranny of fluency, the errors of thinking it can lead to and the unquestioning trust we have in its operation. Communication diversity isn't against language and fluency, and it's not limited to speech disorders, it simply seeks to put all registers of speech and linguistic usage into what Kenyan writer Ngũgĩ wa Thiong'o described to me as a 'network of equal give and take and not as hierarchies of power'.

Embracing this way of thinking has been difficult because of an immense cultural bias stacked against it. It means accepting that fast, fluent, eloquent speech is only one form of good communication. It means embracing ambiguity, being willing to slow down, to listen properly rather than depending on the use of a verbal shorthand that both eases communication and also allows one not to concentrate too closely. Most of all, it means accepting that people whose speech is distorted, fragmented, slow or even entirely absent are not necessarily inferior communicators; they just depend on a degree of engagement and attention we are not used to giving. Steven Pinker's warning about the 'society of hard-working listeners' that must result from 'laziness in pronunciation' is another person's utopia when compared to the errors and confusions that arise daily, not from lazy talking but lazy listening.

The rise of communication diversity is partly a reflection of a confident society that is more willing to encompass and celebrate difference, but it also arises from an increased acknowledgement of the limitations of speech. Yes, it is one of humanity's great creations, a tool that has enabled us to achieve extraordinary things. But where the Victorians unquestioningly praised the benefits of rhetoric and hyper-fluency against the supposed babble of different linguistic registers, there is enough precedence now in acknowledging their limitations. This change, a form of positive disillusionment, is impossible to separate from the failure of that eighteenth-century (or Enlightenment) project of Progress, in which language and technology were seen as the key to a better future. For while that same progress has brought great freedoms and well-being, it has also brought us social and environmental disequilibrium on a scale unprecedented in human history. While we continue to recognise that words help us, we also recognise the extent to which they have failed us too.

I began by asking why King George VI's ability to speak fluently seemed to matter so much. I have tried to show that it has very little to do with the inherent shamefulness of a tendency to get stuck on certain words, but is really about the cracks that run through our civilisation. By putting too much at stake – our knowledge, our institutions and values – in the exercise of fluent language, we put ourselves, as a society, in the ludicrous position where the King's stutter seemed to undermine everything we stood for. The notion is, of course, absurd, yet its very absurdity shows how ill-founded and insupportable our trust in that single mode of hyper-fluent linguistic usage really is. Seen objectively, the King's stutter did not matter, and the conviction that it demeaned not only him, who tried so hard to conceal it, but also – more substantially – the whole society of 1940s Britain, with its values, beliefs and customs, that made him feel he ought to. We need to ensure that this can't and doesn't happen again.

The key to achieving this lies simply in telling stories. We know the familiar ones: the neurotic stutterer, the mentally impaired aphasiac, the obscene Tourettic and the sorry faces of dysarthria. Now it's time to tell the real ones, using whatever means we have available. I spent a lifetime doing my best to hide my stutter. On the occasions when it was unavoidably present, I made it a laughing point, even exaggerated it, as if my only value as a person who stutters was to provide a little amusement for others, apologising as I did so. I played the clown, but I will not do so any more.

Epilogue: Out of the Mouth Trap

One evening in 2009, I found myself in a state of extreme anxiety standing in the dark and drizzle outside Holborn station. The entrance was fanned by a crowd of commuters trying to squeeze their way out of the rain, through the ticket barriers and down to the platforms below. No such escape was available for me though. I had a task to do; one that filled me with more fear than almost anything I had ever done.

For some time, I procrastinated, finding endless excuses, mostly to do with the fanciful notion that those passing me were the wrong sort of people. But finally, fed up with being wet and cold, and disgusted by my own inaction, I made my move. Lurching towards the nearest passer-by, I said, 'Excuse me!' The man stopped. He was a tired, harassed-looking commuter who glanced rather regretfully towards the station entrance but turned nonetheless. I looked him in the eye and smiled. 'Can you tell me the way to …' And then I blocked on a hard C sound. I felt my top lip quiver, my nostrils flare, my chin strain. I hit that 'Co-' sound five times, never breaking eye contact, and then released: 'Covent Garden?'

To my surprise, the weary businessman didn't laugh

or sneer, but simply gave me directions and hurried on without another word. Apparently, he just wanted to get home. Emboldened, I repeated the exercise on another passer-by, then another. I did it seven times in total. I'd like to say they all exhibited the same disinterested reaction as the first, but one gave a quizzical smirk as I blocked and another laughed outright. I then returned to the strip-lit classroom barely a hundred metres away, where ten people with stutters like mine were gradually regrouping. This was the City Lit course for Interiorised Stammering. We were all people who had constructed our lives around avoiding the act of stuttering for the simple reason that, on a good day, we could just about manage to do so. As long as we didn't say certain words, of course, and avoided particular situations, even particular people. We had just made our first out-of-the-classroom foray in the technique of voluntary stuttering.

I am ashamed to say that despite a lifetime of stuttering and avoiding stuttering, I had never looked anyone in the eyes at the crucial moment. Like the Three Sillies of the old English folk story, who live in fear of an axe stuck in the ceiling falling on them without it ever occurring to them that they might reach up and remove it, I had spent my life fearing the disgusted reaction people must have to my stutter without ever looking to see whether it was true. This was behaviour ingrained since childhood and, as a consequence, I had also never really thought about my stutter other than as a revolting trait I needed to conceal. I was thirty-four years old and knew next to nothing about the very phenomenon that had consumed more mental energy than almost anything else in my life. I had no idea what might cause stuttering, how many others experienced it, the different ways it had been treated or how it related to other speech disorders.

That night was a turning point. When I looked that commuter in the eyes, I also looked for the first time at my stutter itself as something I might try to understand rather than hide from. Almost immediately, I began reading into it, beginning with what ultimately forms the first two chapters of this book: an anatomy of the main speech disorders. The ensuing chapters more or less follow, with a little retrospective tidying up, the process of discovery and self-understanding I embarked upon. But there is another story not captured in these pages. In the ten years since that night, stuttering has ceased to be a significant presence in both my spoken and unspoken use of language.

The reason for this is, I think, a perfect storm of elements. There is, of course, the impact of the City Lit course and the excellent speech therapists I was lucky enough to encounter. While endlessly emphasising that there is no cure for stuttering, that they could only help me change my attitude to it, they also made me fear it less, with the outcome that I did it less. While I have met some who are against speech therapy, it changed my life. And I see that reflected in the accounts of others. 'This profession is certainly not given enough credit,' writes Grace Maxwell when describing the impact that speech therapy had on her husband's aphasia. 'The best therapists turn around lives that appear to be wrecked.'[1]

There are other, more prosaic, changes that probably played a role. I was getting older for a start. We still don't know why conditions like stuttering often alleviate with age. It might be about acceptance, it might be about changes in the brain. After all, if the problem is to do with neurological wiring unable to keep up with the activity of different parts of the brain, maybe the brain overall simply slows down a little and that connecting matter finds it easier to keep pace. Then there was my job. I accepted an irresistible promotion that meant I couldn't avoid public speaking any longer. Within a couple of years, I was readily and regularly participating in talks, interviews and debates often on air or in front of large groups of people. I feared it dreadfully at first, neurotically preparing and over-preparing for days, but you can only maintain that level of fear, with the requisite preparation time to compensate, for so long. I learned to speak impromptu. I found that along with the fear was a seed of pleasure which flowered and grew with each event until the anxiety and enjoyment complemented one another. While I still block on words much more when public speaking (and, I should add in self-admonishment, still resort to the sort of word substitution I am trying to avoid), it generally doesn't prevent me from saying what I have to say.

My fluency also increased through researching this book. I became fascinated by those, like Lewis Carroll, Edwyn Collins and Jess Thom, who found a creative outlet for their speech conditions. I felt proud to be associated with what I increasingly saw as a historical and cultural tribe: people with a fundamentally different experience of language going back as far as records allow. Most of all, I found myself deeply moved and inspired by the bravery of those I met: people for whom every sentence was imbued with disordered speech, who in the process of coming out had wrestled with appalling self-loathing, real rather than perceived social discrimination and who in some cases even considered suicide. My own experience of stuttering, mostly interiorised, felt petty in comparison. I am particularly inspired by the younger generation who, still in their teens or in their twenties, openly identify as people with speech disorders and manage to recognise and celebrate the distinctiveness of their speech while also acknowledging the pain it has caused them.

There's a final reason why I think I am more fluent, yet also identify more strongly as a person who stutters than ever before. Shortly after completing the City Lit course, I met a woman whose experience of stuttering was similar to mine. Like many in his time, James Hunt believed people who stutter should avoid one another because it is a form of imitative behaviour and, as a rule of thumb, they still do. But I think it's one thing he got truly wrong. The only way people with speech disorders can change the wider perception of their conditions is by working together. Not only did Constance stutter but most of her family did, simply as my mother had done. Finding myself part of an extended family of people who stutter, although with great variation, was a joy.

In the early years of our marriage, Constance and I found ourselves having to do a lot of public speaking for work. It was a new experience for both of us. We would spend hours rehearsing presentations at one another, which would generally begin with a giant block followed by moments of verbal collapse throughout. We were trying to pass for fluent and by the time the talk came most difficult words had been carefully ironed out. I think the whole process made us less self-conscious and we prepare less intensely now. If we stutter, that's fine. And, of course, just that mental acceptance means we do it less.

At the time of writing, our two children are learning to speak. With so many people who stutter in the family, there is a high chance one of them will too. We find ourselves listening carefully, although we hope not obsessively or neurotically, to their speech development. As a proud father, I keep a track of our eldest's words: mama, papa, caca, goh-goh (meaning both 'crocodile' and 'helicopter'), pah-pah (pasta). All repetitious words like the 'bah-bah' of 'barbarians'; all indistinguishable from what might, in other cases, be a stutter. If learning to speak is a form of stuttering, when does it become considered a 'problem'? And if one of our children does stutter, will we take them to speech therapy, and at what point?

As one of the many born with a speech disorder, I dream, for future generations more than anything else, of their acceptance. But there is an unexpected risk here. Once the shame and the coping mechanisms disappear, once the fear of language and the need to use it differently are rendered obsolete, will speech disorders still have the same creative and productive characteristics I have identified or will they diminish? I want to preserve rather than eliminate such qualities. The solution, I think, is to go one step further. As well as accepting speech disorders, let us all distrust language a little more: vigilant for the delusions and misuses it is put to; more open to experimentation, trying unusual words, strange sentence structures, and resisting rather than striving for more consistent use. Rather than seeking for better inclusion of people with speech disorders in society, let's instead seek to make society use language more like they do. We will, I think, be more tolerant, creative and wiser for it.

Notes

Introduction: The King and I

1. For my account of George VI's youth and coronation I have drawn predominantly from *George VI: The Dutiful King* by Sarah Bradford (Penguin, 2011).
2. Alan and Irene Taylor, *The Assassin's Cloak: An Anthology of the World's Greatest Diarists* (Canongate Books, 2008).
3. Simon Garfield, *Our Hidden Lives: The Remarkable Diaries of Postwar Britain* (Ebury Press, 2005).
4. Cecil Beaton, *The Happy Years: Diaries 1944–48* (Weidenfeld & Nicolson, 1972).
5. David Kynaston, *Austerity Britain, 1945–1951* (*Tales of a New Jerusalem*), (Bloomsbury Publishing, 2008).
6. Johannes von Tiling, 'Listener Perceptions of Stuttering, Prolonged Speech, and Verbal Avoidance Behaviors', *Journal of Communication Disorders* (March/April 2011).
7. www.rcslt.org
8. Mark L. Knapp, Judith A. Hall and Terrence G. Horgan, *Nonverbal Communication in Human Interaction*, 8th Revised Edition (Wadsworth Publishing, 2013).

1. Maladies of Speech

1. Gitogo makes a cameo appearance in *A Grain of Wheat* (1967), referred to by name as a deaf mute who was killed by the British. In *Petals of Blood* (1977), all the major characters

struggle with inarticulacy, often speaking in broken sentences or breaking off halfway through. Nyakinyua's husband is unable to recount a vision because 'something always blocked him, his throat, in the beginning of telling it, and could not continue.' In *Devil on the Cross* (1980), many of the characters 'stutter like babies' when speaking Gikuyu but are fluent in foreign languages.

2. John A. Tetnowski and Kathy Scaler Scott, 'Fluency and Fluency Disorders', in Jack C. Damico, Nicole Müller and Martin J. Ball (eds), *The Handbook of Language and Speech Disorders* (Wiley-Blackwell, 2013).
3. Marcel Wingate, 'Recovery from Stuttering', *Journal of Speech and Hearing Disorders* (August 1964).
4. David Crystal, *How Language Works: How Babies Babble, Words Change Meaning and Languages Live or Die* (Penguin, 2007).
5. Sarah Bradford, *George VI: The Dutiful King* (Penguin, 2011).
6. Mary Robertson and Andrea Cavanna, *Tourette Syndrome*, 2nd Edition (Oxford University Press, 2008)
7. Ibid.
8. Oliver Sacks, *An Anthropologist on Mars* (Alfred A. Knopf, 1995).
9. Gill Edelman and Robert Greenwood, *Jumbly Words, and Rights Where Wrongs Should Be: The Experience of Aphasia from the Inside* (Far Communications, 1992).
10. Henry Head, *Aphasia and Kindred Disorders of Speech*, Volume 2 (Cambridge University Press, 1926).
11. Chris Code, 'Aphasia', in Jack C. Damico, Nicole Müller and Martin J. Ball (eds), *The Handbook of Language and Speech Disorders* (Wiley-Blackwell, 2013).
12. Gill Edelman and Robert Greenwood, *Jumbly Words, and Rights Where Wrongs Should Be: The Experience of Aphasia from the Inside* (Far Communications, 1992).
13. Ibid.

14. Mona Greenfield and Ellayne S. Ganzfried, *The Word Escapes Me: Voices of Aphasia* (Balboa Press, 2016).
15. www.parkinsonsnewstoday.com/parkinsons-disease-statistics
16. www.cerebralpalsy.org.uk
17. www.mndassociation.org
18. Patrick J. Bradley, 'Voice Disorders: Classification', in *Otorhinolaryngology–Head and Neck Surgery* (Springer, 2010).
19. www.selectivemutism.org.uk
20. Ashley John-Baptiste, 'Selective mutism: "I have a phobia of talking"', *BBC News* (15 July 2015).
21. Greta Thunberg, TEDxStockholm talk (24 November 2018).
22. Office for National Statistics
23. T. Benke, C. Hohenstein, W. Poewe, B. Butterworth, 'Repetitive Speech Phenomena in Parkinson's Disease', *Journal of Neurology, Neurosurgery and Psychiatry* (September 2000).

2. The Mouth Trap

1. All quoted in Leon Edel, *Henry James: A Life* (HarperCollins, 1985).
2. Ibid.
3. Ibid.
4. Ibid.
5. Ibid.
6. Letter from Virginia Woolf to Violet Dickinson, 25 August 1907, in Nigel Nicolson and Joanne Trautmann (eds), *The Letters of Virginia Woolf, Volume One: 1888–1912* (Houghton Mifflin, 1977).
7. Leon Edel, *Henry James: A Life* (HarperCollins, 1985).
8. Edith Wharton, *A Backward Glance* (Appleton-Century Company, 1934).
9. Joseph Sheehan, *Stuttering: Research and Therapy* (Harper and Row, 1970).
10. David Crystal, *How Language Works* (Penguin, 2007).
11. Francesca Martinez, *What the **** is Normal?!* (Virgin Books, 2015).

12. Eugene Frederick Hahn (ed.), *Stuttering: Significant Theories and Therapies* (Stanford University Press, 1956).
13. Wendell Johnson, 'The Indians Have No Word for it: I. Stuttering in Children', *Quarterly Journal of Speech* (1944).
14. John A. Tetnowski and Kathy Scaler Scott, 'Fluency and Fluency Disorders', in Jack C. Damico, Nicole Müller and Martin J. Ball, *The Handbook of Language and Speech Disorders* (Wiley-Blackwell, 2013).
15. Mary Tudor, 'An experimental study of the effect of evaluative labelling on speech and fluency' (MA thesis, University of Iowa, 1939).
16. Franklin H. Silverman, 'The "Monster" Study', *Journal of Fluency Disorders* (June 1988).
17. Darcey Steinke, 'My Stutter Made Me a Better Writer, *New York Times* (6 June 2019).
18. Annual Report of Tourette Association of America 2018.
19. Gill Edelman and Robert Greenwood, *Jumbly Words, and Rights Where Wrongs Should Be: The Experience of Aphasia from the Inside* (Far Communications, 1992).
20. Elizabeth Jordan, 'Henry James at Dinner', *Mark Twain Quarterly* (Spring 1943).
21. Ben Brown, 'Ben Brown's Story', Tourette Association of America website.
22. Jon Palfreman, *Brain Storms: The Race to Unlock the Mysteries of Parkinson's Disease* (Rider Books, 2015).
23. Michael J. Fox, *Lucky Man: A Memoir* (Hyperion, 2002).
24. James Hunt, *Stammering and Stuttering, Their Nature and Treatment* (Longman, Green, Longman and Roberts, 1861).
25. Gill Edelman and Robert Greenwood, *Jumbly Words, and Rights Where Wrongs Should Be: The Experience of Aphasia from the Inside* (Far Communications, 1992).
26. Chris Code, 'Aphasia', in Jack C. Damico, Nicole Müller and Martin J. Ball (eds), *The Handbook of Language and Speech Disorders* (Wiley-Blackwell, 2013).

27. Jane Fraser (ed.), *Do You Stutter: A Guide for Teens* (Stuttering Foundation of America, 1987).

3. Talking Culture

1. Daniel Everett, *Language: The Cultural Tool* (Pantheon Books, 2012).
2. Brian Goldstein and Ramonda Horton-Ikard, 'Diversity Considerations in Speech and Language', in Jack C. Damico, Nicole Müller and Martin J. Ball (eds), *The Handbook of Language and Speech Disorders* (Wiley-Blackwell, 2013).
3. John Colapinto, 'The Interpreter', *The New Yorker* (16 April 2007).
4. Brian Goldstein and Ramonda Horton-Ikard, 'Diversity Considerations in Speech and Language', in Jack C. Damico, Nicole Müller and Martin J. Ball (eds), *The Handbook of Language and Speech Disorders* (Wiley-Blackwell, 2013).
5. Victoria Glendinning, *Elizabeth Bowen: A Biography* (Anchor, 2006).
6. Emily C. Bloom, *The Wireless Past: Anglo-Irish Writers and the BBC, 1931–1968* (Oxford University Press, 2016).
7. Howard I. Kushner, *A Cursing Brain? The Histories of Tourette Syndrome* (Harvard University Press, 1999).
8. Ibid.
9. Erving Goffman, *Stigma: Notes on the Management of Spoiled Identity* (Prentice-Hall, 1963).
10. Suetonius, *De Vita Caesarum* (*Lives of the Caesars*), *circa* AD 121.
11. Seneca the Younger (attributed), *Apocolocyntosis*, *circa* first century AD.
12. Tacitus, *Annales,* Book 3, Chapter 12, *circa* first century AD.
13. Erving Goffman, *The Presentation of Self in Everyday Life* (Doubleday, 1956).
14. The popularising of the term Received Pronunciation is credited to the second edition of Daniel Jones's *English Pronunciation Dictionary* (1924). In the first edition of 1917, he used the

term 'public school English'. 'Standard Southern British' is cited in *Handbook of the International Phonetic Association* (Cambridge University Press, 1999).

15. John Hendrickson, 'What Joe Biden Can't Bring Himself To Say', *The Atlantic* (Jan/Feb 2020).
16. Ibid.
17. Lee Ridley, aka Lost Voice Guy, *I'm Only in it for the Parking: Life and Laughter from the Priority Seats* (Bantam Press, 2019).
18. Alessandro Duranti, *Linguistic Anthropology* (Cambridge University Press, 1997).
19. David Crystal, *How Language Works: How Babies Babble, Words Change Meaning and Languages Live or Die* (Penguin, 2007).
20. William Jordan, 'Afraid of Heights? You're Not Alone' (YouGov, 20 March 2014).
21. Quoted in Ronald Carter, *Language and Creativity: The Art of Common Talk* (Routledge, 2004).
22. Steven Connor, *Beyond Words: Sobs, Hums, Stutters and Other Vocalizations* (Reaktion Books, 2014).
23. John A. Tetnowski and Kathy Scaler Scott, 'Fluency and Fluency Disorders', in Jack C. Damico, Nicole Müller and Martin J. Ball (eds), *The Handbook of Language and Speech Disorders* (Wiley-Blackwell, 2013).
24. Mark L. Knapp, Judith A. Hall and Terrence G. Horgan, *Nonverbal Communication in Human Interaction*, 8th Revised Edition (Wadsworth Publishing, 2013).
25. Albert Mehrabian, *Nonverbal Communication* (Transaction Publishers, 1972).

4. The Tyranny of Fluency

1. Chris Anderson, *TED Talks: The Official TED Guide to Public Speaking* (Hodder and Stoughton, 2018).
2. Susan Cain, *Quiet: The Power of Introverts in a World That Can't Stop Talking* (Penguin, 2013).

3. Victor Klemperer, *The Language of the Third Reich* (Athlone Press, 2000).
4. Ronald B. Adler, George Rodman and Athena du Pré, *Understanding Human Communication*, 13th edition (Oxford University Press, 2016).
5. Andrew Solomon, *Far from the Tree* (Vintage, 2014).
6. Ronald B. Adler, George Rodman and Athena du Pré, *Understanding Human Communication*, 13th edition (Oxford University Press, 2016).
7. Patrick Leigh Fermor, *A Time to Keep Silence* (Queen Anne Press, 1953).
8. Christian Laes, 'Silent History? Speech Impairment in Roman Antiquity', in Christian Laes, C.F. Goodey and M. Lynne Rose (eds), *Disabilities in Roman Antiquity* (BRILL, 2013).
9. Friedrich Max Müller, *The Science of Thought* (Longmans, Green and Co., 1887)
10. Johann Gottfried von Herder, *Treatise on the Origins of Language* (1772).
11. Daniel Defoe, *The Fortunes and Misfortunes of the Famous Moll Flanders* (London, 1722).
12. Eugenia Stanhope (ed.), *Letters Written by the Late Right Honourable Philip Dormer Stanhope, Earl of Chesterfield, to his Son, Philip Stanhope, Esq.* (London, 1800).
13. Elizabeth Foyster, '"Fear of Giving Offence Makes Me Give the More Offence": Politeness, Speech and Its Impediments in British Society, c.1660–1800', *Cultural and Social History* (September 2018).
14. Quoted in Susan Cain, *Quiet: The Power of Introverts in a World That Can't Stop Talking* (Penguin, 2013).
15. Erving Goffman, *The Presentation of Self in Everyday Life* (Doubleday, 1956).
16. Mihaly Csikszentmihalyi, *Flow: The Psychology of Optimal Experience* (Harper and Row, 1990).

5. A Muted History

1. Chris Code, 'Aphasia', in Jack C. Damico, Nicole Müller and Martin J. Ball (eds), *The Handbook of Language and Speech Disorders* (Wiley-Blackwell, 2013).
2. Paul Broca's original statements are recorded in editions of *Bulletin de la Société Anatomique de Paris* (1861). I have used translations from Paul Eling (ed.), *Reader in the History of Aphasia: From Franz Gall to Norman Geschwind* (John Benjamins Publishing Company, 1994).
3. James Hunt, *Stammering and Stuttering, Their Nature and Treatment* (Longman, Green, Longman and Roberts, 1861).
4. J.F. Dieffenbach, *Memoir on the Radical Cure of Stuttering* (Samuel Highley, 1841).
5. Elizabeth Foyster, '"Fear of Giving Offence Makes Me Give the More Offence": Politeness, Speech and Its Impediments in British Society, c.1660–1800', *Cultural and Social History* (September 2018).
6. Erasmus Darwin, *Zoonomia, or the Laws of Organic Life* (London, 1794).
7. Allan Ropper and B.D. Burrell, *How the Brain Lost Its Mind: Sex, Hysteria and the Riddle of Mental Illness* (Atlantic Books, 2020).
8. Howard I. Kushner, *A Cursing Brain? The Histories of Tourette Syndrome* (Harvard University Press, 1999).
9. Sigmund Freud, *The Psychopathology of Everyday Life* (Berlin, 1904).
10. This is not the same as the 'psychical' approach of James Hunt for, while Hunt emphasised the importance of negative associations and mental habits in stuttering, these were conscious and easily identifiable rather than repressed.
11. Sigmund Freud, Sándor Ferenczi, Karl Abraham, Ernst Simmel and Ernest Jones, *Psycho-Analysis and the War Neuroses* (The International Psycho-Analytical Press, 1921).
12. I. Peter Glauber, 'Freud's Contributions on Stuttering: Their

Relation to Some Current Insights', *Journal of the American Psychoanalytic Association* (April 1958).

13. Sándor Ferenczi, *Thalassa: A Theory of Genitality* (The International Psycho-Analytical Press, 1924).
14. Otto Fenichel, *The Psychoanalytic Theory of Neurosis* (W.W. Norton and Company, 1945).
15. Isador Coriat, *Stammering: A Psychoanalytic Interpretation* (Nervous and Mental Disease Publishing Company, 1927).
16. Sándor Ferenczi, 'Psycho-analytical Observations on Tic', *International Journal of Psycho-Analysis* (March 1921).
17. Margaret S. Mahler, 'A Psychoanalytic Evaluation of Tic in Psychopathology of Children: Symptomatic Tic and Tic Syndrome' (1949), in *The Selected Papers of Margaret Mahler*, Volume 1 (Aronson, 1979).
18. Margaret S. Mahler, 'Outcome of the Tic Syndrome' (1946), in *The Selected Papers of Margaret Mahler,* Volume *1* (Aronson, 1979).
19. L.S. Jacyna, *Lost Words: Narratives of Language and the Brain, 1825–1926* (Princeton University Press, 2000).
20. Nicholas Mosley, *Beyond the Pale: Sir Oswald Mosley and Family* (Secker & Warburg, 1983).
21. Louise Robison Kent, 'Carbon Dioxide Therapy as a Medical Treatment for Stuttering', *Journal of Speech and Hearing Disorders* (August 1961).
22. Howard I. Kushner.
23. Norman Geschwind, 'Disconnexion Syndromes in Animals and Man', *Brain* (June 1965).
24. Arthur K. Shapiro and Elaine Shapiro, 'Treatment of Gilles de la Tourette's Syndrome with Haloperidol', *British Journal of Psychiatry* (March 1968).
25. Howard I. Kushner.
26. Transcript of interview with Oleh Hornykiewicz conducted by Barbara W. Sommer in Toronto, Canada, 9 February 2007.

6. Unfinished Stories

1. The stuttering Ken in *A Fish Called Wanda* was played by Michael Palin who a few years later gave his name, and a great deal of his time, to the Michael Palin Centre for Stammering Children. In an article for the *Telegraph* in 2011, Palin argued that although the role of Ken was considered cruel by some people who stuttered, others were delighted with it because it got people talking more openly about stuttering.
2. Anne Woodham, 'How My Son Lost the Edge of My Wretched Tongue', the *Guardian* (15 February 1991).
3. Anne Woodham, 'In a Manner of Speaking', *Good Housekeeping* (December, 1987).
4. Ibid.
5. Anna Craig-McQuaide, Harith Akram, Ludvic Zrinzo and Elina Tripoliti, 'A Review of Brain Circuitries Involved in Stuttering', *Frontiers in Human Neuroscience* (2014).
6. Deanne J. Greene, Bradley L. Schlaggar and Kevin J. Black, 'Neuroimaging in Tourette Syndrome: Research Highlights from 2014–2015', *Current Developmental Disorders Reports* (December 2015).
7. Gregory J. Synder, 'The Existence of Stuttering in Sign Language and Other Forms of Expressive Communication: Sufficient Cause for the Emergence of a New Stuttering Paradigm?', *Journal of Stuttering, Advocacy and Research* (January 2009).
8. T.J. Murray, P. Kelly, L. Campbell, K. Stefanik, 'Haloperidol in the treatment of stuttering', *British Journal of Psychiatry* (April 1977).
9. M. Boldrini, M. Rossi, G. F. Placidi, 'Paroxetine Efficacy in Stuttering Treatment', *International Journal of Neuropsychopharmacology* (September 2003).
10. Howard I. Kushner, *A Cursing Brain? The Histories of Tourette Syndrome* (Harvard University Press, 1999).
11. L.S. Jacyna, *Lost Words: Narratives of Language and the Brain, 1825–1926* (Princeton University Press, 2000).

12. Marian C. Brady, Helen Kelly, Jon Godwin, Pam Enderby and Pauline Campbell, 'Speech and Language Therapy for Aphasia Following Stroke', *Cochrane Library* (1 June 2016).
13. Sarah Johnson, 'Nick Robinson: I Never Thought I'd Get My Speech Back', the *Guardian* (28 December 2016).
14. Grace Maxwell, *Falling and Laughing: The Restoration of Edwyn Collins* (Ebury Press, 2010).
15. Nicholas Mosley, *Beyond the Pale: Sir Oswald Mosley and Family* (Secker & Warburg, 1983).
16. Lee Ridley, aka Lost Voice Guy, *I'm Only in it for the Parking: Life and Laughter from the Priority Seats* (Bantam Press, 2019).

7. Extraordinary Minds

1. A person with agnosia struggles to interpret sensations and thereby recognise things; someone with hemispatial neglect loses awareness of one side of vision; someone with somatoparaphrenia may deny the existence of a limb or part of the body.
2. Oliver Sacks, 'The Twins' and 'The Autist Artist', Chapters 23 and 24 of *The Man Who Mistook His Wife for a Hat* (Gerald Duckworth, 1985).
3. Oliver Sacks, 'Witty Ticcy Ray', Chapter 10 of *The Man Who Mistook His Wife for a Hat.*
4. Oliver Sacks, 'The President's Speech', Chapter 9 of *The Man Who Mistook His Wife for a Hat.*
5. Oliver Sacks, *An Anthropologist on Mars* (Alfred A. Knopf, 1995).
6. Landmark reports include Hans Asperger, 'Die Autistischen Psychopathen im Kindesalter' (1944) and Leo Kanner, 'Autistic Disturbances of Affective Contact' (1943).
7. The notion of autism being caused by a 'lack of maternal warmth', effectively leaving children 'in refrigerators which did not defrost', originated in Leo Kanner, 'Problems of Nosology and Psychodynamics in Early Childhood Autism', *American Journal of Orthopsychiatry* (1949).

8. Jason J. Wolff, Suma Jacob and Jed T. Elison, 'The Journey to Autism: Insights from Neuroimaging Studies of Infants and Toddlers', *Development and Psychopathology* (May 2018).
9. Temple Grandin, *Thinking in Pictures: And Other Reports from My Life with Autism* (Random House, 1996).
10. Ron Suskind, *Life, Animated: A Story of Sidekicks, Heroes, and Autism* (Kingswell, 2014).
11. Steve Silberman, *NeuroTribes: The Legacy of Autism and the Future of Neurodiversity* (Avery Publishing, 2015).
12. Maryanne Wolf, 'Dyslexia and the Brain That Thinks Outside the Box', *Dyslexia Review* (2008).
13. Judy Singer, *NeuroDiversity: The Birth of an Idea* (Judy Singer, 2017), based on her 1998 Honours thesis.
14. Thomas Armstrong, *The Power of Neurodiversity: Unleashing the Advantages of Your Differently Wired Brain* (Da Capo Lifelong Books, 2011).
15. www.england.nhs.uk/mental-health
16. Thomas Armstrong, *The Power of Neurodiversity: Unleashing the Advantages of Your Differently Wired Brain* (Da Capo Lifelong Books, 2011).
17. The Union of the Physically Impaired Against Segregation and the Disability Alliance, 'Fundamental Principles of Disability', summary of discussion held on 22 November 1975.
18. Michael Oliver, *Social Work with Disabled People* (Macmillan Education, 1983).
19. Patrick Campbell, Christopher Constantino and Sam Simpson (eds), *Stammering Pride and Prejudice: Difference Not Defect* (J & R Press, 2019).

8. Virtuous Disfluency

1. Sarah Bradford, *George VI: The Dutiful King* (Penguin, 2011).
2. Aneurin Bevan, *In Place of Fear* (William Heinemann, 1952).
3. Nicklaus Thomas-Symonds, *Nye: The Political Life of Aneurin Bevan* (I.B. Tauris, 2014).
4. Michael Foot, *Aneurin Bevan: A Biography* (Scribner, 1974).

5. John Mather, MD, 'Churchill's Speech Impediment Was Stuttering', article for International Churchill Society (2002).
6. Winston Churchill, 'The Scaffolding of Rhetoric' (unpublished manuscript, c.1897).
7. Vernon Bogdanor, 'Aneurin Bevan and the Socialist Ideal' (Gresham College lecture, 2012).
8. 'Putting it Bluntly', *W Magazine* (1 October 2007).
9. Chrissy Iley, 'Dan Ackroyd: a comedy legend's spiritual side', *Telegraph* (28 February 2012).
10. Richard Laliberte, 'Actor Dash Mihok on How Tourette Syndrome Shaped His Career', *Brain and Life* (October 2019).
11. Renée Byrne and Louise Wright, *Stammering: Advice for All Ages* (Sheldon Press, 2008).
12. John Hendrickson, 'What Joe Biden Can't Bring Himself To Say', *The Atlantic* (Jan/Feb 2020).
13. Mona Greenfield and Ellayne S. Ganzfried, *The Word Escapes Me: Voices of Aphasia* (Balboa Press, 2016).
14. Ibid.
15. 'Stammering and Identity: Land of Too Much' (producer Jayne Egerton), BBC Radio 4 (15 May 2013).
16. Steven Connor, *Beyond Words: Sobs, Hums, Stutters and Other Vocalizations* (Reaktion Books, 2014).
17. David Mitchell, 'Let Me Speak', *Telegraph* (30 April 2006).
18. Marc Shell, *Stutter* (Harvard University Press, 2005).
19. David Shields, *Dead Languages* (Alfred A. Knopf, 1989).
20. C.D. Dye, M. Walenski, S.H. Mostofsky, M.T. Ullman, 'A Verbal Strength in Children with Tourette Syndrome? Evidence from a Non-Word Repetition Task', *Brain and Language* (September 2016).
21. Fanny Burney, *Journals and Letters* (Penguin Classics, 2001).
22. Jason W. Brown (ed.), *Jargonaphasia* (Academic Press, 2013).
23. David Crystal, *How Language Works: How Babies Babble, Words Change Meaning and Languages Live or Die* (Penguin, 2007).

24. Steven Pinker, *The Language Instinct* (William Morrow and Company, 1994).
25. Darcey Steinke, 'My Stutter Made Me a Better Writer, *New York Times* (6 June 2019).
26. Jonathan Bryan, *Eye Can Write: A Memoir of a Child's Silent Soul Emerging* (Lagom, 2018).

9. The Art of Disorder

1. Lewis Carroll, *The Complete Works of Lewis Carroll* (The Nonesuch Library, 1939).
2. Morton N. Cohen, *Lewis Carroll: A Biography* (Vintage Books, 1995).
3. Ibid. The original quotation comes from G.J. Cowley-Brown, 'Personal Recollections of the Author of "Alice in Wonderland"', Scottish *Guardian* (28 January 1898).
4. Ibid. The original quotation comes from H.T. Stretton, 'More Recollections of Lewis Carroll – II', *The Listener* (6 February 1958).
5. Collected in Stuart Dodgson Collingwood, *The Life and Letters of Lewis Carroll* (Thomas Nelson and Sons, 1898).
6. Morton N. Cohen, *Lewis Carroll: A Biography* (Vintage Books, 1995).
7. Caryl Hargreaves, 'Alice's Recollections of Carrollian Days, as Told to her Son', *Cornhill Magazine* (July 1932).
8. Morton N. Cohen, *Lewis Carroll: A Biography* (Vintage Books, 1995).
9. Lewis Carroll, 'Alice on the Stage', *The Theatre (*April 1887).
10. J. de Keyser, 'The Stuttering of Lewis Carroll', *Neurolinguistic Approaches to Stuttering* (Brussels, 1972).
11. Morton N. Cohen (ed.), *The Selected Letters of Lewis Carroll* (Macmillan Press, 1982).
12. Ibid.
13. Darcey Steinke, 'My Stutter Made Me a Better Writer', *New York Times* (6 June 2019).
14. Christy Brown, *My Left Foot* (Secker & Warburg, 1954).

15. Mona Greenfield and Ellayne S. Ganzfried, *The Word Escapes Me: Voices of Aphasia* (Balboa Press, 2016).
16. Euan Ferguson interview with Edwyn Collins, '"I couldn't really talk. The words I could say were 'yes', 'no' and 'the possibilities are endless'"', *Guardian* (28 September 2014).
17. Grace Maxwell, *Falling and Laughing: The Restoration of Edwyn Collins* (Ebury Press, 2010).
18. Edwyn Collins, *Understated* (AED Records, 2013) and *Balbea* (AED Records, 2019).
19. Marc Shell, *Stutter* (Harvard University Press, 2005).
20. Charles Dickens, 'Psellism', *Household Words* (November 1856).
21. Ted Morgan, *Somerset Maugham* (Jonathan Cape, 1980).
22. Somerset Maugham, *The Moon and Sixpence* (William Heinemann, 1919).
23. B.B. King, *Blues All Around Me: The Autobiography of B.B. King* (Avon Books, 1996).
24. John Lee Hooker, 'Stuttering Blues', *Don't Turn Me From Your Door* (Atco Records, 1963).
25. Charles Shaar Murray, *Boogie Man: The Adventures of John Lee Hooker in the American Twentieth Century* (St Martin's Griffin, 1999).
26. Van Morrison, 'Cyprus Avenue', *It's Too Late to Stop Now* (Warner Bros, 1974).
27. Laura Barton, 'A Duel with Van Morrison: "Is this a psychiatric examination? It sounds like one"', *Guardian* (31 October 2019).
28. Led Zeppelin, 'Whole Lotta Love', *How the West Was Won* (Atlantic Records, 2003).
29. Dan Reilly, 'Kendrick Lamar Reveals Childhood Stutter', *Spin* (26 June 2014).
30. Ed Sheeran's speech on stuttering, recorded in *Time* magazine (10 June 2015).
31. Susannah Gora, 'How Carly Simon Overcame Stuttering and Migraine', *Brain and Life* (November 2009).
32. John Updike, *Self-Consciousness: Memoirs* (Penguin, 1990).

33. James Boswell, *The Life of Samuel Johnson* (London, 1791).
34. Samuel Johnson, *A Dictionary of the English Language* (London, 1755).
35. Leon Edel, *Henry James: A Life* (HarperCollins, 1985).
36. Grace Maxwell, *Falling and Laughing: The Restoration of Edwyn Collins* (Ebury Press, 2010).
37. Samuel Beckett, *The Letters of Samuel Beckett: Volume 1, 1929–1940* (Cambridge University Press, 2009).
38. Laura Salisbury and Chris Code, 'Jackson's Parrot: Samuel Beckett, Aphasic Speech Automatisms, and Psychosomatic Language', *Journal of Medical Humanities* (June 2016).
39. Samuel Beckett, *Collected Poems* (Faber & Faber, 2013).
40. Oliver Sacks, 'Tourette's Syndrome and Creativity', *British Medical Journal* (December 1992).
41. Steph Harmon, 'Backstage in Biscuit Land Review', *Guardian* (18 October 2016).
42. Letter from Charles Dodgson to Henry Rivers, 19 December 1873: 'Just now I am in a bad way for speaking, and a good deal discouraged. I actually so entirely broke down, twice lately, over a hard "C", that I had to spell the word! Once was in a shop, which made it more annoying.' In a following letter (27 December 1873), he thanks Rivers 'for advice about hard "C", which I acknowledge as my vanquisher in single-hand combat, at present'.

10. Speech Acts of Resistance

1. Siegfried Sassoon, 'They', from *The Old Huntsman, and Other Poems* (William Heinemann, 1917).
2. Siegfried Sassoon, 'The General', from *Counter-Attack, and Other Poems* (William Heinemann, 1918).
3. Siegfried Sassoon, *Memoirs of an Infantry Officer* (Faber & Faber, 1930).
4. Robert Graves, *Good-Bye to All That* (Anchor, 1929).
5. Hugo Ball, *The Dada Manifesto* (July 1916).

6. Anna Lawton (ed.), *Russian Futurism Through its Manifestos, 1912–1928* (Cornell University Press, 1988).
7. Peter Leese, *Shell Shock: Traumatic Neurosis and the British Soldiers of the First World War* (Palgrave Macmillan, 2002).
8. Geoffrey O'Hara, 'K-K-K-Katy' sheet music (Leo Feist, 1918).
9. Siegfried Sassoon, 'Survivors', from *Counter-Attack, and Other Poems (*William Heinemann, 1918).
10. Quoted in Chris Eagle, *Dysfluencies: On Speech Disorders in Modern Literature* (Bloomsbury, 2013).
11. Peter Leese, *Shell Shock: Traumatic Neurosis and the British Soldiers of the First World War* (Palgrave Macmillan, 2002).
12. R.S. Norman, C.A. Jaramillo, B.C. Eapen, M.E. Amuan, M.J. Pugh, 'Acquired Stuttering in Veterans of the Wars in Iraq and Afghanistan', *Military Medicine* (April 2018).
13. W.H.R. Rivers, *Instinct and the Unconscious* (British Psychological Society, 1919).
14. Siegfried Sassoon, *Sherston's Progress* (Faber & Faber, 1936).
15. Quoted in Ben Shephard, *Headhunters: The Pioneers of Neuroscience* (Vintage Books, 2014).
16. L.S. Jacyna, *Lost Words: Narratives of Language and the Brain, 1825–1926* (Princeton University Press, 2000).
17. Henry Head, *Aphasia and Kindred Disorders of Speech,* (Cambridge University Press, 1926).
18. Gilles Deleuze and Felix Guattari, *Capitalism and Schizophrenia*, Volume 1, Volume 2, *Anti-Oedipus*, and *A Thousand Plateaus* (Paris: Les Editions de Minuit, 1972 and 1980).
19. Dambudzo Marechera, 'An Interview with Himself', from *The House of Hunger* (Heinemann, 2009 edition).
20. Ibid.
21. Ibid.
22. Doris Lessing's review of Marechera's *The House of Hunger* in *Books and Bookmen* (June 1979).
23. Donna Ferguson, 'Greta Effect Leads to Boom in Children's Environmental Books', *Guardian* (11 August 2019).

24. Greta Thunberg, TEDxStockholm talk (24 November 2018).
25. Christian Laes, 'Silent History? Speech Impairment in Roman Antiquity', in Christian Laes, C.F. Goodey and M. Lynne Rose (eds), *Disabilities in Roman Antiquity* (BRILL, 2013).
26. Peter Dominiczak, 'Ed Balls: Reaction to My Stutter "really upsetting"', *Telegraph* (22 October 2013).
27. Hélène Mulholland, 'Ed Balls: "I won't apologise for my stammer"', *Guardian* (6 December 2012).
28. For biographical details of Wittgenstein's life I have drawn predominantly from Ray Monk, *Ludwig Wittgenstein: The Duty of Genius* (The Free Press, 1990).
29. Ludwig Wittgenstein, *Lectures: 1930–1932* (Rowman and Littlefield, 1980).
30. Ibid.
31. Lawrence Goldstein, *Clear and Queer Thinking: Wittgenstein's Development and his Relevance to Modern Thought* (Duckworth, 1999).
32. Julian Bell, 'An Epistle on the Subject of the Ethical and Aesthetic Beliefs of Herr Ludwig Wittgenstein', *The Venture* (February 1930).
33. G. Kreisel, 'Critical Notice: "Lectures on the Foundations of Mathematics"', in S.G. Shanker (ed.), *Ludwig Wittgenstein: Critical Assessments* (Croom Helm, 1986).
34. Norman Malcolm, *Ludwig Wittgenstein: A Memoir* (Oxford University Press, 1958).
35. Quoted in Ray Monk, *Ludwig Wittgenstein: The Duty of Genius* (The Free Press, 1990).
36. Rudolf Carnap, 'Autobiography', in Paul Schlipp (ed.), *The Philosophy of Rudolf Carnap* (Open Court, 1963).
37. Ludwig Wittgenstein, 'Lecture on Ethics', *Philosophical Review* (January 1965).
38. Ludwig Wittgenstein, *Culture and Value* (Wiley-Blackwell, 1998).
39. Alison Rourke, 'Greta Thunberg Responds to Asperger's Critics: "It's a superpower"', *Guardian* (2 September 2019).

40. David Shields, *Dead Languages* (Alfred A. Knopf, 1989).

11. Communication Diversity

1. Steven Pinker, *The Language Instinct* (William Morrow and Company, 1994).
2. Ibid.
3. Edouard Glissant, *Caribbean Discourse: Selected Essays* (University of Virginia Press, 1992).
4. Aimé Césaire, *Notebook of a Return to My Native Land* (Bloodaxe, 1995).
5. John Patrick Walsh, *Free and French in the Caribbean: Toussaint Louverture, Aimé Césaire, and Narratives of Loyal Opposition* (Indiana University Press, 2013).
6. Frantz Fanon, *Black Skin, White Masks* (Grove Press, 1967).
7. Jean Bernabé, Patrick Chamoiseau, Raphaël Confiant and Mohamed B. Taleh Khyar, 'In Praise of Creoleness', *Callaloo* (Autumn, 1990).
8. Alexander Graham Bell, 'The Utility of Signs in the Instruction of the Deaf', *The Educator* (1898).
9. Andrew Solomon, *Far From the Tree* (Vintage, 2014).
10. William Stokoe, *Sign Language Structure: An Outline of the Visual Communication Systems of the American Deaf* (University of Buffalo, 1960).
11. Andrew Solomon, *Far from the Tree* (Vintage, 2014).
12. Ibid.
13. For example, Doreen Lenz Holte, *Voice Unearthed: Hope, Help and a Wake-Up Call for the Parents of Children Who Stutter* (Holte, 2011).
14. For instance, as of 2016, the Employers Stammering Network (ESN), launched in 2013 to raise awareness about disability rights and best practice, claims to represent an employed population of 1.5 million. The ESN inspired, in turn, the UK Civil Service Stammering Network and the Defence Stammering Network.

15. Francesca Martinez, *What the **** is Normal?!* (Virgin Books, 2015).
16. Lee Ridley, aka Lost Voice Guy, *I'm only in it for the Parking: Life and Laughter from the Priority Seats* (Bantam Press, 2019).
17. Vyvyan Evans, *The Emoji Code: How Smiley Faces, Love Hearts and Thumbs Up are Changing the Way We Communicate* (Michael O'Mara, 2017).
18. Anna Doble, 'UK's Fastest Growing Language is … Emoji', *BBC News* (19 May 2015).

Epilogue: Out of the Mouth Trap

1. Grace Maxwell, *Falling and Laughing: The Restoration of Edwyn Collins* (Ebury Press, 2010).

Acknowledgements

I am grateful, first and foremost, to those who guided me, made crucial introductions and shared personal experiences. They include: Marina Abramović, Giuliano Argenziano, Nihal Arthanayake, Sebastian Barfield, Mary Beard, Jamie Beddard, Patrick Campbell, Brian Catling, Alison Clark, Oliver Dimsdale, Margaret Drabble, Will Eaves, Max Egremont, Daniel Everett, Robert Douglas Fairhurst, Tim Fell, Hartry Field, James Fox, Betony Kelly, Danny Ladwa and the Stammering Voice Orchestra, Charlotte Mosley, Hans Ulrich Obrist, Scroobius Pip, Janina Ramirez, Rebecca Roache, Uri Schneider, Sophie Scott, Walter Scott, Owen Sheers, Rory Sheridan, David Shields, Jim Smith, Debris Stevenson, Colm Tóibín, Jennifer Vonholstein, Kate Watkins, Tom Wheeler and Harry Yeff.

Ngũgĩ wa Thiong'o, David Shields, Joshua St Pierre and Jess Thom were interviewees who significantly shaped my ideas at critical stages in the writing process. Roland Allen, Dan Fox, Henry Hitchings and Thomas Karshan are writers and friends whose advice I sought and was thankful for on a number of occasions.

While there are many books about speech disorders, there are few on their cultural and historical context. For this reason, I relied on a handful of important exceptions: *Knotted Tongues* by Benson Bobrick, *A Cursing Brain?* by Howard I. Kushner, *Dysfluencies* by Chris Eagle, *Lost Words* by L.S. Jacyna and *Stutter* by Marc Shell.

I have been guided or supported by Elaine Kelman, Frances Cook and Jo Hunter from the Michael Palin Centre for Stammering Children, by Carolyn Cheasman from City Lit, and by Tim Fell and Jane

Powell from the British Stammering Association. The achievements of all three organisations are nothing short of heroic. I am also extremely grateful for the support of Jane Fraser and the Stuttering Foundation of America and to Professor Shelagh Brumfitt who read the book at draft stage. But most of all, I thank therapist Willie Botterill, whose expertise and care I have depended upon at various, often vulnerable stages in my life.

As a needy first-time author, I suspect I have occasionally been a drain on the time and patience of my publishers. The idea for the book was developed in close collaboration with the brilliant Kirty Topiwala at the Wellcome Collection. Andrew Franklin provided invaluable advice and necessary interventions throughout. Ellen Davies is a superb and diligent editor who oversaw the final drafts. The wider teams at Wellcome and Profile have been incredibly supportive, including Penny Daniel, Hannah Ross and Joe Staines.

My greatest thanks go to my family. My parents, Annie and Stephen, and sister, Tamsin, were always supportive when I felt most lost in speech and language. My mother has always encouraged me to write, although probably never expected to find herself copy-editing the last draft of her forty-four-year-old son's book. My cousin Gilly was generous in sharing her own difficulties with words. She is a beacon of kindness and bravery; an inspiration to all who know her. My wife's family, the Wyndhams, all have personal experience, to varying degrees, of stuttering and shared memories and ideas as the book progressed.

And, of course, the endeavour would have been impossible if not for my wife, the wonderful Constance Wyndham, who continued to encourage me even when the reality of life with two small children made the thought of our writing a shopping list feel a stretch too far, let alone a book.

Index

Note: *italic* entries are the titles of books, films, plays or performances discussed.

Index

Index

Index

Index